Harry Takes Off

IRON PEGASUS, BOOKS 1-3

By

Steve Turnbull

Harry Takes Off, Books 1-3 by Steve Turnbull. Second edition July 2016

ISBN 978-1-910342-57-2

Published by Tau Press Ltd.
Cover by Jane Dixon-Smith (jdsmith-design.com).

To the late Capt W.E. Johns

for creating "Biggles" and "Worrals"

BOOK 1

HARRY TAKES OFF

1

Harriet and Khuwelsa had crossed the Usambara Mountains, heading south, only half an hour before. The massive bulk of Kilima-Njaro slowly dropped behind to the northeast, though in this part of Africa the Old Man was never out of sight. At night, with the moonlight shining on the snowy cap of the old volcano, one could believe spirits walked its slopes.

The sun glared down as usual. It was coming on to midday, a couple of hours since the *Pegasus* had lifted from the private air-dock outside her father's home. It was as hot as hell in the single cabin with the sun beating through the glass and the steam furnace going full blast. Harry reached up and unlatched the five catches holding the canopy closed, and the blast of air ripped it open. Squinting against the bright sunlight, she pulled her goggles down over her eyes to protect them from the wind.

"If you keep doing that, one day it'll rip right off." A young woman's voice carried from the rear over the noise of the thumping pistons, the roar of the furnace and the whistling of the air.

Harry glanced back and grinned at her engineer. Khuwelsa was leaning on her shovel taking a rest, in her usual state of undress, and swaying in time to the regular beats of the *Pegasus*'s wings. Her heavy European dress and jacket had been stowed safely in the locker to keep them clean. She wore the minimum to maintain decency—loose cotton top and bloomers billowing in the wind—contrasted by her heavy boots, thick apron, gauntlets and goggles. Harry would have stripped down too, but she wouldn't have time to dress when they landed and there'd be hell to pay if she was seen like that.

They were the same age as far as they knew; Khuwelsa had been rescued from a slave caravan in Mombasa when Harry was six.

Harry's father had taken in the black girl as a companion for his otherwise friendless daughter. And later, when no one had come to claim her, he had taken the radical step of making her his daughter.

"If you could come up with a ventilation system, I wouldn't have to open it," she called back.

Harry felt the wind turning the plane eastward. She adjusted the attitude of the wings and opened the lift power valve for two wing strokes. The *Pegasus* surged twice and brought them back on course.

Daddy had given in and bought her the *Pegasus* two years before. If he thought it was just a mere childish fancy—that it would be too difficult to fly and she'd lose interest before she got into the air—he was disappointed. In fact Harry supposed he'd chosen an ornithopter simply because they were notoriously hard to manage. But she'd confounded him; she loved to fly, and this mechanical bird was everything she'd dreamed of.

Ahead, the bright strip of the river sliced its way through the landscape. At the end of its line to the west she saw the slightly darker patch of the town amid the greens and browns of the savannah. The 'thopter was high enough that it didn't disturb the great herds of wildebeest, gazelles, giraffes and elephants that wandered the plains.

From up here she couldn't see the predators, but she knew they were there. Mrs Hemingway was always warning them about the dangers of the big cats, the snakes and the scorpions. The tutor seemed unaware a bull elephant was far more dangerous than a lion or even a pack of hyenas. There was little that could stop a charging elephant.

Harry peered forward and frowned. The air above the town looked curiously smoky.

She turned back to the cabin, stuck her fingers in her mouth and whistled three times sharply. There was so much noise that she and

Khuwelsa had come up with a system of whistles and signs rather than shouting all the time.

Three abrupt notes from Harry meant their destination was in sight and they were on their approach. To Khuwelsa it also meant she could stop stoking and see about getting her proper clothes back on. Of course, being a black girl she wouldn't rate a second glance from most whites anyway.

Harry took a hand from the helm wheel and tucked her hair back under her heavy cotton headscarf. It didn't matter how tight she made it; strands of thick red hair would always escape and flick her in the eyes—or would have, if not for the goggles. She had considered cutting it off but Khuwelsa had made such a fuss, she dropped the idea.

She stared down at the approaching town, frowning. There was a lot of dust getting kicked up along the main road and many columns of smoke from fires. Didn't they know how dangerous that was? Then she thought better of it. The Germans were always properly organised; they didn't want a fire raging across the savannah either.

A shadow passed across the sun. Shielding her eyes, she looked up. A huge black form like a squat sausage hung there: a Zeppelin.

German army must be on the move, she thought. *I hope Johannes has got time to chat.*

A buzzing like a big and angry hornet, loud enough to be heard over the huffing and panting of the *Pegasus,* filled the air. An airplane shot across her bow from port to starboard at almost twice her speed and then swung round in a wide arc. The black design of the Iron Cross on its fuselage was plainly visible as it flew past in the other direction.

2

The German airplane came alongside on the right and matched airspeed. She glanced across at the pilot. He pointed at the encampment and then down.

She frowned in irritation. An unladylike word that challenged the pilot's parentage fell from her lips. Then she smiled sweetly and gave him a thumbs-up to show she had understood.

The German accelerated effortlessly ahead of her. His vessel had a pusher propeller like the *Pegasus* but it was a fixed-wing design, fast but not manoeuvrable. The wide body looked like it housed a big power plant. Smoke poured from its funnel. He probably had a crew of three or four. The starboard wing dipped and the plane banked towards one end of the temporary military camp, furthest from the town.

Harry cursed again. There was no way she was going to land on some makeshift air-dock in the middle of the German army.

He may have a powerful machine, but he didn't have the *Pegasus.*

She reached back, grabbed the top of the canopy and pulled it down. It latched into place. She gave five quick whistles—*hang on tight*—and opened the throttle, hoping they still had plenty of steam pressure. The *Pegasus* leapt ahead. She pushed the controls forward hard, and the articulated wings folded back to reduce wind resistance but remained open enough to maintain control. *Pegasus* went into a fast dive. They picked up speed and Harry banked smoothly, heading straight for the town.

She was below the German and so, with a bit of luck, the pilot wouldn't notice she was missing until it was too late to catch her.

"Can you see him?" shouted Harry, glancing back to where Khuwelsa was wriggling into her dress. Neither of them had a figure that needed a corset and wearing one in the middle of the day was something only a crazy woman would do.

"I am tied up at the moment."

Harry took a moment to glance out the starboard side and up. The German airplane was nowhere in sight, which was not good news. She hoped he was not trigger-happy. Not only was the *Pegasus* unarmed, but her hull, wings and mechanics were as light as possible because a 'thopter could not afford any unnecessary weight.

A white magnesium trail shot past the starboard wing. She'd never seen a tracer bullet before but she knew what one should look like. Damn and blast it. The town was still at least five minutes away. Plenty of time for the pilot to decide that her behaviour was contrary to the good of the German Empire and knock her out of the sky.

Why not just accept the inevitable? It was not as if she was on some life or death mission. What difference would it make? The German dispute was with the local rebels, not the British, at least not yet. It really wasn't important enough to get killed over.

But somehow all the sane and sensible reasoning in the world was not enough to make her kow-tow to the arrogance of the Kaiser's war machine.

Five quick blasts. Again.

"Harry!"

Harry reached forward and for one fraction of a second her hand hesitated over the Faraday switch. That was the one thing never switched off when in flight, the one that prevented the gravity of the earth's mass from exerting most of its influence. The Faraday device was the one and only thing that allowed the *Pegasus* to fly.

She disengaged it.

The *Pegasus* fell.

Khuwelsa squealed.

Harry wrestled with the controls, trying to keep her bird flying straight. The *Pegasus* accelerated towards the ground, her wings still pulled in tight. They began to roll and Harry adjusted the control flights, but the response was sluggish. She managed to stabilise them.

"Are you crazy?" shouted Khuwelsa.

Harry craned her neck and could make out the German airplane a long way up and behind them, though, as she watched, its nose dipped in a dive after her.

"Harry! The ground!"

She snapped her attention forwards. The savannah was uncomfortably close. A small herd of giraffes had taken fright at the roaring bird dropping out of the sky like some enormous avian predator. She slapped the Faraday switch; the power flowed through the grid and lightness returned. She threw open the wings and the air screamed between the vanes, threatening to tear them from their sockets.

The *Pegasus* swooped low across the grassland. Animals froze in terror as the metal bird flashed over their heads.

The town was coming up fast. Harry fought to bring the nose up and arch the wings to slow them down. She gave two strong down-strokes that lifted them over tall and wide storage buildings on the outskirts.

"Steam's out, Harry," shouted Khuwelsa. They didn't have a code for that. It wasn't supposed to happen.

She wouldn't be able to make it to the military compound. The town square was the only space within dropping distance. The sound from the drive engine faded; Khuwelsa must have disengaged it. That would save what little steam remained for the wings. One quick beat had them hopping another building and careening over the square. The open space in the centre of the town should have been empty, but instead it was packed with German military vehicles, horse-drawn carriages and steam-trucks.

She spotted a space which only contained a couple of market stalls near the statue of Bismarck.

With the remaining steam she back-winged to kill their speed and prayed the stallholders would move. She tried for another back-wing but the steam reserves were all gone. The ship was little more than a lump of metal.

The *Pegasus* slipped out of the sky and, with a thud, sat on her rear end. Then slowly the nose fell forward and crashed to the ground.

"Undercarriage!" Harry shouted belatedly.

"Done," said Khuwelsa.

Harry climbed out of her chair. Her hands were shaking. She reached back and killed the Faraday. No point draining the battery. The ship groaned and sagged. From outside there was a cracking and breaking sound followed by harsh words in Kiswahili.

"What were you doing, Harry?"

Harry took a deep breath. "Maintaining the dignity of Her Majesty's Empire?"

"I should give you a slap," said Khuwelsa, and then she grinned.

Harry laughed. "Remind me not to do that again."

There was a banging on the door and commanding German consonants.

"Oh well, best go face the music."

3

A violent metallic knocking resonated through the cabin as someone banged on the hatch. Harry hastily tightened the drawstrings at the back of Khuwelsa's dress and tied them off in an untidy bow. She brushed down the front of her skirts as Khuwelsa drew the bolts on the door and pulled it inwards.

Harry kicked the steps so they unfolded and dropped to the ground. Bright sunshine flooded in illuminating Harry's slim figure in her cream and red dress. The bobbing silhouettes of soldiers brandishing guns moved towards the entrance. One of them grabbed hold of the hatch to pull himself up and in.

"Don't you dare," shouted Harry and she took a step forward to block the entrance, then realised she still had her goggles on. She pulled them up onto her headscarf and was temporarily dazzled by the reflections off vehicles and guns. "This is my ship, and you do not enter without my permission."

The fact she was female, and young, seemed to stall him. She knew her hair always made a good impression—especially when there was a light breeze to move it around, though that wasn't the case here.

She heard one of the soldiers make a comment in German, something about his little sister crashing a Zeppelin.

"Your little sister would have better manners than a slug like you." She spoke in passable German. It wasn't a good comeback but it had the other soldiers laughing at him instead. "Now, if you don't mind. I am visiting my friend, *Feldwebel-Leutnant* Johannes Schönfeldt."

She descended the steps purposefully and the soldiers at the front made space for her. A murmur went through the gathered group as Khuwelsa appeared. Harry didn't pay a great deal of attention to politics, but the fact that the Germans had been in a state of war with the Wahehe tribes for years meant that many soldiers did not like the blacks.

As far as they knew, Khuwelsa could be one of the Wahehe. But she was dressed in European clothes, which fitted perfectly since they were her own and not cast-offs. And she spoke German as well as Harry—she'd had exactly the same education—so she knew what they were saying. The only word that came across clearly was *Schwarze*.

As Khuwelsa descended the steps behind Harry, there was a motion in the crowd as someone made their way through it. It was blond Johannes in full uniform. She wasn't sure she had ever seen him dressed up like this except at one of the dances. Whatever was going on had to be serious.

"Miss Edgbaston." He clicked his heels and saluted. She raised an eyebrow.

She nodded her head in return. "Lieutenant Schönfeldt." They were being so formal that the presence of her goggles on her head now felt awkward, but trying to remove them would probably dislodge her scarf.

"Accompany me, please?"

"I'm afraid I broke some things landing."

"We will deal with the damages. You could not to know the square would be occupied." He gave a curt bow, and gestured in the direction of the permanent military buildings. A path opened for them through the troops and he led them away under the oppressive gaze of a hundred soldiers.

They crossed the square between the massive Faraday-based mobile fortresses that the Germans favoured. They were huge machines on wide wheels, sporting half a dozen artillery turrets each. With just a few of these and a hundred infantry they could take over an entire city in no time at all. Especially with support from their Zeppelins and attack aircraft.

But there were no cities here, so what were the Germans doing? Their vehicles were of no value in their struggle with the natives who attacked by surprise and disappeared into the savannah when they were done.

Johannes's rank granted them passage through security gates and checks that had not existed on her last visit. The main building of the military outpost was modern and utilitarian. It had been constructed by the Germans to station their local military forces and did not feature the ornateness that typified British-built administration buildings.

Harry had expected to be shown upstairs, but Johannes led them down into the cellars where she'd never been. They reached a small room with a small but clear sign giving Johannes's name and rank.

"What's this?" She gestured round the small room. "What happened to your office, Johannes?"

He crossed to the other side of the desk and stood behind it, facing them. His self-control seemed to break. "My God, Harriet, why are you here? Why now?"

"What's going on? What is all this?"

"I can't tell you that, but you have to leave as soon as you can get up steam, before my seniors know you are here." He paused, then continued in a slightly uncertain tone. "It is good you did not try to land in the compound as usual; they would have shot the *Pegasus* out of the sky."

He paused. She could see the pieces clicking together in his head. She glanced at Khuwelsa, whose jaw was set and lips were firmly closed. . The look on his face as she returned her attention to him told her had completed the mental jigsaw as far as he could.

"Harriet, why did you land in the square?"

She looked at him, not sure how she should frame the answer for the best result.

"What have you done, Harriet?"

Khuwelsa piped up in the middle of Harry's silence. "She got the better of one of your *Todesflug*."

Johannes sat down at his desk with his head in his hands. Harry considered that Khuwelsa's explanation was probably not the most diplomatic, but Sellie had always been one for plain speaking.

Harriet got defensive. "He was firing at an unarmed vessel."

"You did not follow his instructions."

There was the approaching sound of many booted feet thudding in perfect unison outside the door. At a sharp command they came to a halt. The sound of guns being cocked and readied penetrated the room. A shadow moved across the frosted glass of the window.

Then someone knocked.

4

Kommandant Schmidt had been very polite.

He had very politely escorted the two of them from Johannes's office to a room on an upper floor of the main building, a room that sported bars on the windows.

So here they were, with Harry sitting on one side of a bare table, him on the other and Khuwelsa merely allowed to stand near the window.

"Does your girl speak German?"

"I'm sorry?"

"Please do not pretend you only speak English."

"I speak French, if you like."

"Miss Edgbaston, you think this is a joke?" He took out a cigarette pack, tapped out one for himself and lit it with a match. "I assure you this is no joke."

"You can't keep us here."

He drew in a lungful of smoke and blew it out. Harry hated the smell of cigarettes but she was not going to let him know that.

"I *can* keep you here."

"My father knows I was coming here. If I'm not back by this evening someone will look for me."

"Why are you here, Miss Edgbaston?"

"I came to see Jo— Lieutenant Schönfeldt."

"Why?"

Because she often did? Because he was a good dancer? Because she enjoyed talking to him about flying and machines? There didn't seem to be a very good answer.

"Are you spying for your father?"

"What?" She laughed. He, however, did not. It took her a moment to realise it would be better if she expressed anger rather than amusement. "You think that a seventeen-year-old girl would be a spy."

"We know who your father is, Miss Edgbaston. It is very likely he would use you as a spy, even if you did not realise it."

She jumped to her feet and leaned over the desk. "How dare you? I am no spy. My father never asks me about my trips. He has never expressed an interest in what you Germans are doing. Why? Are you doing something he ought to know about?"

Schmidt had maintained his slightly aloof, superior attitude until those words slipped out. Now he frowned and stood up. His face drew close to hers.

"You will remain here until noon tomorrow. Then you will be free to go. If anyone comes looking for you they will be dealt with the same way."

He went to the door and turned. "Miss Edgbaston. You made an unfortunate mistake coming here today. We are not at war with your country. If you behave intelligently you will not be harmed."

"And if I don't, *Herr* Schmidt?" she said, omitting his title. His frown deepened into a scowl.

"I will leave that to your no doubt vivid imagination."

He banged on the door, and it was unlocked from the other side and opened. The *Kommandant* clicked his heels, saluted and left without a further word.

Harry sat down and sighed. Khuwelsa took the other chair.

"It's only a day," Khuwelsa said. "No worse than when Mrs Hemingway manages to keep us in the schoolroom."

Harry stood up and went to the window. She looked out on the entrance to the military compound. Squads of soldiers marched along the main road and there were patrols around the perimeter.

"What's going on, Sellie?" she said, almost inaudibly. "What are they doing?"

Khuwelsa came up beside her, placed her palms on the windowsill and peered out. "They are going to war."

"But who with?"

It couldn't be the Italians; they held so little land it hardly seemed worth it, even if it was along the coast. Most of the natives were on the German side anyway, only the Wahehe fought them. And that left the British. But how could they even dare? The Empire was far too strong.

The Empire might be powerful around the world, but not here in East Africa.

"They must be going against us," she said.

The door unlocked. She and Khuwelsa turned as Johannes entered.

"*I will speak with them alone*," he said to the guard outside.

The door shut and locked.

"What do you want?" said Harry.

He switched to English. "Do not do anything, Harriet."

She laughed. "Do?" She gestured around the bare room. "Do, Lieutenant? I am imprisoned. I cannot *do* anything."

He frowned. "I am your friend. Just wait until tomorrow and they'll let you go."

"If you were my friend, you would have them unlock the door and let me go now."

"I cannot do that, but I will have them move the *Pegasus*. It is in the way."

She turned to face him fully. "Don't you dare break my baby bird."

"Oh no, Harry," he said and enunciated every word. "I will ensure your baby bird is in perfect flying condition."

She paused, absorbing his words, then retorted, "You'd better. If there's a single feather damaged I'll replace it with your skin."

He nodded and knocked on the door. As it was unlocked he saluted with a click of his heels.

"Johannes"—she burst out as he turned to go—"we can't be stuck in here all day and night."

He glanced round and then nodded. The door closed behind him and locked with a solid clunk.

Harry turned back to the window with a grin on her face. Khuwelsa frowned. "You worry me when you smile like that."

"Ha!" Harry threw her arms around her in a tight hug. "He's going to help us get out."

"Are you feeling well?" Khuwelsa said, extricating herself from Harry's arms and brushing the creases from her dress. "He didn't say anything like that."

"You weren't listening with the right ears," said Harry.

"You mean *your* ears. I remember the time you claimed your father said we could go down to the waterhole. And we got chased by that old hippo."

"We were seven."

"And ten years later you're just the same."

"We didn't get hurt."

"Only because hippos can't climb trees."

Harry laughed. "You're still angry because you tore your dress."

"It was a present from your father." She turned away, pouting. "I could never wear it again."

"You wait," said Harry. "You'll see."

5

They waited. At shortly after two in the afternoon the main compound gates opened and the *Pegasus* came through, mounted on a reduced-gravity trailer and pulled by a steam truck. The wings had been folded in. Khuwelsa worried over potential damage to the control mechanisms.

"They don't know what they're doing with a 'thopter," she said.

The steam truck was unhooked, but the electrical cable remained attached. A dozen soldiers manoeuvred the trailer into a space out of the main stream of traffic. One of them disconnected the cable and the girls watched the trailer sink as it took the full weight of the *Pegasus.*

A meal was brought to them mid-afternoon and Harry asked to see Johannes. They ate and drank slowly. The electric fan in the ceiling kept the hot air circulating but, as the sun crept round, the room was bathed with light and heat. Their only escape from it was to sit against one wall until the sun had moved on.

It was an hour later that Johannes appeared. Khuwelsa was sitting near the door as he entered, while Harry stood near the window but in the shade.

"What do you want, Harriet?"

"Well, without wishing to be indelicate, I would like to point out there are no *facilities* available."

He frowned. "Facilities?"

Harry sighed. "No water closet."

Johannes nodded. "We do not have the *facilities* for ladies."

"Well, you should have thought about that before you locked us up."

"It was not my decision, Harriet," he said. "I do not want you here."

"And to think I came all this way just to see you."

"You deliberately misunderstand." Before she could come back with another retort he continued. "I will arrange a visit to the officers' *facilities* in a short time."

He knocked on the door. It was unlocked and he pulled it open.

"Johannes?"

He paused, waiting for her to continue, but she said nothing.

"Yes, Harriet?"

She arranged what she hoped was an expression of concern on her face, and looked down at the floor. She had been to parties where the young women made the men chase them by behaving like prey.

Like the good German gentleman that he was, he moved away from the door and stood before her.

"What is it, Harriet?"

"They will be letting us go tomorrow, won't they?"

"That is what I have been told." The momentary pause before his reply told her everything she needed to know.

She nodded, which he took as his dismissal. The door lock clicked firmly behind him.

"Well?" Harry demanded when the footsteps of the guard had retreated. "Did you get a good look at the lock?"

"I wish we were wearing corsets," replied Khuwelsa. "What we really need is a strip of pliable bone or metal. But at least there's no bolt on the outside."

"You've got your tools, though?"

Khuwelsa patted her skirt and smiled. "I wouldn't go anywhere without them. No chisel, though."

"What about the table?"

"It's designed to be taken apart but there's nothing useful. Though we could use the legs as clubs."

Harry sighed. "Maybe there'll be something in the W.C. that you can use."

Another thirty minutes crept past before Johannes reappeared with an escort of four soldiers with rifles in their hands and pistols at their hips.

"You're expecting us to make a break for it?"

"Regulations."

"Of course."

They were guided through the building and out into the open. The *Pegasus* was only a dozen yards away but might as well have been on the other side of the moon for all the good it did.

"The furnace wasn't properly banked when we landed."

"Our engineers looked after the ship."

"What do they know about 'thopters?

"You are not going aboard your vessel, Harriet."

They were guided to a building, probably constructed by Arab slavers years before. It had smooth tapered columns, and open windows with a ceiling that was high and distant. As they stepped through into the shade and coolness of the interior, Harry breathed a sigh of relief. The German-built structure was not designed for equatorial zones, but the Kaiser's people had only started colonising in the last fifteen years. They were new to the game and did not understand the climate.

The building bustled with officers in deep discussion and messengers moving in and out. Apart from the guards there didn't seem to be a single man of rank below lieutenant in the place.

They passed the open door of a room with a huge map hung on one wall, showing the German Protectorate from the inland lakes to the coast, and the island of Zanzibar from whom they'd wrested control of the land. She knew the Arabs weren't too pleased about it, though in general she did not pay attention to her father's business.

He was on a diplomatic mission to Zanzibar. The old sultan was dead and there was some problem with the succession. Could this German invasion have anything to do with that?

They reached a suite near the rear signposted in German as "refreshment rooms." German was a long-winded language, but at least everything was labelled.

Johannes went in and determined that the rooms were in fact empty. On his return, he held open the door, gesturing for them to enter.

Harry put on her best haughty "maiden aunt" expression and jammed her fists into her hips, elbows out. "You do not expect to be in there *with* us?"

"Regulations state…"

"I don't give a *damn* about your regulations."

Khuwelsa gasped and threw her hand over her face to hide her giggles.

Johannes stood in the doorway, looking for a moment as if he was going to argue. Then he shrugged and came out.

With Khuwelsa in tow, Harry stormed past him and slammed the door. She threw the bolt on the inside and took in the details of the room as fast as she could. There were the usual wide windows along one wall, blocked with elegant wooden grids of complex geometric patterns, one behind the other in such a way that air would flow through but no one could see in or out.

The room was constructed primarily of marble with cubicles separated by alabaster panels, while the ceiling was decorated in patterns that echoed the window ornamentation.

A room off led to a bathing area.

"Those slavers liked the good life," commented Khuwelsa, with a dangerous undertone in her voice.

"See what you can find."

"Better not forget to use the facilities either," said Khuwelsa, grinning as she pulled up her skirt and extracted a leather toolkit from an inside pocket. "They probably won't let us out again until tomorrow."

6

The walk back through town was similar to the outward journey, except for the marching columns of soldiers heading east. Their thudding boots raised clouds of dust that dried the throat. The regular rhythm of their passing was punctuated by barked commands.

Harry made a point of counting them as they passed and had reached a number over a thousand by the time they regained the main building. But there had already been soldiers before those, and more just kept on coming.

Khuwelsa had extracted a strip of lead from one of the cisterns while perched on the toilet lid, and replaced the missing metal with a wad of folded cotton sliced from Harry's petticoat using a small knife. She thought her makeshift replacement would hold for perhaps a few hours. They hoped to be away before they were discovered.

The second part of the plan was trickier.

When they approached the door to their prison, Harry allowed Khuwelsa to go ahead of her and through the open door. Harry turned on Johannes.

"This is completely outrageous. My father will hear of this. There will be stern words to your government."

"Harriet, your father is precisely the reason why you are to be kept here until tomorrow," he said. She kept her head down and sniffed. "*Fraulein* Edgbaston?"

Harry knew she'd never win awards for acting, but she didn't have to do this on the stage. She pulled out a kerchief and lifted it to her face. The handkerchief had been soaked before they left the facilities; she wiped it across her cheeks, dampening them rather than drying. She rubbed her eyes hard in an effort to redden them.

Suffering as she did from the combination of a redhead's complexion and a multitude of freckles, crying always made her blotchy and quite ugly (as Khuwelsa had pointed out on more than one occasion).

She sniffed again and raised her eyes. Johannes shifted his feet and looked uncomfortable. "There is no need for tears, Harriet." He glanced at the guards, all looking at him, and then patted her awkwardly on the shoulder. "You must go into the room now."

She sobbed and pretended to suppress it, which caused something of a problem in her throat and turned into a short fit of coughing. She felt Johannes patting her shoulder again. *Men are so useless*, she thought. Give them a gun with something to shoot and they're all bravado and swagger. Faced with a crying girl, they crumble.

Which was just what she had counted on.

Khuwelsa's voice drifted from the room. "It's all right, Harry, I'll look after you." That was her signal to indicate she had finished. Harry was grateful; if she had to escalate, the next stage involved collapsing to the floor in a dead faint. She hated smelling salts. And as she wasn't wearing a corset, it might be unconvincing.

She sniffed. "Thank you for being so kind, Johannes." She closed on him and raising herself on tip-toes gave him a peck on the cheek. She turned and walked into the room. The door shut with a firm click.

Khuwelsa could barely contain her laughter. She put her hand on Harry's shoulder and mimicked Johannes's concerned tones. "It's all right, Harry, I'll look after you."

"Oh stop it. He was trying to be nice." Then she too had a fit of giggles that she desperately tried to suppress. "Did you do it?"

Khuwelsa nodded. "Of course I did."

Harry went to the window and the humour went out of her. The army continued to march past and she counted a further thousand men as she peered through the window of their prison. And that didn't include the five hundred she guessed must have gone past when she wasn't looking.

The military column changed composition from men to equipment: numerous steam- and diesel-powered automatic artillery units. She had no experience with which to judge how powerful they were but there was a group that had barrels that she thought she could stick her head into. Or Johannes's head.

Finally came a hundred steam trucks carrying supplies and support staff.

Could the Germans really be going to war? How many soldiers did you need for a war? Let's say they had five thousand men. How many had fought at Agincourt? She couldn't remember but it was more than that, and that was hundreds of years ago.

It all went quiet until an hour or so before dusk when the sky was filled with the sound of engines as a squadron of fighters went over followed by four Zeppelins that were so low they filled the sky.

They needed to get out and warn her father.

Below them in the courtyard sat the *Pegasus*–so near and, as yet, unattainable. They might be able to get out of the room, but how could they possibly reach it, get inside, and fire up the furnace, all without being shot?

It was seven in the evening when a meal was brought. She made sure she ate everything, even though it was not very appetising. Khuwelsa never had a problem eating anything that was put before her.

At eleven o'clock the lights went out. The guards still patrolled, but the number of people out in the streets and in the compound was greatly reduced. That was the good thing about armies. They even slept by the clock.

But she couldn't afford to do that. So she continued to stand at the window looking out even though she kept slipping as she drifted to sleep. At one point she caught herself on her knees, having decided in her befuddled state that lying down for a few minutes would be completely fine.

It was then a rattling alarm erupted through the compound.

7

Lights flicked on almost immediately. Khuwelsa pushed herself up on one elbow from where she'd been curled up asleep on the floor.

"What's that?" Her words ran together as she tried to push the sleep away.

Harry grinned. "Told you."

"Told me what?"

"Johannes. He's set off the alarm as a diversion. Come on, get the door open."

Khuwelsa climbed to her feet and made her way to the door. She extracted her kit, undid the buckle and rolled it open. Selecting a spatula-like tool, she knelt by the lock. Harry watched as she inserted the tool into the frame and wiggled it a few times. Sellie glanced up at her and nodded.

"Pull."

Harry grabbed the handle and applied increasing pressure. The door shifted slightly and then edged open.

The sound of the alarm got louder as the gap between the door and the frame opened up. Khuwelsa removed the spatula and together they peered through. There was no guard in sight.

"Let's go," hissed Harry.

"Wait." Khuwelsa brought out a pair of pliers and yanked a distorted lump of metal from the lock. She put it in her pocket, exchanging it for the original metal latch which she carefully returned to its proper position and jammed into place. She stood up and gave the room a final scan while Harry shifted impatiently at the entrance.

"Come *on.*"

Khuwelsa rewrapped her tools and returned them to their hidden pocket. "Just making sure we haven't forgotten anything." She walked past Harry into the corridor.

"And what, pray, could we have possibly forgotten?"

Khuwelsa shrugged. Harry pulled the door shut and it clicked into place.

"That'll keep them guessing," said Khuwelsa.

They made their way along the corridor past a bell still rattling out the alarm. Khuwelsa put her fingers in her ears as they passed. They turned left through an entrance into the stairwell. It was quieter out there with the door closed.

"What if it's a real alarm?" asked Khuwelsa while Harry looked up and down the stairwell.

"It isn't." Harry headed up.

"Don't we want to go down?"

"Down is where all the soldiers are."

"And the *Pegasus*."

"Trust me."

Khuwelsa gave her a look but followed her as she lifted her skirts and took the wide stairs two at a time.

As they reached the next level the alarm stopped, followed almost immediately by the sound of grumbling soldiers echoing up from below them. A final flight led up and terminated in a door. They kept going.

Harry tried the handle. It opened without any trouble. Cold night air flowed in, along with the distant sounds of officers barking orders and the tramp of marching feet.

The two girls slipped out onto the roof and shut the door behind them.

Like a black desert the top of the building lay before them, lights from the streets glowing beyond the edges. They headed towards the wing of the building to the right. The *Pegasus* was located at its far end.

As they reached the corner Harry looked over the edge into the compound below. It was empty but brightly lit. They would never be able to get across it to their ship without being seen by the guards on the gate. She wondered whether perhaps they would have been less awake if it hadn't been for the alarm.

The door they had come out of opened once more, spraying light into the darkness. They froze. Two soldiers stepped onto the roof and shut the door behind them. Against the blackness they became invisible.

A murmur of conversation drifted across to them. *Strange, how German sounds like English when you can't make out the words*, Harry thought. She saw a flare of light as they lit cigarettes. Probably shouldn't be smoking on duty, but it meant they weren't paying attention. She nudged Khuwelsa and, keeping low with their skirts pulled up, they moved on.

They made it to the end of the building where a metal ladder led down to their little ornithopter. There was no way they could get down with the two soldiers lounging around on the rooftop. They'd notice any movement as she and Khuwelsa went over the edge since the side of the building was lit up.

Harry glanced at Khuwelsa. She was removing her dress. It took Harry a moment to understand; it was the only practical way they were going to be able to get down. With a heavy sigh Harry followed suit, reaching round and untying the bows that held the bodice tight.

This will be very awkward if we get caught, she thought as she shrugged the heavy material off her shoulders and wriggled the dress down over her hips. Not only awkward, but unfortunate—they would have to leave the dresses behind, regardless.

Khuwelsa had got hers off. Next she produced a pair of scissors from her tool kit and proceeded to cut three long strips from one of her petticoats. She passed one of the strips across to Harry, then rolled up her own dress into a tight bundle that she tied off with another.

Harry smiled and did the same while Khuwelsa was folding and tying the last strip into knots, or so it looked to her. Harry shoved her arm through the cotton strip holding her dress and pushed the bundle back so it was on her shoulder, giving her complete freedom of movement.

Whatever Khuwelsa had been doing, she was apparently finished. She delved into a pocket of her bloomers—*when had she put a pocket in?*—and there was a quiet chink of metal on metal. Khuwelsa held the ends of her knotted strip and placed the whatever-it-was into the loop. She got up on one knee and spun the slingshot, getting up speed, and then released it towards the far corner of the building beyond the soldiers.

There was nothing to see.

And nothing to hear.

Khuwelsa sighed quietly and rummaged for another missile. She wound up and let fly again. Harry got the impression it was with less force than before. Two things happened in quick succession: glass shattered, and the soldiers swore. The glow of their cigarettes dropped to the rooftop and vanished. They unslung their guns and headed round the top of the stairwell to investigate the noise.

Harry squeezed Khuwelsa's arm. Staying low they made it to the edge and swung over onto the ladder. First Harry and then, after she had descended a few steps, Khuwelsa. They were completely exposed; it would only require someone to look up, or look out from a window, and they'd be seen. The guards on the roof would probably head back and see them easily, too.

Halfway to the ground they heard the sound of someone in the compound. Harry looked down. A soldier stood by the gate, talking to the guard. They laughed about something. Harry glanced up at Khuwelsa but could see nothing more than her legs. Finally she took a look at the roof; as yet there was no sign of the guards. She tried to will the soldier to leave.

Instead he moved forward until all she could see was his legs. The rest of his body was hidden by the guard house roof. Harry tapped Khuwelsa twice on the leg and headed down again. She kept peering over her shoulder as she descended; more of the guard came into view. Before he could have seen them, they were safely hidden behind the body of the *Pegasus*. They reached the ground and then clambered up on to the trailer. Shucking off their bundles the girls sheltered in the shadow of their 'thopter. Harry almost kissed it.

The main hatch was on the other side of the fuselage, and there was no way they would be able to use it without being seen. So while Khuwelsa set to with a screwdriver on one of the portholes—it was going to be a squeeze—Harry crept to the rear and unbuckled the straps that had been used to tie the *Pegasus* to the trailer. She wouldn't be able to do anything about the one on the other side, but she hoped unbuckling this side would be enough.

She headed forward as Khuwelsa gently removed the metal-bound glass from the porthole. Khuwelsa shoved the dresses inside and, using a protrusion on the hull for a foothold, got her head and shoulders through, then wriggled her way inside. Harry knew she had no need to tell Khuwelsa to get the furnace going, though she was puzzled when she saw her sister pulling one end of a rope into the ship as well, leaving the rest dangling out.

Harry crept to the forward strap and worked to undo it. She was almost fully exposed, though still in shadow. Of course this one had been buckled tighter than the other, so she had to spend time straining at it. Finally she got it released and pulled the leather through the loops.

At a premonition of danger, she jerked her gaze up. Straight across from her, looking out of a downstairs window, and directly at her, was a face. Johannes. He watched her for a few more moments, then disappeared into the interior shadows.

Harry shook herself and crept back behind the ship. Hand over hand she went up the side, using Khuwelsa's rope—no, it was a cable for electrics—to reach that porthole, then squeezed through, tumbling headfirst to the *Pegasus*'s deck. She could hear Sellie shovelling and see light coming from the furnace. It wouldn't take long to heat the water, but at that point the ship would begin to make noise as the metal expanded and the generators spun up to speed.

The pilot's chair was waiting. She clambered forward and into it, running her fingers over the familiar controls as she settled. There was nothing she could do until steam was up. Worried, she clasped her hands before her chin and idly gnawed her thumb. She desperately wanted to be away. The Germans would start shooting when they knew the *Pegasus* was going to lift. Someone could die. It could be Khuwelsa. Or her. And she did not like the prospect of either.

8

There were two reasons Johannes had set off the alarm. The first was to provide a distraction to help the sisters get to their ship. He was worried at first that they had not even succeeded in getting through the door of their prison. However, he knew that Harriet was very determined, a trait that was simultaneously appealing and infuriating, and also that Khuwelsa was clever with mechanics. Surely they had found a way.

He considered his course of action, which ultimately could be considered a betrayal of his country. Officially Germany and Great Britain were not in conflict, though imprisoning the daughter of a representative of Her Majesty's government and her companion might be considered an act of war. But the words of the commandant before he left had helped Johannes decide.

"I shall release the girls at midday, then, sir?"

"No, Lieutenant," he had said without a moment's thought or consideration. "You will keep the daughter locked up, as she may prove a useful bargaining tool. You can do what you like with the black. Sell her."

Johannes considered himself to be a good soldier, and part of that was keeping one's word. He had told Harriet she would be released the next day. He would not be made a liar. Nor would he be made a slaver.

To that end, he had not caused a fuss over the time the girls had taken in the officers' convenience—after all, everyone knew how long women usually took—nor had he taken any steps to have the place examined afterwards. Luckily the other officers were not familiar with the two.

But he had not seen them escape by any of the routes he expected, and after the alarm had been switched off he had taken a squad up to their room and tried the door. It was still firmly locked and showed no signs of having been tampered with, at least from the outside. That had been the low point, where he had concluded they had not been able to escape. To be honest, he had been disappointed.

He had dismissed his men and gone down for a look at the *Pegasus* still lying there in the courtyard.

And that was when he had seen them coming down the ladder, in their underclothes. He smiled. They had gone across the roof. *That was daring and completely foolhardy*, he thought as he watched them descend—Harriet's bare white limbs, Khuwelsa's dark ones and their clothes so white it would take a blind man not to see them even on a moonless night.

Both Harriet and Khuwelsa were handsome women in their own ways, and they were not shrinking violets—they were willing to risk their lives for their country. Or perhaps, in Harriet's case, it was simply that she was as stubborn as a mule. Somehow that description seemed to fit her better. Khuwelsa would probably follow Harriet to the ends of the earth and then devise a means of returning.

He watched as one of the guards crossed the courtyard and failed to check his surroundings. Johannes made a mental note to have the man disciplined for his incompetence. The soldier then compounded his crime by starting up a conversation with the gate guard, thus distracting him as well. This might, however, work out for the best.

A glance back at the ladder showed him that Harriet and Khuwelsa were gone. They must have completed their descent. Khuwelsa would have entered the vessel in order to fire up the furnace and bring up the steam pressure before they would be able to take off. That could not happen without alerting the base.

Which brought him to the second reason he had set off the alarm. If one alarm were proven to be false, and another followed quickly, the men would be less enthusiastic in their response since the second would just as likely be false. There would be no mad rush to their stations.

He watched a shadowy form he guessed to be Harriet moving to the front of the carrier on which the *Pegasus* was loaded. She wrestled with the buckles on the strap and got it loose. He glanced at the two guards who were still chatting; they had even lit up a couple of cigarettes.

He looked back at Harriet to discover she was looking straight at him. He paused for a moment and stepped backwards out of the light.

She slipped back behind the ship.

* * *

Harry watched the steam pressure gauge creep oh-so-slowly towards the range in which she could engage the wings. *The wings*, she thought in horror and looked to her left through the canopy. The left side was tight against the wall with no space for a wing beat. They would need to be near the centre of the compound to accommodate the full span.

She pulled herself out of the chair and headed back to where Khuwelsa was pumping the furnace manually to keep the noise down. The heat from the fire was already turning the 'thopter's interior into an oven.

"We need to move the ship," said Harry.

Khuwelsa nodded and pointed to a jury-rigged set of electrical connections. "When we power up the Faraday it'll do the same for the trailer. We'll be able to move it."

"When were you planning on telling me?"

Khuwelsa smiled. "I knew you'd work it out."

Harry did not smile but put her hand on Khuwelsa's arm. "Once we get going you need to stay down."

"You're the one that's at risk, Harry," said Khuwelsa. "I'm surrounded by metal."

* * *

Outside in the compound the German soldiers chatting by the gate were interrupted by the chuffing of a steam engine. They ignored it at first; heavy equipment on the move was not unusual at any time of the day or night. Especially now.

But the sound grew to the point where it could no longer be ignored.

The guard took a couple of steps back into the open part of the compound and stared in astonishment at the smoke pouring from the British ornithopter's stack.

"Alarm!"

He unslung his rifle as the soldier in the guard post set off the jangling bells throughout the building.

* * *

Khuwelsa gave two shrill whistles. Harry reached forward, flipped the Faraday and the feeling of lightness swept through them.

A bullet ricocheted nearby, the sound zinging across Harry's head. Instinctively she ducked but felt no pain. She glanced out to the right; two soldiers, one with a rifle and the other with a pistol, trained their weapons on the ship.

After so many years in the *Pegasus* it was as if the vessel were an extension of her own body and she reacted without thinking. Grabbing the controller for the right wing, she slammed it forward and to the right. The starboard wing flicked out and smashed into the two men, sending them flying into the far wall where they fell to the ground and lay still.

It took her a moment to take in what had happened. She whispered an apology and hoped they weren't dead. But now she realised what she needed to do.

She worked the left wing with more finesse until the metal arm was against the wall at their side, and then she pushed. The *Pegasus* slipped to the side before catching on the trailer straps. She pushed harder, and the *Pegasus* tilted. That wasn't working.

She let off the pressure and the ship righted. Harry angled the right wing to the ground and pushed down as she applied pressure to the wall again. There was a terrific crash of shattering glass as the left wing went through a window.

She cursed herself and pulled it free, making sure she jammed it against the brickwork for her next attempt. This time she pushed down with the right wing to take some of the weight, pulling the trailer up as well. Success. The lateral force from the left wing turned the front of the *Pegasus* toward the middle of the compound…

… where she saw a squad of soldiers pouring from the main doors.

They were about forty feet away. She ploughed both wings into the ground and then drove them backwards, forcing the ship and trailer forward. The men in the squad jumped at the movement. Harry was pretty sure nobody had done that with an ornithopter before.

It also gave her an idea. Bullets pinged off the fuselage as she threw the *Pegasus* into a crazy walk across the courtyard, thrusting it forward again and again. The soldiers dived in all directions as the ship crashed into the space they'd been occupying.

She glanced at the steam pressure. Nearly there.

She tried to do the same manoeuvre in reverse to get them back to the centre of the compound, only to discover the weight of the ship and trailer at the rear made it impossible.

There was banging on the hatch as the soldiers tried to gain entry. Two appeared above the canopy, their guns aimed straight at her. In a reflexive move she slammed the right wing into an upstairs window. Broken glass and wood showered down; the two soldiers slipped off, covering their heads. Using the same technique as before, Harry got the *Pegasus* turned around.

Two long whistles from Khuwelsa meant that they were ready to go. Harry engaged the propeller. She hoped there was no one near it as she heard it spin up to speed. She could feel the force of its thrust trying to edge the ship forward, towards the gate. Harry glanced at the steam gauge. It was on full pressure.

She gave the wings a powerful stroke and felt the ship lift slightly. The soldiers she could see in front were knocked down by the air blast.

She engaged the highest gearing for the propeller. The *Pegasus* surged forward. Harry gave a powerful beat that should have shot them into the air. They gained only a few feet and dropped again. Another beat and another and another. Harry worked the controls and they crept upwards. They were still carrying the trailer.

They ran straight into the gate. The *Pegasus* lurched forwards and the ground loomed in Harry's face. She thrust again and again. The propeller tore the air. The ship was like a bird caught in a snare, desperately flapping its wings to pull itself free. Something had to give. And something did.

The *Pegasus* rocketed forward, then swung to the side. Harry realised the trailer must be unhooked, but the electrical power cable still tied it to the ship. Then that dragging weight was gone too, and the *Pegasus* jerked free. She heard a cry from Khuwelsa but had no time to look.

There were buildings on both sides of them but the sky above was clear. Wingtips scraped the walls, and the nose tilted upwards.

With its wings beating and the propeller whirling like a tornado, the *Pegasus* erupted from its cage.

9

As they rose above the rooftops and into clear air, Harry looked back over her shoulder. Khuwelsa was sitting on the deck, cradling her arm.

Harry pulled the *Pegasus* into a gentle climb into the east, put the wings in an arched position and locked them off. She clambered out of her chair and headed into the body of the ship.

Khuwelsa leaned with her back to the fuselage. A ragged gash along her left forearm leaked blood. Her white chemise and drawers were splattered with red.

Harry found the tied-up parcel of her dress and untied the length of linen Khuwelsa had torn from her chemise. Using it as a bandage, she wrapped it firmly around Khuwelsa's arm and pulled the two edges of the gash together.

Khuwelsa opened her eyes. "Thank you."

"What happened?"

"Power cable."

Harry looked across the ship to where she expected to see the cable. Instead there was a deep scar in the inner hull leading directly to the dismantled porthole. The cable Khuwelsa had used to power the Faraday from the trailer had torn free as they took off. The end must have lashed her arm as it was yanked through.

In the galley area, Harry rummaged around until she found a bottle of water. She brought it back, unscrewed the cap and handed it to Khuwelsa, who took a long drink. Harry returned to the pilot's chair and checked the dials. They were still climbing but hadn't exceeded one thousand feet yet. *Pegasus* could manage nearly eight thousand feet before things started to get uncomfortable for them.

She looked out. It was several hundred miles to the coast. There were no mountains or even tall hills between them and the sea, so she was not concerned about that. She was worried about the German airplanes and Zeppelins that had set off earlier. They would have stopped for the night but she was not sure how far they would have travelled, or when the *Pegasus* might run into them.

Flying by night was avoided where possible because it was so easy to lose one's way. The wandering silver line of the river below them showed her they were still on the right heading. As long as she kept their course to the east, following the river, they should be fine. But if they had to evade any Germans during the night, or lost the river, they could end up anywhere along the coast.

"Pressure's going to drop soon," said Khuwelsa. Harry glanced back and saw her trying to stand.

"I'll do the stoking." Harry said and strode past her to the furnace. "You need to rest."

Even with the door closed the heat coming off the metal warmed her bare skin.

"You'll need me when we land."

"I know, Sellie. But try to get some sleep for now. I can keep us in the air."

* * *

The sun crawled above the horizon shortly before seven. Far below them a dozen giraffes cast extra-long shadows across the undulating savannah. They passed over a waterhole where a herd of gazelles and wildebeest drank. Mists hung in the dips before they were burnt away by the heat of the day.

Harry pulled down her goggles over her eyes. Their tinted glass blocked some of the rays but the brightness dispelled her tiredness. Khuwelsa still slept, her head cushioned on her rolled-up dress.

The horizon looked blurred. Harry squinted, pulled up her goggles and rubbed her eyes. It remained blurred; small dark clouds lay between grass and sky.

Zeppelins. It was the German military force. No more than fifteen miles away.

She checked the steam pressure and cursed on seeing it was almost out again. She realised she must have dozed off in the chair. Indecision froze her. The Germans would cover the distance in less than ten minutes. The *Pegasus* needed more altitude, but without power she could do nothing; it would be like the landing in the town all over again. Except this time the Germans would shoot to bring the *Pegasus* to the ground.

Harry lifted the nose a little and increased the power to the propeller, then made her way back to the furnace. She lifted the latch with the shovel and swung the door open. The heat blasted out as she piled in the coal until she thought she had enough. She paused beside Khuwelsa as she headed back to the chair. The bandage on Khuwelsa's arm was discoloured by dried blood but there was no sign of new bleeding.

She climbed back into the chair. The steam pressure was rising. As she opened the drive valves to maximum, the roar of the propeller increased. She pulled the ship into a steep climb; this would have the double effect of getting them out of sight and slowing their ground speed so they did not reach the German encampment, wherever it was, so quickly.

By the time the *Pegasus* reached seven and half thousand feet she was struggling. Harry reduced the rate of climb, seeing that the Zeppelins were still a few miles out. She closed off the drive valve to cut power to the propeller. The 'thopter went quiet. Wind whispered through the feathers; the soft sound filtered into the fuselage.

If no one looked up, they should be safe—if they had not been heard already. And even if someone did look up, even if they had heard the *Pegasus*, they would just assume it was another German vessel. Wouldn't they?

Harry felt a presence beside her. Khuwelsa's hand came to rest on her shoulder. "Where are we?"

Their air-speed dropped, and to prevent a stall Harry tilted the nose down a little. The horizon came into view, the broad savannah and the massed encampment of the German army with the Zeppelins floating above it. To the right Harry could see the cross-shaped outlines of their fliers on the ground.

"Oh," said Khuwelsa.

"How are you feeling?"

"My arm's throbbing. My head feels like it's filled with mud," said Khuwelsa. "I'll live."

"I'm glad about that."

"You're filthy."

"I've been doing your job as well as mine."

"You should have woke me."

"No," said Harry. "Can you keep an eye on their airplanes? Let me know if anything happens."

Khuwelsa moved to the starboard side and peered through the porthole. "You mean if one of them's taking off?"

"Yes."

The silence that followed tugged at Harry's tired mind. "Why do you say that?"

"Because one of them's taking off."

"Oh hell."

Harry slammed open the propulsion valve and the propeller roared to life.

10

Harry jumped to her feet and peered out through the canopy. A trail of dust ended in the cross-shaped shadow of an airplane. The shadow separated itself from the ground.

"Can you stoke?" Harry asked.

"Yes." Khuwelsa nodded and headed into the back. Harry watched as she awkwardly put on her heavy apron.

There was little point watching the plane; it wouldn't reach their height for several minutes, if indeed it was coming after them at all. She checked to ensure the controls were stable and went to the starboard porthole. The temporary air-dock was slipping behind; she had to get up close to the glass to peer out. She saw two more airplanes on the move.

She went back to her chair, making plans based on the principle they had seen her and would be giving chase. Squinting and staring forward, towards the rising sun, she wondered how far they were from the coast. It couldn't be very far now. Maybe fifty miles. Then there was the twenty miles of sea to cross to Zanzibar.

What could the Germans possibly be hoping to achieve? She tried to remember the boring politics her father talked about. The previous sultan of Zanzibar had been poisoned and the new one favoured the Germans. The British preferred another man who was anti-slavery. Her father had said something about diplomatic moves to replace the current leader.

Perhaps the Germans wanted to make sure the British didn't have their man in charge. And she and Khuwelsa were the only ones who knew about the German force. She was patriotic enough to want to do her duty, though her one trip to Britain had convinced her she didn't want to live there—it was a grey place and seemed to rain all the time.

The fact that her father would be in the middle of the trouble was even more important.

Below them the Wami River grew in size as it was fed by tributaries. It was already too wide to cross easily and would only get wider. Even worse, its banks became swamp as it got close to the sea. The only towns were Bagamoyo or Dar es Salaam even further south. The British-built bridge on the road from Mombasa was the only way across for people on foot. Harry checked the chronometer; it had been five minutes since they watched the German plane take off.

She set the *Pegasus* into a slight descent; the ship's airspeed increased. She had no hope of matching the speed of the fixed-wing craft in level flight (or any direction of flight, if truth be told). However, if the other plane wanted to intercept her it would have spent the time climbing to her altitude.

Khuwelsa came up beside her.

"Can you see if the Kaiser's little pet is following us, Sellie?"

Khuwelsa went to each porthole in turn. "I can't see a thing."

Harry frowned. "Maybe they didn't see us after all." She tried to think. The portholes did not provide a good view. "We have to have a proper look. I'll do a complete circle. You keep your eyes open, out the starboard side."

Harry took hold of the controls, feeling the wind through the wings. She disengaged the propeller and the *Pegasus* went silent. Gently Harry pulled on the controls and the plane swept round. The sun disappeared from the canopy and threw the interior into shadow. The compass rotated in its mount. Harry scanned the sky for telltale shapes, even a trail of steam or diesel exhaust, against the intensely blue sky.

"Level out, Harry!" shouted Khuwelsa before they had even turned all the way west. Harry adjusted the controls and let *Pegasus* glide in a gentle descent without re-engaging the rotor. She joined Khuwelsa at the porthole.

A cloud of dust was rising across the savannah behind them. It was not an uncommon sight; they often saw racing herds of wildebeest, zebras or gazelles spooked by a predator or maybe just their own shadows. But this wasn't any grazing animal on the run.

They could see perhaps two dozen vehicles, all with mounted artillery, ripping across the terrain, airplanes flanking them and the Zeppelins following not far behind. Harry stared for what seemed like ages but was probably only seconds, then threw herself back to the pilot's chair.

She yanked the controls and turned the *Pegasus* on its wingtip. As it stalled and began to fall she re-engaged the propeller, and they shot forwards. Barely caring if they were seen now, she beat the wings to push them forward before the power from the engine thrust them faster than the wings could.

Harry estimated it would take the German motorised forces half a day to get to the coast, maybe less. The infantry would be a few days behind, but they would have to cross the bridge or sink into the swamp. The Wami never dried up, even at this driest time of year.

Tracer bullets streamed up from beneath them, crossing towards the right. That answered that question. The German plane was trying to take out her Faraday grid. She veered off to port and dived. There was a cry of annoyance from Khuwelsa. "Sorry," muttered Harry. She threw the *Pegasus* to starboard and the German plane shot across her bow, so close she could see the pilot's face.

She gunned the propeller to maximum, diving towards the river. A crazy plan formed in her mind.

"Next time you get the chance, Sellie, can we have some guns on this thing?"

"Oh, yes! It will be my pleasure."

Harry glanced at the steam pressure; it was at the top of the gauge. "Better strap in, this is going to be interesting."

"In what way interesting?"

"Fatally."

"You know, as you're not really family maybe I could just get off while you kill yourself?"

Harry grinned and willed the *Pegasus* to fly faster. She trimmed the wings to reduce air resistance. They lost altitude more rapidly but their airspeed increased.

"Apart from the guns, I'd like to be able to see downwards, out the front," she shouted.

"You want me to make a list?"

The *Pegasus* plummeted out of the sky. Harry glanced at the altitude gauge: two thousand feet.

"And a mirror so I can see backwards, above and below."

"Nothing complicated then."

Harry wished she could see behind her right now. The German would be there somewhere. But how close?

A series of metallic impacts rang through the ship in answer to her question. Harry felt one of the wings vibrate oddly. The port wing wasn't responding well.

"He's ruptured one of the pipes!" shouted Khuwelsa.

"Can you fix it?"

"Mind if we pop back to my workshop?"

Harry twisted the starboard wing and the *Pegasus* slipped sideways with its body and wings against the direction of motion, killing their forward speed. The German plane shot past them, passing them in a fraction of a second. He must have been right on their tail and lining up the shot, confident that not only were they unarmed but that they had no idea he was there. If he had been right they would be dead.

They had dropped to one thousand feet.

"Try not to use the wings for a minute," said Khuwelsa.

Harry felt the ship sinking but the propeller was increasing their velocity in the new direction. They would get enough lift in a few moments. She locked off the controls and scanned the sky. No sign of him.

She jumped down and joined Khuwelsa, who was wrapping an oiled cloth around a pipe. "Best I can do is bind the hole. It won't maintain good pressure and won't last."

"Can I help?"

Khuwelsa nodded her head at the tightly wrapped cloth she was still holding. "Keep this tight." Harry took over while Khuwelsa grabbed some wire and a short metal rod. She wrapped the wire round loosely then inserted the rod. She turned it, steadily tightening the wire until it gripped tightly. Harry let go and Khuwelsa tied it off.

Harry went back to her chair and tried the wings. They responded, but the port side was still a bit mushy.

The German would have had time to come around, thought Harry. She kept climbing away into the southeast. Something caught her eye; she turned her head. The German. She whipped the *Pegasus* about and dived back towards the bridge—a monstrous stone thing built along the lines of London Bridge and looking completely out of place on its own in the middle of the African grasslands.

"Let's get it right this time, shall we?" she muttered as the German opened up on them again. Bullets ricocheted off the fuselage.

11

Werner Klauber had joined the Imperial German Air Corps shortly after the Kaiser had announced the new policy: to build an Empire across the world and into the Void. Werner had wanted to go into the Void and he had been there. Just once.

He had been taken above the atmosphere, and had seen the earth as a ball below him. He was confronted with the infinite black beyond filled with the pin-prick lights of crystalline stars. The constant sensation of falling without moving had filled him with a terror so intense it threatened to overwhelm him. It made him shake even when only a memory. He had known there were people that could not bear the Void and, with his comrades, he had laughed at them. He had not thought he would be one.

The only saving grace was that the terror brought out in him a great sickness of the stomach. Something that even afflicted those who did not fear the Void. As a result he was able to disguise the terror that stained his very soul. He hated his weakness. He could not work in the Void, but he became a pilot and funnelled that consuming hatred into a dedicated and murderous streak. He did not care who he killed in the service of the Kaiser—or indeed outside of it, either.

His temper was feared even by his comrades. That brought some satisfaction, though it did not assuage his failure. He worked as a man driven by the devil, even though that devil was himself. In piloting skills and in gunnery he excelled; he took risks and they paid off. His superiors did not like him, but they acknowledged his usefulness.

Werner had been awake early and tending to his airplane when the faint and distant sound of a pumping engine had attracted his attention. He had seen the foreign ornithopter when the light from the rising sun glinted on the metal of its wings. The story unfolded in his mind. The girls had escaped and were even now on their way to warn the British forces in Zanzibar.

He had already had the engine ticking over. There had been no time to alert anyone else. He threw himself into the cockpit and took to the air. He would bring it down, save the expedition and they would give him the credit he deserved.

But the damned British plane would not go down.

He knew he had hit something important because it went into a holding pattern, but he was unable to capitalise on it. His speed shot him past the ornithopter, giving him only a glimpse of the girl in the pilot's seat before he flashed beyond it and had to pull round in a long sweep.

The ornithopter was in a climb away from the bridge on the ground before he managed to get into position for another attack. This time he throttled back; he would not make the mistake of overshooting again.

They must have seen him because they turned back towards the bridge. He was at a loss to understand the pilot's thinking but then she was just some stupid girl, not a professional combatant.

He watched as she pulled the wings in, like a bird diving, and the ornithopter accelerated. He laughed. There was no way she could outrun him. As he closed on them, taking his time, he lined up behind them. It made the target smaller, but she was effectively motionless in front of him.

Werner opened fire and watched the tracers rake across her stern. One of them sparked off the propeller, the others deflected from the fuselage.

The nose of the ornithopter dipped abruptly, the wings folded into the body and the machine fell away from him.

He grinned. All the pilots had made fun of Tomas when she had switched off her Faraday to escape him and landed—crashed—into the town square. Seems she only had this one trick.

Werner opened up the power and dived after her. She was already out of range but he would catch her soon enough. The ground was approaching fast. They were at only a few hundred feet when she re-engaged her Faraday and flipped the wings out halfway—enough to give her control.

He was about to revise his opinion of her—thinking perhaps she was not entirely unskilled—when she dipped into the river. A wall of water exploded upwards. Clouds of flamingos erupted into the air. Hippos charged from the water. She lifted again, her speed reduced to almost nothing, and crashed down on the far side of the bridge.

The ornithopter landed hard on the parapet. She smashed through the wall and into a lamp post, which toppled down the far side. The British were crazy. They built a bridge that should have been in a city in the middle of the savannah *and* gave it lamp posts when there was no gas or electric for a hundred miles.

The 'thopter back-winged furiously to arrest its remaining momentum and came to rest half off the bridge.

The bridge was coming at him at one hundred kilometres an hour. He pulled the firing trigger and raked it with powerful machine-gun fire as he yanked hard on the control stick to lift the nose. The plane responded by shooting over the bridge with barely thirty feet of clearance. He was not concerned. There was as much space beneath it; he could have gone under just as easily.

Werner pulled up and craned his neck. The 'thopter was a sitting duck. He pulled his craft into the tightest turn he dared. It was critically important to keep the active Faraday beneath the main portion of the airplane. Otherwise, it would have no effect, and the plane would fall out of the sky—just as she had done deliberately, but upside-down.

The 'thopter had not moved from its position. The right wing was flapping, the left one moving a little but not enough to provide any lift. Not just a sitting duck, but a wounded one.

This time he would make sure. He prepared one of his bombs. While this was his least favourite method, against a ground target it was the best option. He lined up for the final run. The 'thopter was still flapping its right wing. He hoped they wouldn't abandon ship. Destroying the plane was his main target, but he'd prefer to kill the girls as well. Get the whole job done properly.

He kept the speed down to fifty, to ensure his aim was good. Descending to skim the surface of the river, he headed towards the bridge. The smile on his face grew in anticipation. His thumb held firm on the bomb-drop mechanism.

Barely three hundred feet from the bridge, the river rippling from his low-level flight, it happened. Both the 'thopter's wings beat in wide forceful strokes. At two hundred feet out, the nose of the 'thopter lifted. At one hundred feet, it was sitting almost vertical, wings outstretched, the propeller driving so hard it created a miniature whirlwind on the bridge.

Werner was too close, and there was no time to pull up. He might want to kill the girls but he did not want to die in the impact. With a grim laugh he pushed the control forward and dived beneath the bridge.

He panicked for a second when he saw the pile of rubble from the damaged bridge in the water ahead of him, but there was still enough of a gap. Except for the fallen lamp post protruding from the river bed, and the 'thopter dropping towards the river on the far side. There was no way out.

His instincts took over and he tried to turn away. His right wing dipped and hit the water. The plane attempted to cartwheel. The left wing ripped off against the underside of the bridge and the airplane smashed into the shallow water.

* * *

The air blast from the exploding plane slammed the *Pegasus* forward. Harry barely managed to maintain control as a ball of fire engulfed them, then dissipated. She kept the wings beating as broken pieces of masonry and metal peppered the ship. Something ripped a hole through the fuselage above her.

And then it was over.

She gained height with strong wing beats and brought the *Pegasus* round. Khuwelsa came to stand beside her.

They looked at the wreckage of the bridge. An entire arch had been blown out and the adjoining sections didn't look too stable.

"He was carrying bombs," said Harry in surprise. "So I guess that went all right."

"All right?"

"Better than expected, really."

"*Better than expected?*"

"Well, we're not dead," said Harry. "I'd call that a success."

"Harry," said Khuwelsa. "Can we not do that again?"

"Yes," said Harry. She brought the ship round and made as much speed as she dared towards Zanzibar. "Let's not."

12

The *Pegasus* thundered across the sea between the African mainland and Zanzibar. Small fishing boats with triangular sails dotted the water. A large ferry steamed for the island and two British gunboats—outmoded and obsolete in the Faraday world—stood at the entrance to the bay. Harry could see their guns following the *Pegasus* as they went past. *Probably just practising*, she thought.

Stone Town of Zanzibar was a different world. The influence of the Arabs on its architecture and culture was evident along the slave trade routes across East Africa.

But Stone Town was Araby. The city had been ruled by the sultans for hundreds of years; they had made their mark, not only in the buildings, but also in the people. The skin tones and features of Africa were far less common than those of the Middle East.

Harry would have preferred to skirt around the city and approach from inland, but Khuwelsa was fussing about the damaged steam pipe. Harry couldn't deny that her bird was not behaving normally. The propeller vibrated unnaturally at high revolutions and she could feel the lack of response in the port wing.

She had never been to Zanzibar and had no idea of the best place to land. The city was built on a promontory sticking out into the sea, surrounded by an ancient wall. A difficult place to attack from the sea but the advent of air transportation made all such defences redundant.

Inside the wall the buildings were crammed together with barely more than alleys between them. To the north was a massive fort. Just to the fort's south was a large building with the only open spaces in the city. From what her father had said, Harry guessed it must be the sultan's palace.

"You're not planning on landing there," said Khuwelsa, leaning on her chair.

"How's your arm?"

"It aches but I'll live," she said. "And you didn't answer my question."

Harry yawned and rubbed her eyes. "Technically, you didn't ask one."

Khuwelsa slapped the back of her head.

"Can you see anywhere better?" said Harry. She rubbed her eyes, she would be glad for the chance to rest.

Khuwelsa said nothing for a while as Harry put the *Pegasus* into wide turn so as not to stress the damaged wing.

"We could land outside the walls inland."

"Every minute counts."

"You've decided then."

Harry hesitated. "Yes."

"Fine, I'll just get dressed."

Harry checked the steam pressure. It was down, but that was probably a good thing; landings and take-offs put the greatest strain on the wings. This was going to be a bit of a ticklish landing.

"What on earth!"

As she circled for the final time a tethered balloon drifted up from the sultan's garden. She saw several others being prepared. Turning again she saw big baggy balloons, attached to great winches, rising all across the city. What was more, they had gondolas hanging beneath holding two or three men, soldiers, with what looked to be small artillery weapons.

"Why is nothing easy!" Harry shouted in despair, remonstrating whatever god might be listening. Something shot across the bows. "Can't they see the flag?"

"Maybe the other side is still in charge."

The *Pegasus* jerked and the tail went sideways. Their airspeed dropped fast. "We've lost the rotor!" shouted Harry.

"I can't fix that up here."

There was no choice now.

"Lie down, Sellie, this is going to be rough."

"Again?"

Harry angled down and hoped they didn't take out any part of the Faraday grid. Another hit blew a hole through the fuselage.

It was difficult to focus. Harry dipped the nose and let the *Pegasus* have her head. There was no point worrying about the wing giving out; they couldn't stay up here any longer.

Harry saw the cable tethering one of the balloons just in time, yanked the controls instinctively and banked sharply. She knew immediately something was wrong. The port wing had ceased to respond. But it was still providing lift, so it must be locked open.

She took a deep breath and continued the turn which took her away from her landing point. She kept the turn going. When the ship had done a full rotation she saw the flat area again. It was too far away. Without wing or propeller there was no way she could get over the wall.

The guns had stopped firing. She was below all the gondolas now, which meant they would be firing on the city itself. That was a small mercy.

Could she land in the road approaching the gate? No, it wasn't wide enough to accommodate the wings. Did she have any choice? No.

She took a deep breath and made another full turn. At the end of it *Pegasus* was heading directly at the wall around the palace, a few yards to the left of the gate. She used the remaining steam to back-wing furiously with the right.

Pegasus almost spun on the spot. When they were over the road and sideways on, she killed the Faraday and the ship crashed to the ground. Harry was thrown from the chair and fetched up against the control panel. She found herself hoping for the second time in as many days that she hadn't hurt anyone. And then she thought of nothing at all.

* * *

Khuwelsa pulled herself to her feet and checked the cabin. The furnace had been banked and was designed to work at almost any angle. There was no hint of breakage or embers leaking out. The water reservoir was likewise solid. Steam leaked from a few places and the temporary mend they had performed on the main port pressure tube had blown apart. The cloth they had tied around it was in tatters.

The damage to the fuselage had not broken anything more important; they were just a couple of holes. It could have been worse. Repairs to the pipe and replacing the propeller would get them airborne again. The feathers and wing controls would need a more thorough check.

It occurred to her there had been no smart comment from Harriet.

The deck was at an angle and she had to climb to reach her sister who was lying curled up with her head resting on her arms. Khuwelsa checked her over and couldn't see any bleeding, or even bruising. In fact she could have sworn Harry was sleeping which, considering the fact she had barely slept since yesterday morning, was entirely likely.

She stood up and looked out but couldn't see anything except a wall. She clambered back to the main hatch and undogged it. Taking a deep breath she pushed it open and peered out along the port wing and into the streets of Zanzibar.

Her heart sank as a man in a dark suit and a wide-brimmed straw hat strode towards her.

"Khuwelsa Edgbaston! What on God's green earth are you and your damnable sister playing at?"

Khuwelsa stepped down awkwardly from the hatch, having to jump the final distance into the sun-baked dust, stone fragments and broken roof tiles. She turned to face him, expecting the full force of his anger. Again.

"Good morning, Daddy."

Jonathan Livingston Edgbaston did not make an impressive figure. He was neither tall nor short, thin nor ample. He kept out of the sun so had managed to maintain a fair complexion despite living in Africa for so many years. Like his daughter he had red hair, though his was thinning on top. He did not attempt a moustache because, as he said, unless one were a burly Scotsman, ginger facial hair invited ridicule.

Though his physique was less than imposing, he had risen through the ranks of the British diplomatic service to be … well, Khuwelsa didn't actually know what he was, except important. He often had official house guests with names that began with significant titles at the family home outside Mombasa, but she and Harry were instructed to stay out of their way.

He was often away for weeks at a time. The only person they had to obey was Mrs Hemingway, their tutor, and then only in regard to lessons. Khuwelsa and Mrs Hemingway did not get along. In some ways Khuwelsa was grateful because the situation had taught her how some white people felt about the blacks.

It had prepared her in some ways for the treatment she received when she and Harry went into Mombasa, or even smaller towns. The sisters had come to an agreement over how they would conduct themselves in such situations. It had taken a fight—a real fight that had started with hair pulling, pinching and slapping, then degenerated into punching, arm twisting and throttling—before Khuwelsa had forced Harry to agree. And she had sulked for days afterwards.

They pretended that Khuwelsa was not Harry's equal, just a native companion, while Khuwelsa kept her mouth shut and followed behind. Khuwelsa didn't like it but the alternative was worse. They hadn't told their father though; he might dislike it as much as Harry did. And Khuwelsa suspected a twisted arm would not persuade him.

"You're bleeding," he said as he clambered beneath the wing. She looked at her arm; she'd almost forgotten about it. It wasn't bleeding but the temporary bandage was still stained.

"Just a scratch, really," she said. He grabbed her hand and stretched her arm for a closer look, prodding at the bandage. She suppressed the sudden intake of breath as the pain shot up to her shoulder, and forced a grin onto her face. "It's fine."

The look he gave he suggested he was not convinced. "Where's Harriet?"

"Asleep."

"Unconscious?" he said with alarm. Khuwelsa thought he had good reason; the *Pegasus* looked a complete wreck, though she knew it was superficial damage, apart from the propeller.

"No, really, she's just asleep."

His eyebrows knotted. "And that's why you crashed? She was asleep?"

"Oh no, she was awake for that bit," she stopped, realising she wasn't making it any better.

"So she crashed the ornithopter."

"The propeller had been shot off."

"Yes. I saw that."

"And the port wing was out of commission so we couldn't manoeuvre properly."

"I see."

"She was aiming for the palace." She pointed and then thought that he probably knew where the palace was.

"She missed."

"Under the circumstances this was a really good landing, *Papa*." Khuwelsa had discovered that word was very good for softening him when his sentences were getting this short. "We're alive."

"Yes." He sighed and squinted through the shadows of the buildings towards the palace. A number of guards in sand-coloured uniforms and turbans had accumulated on the inside of the fence and more were arriving. Every one of them was brandishing a rifle and looking quite unfriendly. The bystanders hanging out the windows and in the side streets faded away.

"You can't just fly into a potential war zone, Khuwelsa, it's dangerous."

"Yes, *I know*," she replied with such vehemence that he looked at her askance before returning his attention to the soldiers.

"Are you sure Harriet is all right?"

"I checked her before coming out," she said. "She hasn't slept since yesterday morning. She was really tired." She realised she had said something else that would need explaining. Khuwelsa didn't mind doing the talking but it was a lot better when they were both together, because then he had to divide his anger between them.

"Very well," he said his tone changing from concerned father to efficient civil servant. "You stay here. Check on your sister while I smooth things out."

With that he squeezed her hand and set off, picking his way through the debris toward the palace soldiers.

* * *

He had not told Khuwelsa quite how untimely their arrival was. The anti-British successor was in power and the British government had ordered that he be removed. As the diplomat on the ground, he had attempted to persuade the new sultan to abdicate but to no avail. This left military action as the only option.

Ostensibly the reason for removing this new occupant of the sultanate was his desire to maintain slavery. And this was even true as far as it went. It was a convenient reason for a slavery-hating nation such as Britain to take action which could be justified to the people and, more importantly, her international allies.

The real reason was far less altruistic. Germany, though a latecomer to empire building, had already obtained a very strong foothold in Africa, occupying all the land between Lake Victoria and the Indian Ocean, as well as areas on the Atlantic coast.

Stopping Germany's attempt to build an empire in Africa was seen as imperative to British interests. Control of Zanzibar was key to the German empire, just as Ceylon was key to Britain's. Germany's control of central Africa interfered with Britain's control of the south and her interests in the north.

His diplomatic powers were limited and he maintained only a small office here. The gunboats in the bay were quite sufficient to wrest control of the city from the new sultan and to install their own.

But the crash landing of his daughters on the palace doorstep introduced a random factor.

He approached the gate with his hands open and outstretched. The guards were jumpy. He did not want to alarm anyone and, most importantly, he did not want to get shot.

13

Harry yawned into the pillow that pressed against her right cheek. She reached her arms forward under the pillows and stretched. She groaned as every muscle ached and protested. *Why*?

Memories of the final crash landing in Zanzibar.

Then she realised the pillow against her cheek felt considerably smoother than the ones at home. She skimmed a hand between pillow and sheet. They were silk.

She opened her eyes but all she could see was pillow. Ignoring the objections from her neck muscles, she raised her head and looked across the undulating terrain of sheets glistening in sunlight that filtered through curtains around the bed.

A wooden post marked the corner, its surface etched in intricate geometric shapes. She pushed herself up and turned until she was sitting—in the middle of a four-poster bed hung with white folds. The canopy draped in almost-perfect symmetrical pleats.

She pushed herself to the edge of the bed and peeked through the curtains. The room beyond was reminiscent of the Arab building back in the African town on the mainland. All cool marble and polished tiles in squares and triangles.

As she slipped from the bed to the floor she discovered she had been clothed in satin nightwear, a baggy top with loose pantaloons.

She stepped across to the windows. These too had complex lattice screens that let her see out but prevented others from seeing in. She was two floors up. Gardens and grass stretched away from her to a tall fence in the distance. Beyond it were the close-packed buildings of Zanzibar that she had become acquainted with in such a sudden manner. Soldiers patrolled the boundary.

She must be in the sultan's palace.

A sudden fear ran through her. Where was Khuwelsa? She knew she had landed the best she could but accidents could happen. And the German Army … She needed to find her father.

"*Sahiba*."

Harry turned toward the voice. On the opposite side of the room, directly in front of the door, stood a woman covered in an embroidered flowing Arab dress. She wore a headdress tied with wide cords but her face was not covered. Harry could tell she was older than herself, but only by a few years. Realising she was staring, Harry smiled.

"How do you do?"

"I am Basmah bint Barghash," she said bowing her head slightly. "You are Harriet Edgbaston."

She separated the word sounds carefully to ensure she said them correctly.

"Yes, that's me. What day is it?"

"The eighteenth day of Rabi Al Awwal."

Harry frowned, and shook her head. "I don't know what that is." She looked out at the sun; it was still morning. "How long have I been asleep?"

"My father, the sultan, gifted you his benevolent hospitality one day ago."

"Only one day?" She was both relieved and driven. "What about my sister?"

It was Basmah bint Barghash's turn to frown. "Sister?"

"Khuwelsa."

No response.

"There was another girl with me?"

"The African? Your servant is unhurt. She is with her machine."

Harry felt some of the tension lift but it was at this moment her body chose to point out, noisily, that she had not eaten properly for over a day. She felt faint and sat heavily in the chair by the window. Warm air breezed in through the lattice.

The woman took a step forward and betrayed the first emotion Harry had seen. "Are you ill, *sahiba*?"

"Haven't had much to eat in the last couple of days. Nothing yesterday." Then she shook herself and got to her feet. "I'm sure the sultan wouldn't like me to starve to death."

"I will send for food." She turned to the door.

"And I want to get dressed. Where are my clothes?"

"They have been sent to be refreshed." Basmah paused halfway through the door. "I will send a maid for you."

"I don't need a maid, I just need some clothes."

But she was talking to a closed door. Despite her light-headedness she strode over to it and turned the handle. Finding it locked was no great surprise. It seemed to be par for the course on this journey.

She cast around the room. There was the outline of another door in the wall adjacent to the window. As she drew closer, the handle—which had been moulded to appear as part of the decoration—became obvious.

This one was not locked and opened into a dressing room. It had no windows but was equipped with electric lights—the sultan must like his modern contraptions. Wardrobes contained Arab-style clothing in a multitude of rich fabrics. Not much would take the wear and tear Harry's clothing usually suffered.

Past this was a bathroom beyond her imagining. Steps led up to the rim of a basin of almost volcanic crater proportions. Harry looked longingly at it. A thorough bath was one thing that she really could do with, both for the dirt and for her aching muscles. Above the tub were a multitude of shining brass pipes and two outlets with valves.

She turned the tap and water began to flow, splashing at first and then thundering. One of the pipes expelled hot water. She would have to have a word with Sellie and see if she thought they might rig something like that back at home.

Sellie. They would be treating her like a slave. She wouldn't like that—and who could blame her. Harry hoped she was all right.

14

After their father had negotiated with the soldiers outside the gates, the sultan himself turned up. He was an enthusiast for all the new mechanical devices. An ornithopter was something new to him and he had insisted it be brought inside the grounds—along with Harry and Khuwelsa.

The look of helplessness on their father's face almost made Khuwelsa cry, but she knew he wouldn't want her to betray any emotion.

While the sultan's engineers brought up a mobile Faraday crane and steam-truck, her father explained the situation to her. He had told them she was Harry's servant. He held his face rigid as he said it and she wanted to kiss him to show that she understood. As a servant, he said, she would have more freedom than Harry.

And it was just as he said.

Harry was carried away on a stretcher after it had been ascertained that she really had not suffered any major, or even minor, injury. It might have been better if she had, because then their father would have had an excuse to visit her. Instead she was taken up into the palace under armed guard and neither her 'servant' nor her father was allowed to go with her.

Khuwelsa stayed with the *Pegasus* and discovered the wonders of the sultan's engineering workshops. There were half a dozen sheds with closed doors; she wasn't sure what they contained, but there were the marks of large wheels in the grass outside.

The sultan possessed three small Zeppelin-style airships and a British fixed-wing made by the Brunel company, with its typical rear-mounted propeller. The corps of engineers numbered about ten as far as she could see, mostly young men. They were all Arab by their features but wore uniforms rather than the flowing robes typical of their culture. The overalls were far more practical.

The arrival of the *Pegasus* caused quite a stir and the engineers were all over it in moments, which caused Khuwelsa considerable concern.

"Stop!" she shouted. She pulled up her skirts and climbed onto the truck bed, feeling herself lighten since the Faraday was still switched on. "Stop. This is my ship—my mistress's ship."

There was considerable laughing, though she did not think they could understand her words. An older man walked up to her.

"Get down, little girl, before you are hurt."

"I am the engineer of this ship," she snarled. "And if my mistress is not here, I say who touches her."

He said something in Arabic and the men laughed. "Woman is not engineer, girl."

"Is that a challenge, old man?"

He eyed her for a moment and said something to the men, who backed off. "Come down, little one. Your bird is safe. We see if you are engineer."

He held out his hand and she took it as she jumped down, but his reason was not to assist her. Once she was down he ran his fingertips across her palms and felt the calluses formed from hard physical labour—but only around the thumb and first fingers, plus the thicker pad at the lower part of the palm. He nodded his approval.

He led the way through to the back of the nearest workshop, past some sort of small military flyer with enough room for a pilot, a stoker and someone to man the Maxim mounted on the front. It had a horizontal rotor rising on an axle above the machine and another to drive it forward.

"Here," he said, pointing at a big steam turbine unit sitting on a work bench. "You say what is wrong with this."

She hesitated. It was not a design she was familiar with; an Italian name plate was riveted to the side. She had only worked with British and French machines. There was a muttering among the men, so she knew she hadn't made a good impression. Then she stepped forward and examined the range of tools available. She was pleased to see that each screwdriver, ratchet and wrench had its place.

Then she turned her attention to the machine itself. *How hard could it be?* She knew how a steam turbine worked; different makes had to be the same under the skin. And if he was asking what was wrong with it, when it was not even hooked up to a boiler and furnace, it should be something easy to spot.

It was hot in the workshop. The ceiling and walls were made of corrugated metal that seemed to absorb the heat from the sun and radiate it at five times the strength. She unscrewed and stripped off the inspection plates.

Her hair was falling forwards and getting in the way. Almost absentmindedly she picked up a greasy cloth and wrapped it around her head.

The steam inlet pipes seemed to be all right, though there was no foolproof way of testing their integrity without running steam through them under pressure. She checked the blades of the turbine and saw that several had been replaced. It was a decent job and striking each blade in turn with a screwdriver gave a consistent tone. She nodded to herself.

Next she gave her attention to the outlets and once again found nothing. Puzzled, she rechecked everything. Finally she replaced the inspection plates and used a torsion screwdriver to ensure they were tightly sealed.

She stepped back. "There's nothing wrong with this. The broken blades have been fixed and the job was done well."

The man looked at her without any expression. He then spoke again, apparently translating what she said. This time there was no laughter. Some of them nodded.

"You are engineer," he said. "Woman engineer."

He passed her a flask of water which she drank gratefully.

15

The other engineers were so impressed with the *Pegasus* that they seemed willing to work on it with her. She showed them how each of the flight feathers was connected to the power—each one had its own Faraday grid. There were at least two dozen that had been damaged by the German airplane; a few along the trailing edge had been cooked by the final explosion.

She was grateful that none of them spoke English because they were unable to ask her about the bullet holes and scoring marks along the hull. She hoped they assumed the damage had been done by their own defensive balloons. It would have been awkward to explain.

Being so busy, she barely noticed the time passing. In the early evening she heard the call to prayer from a nearby mosque and they all disappeared for a while. From her viewpoint she preferred having to attend church services just on Sunday.

Only a few of the engineers returned, but one of them brought some food. He didn't actually give it to her, but left it on a bench. Most of the feathers had been replaced by the time she remembered to eat, and in stopping work she discovered how tired she was.

There were lights in the workshop but she ran a cable to the *Pegasus* and used its internal lights. She went out into the open air and breathed deep as it cooled. The lights were on in the palace across the lawn. She wondered what Harry was doing, whether she had woken up or was still sleeping off the past couple of days.

Father had told her about the deadline and also explained that they had at most two days.

"You can come with me and be safe," he had said.

"And leave Harry?"

He said nothing.

"And leave the *Pegasus*?"

"Your life is more important than that lump of metal, Sellie."

He almost never called her that.

"I can't leave Harry."

He had reached out to her and drawn her into a warm hug. "I know. I'm scared I'll lose you both."

"Oh, we'll be okay. I'll get the ship fixed and we can just fly out of here before the attack."

He still held her. She could feel his heart pounding. He did not speak for a long time; when he finally did it was the sound of a British gentleman trying hard to suppress his emotion. "Just make sure the two of you are out of here before it starts."

Then he had pulled away and strode off towards the main gate, surrounded by guards.

And with that memory she returned to the *Pegasus,* connected the power to the Faraday and curled up in a corner to sleep. With the reduced gravity the metal did not feel quite so hard.

* * *

The call to prayer woke her before the sun was up. She clambered out of the *Pegasus* and stood outside the building. The sky was turning blue in the east; only the brightest stars remained visible.

Turning her back on the rising sun, she looked up to where the Albert Void Station hung bright in the sky. Unlike the Victoria Station over Ceylon, Albert was purely a naval base. Sometimes a person could see its enormous heliograph winking, transmitting encoded messages around the world and down to the surface. Not today.

The palace was quiet, apart from the guards marching the perimeter. Khuwelsa wondered if Harry was inside looking out.

Back inside the workshop she rummaged around for pipes of the same diameter to replace the ruptured ones. Once that was done the only thing missing would be the propeller. The holes could be patched easily enough or just left as they were for the time being, but without a rotor their wounded bird could not fly.

After another hour the workshop had come alive again with the other engineers, but their earlier interest in her and the *Pegasus* seemed to have waned. Of course they had their own work to do so there was no reason they should hang around to help.

Khuwelsa would have liked to have some proper work clothes; the overalls would have suited. But there were no spares to be seen—there was little chance they would be offered—and all she had were the dirty and slightly torn clothes she had been wearing for the last two days.

"I bet Harry's dressed in finery," she muttered to herself as she wrenched the damaged pipe from its mount and commenced hack-sawing through the joint. She found hitting it with a hammer to be quite satisfying.

She had just finished welding the new pipe in place and was thinking about lighting the furnace to perform a pressure test when a well-dressed factotum had turned up and, in very good English, instructed her to accompany him to see her mistress. She bridled but managed to keep her annoyance under control.

* * *

While the water continued to fill the bath, Harry went through to the next room. It was a water closet. Despite having been asleep for so long, and all the flying before that, Harry did not feel the need to utilise the convenience. She suspected this was not a good thing, and made her way back to the bedroom.

It was a mark of her present weakness that she jumped at the sight of a girl in the bedroom where she had not expected there to be anyone. The maid was carrying a tray of food, the smell of which was delicious.

The Edgbaston household had a good stock of servants, both native and white, but Harry did not warrant a personal maid. That said, she knew the kind of thing to expect and did not find having someone to help her undress—particularly when she was feeling under the weather—or to wash her back in the bath at all unpleasant. And the decadence of lying in hot water, scented with jasmine, while eating delightful snacks was an experience to which she felt she could easily become accustomed.

* * *

Sellie tidied herself as best she could and remembered to remove the greasy cloth she'd tied around her head. Then she followed the factotum across the grass and through a side door into the palace.

He guided her through servants' passages with walls of bare stone and flooring of simple brown tiles. They mounted two flights of steps and came out through a door into a corridor that appeared to run the entire length of the building. The walls were plastered and decorated at intervals with tapestries. It was cool despite the heat of the day.

A short distance along the corridor a guard stood at attention outside a door. The two men spoke briefly in a language Khuwelsa didn't understand; then the guard unlocked the door. The factotum knocked lightly, and on receiving no response he pushed the door open.

He stepped back and gestured for Khuwelsa to enter. She passed through into an airy bedroom and heard the sound of water splashing through a doorway.

She had been right; Harry was in the lap of luxury.

* * *

When they were younger Sellie and Harry had always bathed together (never mind the times they ended up in rivers and lakes), but once they had reached thirteen Mrs Hemingway had decided they were too old to share.

With her hair washed, her back scrubbed and her stomach filled (though there was plenty more to eat), Harry lay in the water, drifting back to sleep.

"Replaced me already then, have you?"

16

Harry sat up in the bath. "Where have you been?"

Khuwelsa sat heavily on the side of the tub and splashed the foam, then picked at the tray of food. The maid looked horrified at her presumption. "You know, I could really do with a bath too."

"I'm not entirely sure that would be allowed," said Harry. "They're a bit funny about servants having a soak in their mistress's pool."

Khuwelsa raised an eyebrow. "You know that's not even funny."

"Do I look like I'm laughing?"

"I saw Dad."

"Is he all right?"

Khuwelsa sighed. "You know how he gets when he's really angry?"

Harry grimaced. "Sorry I wasn't there to back you up."

"Not at us, Harry," she said. "Well, not directly. At the sultan, at the whole situation."

"I don't understand—you mean the fact we're not exactly privileged guests."

"Well, I'm just your *servant.*"

"Not my fault, Sellie."

"I know." Khuwelsa glanced at the maid who was sitting back on her haunches, apparently paying no attention to their conversation. "Does she speak English?"

"I don't know, probably not."

Khuwelsa pursed her lips and looked serious. "You're a hostage."

"I thought it might be something like that. They don't usually lock guests in their bedrooms."

Khuwelsa took another of the small parcels of food from the plate and bit into it.

"At least they feed you well."

For a few minutes they didn't speak. But Harry could tell from the way Khuwelsa didn't meet her eye there was more.

"Spit it out."

"I will not, it's delicious."

Harry gave her a look. Khuwelsa swallowed the food.

"Dad said that he won't be able to stop the navy from attacking."

"You told him about the Germans?"

"Of course."

"And?"

"He said they'd have to check it out themselves." Khuwelsa's voice became strained. "He said they wouldn't believe a couple of girls." She looked as if she were holding in a volcano of anger as big as Kilima-Njaro itself. "He said they would say *I* was not a credible source of military information." She got up slowly and turned to face the wall.

Harry stood up abruptly; the maid jumped and pulled a bath sheet from where she had laid it earlier. She went to wrap it around Harry, but Harry just grabbed it from her and did it herself.

Khuwelsa had her palms pressed against the wall and was taking in deep steady breaths. Harry put her arms round her. Khuwelsa tried to shrug her off but Harry just held her more tightly.

"It's not fair, Harry."

"They wouldn't believe me either, Sellie."

"I wish I wasn't black."

"I wish I wasn't a redhead."

It was old ground. Every once in a while the prejudice would get too much, and over the years they had developed a formula.

"I wish you weren't a redhead too." There was a hint of a smile in her voice.

"And I wish your feet didn't smell."

"Yours smell worse."

"Zebra breath."

"Hippo fart."

Khuwelsa turned round and they held one another for a short while.

"You really do need a bath." Harry sniffed and pushed her away. "And some clean clothes."

"Thanks, I've been slaving over the *Pegasus* while you've been living like a queen."

"Like an imprisoned queen, who's been asleep for most of it so didn't get to enjoy anything."

"Except the bath."

"Except the bath," Harry agreed. "Look, why don't you have a dip while I see what they've got that'll suit me."

"As you wish, your majesty."

"I should slap you."

Harry grabbed up the plate of food and carried it through into the dressing room, leaving Khuwelsa to her bath.

"Did Dad say how long we have?" she shouted.

"He didn't know exactly," came the voice from the bath. "But, Harry, he was really worried. He said they would shell the palace."

"But not today?"

"No, the deadline is tomorrow morning."

The maid rummaged in wardrobes and drawers, pulling out diaphanous tops and pantaloons which Harry rejected with an imperious wave of her hand.

She grabbed the maid by the wrist and went back into the bathroom where Khuwelsa was in the process of submerging her head and scrubbing at her scalp. Harry picked up Khuwelsa's heavy skirt and almost shook it at the girl. She held up the cloth and pointed at it.

"Like this," she said slowly and loudly, then followed up with French and German. She was not sure that the maid had understood any of the words but she went back into the dressing room and opened a different wardrobe. This time she brought out a dress similar to the one worn by the sultan's daughter. Heavier cloth. It would have to do.

Half an hour later Harry and Khuwelsa were in the bedroom, seated beside a small table. Khuwelsa had put her dirty clothes back on. Harry was in a voluminous robe which she'd tied round the middle much to the disgruntlement of the maid, who had apparently decided that this European woman had no breeding and therefore did not require as much respect as she had initially shown.

She did, however, leave the room—Khuwelsa confirmed there was a guard outside the door—to fetch more food along with coffee. Harry and Khuwelsa seldom had coffee. It certainly seemed to sharpen the mind.

"We do have one advantage," said Harry, smiling secretively over the top of her coffee cup.

"What's that?"

"We're women."

"How does that work then?"

"Men always underestimate us."

Khuwelsa looked sceptical. "That's all very well, Harry, but at this moment in time they seem to be holding all the cards."

17

Jonathan Edgbaston sighed and put down the dispatch his secretary had placed on his desk a few minutes earlier. Cyril returned with a fresh cup of tea and hovered expectantly.

"Any response, sir?" he said finally.

"There's nothing to say, Cyril. Just send an acknowledgement in clear."

"Yes, sir."

Jonathan picked up the dispatch again. The top part was filled with the verbatim transcription of the encoded message from the gunboat in the bay. Below it was Cyril's translation, written in the man's excellent copperplate hand.

"No change of orders received. Attack will commence at 08:30. Recommend evacuation of any British subjects within a half mile of the palace."

The final sentence had been in direct response to his plea to delay the attack until something could be done about his daughters. The Empire would not stay its hand, even for his family.

Jonathan looked at the tea that was slowly cooling in the delicate porcelain cup on its matching saucer. He thought how easy it would be to break. A trifling bump would knock it to the floor where it would smash into a myriad pieces, spilling the liquid everywhere.

He stood up firmly and went to his drinks cabinet and poured himself something more potent than tea.

* * *

Khuwelsa left Harry and was escorted to the exit through the servants' passages. She made her way down a flight of steps at the side of the palace and headed out towards the workshops. Plans swirled in her head; mentally she rehearsed how things needed to go, for her idea to succeed. The men were already hard at work when she strode into the room where their bird sat.

She pointed at the propeller still mounted on the ship that had been gutted. The man she had come to think of as the one in charge shook his head. "No."

She wanted to press the point but the disagreement was already drawing attention from a couple of the soldiers who patrolled the area. She did not want to risk what little freedom she already had.

Instead she returned to the *Pegasus* and sat in the pilot seat, staring out at the wall.

Harry was right. The pilot could only see ahead and up from this position, and if the plane was climbing even "ahead" was mostly hidden. Whatever had possessed the builders to design something like this? Hadn't they ever flown?

She got down on her hands and knees under the control display. There really was nothing important from the edge of the Faraday grid to where the dorsal support strut went across the front, with the movable canopy above it. The control wires and cables went behind a panel at the front but they could be easily rerouted.

She remembered noticing spare window sections from one of the defunct military vehicles in a corner of the next building. Khuwelsa climbed to her feet thoughtfully, went out into the workshop and gathered tools.

* * *

They had fed Harry in the afternoon. She had another visit from the daughter of the sultan. The young woman was polite and seemed most interested in where Harry had been, and in her flying machine.

Harry was not stupid and did not mention the German task force, which must be massing on the coast by now; taking down the bridge would only have delayed them for a short time. It would not have stopped the Zeppelins at all. In fact, now she came to think of it, if she were in charge of the German force they would set down an airship and use it as a bridge, at least for the infantry.

The interrogation lasted through the meal and into the evening. The subject moved from her activities during the last couple of days to her father. She had no difficulty in pretending ignorance, since that was more or less her normal state in regard to her father's job.

The approach of the evening prayer took her inquisitor away. Darkness fell and she switched on the electric lights in the room.

Harry chafed. She was not used to being cooped up in a cage, even a gilded one. She went to the window. Her room was two flights up. Khuwelsa had said she was in workshops close to the boundary fence, but there were no buildings on this side. Harry went into the dressing room, pulled a dozen dresses from the wardrobes, and set about plaiting and knotting them. She hid the completed escape rope under the bed.

More food arrived later in the evening. At least they weren't trying to starve her. The maid returned and sat in a chair beside the door. Did they really expect her to make a break for it through the door and into the palace?

Perhaps the idea she might climb out the window seemed unlikely for a woman.

Well, let them think that.

There was nothing to do and Harry found herself drifting off. She would wait for the late evening prayer, and when the maid left the room she would tie the sheets and make her escape through the window. Then it would just be a matter of finding Khuwelsa and getting out. She had no idea how they would achieve that. She would just have to make it up as she went along.

That was what she usually did.

She jerked awake as the call to prayer drifted across the city. She glanced across to the door. The maid was still sitting there. Harry frowned. Why hadn't she left? The maid got to her feet and pulled out a mat from behind her which she laid out on the floor, then knelt on.

Harry turned away partly in annoyance and partly because it felt like an intrusion to watch the girl at prayer. She knew how embarrassed she got in church, at least on the occasions she went.

Now what?

She glanced at the bathroom and an idea formed. While the maid was on her knees, Harry went through and opened the valves that let the water in. In truth it was very tempting to have a bath and wash away the sweat of the day. But now was not the time. She took up a position leaning over the incoming water as if she were studying something.

She wasn't sure how long the praying went on, so she waited. Her muscles began to protest at being held in such an awkward position for so long. Finally she heard the maid coming through the dressing room and glanced round.

"Hey!" She gestured to the maid and pointed at the water. The girl innocently leaned over to see what Harry was pointing at. Harry stuck out her foot in front of the girl's legs, reached back and heaved her into the water.

The girl pitched forward with a cry and went headfirst into the foamy water. Harry did not leave immediately; she waited until the girl twisted and righted herself so her head was out of the water. Drowning the poor maid was not Harry's plan.

Once she was sure the girl was safe enough, Harry dashed back down the corridor and slammed the door. There was no lock on it but with an effort born of desperation she pulled a chest of drawers in front. Then she went to the other door and jammed the chair under it. Hopefully it would hold long enough if someone tried to enter.

She pulled the knotted dresses from under the bed, tied one end around the bedpost nearest the window and threw the rest through the opening. She took a moment to switch off the light and headed back to the window.

There was a thump on the door to the bathroom, then a louder one. She was unable to see if the door was being opened, but it went quiet again.

She hitched up her skirts and tied them off around her waist, giving herself reasonable freedom. Looking out it seemed further down in the dark and she wasn't even sure the rope reached all the way to the ground.

But she was committed. She swung herself out and clung to the knotted dresses as she edged her way down. There was a window directly below her with the flicker of fire or candlelight so she pushed herself to the side and continued down.

There was a resounding crash from the room she had vacated. She ignored it and kept going. Another crash. Then some shouting. She reached the end of the rope. Closing her eyes, she let herself down until she was hanging from her straining arms—and let go.

18

She hit the ground with a jarring thump. Her knees were bent as she landed so she ended up sitting on the damp earth of a flower bed. *Easy as falling off a log*, she thought. *And considering some of the logs I've fallen off, a lot drier.*

Two floors above her, a woman continued to shout. She looked up and saw the maid's outline against the light. It disappeared and was replaced the silhouette of the guard and his rifle.

Harry glanced both ways along the building. The nearer corner was toward the south. She set off at a slow run as her eyes hadn't adjusted to the dark yet and she couldn't see the ground ahead of her. She passed darkened windows. The first gunshot made her jump. She kept going. The farther she got from the window the harder it would be for the guard to get a good angle on her.

A second shot ricocheted off a stone to her left. She decided this was a sign she was right, and kept moving. She was almost at the corner. There was another shot from behind but she didn't notice it striking anywhere close.

Her experiences of the last two days came to the fore. Instead of running round the corner, she came to a stop and flattened herself against the wall. There was no way the rest of the guards could have failed to hear the shots and the shouting. And by now the maid would probably have alerted more of the soldiers within the palace so they would be joining the ones from the perimeter in looking for her in very short order. The air was filled with the scent of jasmine from the plants on which she was standing.

A wave of fear washed across her, pricking at her skin. Her hands were cold even though the day's heat had not yet leaked into the sky. Where was her sister? Why hadn't they arranged something?

They had had all that time together, and the only plan they had made was to escape before the British artillery opened up on the palace? Perhaps she deserved to fail.

But if she didn't succeed, what would happen to Khuwelsa? At best she would end up a slave again, more likely dead. And her father could be killed, too.

She pursed her lips and stared into the blackness ahead. In the distance she could see dark shadows of soldiers on the move. They could not see her now but as soon as she moved it would only be a matter of time before they could.

If only her skin were as dark as Khuwelsa's. Well, she could do something about that. She crouched down and dug her fingers into the soil beneath her feet. Taking it up by handfuls she rubbed it into her face. She tied her long hair back in a rough knot to stop it flying about and rubbed the dirt into that as well. The maid had oiled her hair to make it shine, and now that made the soil stick. She had no way of knowing how effective it was but simply doing something positive helped.

She listened. There were still no shouts nearby. The guard in the bedroom window was no longer there. Still in a crouching position, she held her hair back and peered round the corner, keeping as much of her face hidden as possible.

The gardens were dark but there were groups of figures marching and running, criss-crossing the lawns. One might have hoped the grass would have been interrupted by artistically placed bushes, trees and flower beds. Unfortunately it seemed that military sensibilities prevailed. The lawn was devoid of any cover she could use.

Harry could see the workshops Khuwelsa had spoken of. They were dark without any sign of life except for a line of smoke rising from the one at the nearer end. What if Khuwelsa had been arrested?

Some of the soldiers had torches and were quartering the open space. The glare from the light spoilt her night vision and she had to blink away the spots.

If it stopped her from being able to see properly in the dark, it must do the same to them. Who would be crazy enough to go straight into the midst of the search?

Apparently she would. Harry crept from her hiding place. Keeping low and moving in fits and starts, she headed directly across the lawn towards the workshops. She kept checking the progress of the different groups. Whenever one turned in her direction she flattened herself against the ground.

Sometimes she crawled. More than once a group of soldiers would pass so close that she could see their lights reflecting on their faces.

For a long time it seemed as if she was making no progress. But the workshop slowly grew in size and the palace diminished behind her. The concentration of the search moved away, further round the building. The fact they had not found her apparently made them think they were looking in the wrong place. More troops were being concentrated on patrolling the outer fence.

Harry's heart lifted. It seemed like she was going to make it to the workshop. She counselled herself to continue at the same rate. To make no assumptions. To keep her eyes open for any possible threat. But somehow she could not take her eyes off the building ahead. The great double doors stood wide open. Inside was an even deeper black. The smoke trailing from the interior rose grey against the black, star-filled sky. Somehow it made her think of a dragon's cave.

The grass ran out and her fingers rasped on stone and gravel. She realised it would be nigh on impossible for her to cross this part of the yard without making a noise. She could hear the soldiers' boots crunching in the distance.

She reached down and slipped off her shoes, which were more like slippers suitable for walking around in a palace if one never stepped out into the real world. But she would need them to pilot the *Pegasus*, if her bird was going to fly.

Harry pulled up her skirts and rose into a crouching position. She took another look round. There were no soldiers closer than two hundred yards. If she did not take the risk she would be stranded here until dawn revealed her. The workshop was no more than twenty yards, just a few seconds.

She rose up so she could walk in long low strides and stepped out into the gravel. It cut into her feet as she took stride after stride. A figure stepped out of the workshop, tall and erect.

"That is quite far enough, *Fraulein*."

19

Harry felt like weeping. She had come so close. But she did not weep. She stood up straight.

The man stepped towards her. He wore a German uniform. As he emerged from the shadows the gun he held became apparent.

"You and I both know the sultan is a fool," he continued. "He thinks that your boats will not fire on the palace because you are here. He thinks there is some kind of honour in war.

"But we know differently, don't we?" He paused for dramatic effect. "We know they will attack, and I knew you would try to reach your vessel in the vain hope it had been repaired."

Vain hope? Had Khuwelsa not fixed it? Where was she?

"You are wondering where the *Schwarze* is? It seems your faith in her is misplaced."

Harry's heart leapt. He didn't know where Khuwelsa was, which meant she was still free. Harry noticed an increase in the amount of smoke flowing from the workshop and took a step backwards.

"Where are you going?" he laughed and followed her. She kept backing until she reached the grass and decided that was far enough. He stopped too.

Keep him talking. "What are you going to do with me?"

"I will take you out of here and return you to your father, of course," he said. "I am not an animal. You are just a girl. You are not part of this war."

"I took down one of your planes and blew up the bridge to slow down your troops."

"Really? In that sad little construction?"

"Yes." She gritted her teeth at the insult.

He bowed. "I am impressed."

"And I'll do it again."

"One antiquated machine against the military might of the German empire? I am afraid I do not find myself—"

Light poured from the interior of the workshop and the *Pegasus* roared as her propeller spun up to speed. Harry was blinded for seconds and then as her sight adjusted she saw the wings twist and beat. Inside the canopy she could make out Khuwelsa at the controls.

Harry's hand went to her mouth: Khuwelsa wasn't very good at this. The propeller screamed at a pitch higher than Harry had ever heard before, the wings gave a massive thundering beat and the *Pegasus* leapt upwards. She erupted through the roof of the workshop. Harry saw what was coming and threw herself to one side as the *Pegasus* came crashing down to earth, with pieces of the workshop clattering in all directions.

The German officer climbed to his feet, his gun trained on Harry. In the bright light his face was twisted in anger. To Harry's horror he fired. She felt the bullet tear at her clothing as it passed through.

In slow motion she watched a piece of the workshop come tumbling out of the sky and strike the propeller. The voracious rotor shattered it on impact. Shards flashed in all directions. The German screamed and fell to his knees, a length of wood protruding from his leg.

Two long whistles pierced through the noise: *Ready to go!* Khuwelsa was at the hatch holding it open. "Stop dilly-dallying!"

Harry ran to the ship and grabbed Khuwelsa's hand, transitioning to low gravity as Khuwelsa pulled her inside.

She fairly flew to the pilot's chair and landed in it, as Khuwelsa slammed the hatch and dogged it firmly. "Let's get the hell out of here, Harry."

"My pleasure!"

Above the noise of the furnace and the generators she heard bullets pinging off the fuselage. Through the front screen she could see the soldiers gathering in ordered lines. An officer had taken charge; they were preparing to fire. Harry opened up the power to the propeller. The pitch of the spinning rotor screamed even higher. Harry did not pause; whatever Khuwelsa had done, it was good. Harry could feel the extra force at her disposal.

She beat the wings carefully once, just to get the feel. There were slight differences in the way they felt but nothing significant. She beat hard and fast; each thrust took the bird up. The powerful new propeller accelerated them towards the palace faster than she expected. The wall was coming at them. She backwinged with an air blast that knocked the soldiers on their backs.

The nose of the *Pegasus* came up and they shot skywards with plenty of room between them and the palace roof.

Harry checked the compass and saw they were heading east. She soared round to the north, the fastest route to the sea from the palace. Not bothering to gain any more height she headed out to sea. The city fell behind. Zanzibar Island was a dark mass to their right.

She maintained the course for less than a minute before turning towards the mainland. The needle of the airspeed indicator was pushed hard over against the pin. They were travelling at over one hundred miles per hour already.

"Like it?" said Khuwelsa in her ear.

"What did you do?"

"They had a lot of very nice equipment just lying around the place. I improved the pressure seals, added new gearing on the rotor train, and the new prop is beautiful."

"Just what we need."

"What? Why?"

"We need to stop the German airships."

"We do?"

"Our side doesn't believe us and we're the only air power round here."

Khuwelsa sighed. "Silly me, I thought we might just go home."

"And leave Dad?"

"Fair enough," said Khuwelsa. Harry adjusted course more to the east so they would intercept the coast. "So what's the plan?"

"Land on the coast, have a sleep, head south before dawn and catch them napping."

"Catch them napping? Good plan."

20

They had managed four hours' sleep. The constant crash of breakers on the beach had become a lullaby when they had lain down to sleep. They had woken to seagulls screaming.

In the cold pre-dawn light Harry splashed sea water on her face and tasted the salt. Sea birds were diving into the surf and rising again with their prey. The beach stretched for as far as she could see both north and south, curving away into the half-light.

She turned and walked up the gently sloping sand. Smoke was already pouring from the stack as Khuwelsa got steam up. Harry admired the work her sister had done on the front of the *Pegasus*. The new glass allowed her to see forward and down. Looking up through it she saw Khuwelsa, half her body lit up by the furnace, already in her apron over her underclothes.

The fact she could see in so easily meant other people would be able to as well. Harry's feet and ankles would be on show. They would have to see about some sort of curtain and modesty panel. She could imagine how Khuwelsa would react to that comment after working so hard to replace the metal. Perhaps, Harry considered, she should see about wearing men's clothes when flying. There would be definite advantages.

She swung up into the cabin. What she wouldn't have given to be back in her proper clothes and out of this ridiculous thing from the palace. And the sandals were terrible for flying.

"Ready then?" said Harry.

Khuwelsa's very serious face looked back at her. "As ready as we'll ever be."

They had discussed the options. They had no armament of any sort beyond some knives and cutting equipment. And the *Pegasus* itself. Their options were limited but they had no choice.

Harry hesitated. This might be their last chance to say anything important to each other but her reserve was getting in the way. Khuwelsa saved her the decision. She simply walked over and hugged her sister.

"I love you, Harry."

"You too, Sellie."

"'*You too*', Harry? What is that supposed to mean? Mrs Hemingway would not be impressed."

"You know what I mean." Harry reddened with embarrassment.

"I know," said Khuwelsa, gave her an extra squeeze then released her, and stood back.

"Is she hot?"

"Raring to go."

Harry smiled. "Let's do it then."

They turned from each other. Khuwelsa went to the furnace and Harry to the pilot's chair. She ran through the pre-flight checks quickly. Tested the pressure, flapped the wings tentatively. The *Pegasus* responded with precision. Harry nodded to herself.

She gave one long whistle, paused and engaged the Faraday. The loss of weight was comforting. She engaged the drive and the low thunder of the furnace was drowned out by the increasing whine of the propeller. Two long whistles and a count to ten.

Harry pulled on the controls; the *Pegasus* responded with a powerful upbeat. The nose lifted. Harry stroked hard and they lifted in smooth steps. The propeller pushed them forwards, and soon they were soaring.

Before Khuwelsa had added the lower window, Harry had always taken care to fly at a safe height as it was impossible to see what was immediately ahead. But now the coastline raced beneath them as Harry flew as low as possible to prevent the sound of the engine carrying too far ahead.

Harry steered a course as straight along the coast as possible, but at the speed they were going sometimes they found themselves over the sea, startling seagulls out of the sky, or crossing inland as some promontory stuck out into the water.

The terrain flashing by was exhilarating. Khuwelsa came forward and became mesmerized by the ground rushing past. Rivers and streams appeared ahead and then were gone. Startled gazelles, elephants, wildebeest and giraffes had no time to flee as the flying monster was upon them and then passed just as quickly.

Harry and Khuwelsa had no real idea where the Germans had set up camp. It seemed unlikely they would have gone far south because they would want to reach the coast as close to Zanzibar as possible. Additionally, the large towns to the south would be able to send messages to the capital.

At their speed of something well over one hundred miles per hour (Khuwelsa could not determine exactly how much over) it did not seem likely they would need more than an hour to reach the German camp.

And so it was that forty-three minutes later by the chronometer, they sighted a dark blob against the brightness of the rising sun: a Zeppelin already several miles out to sea heading towards Zanzibar. Half a mile behind it a group of three more Zeppelins was rising into the air.

As far as she could see there were no fighters.

Not yet.

"Are you ready?" said Harry, turning to Khuwelsa. Her sister nodded and went back to the furnace.

Harry focused on the vessel ahead. It was flying at about five hundred feet. And it was a monster. The massive gondola, almost as big as the balloon envelope, carried major artillery. Harry whistled four times and pulled back on the control feathers. The *Pegasus* climbed smoothly.

There was a chance they had not been seen; after all, no attack was expected.

She levelled out at two thousand feet. They were overtaking the leading Zeppelin fast. It was probably making less than thirty knots. There was a puff of smoke from one of the guns on its side, and then a line of explosions along the entire length of the gondola.

Harry had no sense that they were under attack. If any of the shells had come close, she did not see or hear them. Within moments the angle was too high for the main guns; they were safe from those, but not from the smaller weapons mounted along the top.

It would have been too much to hope that the *Pegasus* could have attacked without any response from the enemy vessel. In a strange way Harry was glad, because shooting fish in a barrel seemed a dishonourable way to fight. Assuming Khuwelsa's idea would work.

Harry felt the air pressure inside the cabin change as Khuwelsa removed the temporary repair she had made over the damaged fuselage.

Two short whistles, one long. It was a new code: Attack dive. Harry banked the ship and pushed the controls forward.

The *Pegasus* responded and nosed into the dive.

21

Harry could feel the wings vibrating through her fingertips. She pulled them in so there was less resistance to the air. Unlike the time when she had simply switched off the Faraday, this dive was fully controlled: like falling through water.

Still the *Pegasus* had been moving swiftly enough when the dive commenced, and with fifteen hundred feet to go there was plenty of time to build up a powerful velocity.

At each end of the Zeppelin was a gun turret. Harry was not worried about the further one. She was aiming almost directly at the rear one that was spewing shell after shell in their direction. She had heard her father's friends talking about the pom-poms, quick-firing small-bore artillery. If just one of those shells ripped through the fuselage, their attack would be over.

She prayed they would miss.

* * *

Khuwelsa held the bucket in her gauntleted hand. She could feel the heat coming off it despite the leather. She had rigged a harness around the hole in the wall of the ship so the buffeting of the dive did not cause her to spill the contents.

The noise of the wind increased in volume and pitch, drowning out the thumping of the engine and the scream of the propeller. The smell of burning tar filled her nostrils.

The modifications she had made to the front view meant that from her position she, too, could see the approaching Zeppelin. It was terrifying. She could see only the prospect of an imminent collision. But she trusted her sister.

She saw Harry pull back on the controls and felt the inertia driving her into the floor. As if on a signal, she hauled on the bucket, lifted its bottom and poured the contents from the ship.

Boiling hot tar (along with screws and bolts, which until a few minutes ago had been roasting in the furnace) slipped from the bucket. Already travelling at perhaps a hundred and fifty miles per hour, and then subject to the natural force of gravity, the burning liquid rained down the balloon, spreading out across a wide area as it did so.

Khuwelsa gave one short and one long whistle, then hung on tight. Harry pushed gently on the left control and the *Pegasus* rolled to the right. It slipped sideways as it passed the top of the Zeppelin and slid away from the bulk of the balloon. Khuwelsa could see the fabric of the envelope shooting past them, so close that if Harry extended the wings they would touch it.

They flashed past the decks of the gondola. For the briefest moment she saw the astonished face of a sailor as the *Pegasus* dropped.

Harry opened the wings and they decelerated. She flew beneath the Zeppelin hoping to confuse their artillery and escape before they could open fire.

The propeller screamed and the *Pegasus* leapt forward like an eagle in pursuit of a flamingo. Khuwelsa shook herself to release the tension, detached the bucket and headed back to the furnace to fill up.

* * *

Harry tore the *Pegasus* round in the tightest circle she dared, losing speed and altitude. They had come out on the port side below the Zeppelin, but she needed to get away from their guns.

With the propeller at maximum she stroked hard to get their speed back up.

She had no idea whether their improvised weapon had done any damage at all. Modern military Zeppelins used helium instead of hydrogen, so there was no risk of it going up in flame. All she could see above them was the dark underside criss-crossed with the Faraday mesh. If only they had some way of destroying *that.*

She looked up again and frowned. She checked her altitude. She wasn't climbing but the airship was closer. It was coming down right on top of them. She dived for the waves.

The sun was above the horizon and its bright rays glinting off the waves blinded her as the *Pegasus* pulled out from underneath the falling ship. She pulled into a turn and saw the whole rear section of the outer envelope was loose and flapping; balloons of helium gas were escaping and floating into the sky.

It had worked.

Men were throwing themselves from the gondola as the doomed vessel hit the water. Harry kept turning. She knew what would happen next. When the ship hit the water the Faraday grid would short-circuit and the ship would sink fast.

She whistled the first line of the "Sailor's Hornpipe" to let Khuwelsa know they had succeeded. Then she looked ahead. The three following ships were heading towards them. Probably at full thrust. And if the people on the shore had seen what had happened, the fighters would not be far behind.

She and Khuwelsa had discussed what they would do if faced with impossible odds.

Harry looked about. The sun continued to rise in the east; the landmass of Zanzibar was a dark smudge on the horizon. The coast of Africa was five miles away, and three heavily armoured Zeppelins were coming their way.

Impossible odds.

Harry pulled the *Pegasus* round with her stern to the coast away from the Zeppelins, and kept up full throttle.

She brought the nose up and climbed to three thousand feet, putting more distance between them and the enemy. She held her hand over her eyes; the sun was directly ahead. She let the airspeed drop until it was barely a crawl.

They had considered all the possibilities and the consequences of their actions.

Impossible odds.

At stalling speed Harry flipped the *Pegasus* around and lined up on the Zeppelins, with the sun directly behind her.

Running away had not been among the options.

22

The three Zeppelins were flying in close formation, one at the front and the two others behind to the port and starboard, slightly offset from one another. They maintained the same altitude as the first.

They did not see the *Pegasus* as she came out of the sun until she was right on top of the first vessel. Harry had to bank slightly to port to line up with the balloon and then banked hard to starboard as Khuwelsa poured out a second bucket of steaming tar and red hot metal.

Harry kept as low to the top of the balloon as she dared so that the artillery would think twice before opening fire in case they hit each other.

They only had three buckets' worth of that weapon. She could not wait to see if they had been successful but dipped over the first ship and throttled back. Going more slowly made them easier to hit but she could spend more time among the balloons where, perversely, they were safer.

Only one bucket remained and Khuwelsa needed time to refill.

Lines of tracer bullets filled the air. A fighter was streaking up towards her from sea level. With barely a thought Harry let out five abrupt whistles and flipped off the Faraday. The *Pegasus* fell. Harry fanned out the wings to slow their descent as the fighter airplane shot above them. She re-engaged the Faraday and found herself below the level of the Zeppelins. Now there was no risk of them hitting each other and they opened fire.

She pushed forward and slid under the first Zeppelin on the right.

Khuwelsa indicated her readiness with two short whistles and Harry opened up the power. She steered the length of the airship accelerating as she went, explosions filling the air around her. Some sort of proximity shell? As she came out from beneath the gondola she saw a squadron of fighters moving across the sky above her.

There was no time to worry about them.

She climbed between the two airships. The artillerymen on the trailing ship had apparently decided they did not care whether they hit their sister vessel and opened fire on her. Harry dipped and twisted randomly as she climbed, to upset their aim. As she lined up for the run, she could see the gunners take a few pot shots but then abandon their position, climbing down the outside of the envelope.

They clearly knew what was coming.

Tracers ripped past her and bullets pinged off the fuselage. Some of the bullets hit the balloon; others sparked off the gun mounted on the ship. She laughed at her own arrogance; it wasn't her they were afraid of, it was their own fighters because a few bullets through the envelope were not going to bring down the airship.

The *Pegasus* made her run with tracers from more than one plane crossing in front of her. Harry banked the ship and hoped Khuwelsa was releasing the bucket's contents.

She brought the *Pegasus* round in a full turn. For the first time they saw the results of the second bucket: The leading airship of the three was in the water with its envelope sagging and straining. Dozens of men floundered in the sea, swimming away from the sinking gondola.

She could only hope Khuwelsa had been successful with the final bucket. They could not wait to find out.

With only one Zeppelin remaining, no more tar and a dozen fighters taking pot shots at her, Harry barely even considered her next action. There was no way she was going to let the final airship cross to Zanzibar.

She engaged the highest propeller gearing and dived for maximum speed. The fighters were fast but with the new propeller the *Pegasus* could outdistance them. Still, without guns a stern chase was the last thing she wanted—they would just shoot her out of the sky.

With the artillery fire exploding around her she drove hard beneath the final airship. As the *Pegasus* emerged on the other side, out of sight of the pursuing fighters, she disengaged the propeller and back-winged hard. Her forward speed dropped to nothing and wing beat by wing beat she flew up the side of the balloon as the fighters shot out beneath them. As far as they were concerned she had simply vanished.

The men on the Zeppelin knew where she was but she was so close they could not bring their artillery to bear. It took barely twenty seconds for her to reach the top of the balloon, to manoeuvre over the top and set down. She switched off the Faraday but they remained light, because they were inside the effect of the airship's Faraday grid.

"What are you doing, Harry?" Khuwelsa's voice had an odd strained tone.

Harry looked round. Khuwelsa was wrapping a cloth round her leg. There was no time to talk. A couple of the fighters had come around and seen her. Not that there was much they could do.

"Do you trust me, Sellie?"

Khuwelsa stopped her bandaging. "Like a sister."

Harry smiled and reached for the propeller control.

* * *

The British ornithopter was sitting motionless on the top of the *Graf Joseph Kreisler.* Hans Pietsch throttled back his fighter plane. Was the British ship surrendering? Whether it was or not, they could not attack it. While the air-ship could take many bullets before its integrity was harmed, a concentrated attack would provide exactly that harm.

He was unclear exactly what had happened to the other three ships. The ornithopter had no guns, and yet it flew across the top of a Zeppelin and within moments the warship was falling out of the sky. That one small craft could do so much harm was quite disturbing.

What was the British ship doing now, just sitting there?

Suddenly its propeller burst into life. It ripped through the wooden planking above the balloon envelope and tore into the outer skin. He watched in fascinated horror as the balloons just beneath the skin were shredded. As the propeller destroyed the balloons the 'thopter lost its support and its nose tilted upwards. Its weight pressed the propeller deeper into the body of the Zeppelin like a knife cutting through skin. The ship tilted almost vertically and sank out of sight into the heart of the airship.

The Zeppelin lost height, slowly at first then faster. The one remaining airship of the task force touched the water. Men threw themselves into the water to save themselves from drowning. There was that moment when the Faraday grid ceased to function and the vessel sank fast, the windows of the gondola exploding under the air pressure.

Then something moved beneath the rippling skin of the crippled Zeppelin's envelope. A dark shadow, like a baby crocodile inside an egg, it seemed to twist and turn. A tear in the skin opened and ripped forty feet across. Struggling like a baby bird to escape its shell, a winged creature crawled out. Barely a dozen feet above the churning and bubbling sea, it seemed to pause and then leapt skywards. Strong wing-beats thrust it into the air like a living being, like a dragon.

It accelerated hard and flew across the waves, heading towards Zanzibar.

Hans Pietsch watched the creature of living metal beat its wings across the sea.

He saluted them and turned his fighter to the African shore.

BOOK 2

HARRY IN THE WILD

1

Harry shifted her weight, trying to find a position on the boulder that was a little more comfortable. She was shaded from the morning sunshine by an ancient fir tree with a gnarled trunk. The air was still cold up here in the mountains and wouldn't warm until the afternoon, but that didn't stop the sun's dazzling rays reflecting off the small lake.

This was the hideaway she and Khuwelsa had found deep in the heart of the Usambara Mountains. It was what remained of a volcano. The eroded lip of its rim made a circle all around them and, except for the lake, it was filled with tall Christmas trees. It was strange to see them here, but they grew profusely on the upper slopes of the mountains.

There was little in the way of animals, mostly wild goats that had probably become separated from their herds and made their way in here. The outer slopes were very steep, but mountain goats could climb anything. Birds did not need to climb; there were plenty of them here.

And the *Pegasus*, of course. She did not have a problem coming over the rim, either. Harry glanced round at her air-plane perched on a small plateau of rock a few yards up the slope. Her wings folded in around her body, sitting there as if she were roosting. A thin trail of smoke drifted up from her chimney.

A splash from the water brought Harry's attention back to the glassy surface of the lake, reflecting a blurry image of the trees and cliff on the opposite bank. Khuwelsa swam into view using a strong over-arm stroke.

Their tutor, if she were here, would have been horrified. Swimming was not something ladies did. Not to mention that swimming in the nude in a mountain lake, no matter how secluded, was scandalous.

Khuwelsa steered towards the shore below where Harry was sitting and glided up to the bank. She pulled herself out of the water and shivered. Harry threw her one of the large towels they had stolen from the house. Khuwelsa rubbed herself down.

"You should come in," she said. "It's lovely."

Harry shrugged. "Really not feeling like it."

"You've been moping around for weeks."

"I know." Harry stood up on the rock and looked out across the water. "Just … well, you know."

Khuwelsa nodded and wrapped the towel about herself the way the native women wore their wraps, their *kitenge*. It always struck Harry as strange when her sister did that. Of course, she had been wearing one when their father had brought her home, so she must have put it on every day. It was second nature to her.

"We haven't done anything really naughty for ages," said Khuwelsa.

No, they hadn't. After they had destroyed the four German Zeppelins they had been confined to the house for days. Mrs Hemingway had been apoplectic and retired to her bed with the vapours.

Harry had not minded being kept at home, at least at first. After the reality of what the two of them had done hit her, she spent a week alternating being physically sick with nervous distraction. Men had died. She and Sellie had killed them.

Things did not improve when her father returned home one day with the news that the official German report was that less than twenty had drowned in the end. It did not make Harry feel any better. Even one was bad enough. Sellie seemed to cope better, but they had bouts of mutual crying.

"You did the right thing," said her father. "Even though I would have forbidden it if I had known what you intended."

It was easy to rationalise: If they had not done it, many more British sailors and soldiers would have died—possibly even their father.

But it made no difference.

So for three long weeks she had moped around the house while Sellie tinkered with the *Pegasus*.

Harry sighed, then blinked as a movement on the far side of the crater caught her eye. Something moved in the dark beneath the trees like a liquid shadow. She frowned. It faded into the background.

"Did you see that?" she said.

"What?"

Khuwelsa looked where Harry pointed across the water. Khuwelsa raised her hand to shade her eyes, then shook her head. "Imagining things now?"

"No, there was something."

Harry glanced around the edge of the lake to the left and right; she knew from experience that it was very difficult to get round. This small area was the only place with the magical combination of a not-too-steep slope and a landing spot.

She started to strip.

Khuwelsa harrumphed. "Oh right, so now you want to go in the water. Just when I've managed to get dry."

Harry wriggled out of her dress, leaving just her bloomers and chemise. She climbed down to the water's edge and placed her toe in it. "It's freezing."

Sellie shrugged. "You get used to it." She gave no indication she intended follow. "You know, when you get back, you'll have wet underthings."

Harry did not rise to her taunt. "Are you coming?"

"No," she said. "You go off and have your big adventure. I'm going to get dressed and read a book."

"Fine," Harry said with annoyance. "Read your bloody book."

"Well, someone round here needs to acquire an academic education," she said. "And it would be wasted on you."

Which is what Mrs Hemingway always said about Khuwelsa. The woman did not like teaching Sellie; an education was wasted on a black girl. Not that she thought an education was a great deal of use to a white one either, since a woman's sole purpose in life was to marry and have children.

Harry stepped out onto a submerged boulder and shivered as the cold seeped into her calves. She crouched down and pushed off into the water. The numbing cold stole the warmth from her skin, but it was invigorating. As she moved out from the shade the sun beat down on her head and back.

She was more comfortable with the breast stroke because it allowed her to watch the opposite bank as she moved smoothly across the lake. Nothing unusual presented itself: just the pine trees and, on the higher slopes, small groups of goats. Their occasional bleating echoed round the caldera.

It took her a few minutes to reach the other side, the last few yards through a surface covered in floating pine cones. On this side there were no boulders or convenient shore line. The crater's slope emerged directly out of the water and climbed at a sharp angle. The trees were perched precariously, but they, too, were old and had not fallen yet.

Harry peered into the pine-scented dark. She heard a low growl. Not threatening, it reminded her of the sound the family cats made when they were tearing a rat to pieces.

Then she saw it. The dappled colouring of the cheetah merged perfectly with the half light of the wood. It was eating something.

Probably a goat it had brought down. Then she heard the clink of metal against stone. Again. And again.

Grabbing hold of a tree root that thrust out into the water, she hauled herself up onto the slope. The floor was covered in pine needles. It meant she moved quietly but every now and then one would stick into the water-softened sole of her foot. She had to clamp her mouth down on the unladylike words she wanted to utter.

She looked back across the water. The *Pegasus* gleamed in the sunshine, and next to it in one of the deck chairs they had brought sat Khuwelsa, her attention thoroughly on the book.

Harry turned back to the slope. She climbed around the tree and pushed herself up towards the next. The sounds of eating stopped, and she peered forward. A few yards up the slope the cheetah's eyes glowed silver as it studied her. She was still unable to make out what it was eating.

She grabbed a branch of the next tree and climbed closer. The cheetah growled a warning. The cat was not planning on letting this meal go if he could help it. She entirely appreciated his position but was not about to be put off.

There was no handy branch lying about but many pine cones. She gathered up a handful, took aim, and threw the first. Throwing uphill as she was, she did not get close. The cheetah followed the pine cone's path through the air until it landed and rolled back. Turning its attention back on Harry, it lashed its tail.

This was not going so well, Harry thought. She needed to get more aggressive.

She gathered a large pile of cones on the slope in front of her, and with her back against a tree threw them one after the other, using both hands to maintain the barrage. And she shouted. "Get out. Get lost. Run away!" Again and again.

Under the onslaught the cheetah held its ground for almost twenty seconds, but as Harry's supply of cones was running down it decided to find its dinner elsewhere and loped off up the slope.

Relieved by the big cat's capitulation Harry climbed to the next tree. And then stared down at the dead man in a military uniform lying on the ground in front of her.

2

Harry recognised the uniform. This was a deckhand from a German military airship. It was as if one of the men whose deaths she had caused had returned to haunt her. The man had not been lying here long; the cheetah had had a go at his hand but apart from a few scrapes and scratches he was in one piece. Only the flies were interested.

His clothing had a sprinkling of pine needles across it, which suggested he had rolled when he hit the ground. He had come to rest against the tree above her on the slope.

Probably just an accident, she thought. Nothing to get excited about.

The simplest course of action would be to leave him. Let the cheetah and other wildlife eat the evidence. In a few weeks there would be nothing left except bone, cloth, and metal.

His face was turned to look down the slope towards the water and his eyes were open. He wasn't much older than her, just a few years at most. She should just leave him. Except she would always know he was lying here, rotting away. She and Khuwelsa could never come back if he remained.

She knew what Khuwelsa would say: He has a family somewhere. Because she had a family somewhere, her real family. Her abduction from her tribe was the one thing she would never talk about. She said she didn't remember but Harry knew she was lying.

Harry sighed. No two ways about it; she would have to do the right thing.

She clambered up the slope until she was above him. There was no elegant way she could do this on her own. She grabbed his legs and lifted. The body was stiff which, she understood, happened for a few hours after someone died. So he had been here since before she had arrived.

She had not seen any other flyers when they approached, but she hadn't been looking hard. This area was not on any regular route.

Heavy as he was, she managed to twist his body until it was no longer being blocked by the tree and in the process she turned him face up. She hung on to his trousers and dug her bare heels into the ground as his weight dragged them both down the slope towards the water's edge.

She held on tight and cringed every time his head hit a root or a rock. As they reached the shoreline she twisted him once more until another tree and its roots supported his weight. Sweating with the exertion, she sat on the root by his head to rest.

Harry noticed a "V" of ripples in the lake, which converged on Khuwelsa's head. A little distance out she trod water and spotted Harry sitting with the corpse. The sunlight glistened on her wet black hair.

"Are you all right?"

Harry shrugged. "Better than him." She gestured at the head beside her.

Khuwelsa squinted. "What are you—" She stopped and peered into the dark shadow. "What have you done, Harry?"

"Done?" said Harry in annoyance. "Oh well, I flapped my arms, flew up to the nearest Zeppelin, coshed this lad over the head, brought him back, and then killed him. You know, like all the others."

Khuwelsa swam to the shore, clearing a path through the floating pine cones. She came in under the shadow of the trees and grabbed on to a root below Harry. She studied the man's face.

"Is he what you saw moving in the trees?"

"No," said Harry. "That was a cheetah planning to make a meal of him. I chased it off, found him. He's been dead a few hours, I think."

"You thinking of getting him back to the *Pegasus*?"

Harry nodded. "Can't leave him here, but I'm not sure how to get him across."

Khuwelsa made a face. "Dead bodies fill up with gas like a balloon pretty quick."

"Well, if he doesn't float I suppose the fish will eat him and we can say we tried."

As Harry spoke she saw a far-away look in Khuwelsa's eyes, the one that meant she was having an idea. "Fill his pockets with pine cones and shove more of them inside his shirt."

"You expect me to touch him?" said Harry.

"You already have."

Harry didn't bother arguing. She got to her feet and clambered round to the other side of the body. Khuwelsa picked the least-waterlogged pine cones from the water and tossed them up to her. Eventually they had his clothes packed with as many as Harry could find space for, and she called a halt.

Harry grabbed his legs once more and moved him round the tree. With the extra weight he slipped from her fingers, slid with barely a splash into the lake, and disappeared beneath the surface.

"Oh," said Khuwelsa, staring at the eddying surface where he disappeared. Although the water in the lake was perfectly clear, the sun reflecting on it prevented them seeing into its depths.

"We did what we could." Harry was about to speak again but was distracted by a disturbance in the water about ten feet out. The body surfaced. It drifted towards the opposite bank at a sedate pace.

Khuwelsa pushed off to catch it. Harry clambered down and let herself into the cold water. She caught up with Khuwelsa, who was holding on to an arm and sculling towards the opposite shore. Harry took the other and they propelled him across the lake.

Working together they pulled the dead man up on to the further bank and removed the pine cones.

"If we let him drain and dry in the sun for a while, he'll be easier to move," said Khuwelsa. "And it'll give time for your clothes to dry, too."

"Well, I'm not taking them off with him here," said Harry.

"Seriously?" said Khuwelsa. "Your body is the last thing he's interested in."

"Well, you obviously don't care," said Harry referring to Khuwelsa's undressed state. "It's the principle."

Khuwelsa laughed. "Whatever you like. I'm going to put my dry clothes on and read a bit longer."

Harry watched her go, then turned her attention back to the dead German. Now that the water had washed him clean she could see a dark, round bruise about three inches in diameter on his close-shaven head where the skull looked unnaturally flat. She sighed and hoped he had not suffered. Well, no more than anyone would suffer falling out of a flying machine.

Perhaps it was true what they said, that one died of fright before hitting the ground. It would be a comfort if that were true. There was a badge sewn into his lapel. Harry leaned over to get closer. Wings denoted an air service but they were attached to a round shape with criss-crossed lines. It meant nothing to her.

The sun was warm on her back. Their governess was constantly warning Harry about being out in the sun. But the worst that had happened to Harry was an increase in the number of her freckles. Khuwelsa thought her freckles were interesting, and that was good enough for Harry.

His right hand caught her attention. It was clenched as if he was holding something.

She glanced up at Khuwelsa engrossed in her book. The man's fingers would not move; the body's stiffness included those muscles. She studied the fist. He was definitely holding something white. She poked at it, squeezing her little finger into the gap. Her nail hit something hard. It wasn't metal, nor was it wood.

Her curiosity got the better of her and she prised the fingers apart until they opened with a crack. She glanced at Khuwelsa guiltily, and mouthed an apology to the body.

After a few minutes of rooting around with a stick she managed to retrieve the object from the gap between the boulders where it had fallen. It was roughly two inches long, off-white and slightly marbled on the outside, with a curved pyramidal shape. Holding it up to the light she could see it wasn't smooth but had ridges running along its length. The sawn-off side revealed concentric rings that went from white on the outside to slightly greenish in the middle.

What it most resembled was a large tooth.

3

"Where shall we go?" Harry said.

The *Pegasus* was still perched on the plateau overlooking the lake. Steam was up, the body wrapped in a blanket and tied down out of the way behind the pilot's chair. Harry was ready to go but was not sure where.

"Home," said Khuwelsa.

"Everybody will think we killed him," said Harry.

"We need to talk to Dad. He'll believe us."

"Will he?"

"Of course."

"I was thinking Johannes."

"Your pash for him will get us locked up," said Khuwelsa.

Harry turned with a flush of anger. "I do not have a pash for him," she said. "I just think he'd be the best choice to find out where Hans here came from."

"Hans?"

"Have to call him something."

Khuwelsa came up beside Harry and looked out across the peaceful water. "It's a nice idea but we're not exactly popular with the Germans, are we?"

"I was thinking you might go in wearing a disguise."

"Oh fine," said Khuwelsa. "Send the black girl into danger while you keep your precious freckly white skin safe and sound."

"Well, I can't go."

"We haven't established that talking to Johannes is the best idea."

Harry reached out and took Khuwelsa's hand in her own. "I need to make up for what I did, Sellie."

"What we did," said Khuwelsa. "Don't you think I feel guilty too?"

Harry gave her fingers a gentle squeeze. "You never said."

"No."

* * *

Harry gave one long whistle and flicked the switch to engage the Faraday. The familiar and comforting lightness pervaded the ship. She took hold of the controls and spread the wings. She tested them with a couple of experimental strokes. They felt good—in fact they felt more powerful. Khuwelsa had definitely done something in her recent tinkerings.

Two long whistles. She engaged full power on the propeller and beat the wings in strong lifting strokes. The *Pegasus* leapt from the rock, dipped momentarily as she raised the wings for the next stroke. The nose lifted and the roaring propeller thrust them away from the roost.

As the wings rose the ship dipped again towards the bright surface of lake. The next beat swept them upwards, causing ripples in the water. Harry thought she saw a pair of yellow eyes peering out the 'thopter carried them above the tops of the trees opposite.

The craggy lip of the ancient volcano slipped beneath them and the ground fell away a thousand feet into a deep valley. They were facing north. In the distance the great mountain Kilima-Njaro was a blue shadow against the sky, save for its snow-encrusted peak.

Around them were the rain-eroded peaks and ridges of the Usambara range, from their bare tips to the thick forests of the valleys. Each valley held a river that cascaded down the rapid drops, spread out in the flat floors, or tumbled hundreds of feet in sparkling waterfalls.

Harry side-slipped slowly, bringing the nose round until the compass showed them on a southwesterly course. She adjusted the air-plane's attitude into a steady descent and locked the wings in the rising V-shape she had discovered had a natural stability.

With the new propeller installed, Khuwelsa had adjusted the airspeed gauge and changed the speed positions. They could now make one hundred and fifty miles per hour. Khuwelsa had indicated she was tired of having to be the stoker as well as the engineer and wanted to fit the 'thopter with one of the new coal-dust furnaces, even though they were potentially explosive, or a diesel, which wasn't.

However, after recent events neither of them thought it would be appropriate to approach their father about buying one. He had indulged their hobby thus far, but the events leading up to the Anglo-Zanzibar War meant he was unlikely to accede to any request for some time to come.

The war itself had lasted twenty-five minutes: from the deadline given to the resident sultan to abdicate in favour of the British choice of leader, to the moment when the British troops had landed in the palace grounds in their flying assault craft and seized the throne.

The new sultan had taken up his post and the British were content. The Germans, who favoured the original incumbent, were not happy at all. It was their task force that Harry and Khuwelsa had taken apart, downing the four Zeppelins in the ocean.

So she and Khuwelsa were unlikely to get any improvements unless they bought them themselves. Granted, they were provided with some pocket money, but it was not enough to buy heavy machinery. Khuwelsa was reduced to tinkering with what they already had.

Harry pulled the tooth from her pocket and examined it. Why would a dead man have a tooth in his hand? Perhaps it was valuable.

"She's fully stoked for now," said Khuwelsa right beside her. Harry jumped, having been so engrossed in her own thoughts. "I think I'll read some more."

Harry frowned with an annoyance she did not quite understand. "Whatever you want."

"Unless there's some bowing and scraping you'd like me to do, your majesty."

Harry shook herself. "Sorry."

Khuwelsa glanced at the gauges. "At this rate of descent we won't hit the grass for about an hour or so. You could catch forty winks, paint a picture, or read a book yourself."

"Yours is the only one on board," said Harry.

"Oh no," said Khuwelsa, clutching the book to her breast. "You're not reading my Jules Verne." She wrapped her arms around it protectively.

Harry cocked her head to one side and looked at the spine. "Vingt mille lieues sous … your fingers are in the way."

"Vingt mille lieues sous les mers: Tour du monde sous-marin," said Khuwelsa. "Twenty thousand—"

"I know what it means," said Harry huffily. "In French?"

Khuwelsa shrugged. They both knew that her French was better than Harry's German. It was just that Harry wouldn't bother reading in a foreign language if she could avoid it.

Harry took a breath to say something but Khuwelsa was looking down through the lower window of the plane. Harry looked too. They were coming out of the mountains and crossing the foothills.

Several rivers joined together and ran into the flat open of the savannah. They reached a depression in the landscape and widened out into a broad, flat expanse of flowing water edged in grass and trees. They could see crocodiles floating across the surface and a herd of giraffes feeding in the west.

But Khuwelsa's attention had been caught by dozens of dark blobs on the shoreline, with perhaps hundreds of vultures flapping about on the ground and many more circling above. The blobs could only be the carcasses of animals, but she was unable to make out what kind.

"That doesn't look right, Harry."

Without a word Harry took the controls. She cut the power to the propeller and put them in a spiralling descent.

4

Harry held the *Pegasus* in a tight circle as they went down rapidly. The vultures had enough sense to get out of the way as the huge metal rival fell through their ranks.

Khuwelsa released steam pressure by opening the whistle, and the *Pegasus* gave a long mournful hoot. The steam whistle had an "alive" quality that launched clouds of terrified flamingos and vultures into the air, and cut short the crocodiles' investigation of a free lunch, sending them sliding back into the water.

The air was filled with carrion-eaters as Harry engaged the engine again to give the *Pegasus* manoeuvring power. She stroked the wings to bring the ship down to a gentle landing in a space a short distance from the dark mounds.

The turbine powered down and the vessel went quiet. Almost automatically she flipped the Faraday switch and the *Pegasus* groaned as it sagged under the returned weight. From the rear of the ship came a thump.

"Ow!" shouted Khuwelsa. "What about the signal?"

Harry did not reply. She stood up in the bow and leaned forward, resting her arms against the window and gawking at the expanse of ground between ship and water.

"Oh, God," she said. "Sellie!"

Khuwelsa came up beside her, and followed her gaze. Her breath caught in her throat at the sight ahead. "Oh, Harry, no."

Scattered across the grass leading down to the water's edge were the mutilated corpses of at least fifty hippopotamuses. Their glossy black skins were dried, cracked, and pierced repeatedly with machine-gun wounds.

But worse, their mouths had been forced open and their teeth hacked out.

Harry's hand flew into her pocket. She pulled out the tooth and flung it away as if it were poison. It clattered on the metal. "Burn it, Sellie."

They gazed at the appalling scene of death and destruction while bolder, perhaps hungrier, vultures returned and floated down to the carcasses.

"Their teeth?" said Harry, shaking her head. "What's so special about their teeth?"

"Ivory," Khuwelsa said almost in a whisper. "Hippo teeth are ivory, and better quality than elephant tusk." She turned to look at the wrapped body lying behind them. "Soldiers did this. German soldiers."

Harry nodded and moved round to the other side of her chair, bent down, and unlatched a wooden box bolted to the deck. She pulled out a shotgun and broke it open. Holding it out to Khuwelsa, she grunted softly at her sister's head-shake of refusal. So, Harry put it on the pilot seat, then took out the second one and a box of cartridges.

"What are you planning to do with those?" asked Khuwelsa.

"They might not all be dead."

Khuwelsa sighed and glanced out at the bodies. The vultures were back, in the hundreds. "Yes, all right." She picked up the weapon. "You didn't land in the middle, did you?"

Harry shook her head. "No. If there are any alive they won't try to charge us here, but keep your eyes open." A shotgun wouldn't stop an enraged hippo.

They opened the door, admitting the stench of rotting bodies on the breeze. Under the baking sun they climbed out onto the grass. The air was thick with flies; the sound of their buzzing drowned out all other noises. Walking through the clouds of insects was like walking through a sandstorm except the grains were too large and landed on them. They pulled their flying goggles down over their eyes and kept their mouths shut.

The vultures were unwilling to lose their dinner to a pair of apes. They arched their wings threateningly and squawked at the girls. Harry and Sellie steered a course between the bodies, keeping their guns at the ready.

They reached the shoreline without incident. The flies thinned out a little and Harry pushed up her goggles as she looked back at the bodies. They had found nothing alive. Her best guess was that the soldiers had chased the hippos from the water somehow, using whatever flying machine they had, probably a Zeppelin. And then machine-gunned them.

The native tribes sold ivory to the traders but they did not have the advantage of flyers and machine guns. The traders brought it to the coast and sold it to people who carved it. They then sold it on to the Europeans and the Arabs.

She had not known hippo teeth were ivory. They must be easier to bring down than elephants. Hippos were very dangerous but not if you were flying above them.

As she imagined what had happened, she grew angry. Angry enough to use her gun on the men who had done this. This was not like Zanzibar. Yes, those men had been the enemy and threatened her father—and the Empire—but she did not hate them. She was not angry with them.

These men she would harm without a thought.

"Harry?"

"What?"

"We're not doing anything useful here."

"No." Harry shook herself. "Sorry."

Khuwelsa laid her hand on Harry's arm. "I know."

There was a disturbance along the shoreline to the left where a crocodile had snapped a vulture and had it by the leg. The other vultures in the area exploded into the air. Panic went out like a wave across the field of death. They watched as the crocodile retreated into the water, the vulture flapping its wings helplessly as it was dragged under.

She looked around behind them. More crocodiles were heading towards the shore.

"Let's go."

Back on board the *Pegasus* they stowed the guns. Khuwelsa got the furnace roaring and pressure up. The ship stayed firmly on the ground with Harry staring into space.

"Do you want me to fly, then?" asked Khuwelsa.

"I don't know what to do."

Filling the silence was the hum from the flies that had got into the cabin and were taking an interest in the body.

"We need to get rid of him, for a start," said Khuwelsa. "He'll start to stink soon."

"Johannes then," said Harry. "We'll go with plan A."

She flipped on the Faraday and took them into the air with strong strokes, then headed southwest at low height and high speed.

5

Khuwelsa decided she was not keen on plan A. Stars filled the black sky on either side of the strip of the Milky Way snaking across it. She felt under-dressed and very cold, wearing nothing but a native kitenge they had bought with the hippo tooth from a family by the roadside.

It was all very well, Harry saying that it was a perfect disguise and that Khuwelsa was used to it. Perhaps it was a good way to blend in, but she hadn't worn one in thirteen years. In addition, just because her skin was black and she swam naked in private did not mean she was happy to go about in public in a state of undress. She was used to proper clothes and, worse, she was separated from her toolkit.

But Harry was probably right; it would be better to find Johannes and get him to deal with the dead soldier. Of course they had no idea whether he was still stationed in the town. He might have been court-martialled for helping them escape. He might have been shot for treason. She went cold at the thought.

She walked through the dark streets. There were plenty of people about—native Africans selling fruit at the roadside, Arabs and soldiers—and none of them gave her a second glance.

Khuwelsa headed towards the officers' building they had been taken to when imprisoned. Exactly how she was going to get to see Johannes even if she found the right building was something Harry had glossed over: "improvise," she said. Which was all very well for her.

Something dug into Khuwelsa's foot. She suppressed a squeal of pain and hopped to the wall to pull out a sharp stone.

That was another thing. Unlike natives who spent their lives going about without shoes, Khuwelsa was used to having a layer of thick leather between the soles of her feet and the ground.

She limped round a corner. The old Arab building stood there with light pouring from almost every window. There was a wall, though not a high one, and guards on the main gate. She turned away and tried to think of how she would get in.

"Hey, you!"

She glanced up to see one of the gate guards heading her way. Her mind raced. Should she flee? No, she had no time and he had a gun at the ready.

He loomed over her. She went for an innocent look, though in the dark he probably couldn't see it.

"What are you doing?"

If she didn't answer soon he would think she didn't understand him. She spoke in halting German. "I want to see Johannes."

The fact that she spoke in his language took him back a bit. He hesitated.

"Johannes?"

"Johannes Schönfeldt."

"Why?"

She thought quickly: perhaps she should pretend to be an informant. The Germans were paranoid about the Wahehe tribe, a constant thorn in the sole of their collective foot. "I have information."

"You tell me your information and I will tell Feldwebel-Leutnant Schönfeldt."

"Will you pay me?"

That stopped him but only for a moment. "I will beat you if you do not tell me."

"Johannes will be angry if you strike me."

He thought for a moment. "Come with me."

Even though he had told her to go with him, he expected her to go first while he kept a lookout behind and his gun trained on her back. The shiver of fear that ran through her was not a fake.

The guard conferred briefly with the other on the gate and then took her through into a shed just inside the entrance. Khuwelsa took in the lists of postings on the wall; the map of the area; rules about who could be admitted and what documentation was required. The Germans were always very well organised.

There was a chair but he did not tell her to sit, so she did not. It seemed the building was equipped with the new telephonic apparatus. She watched in interest as he wound the handle to generate the power needed to communicate first with a switchboard and then somewhere else within the building.

He spoke briefly asking that the Feldwebel-Leutnant come to the guardhouse. He did not give any further information, which worried Khuwelsa; how would Johannes react when he saw her? Would he give the game away?

She was not facing the door when it opened behind her and the guard snapped to attention and saluted.

"What's this about, Sergeant?"

"This girl said she had information for you, sir."

She turned to face him. His gaze raced from her feet upwards. Her legs and knees were completely bare—she blushed but knew it was almost invisible—and he paused around her bare shoulders. Then he looked at her face.

For a moment it was obvious that he did not recognise her. Then his gaze became stony. He turned to the sergeant. "You can go back to your post."

"Yes, sir." He saluted again and left the room.

Johannes turned back to Khuwelsa. She got the very strong impression that he had no idea of what to say.

"Good evening, Johannes," she said in English.

"God in Heaven, Sellie," he said at last. "What are you doing here? And what are you wearing?"

"I am in disguise."

He sighed. "Yes, very well. Disguise. If they knew who you were, you would disappear and be talking to Saint Peter instead of me. Why are you here?"

"Long story."

"Make it short."

"Mind if I sit down? My feet are killing me."

He gestured to the chair beside her, while he took the one on the other side of the desk. "I am all ears, as you British say."

As Khuwelsa related the events of the day he looked steadily glummer. He had a nice enough face, thought Khuwelsa, but she really didn't see what Harry saw in him. Harry may have claimed she did not have a pash for him, but she was only fooling herself.

"What do you want me to do about it?"

"Well, first thing is for you to take this body off our hands," she said. "He must have a family somewhere."

"And then?"

Khuwelsa shook her head. "Not really sure. Perhaps you can shed some light on how a bunch of German soldiers came to be slaughtering hippos for ivory."

Johannes pursed his lips and brought his hands up onto the desk. "In order that Harriet and you can go chasing off to stop them?"

She shrugged. "That's not my idea of a good plan."

"You are not Harriet."

"No, I'm not."

He sighed and sat back in the chair. He kept glancing at her shoulders, which was quite embarrassing for her. She was never going to do this again.

"I'll come and look at the soldier."

"And take him off our hands?"

"I'll decide what to do when I've seen him."

They left the gatehouse and headed out on to the road. There were sidelong glances from the guards, but they could not say anything and Johannes did not have to justify himself.

They rounded the first corner. "You walk ahead," he said. "I'll follow at a discreet distance."

6

Harry jerked awake at the hammering on the hatch of the *Pegasus*. It took her a moment to get her bearings. She had made a nest near the furnace to ward off the cold of the African night, then spent half an hour working her way through the opening chapters of Khuwelsa's book before falling soundly asleep. She vaguely recalled dreaming in French about Zeppelins and sea monsters.

The banging on the door came again. This time, she came properly awake.

"Come on, Harry," shouted Khuwelsa. "It's bloody freezing out here."

Harry pulled herself stiffly to her feet and staggered over to the door. Her left leg had gone numb; she must have slept on it in a funny way. She unlocked the hatch, nearly tumbling out as Khuwelsa yanked it open. She pushed past Harry, went straight to the furnace, and plastered herself against its riveted iron skin.

"I am never ever dressing like this again, I swear," she said. "You can do it next time, Harry, and I don't care if your skin's not the right colour, we'll use boot black."

Harry turned her attention to the half-lit figure still outside. "Hello, Johannes. You can come in."

"No, he bloody can't!" shouted Sellie. "You can both get out while I get changed into some proper clothes."

Harry smiled and shrugged. She put her foot down on the outer steps and Johannes offered her his hand to steady her descent. She pulled the hatch closed behind her.

It was very cold. The air was crystal clear and very still. The stars barely twinkled against the blackness of the Void. There was an awkward moment of silence.

"Thank you for coming," she said.

"It was very foolish of Khuwelsa to enter the town, Harriet," said Johannes. "If someone had recognised her I don't know what would have happened."

"Nobody looks at the natives," Harry said quietly as if she was worried Khuwelsa would hear.

"But if she had been recognised—"

"She wasn't," said Harry with finality. If Johannes had been going to argue more, he chose not to.

A silver glow on the horizon to the northeast foretold the moonrise.

"Did you get into trouble?" she asked.

"When they discovered you were missing, there was a great deal of shouting and anger," he said without a trace of emotion. "The gate guards have been returned home and will be punished."

"What about you?"

"It has gone on my record that you escaped from my custody, but I am not accused or suspected of aiding you."

"Well, you didn't," she said with a hint of warmth in her voice. "Did you?"

"No, I did nothing intentional to aid your escape."

Like having the *Pegasus* moved inside the compound, or setting off the first alarm to provide a distraction. And Harry knew he had seen her untying the *Pegasus* before they took off, and had not raised the alarm at that moment.

"The trick with the lock was very clever," he said. "And the failure of the WC in the officers' quarters was not connected to your escape."

"Sellie's a magician."

"What did she do?"

Harry shrugged but realised he couldn't see her in the dark. "A magician never reveals her secret."

"You mean you don't know." He was teasing her.

"No," she said. "I have no idea."

Light flooded out from the *Pegasus*. They turned and saw Khuwelsa silhouetted against the bright interior. Johannes paused to allow Harry to ascend the steps first and then followed her in. Khuwelsa slammed the hatch behind them.

Harry gestured at the rolled blanket on the other side of the cabin. "There he is, take a look."

Johannes knelt beside the body and unwrapped the cloth about its face. The taint of death in the air intensified. It made Harry's stomach turn over.

"I do not recognise him," Johannes said and then pushed the cloth down to reveal the uniform. "Zeppelin deckhand."

"Even I knew that," said Harry. "He's got a badge on his lapel."

Johannes checked it and shook his head. "I don't recognise it," he said. "Did he have any papers on him?"

"We didn't find any."

Johannes pushed the body up on one side to release the blanket tucked beneath it, and unwrapped it further. He reached inside the jacket and went through the pockets. He pulled out a small oval object and held it up.

"Pine cone?" he said.

Harry moved forward and took it from him. "That was us."

Finally Johannes rewrapped the body and stood up.

"Well?" said Harry.

Johannes shook his head. "I am not sure."

"But you have an idea."

"I should not speak of this," he said. Harry put an innocent expression on her face. Johannes sighed. "There is a vessel that went missing. Three months ago."

"So you think he's from that?"

"How can I know?" said Johannes. "Ships disappear from time to time. There was a search but it was not found. It was assumed to have been lost, and we thought perhaps one day we would find it, or perhaps a survivor would appear."

Harry knew it was true. Vessels were lost over oceans, mountains, deserts, and in the Void, of course. Anywhere that no one would see them fall.

But Johannes was not finished. "You did not report about his wrists."

Harry frowned. "There was nothing unusual about his wrists."

Johannes bent down and unwrapped the man again. Harry knelt beside him. He lifted the man's hand. The uniform slipped back and revealed bruise marks all the way around the wrist; the other was the same.

"They weren't there before," Harry said.

"Perhaps it takes time," said Johannes.

"It looks as if he was tied up," said Harry, "and must have fallen when he was escaping. Could it be pirates?"

"Pirates are unlikely to attack a military vessel, Harry," he said. "Nor would they keep a man alive if he did not cooperate."

"So," said Khuwelsa, making both of the others jump. "He was cooperating and then found a reason not to. He was tied up, escaped, and fell. With a hippopotamus tooth in his hand."

They turned. Khuwelsa was behind them with both hands wrapped around a steaming tin mug. "Want a cuppa? Kettle just boiled."

7

They only had the two deck chairs so Johannes sat on a toolbox. They all drank from the mugs.

"This is fresh milk," said Johannes.

"Sellie put together a cold store," said Harry. "Don't bother asking her how it works because she'll start talking about the furnace, which makes no sense to me at all."

"It makes perfect sense," protested Khuwelsa. "Just because you are a complete dunce when it comes to science, you think it's nonsense."

"I didn't say that!"

"No, but you were thinking it, and you were trying to get the Feldwebel-Leutnant to agree with you."

"Ha, you have a pash for him too," crowed Harry.

"So you do have a pash for him then," said Khuwelsa. "I knew it."

"I am still here, ladies," said Johannes in a tone probably reserved for admonishing the lower ranks. "And my hearing is in perfect order."

Harry glanced at him; there was a redness to his cheeks.

Johannes continued. "We must decide what to do about your passenger."

"It's really simple," said Harry. "You have to take him off our hands."

"I do not think I can have anything to do with him," said Johannes. "It would be very difficult to explain how he came into my possession."

"Well, we can't keep him," said Harry. "He's already attracting flies and starting to smell."

"And what about the hippos?" said Khuwelsa.

Johannes held up his hands to quiet them. "There is only one choice. You must leave him on the road where he will be found by someone. They will come to us and we will collect him in that way. There will be no way to connect him to you or me.

"Once it is established he came from the missing vessel, the authorities will send out ships to search again, and this time they will be looking for a vessel that is flying instead of one that has crashed."

Harry nodded. "Yes, that makes sense."

"And what about the hippos?" said Khuwelsa again.

Johannes shrugged. "They are of no importance to me."

Harry glanced at Khuwelsa fuming in her chair. She looked like she was going to explode. If she did have any feelings for Johannes, they had probably evaporated in the heat of her anger.

"All right, Johannes," Harry said as she climbed awkwardly to her feet. It was impossible to get out of a deck chair with any degree of elegance. Johannes also stood out of good manners. "You better get back to the town. We'll put the body out on the road before we leave."

She went to the door and held it open for him, giving him no choice but to leave. And it would be ill-mannered of him to imply that the dismissal was, to any degree, rude or abrupt.

"Good evening, Miss Edgbaston and Miss Edgbaston," he said formally. He saluted and clicked his heels. Harry shut the door behind him as he disappeared into the dark.

Khuwelsa's tin mug flew past Harry's head and clanged off the door.

"I hate him," said Khuwelsa. She looked down at her dress and brushed it with her fingers. "I got tea on me."

"You don't hate him," Harry said.

"Germans are stupid, Harry," said Sellie. "I honestly don't know what you see in him."

"He's a good dancer."

Khuwelsa harrumphed.

"Let's get airborne," said Harry. "Dump this fellow on the road and head home."

"You have noticed the sun's not up yet?"

"Full moon, clear sky," said Harry. "It'll be as good as daylight. I had a sleep while you were out. You can have a nap once we're off."

"When were you thinking of getting some sleep?"

"I just want to get away from here," said Harry. "I'll give it a couple of hours and then set down."

"All right."

It took Khuwelsa twenty minutes to get the *Pegasus* up to full pressure. They moved the body to a position beside the hatch and took off. The moon was high enough to provide good illumination across the savannah; across the darker shades of grass, the main road was a distinct grey ribbon.

The *Pegasus* could take off and land vertically but could not hover, so Harry brought her down steadily. Khuwelsa got the hatch open and pushed the body out. She leaned out to ensure it was on the road—dead centre—then gave two long whistles. As Harry fed full power to the propeller and stroked away from the ground, Khuwelsa slammed and locked the hatch.

* * *

The morning sun poured in through the front window. Harry rolled over away from the brightness and bumped her head on a metal strut. She sniffed; a delicious scent filled the air. Frying bacon.

"Breakfast," said Khuwelsa.

"What time is it?"

"Half-past eight" came the reply. "I've been up for hours."

A thought struck Harry. "Bacon?"

"Wild boar."

Harry pushed herself up on her elbows and craned her head round. Khuwelsa was standing by the furnace holding the handle of her coal shovel. The other end was inside. There were hacked strips of meat on the box beside her. Some were cooked.

"I had to improvise."

"Lucky you found one," said Harry. "Was it already dead or should I be impressed? Where's the rest of it?"

"Outside," said Khuwelsa, then grinned. "You think I actually went out, shot a boar, and then butchered it?"

"Didn't you?"

"I'm not entirely sure whether I should be flattered you think I did, or insulted that you think I could because of my birth," said Sellie, and Harry squirmed until her sister grinned. "No, some natives were passing. I bought it."

Harry got up and stretched, trying to get the kinks out of her muscles and joints. She groaned as she twisted her back but it felt better once she stopped.

"I'm still impressed," said Harry. "Is it ready?"

They tucked the cooked bacon inside pouches of unleavened bread, took them outside, and sat on the steps of the *Pegasus* with cups of tea.

"The bacon should keep for a couple of days in the cold store," said Khuwelsa.

Harry looked round. She had landed the *Pegasus* in a small dell surrounded by wooded ridges; about thirty yards away was a watering hole. Between the *Pegasus* and the hole a group of ten warriors sat around a fire, talking and laughing. Harry smiled. People who thought the natives were different from Europeans had no idea what they were talking about.

"Do they know anything about the hippo killers?" said Harry.

"I didn't ask."

"Perhaps we should."

8

They finished their food and cleaned up. Khuwelsa watched Harry pulling her scarf around her head. She knew that Harry was expecting to run the show as usual, but this time was going to be different. If she chose her words carefully, sticking to facts, maybe Harry's reaction would be less dramatic than she feared. She hoped so, anyway.

Khuwelsa collected up the plates and placed them just inside the hatch.

"There's just one thing, Harry," she said. "I'll be doing the talking."

"Of course," said Harry. "I can't speak—what? Bantu?"

Khuwelsa stood in front of her. "That's not exactly what I mean."

Harry tucked loose strands of her long red hair behind her ears and under the scarf. "What then?"

"I gave the impression I was in charge."

Harry stopped with the fingers of her right hand pushed up under her headscarf. "Why?"

"You know most natives don't like Europeans, right?"

"Of course."

"They'll be more cooperative."

Harry shrugged. "That's fine," she said. "Doesn't matter." She turned back to the ship and made a big show of noticing a dead insect on the glass and wiping it off with the sleeve of her jacket.

"Harry!"

"What?" Harry turned back to her. "I said it doesn't matter. It's fine. No reason I should be the one in charge. We're sisters."

"But you always are, aren't you?"

Harry stopped again. "I … don't mean to be."

Khuwelsa smiled and put her hand on Harry's arm. "Of course not. But you can be a bossy cow, you know?"

"Thanks for nothing."

"Honestly, I don't really care," said Khuwelsa. "But these are Kikuyu, and they really don't like the British."

"Any relation to your tribe?" asked Harry.

"Not really, they're from further north."

Harry hesitated. "Am I supposed to be your slave?"

"They aren't slavers, so you don't have to grovel. They're mostly just farmers."

Harry glanced across at the men; from what she could see they were armed to the teeth. "Farmers?"

Khuwelsa shrugged. "Come on, just stay behind me, and don't look them in the eye."

The two of them, Khuwelsa in the lead and Harry following, pushed their way through the long grass. The men saw them coming. There was a quick conversation and then three of them left the group and met the girls halfway.

Even though Harry had said "Bantu" as if it were a single language like English, they both knew there were hundreds of variations. Still, the core remained the same. Those differences should mean the men would not realise she wasn't good at the language at all. Khuwelsa had started using it again only in recent years, and was very rusty with it.

"Greetings, Bakari, brave warrior of the Kikuyu," she said in simple Bantu.

"Greetings, Khuwelsa, sky rider of the iron bird," said the one in front. She smiled at the appellation he had given her when they spoke earlier. Thin but not bony, he had muscles like whipcords. She did not often get close to young men without layers of clothes. He was quite handsome.

"If it is acceptable to you, Bakari, I have questions," she said. She was sure there were more polite ways of asking, but she had no idea what they were.

"We also have questions, Khuwelsa," he said. "We shall give — and — ."

Khuwelsa panicked for a moment. She had no idea what he had said; if she agreed, would she be committing them to something that she shouldn't? Harry would never let her forget.

She pulled herself together. Misunderstandings in communication must happen all the time. Just say so. "I am sorry. I did not understand."

He nodded and gestured with his hand towards their camp. "Come, we will sit and ask questions."

He backed away, then turned and retreated.

"What are you saying?" hissed Harry. "This is really hard, you know?"

Khuwelsa rolled her eyes. One short conversation Harry wasn't involved in and she was already climbing the walls. "I said we have questions, he said he has some too, and now we're going to sit down and exchange information."

"All right." Harry started off after the warriors and then remembered herself. She stopped and gestured for Khuwelsa to go first. "Sorry."

Khuwelsa smiled as she passed Harry. "Don't sit down when I do. You should stand behind me a couple of paces away."

"You're not serious?"

Khuwelsa did not respond but traced her way through the long grass with Harry behind. She could get used to this.

The warrior sat on a boulder and she had the trunk of a fallen tree. Between them the remains of a small fire were burning out. Harry had taken up her prescribed position and the four other warriors, all looking younger than the one who was in charge, stood a short distance away, leaning on their spears.

Khuwelsa waited for him to speak first.

"You travel in the sky," he said after an uncomfortable silence.

"Yes."

"You fly across the mountains like a bird."

"Higher than birds."

"You look down upon the ground and see all."

Khuwelsa hesitated. "Only what a bird sees."

"I understand," he said and nodded. "Ask."

"Warriors of the white man kill many … hippopotamus." She was not sure if na kiboko was the right word. But the more she listened and spoke, the easier the words came and this one seemed right.

He nodded. "The white warriors with their guns. They are — ." Another word that meant nothing.

"We seek them. Have you seen them?"

"Three days ago. The bag of white warriors passed over us."

Khuwelsa barely suppressed a laugh. Of course he did not have a word for balloon so he called it a bag, which it was.

"Which way?"

"Over the mountains." He pointed north.

Khuwelsa sighed. They already knew that; their valley was to the north of the place the hippos had been slaughtered.

"Do you go to kill them with your metal bird?"

She did not know the answer. What did Harry really want? The killing of the hippos was upsetting, but there were a million hippos in

Africa; what did it matter that fifty or even five hundred had been killed?

"We want to know what they are doing."

He nodded, then looked up at her. "We seek one of our people. A bad man. Have you seen him from your iron bird?"

"We fly like the fastest wind," she said. "I have not seen a man of your people. I will ask my sister."

She could not bring herself to say servant and although he stiffened at the word, he said nothing. Khuwelsa craned her head round and switched to English. "He's after some criminal from his tribe; did you see anyone last night?"

"What did he say about the Zeppelin?" Harry demanded. "I saw him pointing."

"They saw the ship but that was a couple of days ago," said Khuwelsa. "So did you see anyone?"

"No, but it was night," said Harry. "We could offer to take him and his men up to could scout around; they know what they're looking for better than we do."

Khuwelsa liked that idea and passed it on to Bakari. Thoughtfully, he glanced at the *Pegasus* nestled in the long grass. Then he nodded.

9

Harry climbed into the pilot's chair. Khuwelsa had rigged a rope across the width of the cabin for the warriors to hold on to, then put her apron on over her clothes rather than stripping off, which meant they were going to get filthy.

The men climbed aboard with much bravado. They tried not to show their fear but their eyes were wide as they tried to take in everything. Far from being ignorant savages—the term their governess liked to use, regardless of the insult to Khuwelsa—they were simply encountering something almost entirely outside their experience. Seeing such a wonder from a distance was one thing, but this?

Now five Bantu warriors stood behind her, which made Harry feel odd and self-conscious though the rope also helped as a barrier so they would not crowd her. Khuwelsa had tried to explain what would happen when Harry engaged the Faraday, but the closest she could come was to describe it like swimming. Their response had been blank stares.

The girls had agreed they would take things slowly. Khuwelsa stoked up the furnace, and they waited a few minutes for the pressure to build. The first thing Harry did was engage the turbine that drove the generator. Its whine caused some jitters but no panic.

Harry wondered again whether this really was a good idea. Except it had been hers. If the warriors panicked mid-flight, they could all die. She calmed herself. These were grown men. The important part of that statement was "men": It would be a competition between them not to show any fear. Hopefully that would work in the *Pegasus*'s favour. Two short whistles from

Khuwelsa broke into her thoughts. The signal meant steam pressure was high enough to "go light".

She reached for the Faraday switch and gave a long whistle, pausing afterwards to give Khuwelsa the chance to shout a warning to the warriors. Then she flicked the switch.

Harry did not embarrass them by turning to watch, but she heard quite clearly. The lightness was accompanied first by gasps of amazement and fear. Then she heard one of them being sick. A couple of the others laughed, and finally she heard their leader bark an order which brought silence.

It wasn't the first time someone had been sick in the *Pegasus*.

Harry took a deep breath; the sooner they were on their way, the sooner the air flow would clear out the smell and whoever had lost his breakfast could damn well clean it up.

She engaged the propeller, which started with a roar that rose in pitch as she increased the power. If she had been able to lift off without it, she would have. She did not run it up to maximum revolutions, because that would probably be terrifying for her passengers.

She took hold of the wing controls and spread them out. There were more gasps as the warriors watched the wings moving through the portholes. At least they should be able to understand that part, Harry thought. She gave a couple of experimental beats. The port wing was a sluggish again; it had not been right since Zanzibar. It felt a little heavy which probably meant one of its feathers had lost power so its individual Faraday grid was not operating. Not enough to worry about.

The *Pegasus* gave two strong down-strokes and hopped forward a yard. Harry smiled. She loved this part. Two long whistles and another pause while Khuwelsa shouted to the men. This was the reason they used whistles; it made communication much simpler.

Harry made the decision to lift and gave full power to the wing beats. The *Pegasus* lifted smoothly. Even at half power the propeller pushed them forward. There was a clatter from the back; one of them probably had not been holding on.

With stroke after stroke the ship lifted. Harry applied full power and the rotor screamed in response. The *Pegasus* ploughed upwards through the air.

Once they had reached a safe airspeed she throttled back, and the whine decreased. Since their velocity alone was now sufficient to maintain their altitude, she locked off the wings.

With everything under control, Harry sat back and relaxed. The savannah rolled beneath them at a sedate seventy miles per hour. She closed her eyes.

There was movement behind her as Khuwelsa came up beside her on the left. The one Khuwelsa said was called Bakari appeared on her right. His hand clamped the arm-rest of her chair like an eagle's talon.

She gave him a sidelong glance. He was fixated on the rolling landscape beneath them. They were at about five hundred feet so every tree, stream, rock outcropping, and animal was perfectly clear below. They passed over a small herd of gazelles that took fright at the huge avian predator and bounded off into a stand of trees.

Bakari said something.

"He is very impressed," said Khuwelsa as she put her hand on Harry's shoulder and gave it a squeeze.

"Now who's got a pash?" said Harry.

"Shut up."

Harry took the controls. "Tell him I'm going to circle back to the camp, and then ask him where he wants to go."

Khuwelsa passed on the message as Harry brought the *Pegasus* round and increased power to bring them back quicker.

After some to-ing and fro-ing with Bakari, Khuwelsa told her that the warriors had been pursuing the fugitive east but had, not to put too fine a point on it, lost his trail. They had been on the verge of going home even though they would be in trouble.

"So I'll spiral out from that centre point," said Harry. "But we can't spend too much time on this. We have our own mission."

"I know, Harry, but you suggested it."

Harry chafed at so much time, especially as they had got nothing useful from the warriors. Then she chastised herself for being so uncharitable.

"We'll give them until midday."

She settled down for a boring morning.

10

The sun was high and it was hot in the cabin. It was probably just her imagination, but Harry felt as if there were no air, with seven people where usually there were only two. The warriors had become used to the strangeness of the vessel and called to one another, even cracking jokes she did not understand and laughing.

It was unnerving, as if her bedroom had been invaded. She was grumpy; she knew perfectly well it was because Khuwelsa could talk to them and she herself could not. Knowing did nothing to alleviate the effect.

She had chosen a spiral search pattern. Starting at the camp, she made larger and larger circles. The turn she was making now was about eight miles out, which meant the total distance covered on this circle would be about sixty miles. She had upped the speed to about one hundred miles per hour, which struck a reasonable balance between speed and noise.

About forty minutes to go round, then move out another mile and do it all again.

The savannah was a beautiful place, but this was tedious. They were not going anywhere. The warriors peered out, one on each side of her and the others at the portholes. They were fascinated. Every now and then one of them would spot something of interest—to them—and comment on it to the others.

Perhaps they were places they had remembered from their journey. She had no idea. She tried to distract herself from the tedium. What did the renegade Zeppelin want with hippo teeth? Yes, they were ivory and would fetch a price, but were they really worth anything uncarved?

How long did it take to carve a hippo tooth, and how much money would it bring? She was sure it would not be significant to a bunch of Germans in an airship. It seemed pointless.

And if you dumped two or three hundred ivory teeth into the market all at one time, wouldn't that bring the price down? Economics was not a subject she studied, but it stood to reason. When things were scarce their price went up, that was easy to understand; so logically, if there was a lot of something, the price would come down.

And the Germans had a lot of hippo teeth.

A strong gust of wind buffeted the *Pegasus* she adjusted without even thinking about it. The sun had gone behind a bank of cumulonimbus clouds building in the south. Storm coming, but it might miss them.

"Khuwelsa?" she called above the noise of the engine.

Her sister turned up a few moments later, squeezing between the chair and Bakari. "Problem?"

"If you call intense boredom a problem," Harry said. "No, not that. What else can you use hippo teeth for?"

"As opposed to … ?"

"Carving and selling. It doesn't make sense they would want it for that."

At that moment the little weight they had vanished completely as the *Pegasus* dropped for a few seconds. Reacting instinctively, Harry put the nose down and shoved the throttle to maximum. The propeller roared and shot them forwards into solid air.

Khuwelsa explained to Bakari in halting Bantu that sometimes there were pockets of bad air. They had been driving towards the ground at increasing speed until Harry felt lift under her wings again and she pulled up, letting the power off the propeller at the same time. The ship tilted nose up and she regained altitude.

There were a few anxious faces as Bakari communicated his limited understanding to the rest of his men. One of them forced a laugh and the others joined in. Harry was not impressed by their posturing.

"We're going to have to put down," Harry said to Khuwelsa. "That storm is going to be bad enough on the plain, but that's the Usambaras ahead. The air's just going to be too messy and we daren't take a lightning strike so far from the ground."

Bakari gave a cry and pointed down. Following his pointing finger, the sisters recognised the hippo killing ground they had landed at before.

"Tell them we're going down," said Harry.

Khuwelsa passed it on and asked them to get on the line again. Harry was grateful, as she felt crowded with the two so close beside her. She had enjoyed going to dances with Johannes, but not when they became too crowded. She preferred open sky where you could see the horizon fifty miles away at any given moment.

Unlike this moment, when the horizon was rapidly disappearing in the grey mist of the approaching storm. Flashes of lightning zipped across the surfaces and the inner parts of the cloud lit up again and again. This was a bad one.

There was no time to be delicate. She glanced back to make sure the passengers were holding on tight, then put the *Pegasus* into a powered dive at a high angle. The nature of the Faraday device was that it only reduced gravity directly above it, in relation to the source of gravity. The grid of the *Pegasus* ran along the bottom of its fuselage and into the individual feathers. So if it tilted off being completely flat, parts of the ship extended beyond the field and increased in weight.

It was a problem with all flyers; tilting too far meant you no longer had lift, and that could be fatal. On this occasion she was using it to increase her fall towards the ground. It was coming up fast. She flipped the wings out to act as brakes, killed the power to the propeller, then beat hard and fast to arrest their speed.

A moment before they touched down, lightning pierced the increasing gloom and touched her starboard wingtip. The Faraday cut out and they hit the ground with a crash.

11

The sky was thick with clouds, and rain lashed down. Gusts of wind made the hull shudder; lightning gave tantalising glimpses of the interior. The thunder boomed. An acrid smell meant the batteries had spilt their acid on to the deck. Hopefully not too much.

Harry flicked the switch to bring up the interior lights. Nothing happened.

"Power's completely out, Sellie," she shouted and climbed out of her chair.

The warriors still stood, resembling shadows clinging to the rope. Harry couldn't see their expressions but supposed they were probably not very happy. She made her way towards the hatch, ducked under the rope, and unlatched it. Flinging it open, she let in the gale and the rain. It cleansed the air in seconds.

Harry was soaked to the skin immediately but she was more concerned with checking the sky. The clouds were moving fast; the storm would probably blow itself off to the north within the hour. As the wind chilled her wet clothes, she shivered.

A gleam of light illuminated the interior. She turned to see Khuwelsa with one of the oil lamps they kept for this contingency. Electrics could be unreliable. And if one part burnt out, chances were they all would.

"The fuses have blown," said Khuwelsa.

It was just as well they had been about to land. A fall from twenty feet could have made the *Pegasus* unflyable, while one from fifty feet or higher might have killed them. Any vessel that used a Faraday device had the same problem, even the Zeppelins, though they were less attractive to lightning than a vessel composed entirely of iron like the *Pegasus*.

"I'll get the lightning rod up," shouted Harry as another crash of thunder exploded around them. She headed into the space beside the coal bunker—which was looking a bit empty—and rummaged around for the gauntlets, then turned to the warriors.

"Bakari!" she shouted. He turned at his name though she couldn't see the expression on his face. "Here!" She threw the two pairs of leather gloves in his direction and untied a long metal pole from the wall.

There was still chance they might get hit, and while lightning might not wipe them out it was very hot and could possibly melt something important. As she pulled the pole from the wall she heard Khuwelsa saying something behind her. Moments later two of the warriors were helping.

She let them do it but as they headed outside she stopped them. Bakari was examining the gauntlets. She took one pair from him and handed it to one of the men. She mimed putting them on. Bakari put on the remaining pair and took the poles from the man who did not have gloves.

Harry grabbed the guy ropes and the mallet, then led the way outside into the deluge. It would take no time for the warriors to dry, since they were wearing almost nothing in the way of clothes. She, on the other hand, would be condemned to steaming beside the furnace for several hours.

She hooked each guy rope to a collar mounted on the pole and stretched them out, then drove the pins into the ground. The cords were adjustable. One by one she tightened them until the pole stood on its own.

They went back inside just as the electric lights went on. So far so good, but Khuwelsa would have to check all power lines in the Faraday grid.

Harry sat in the corner next to the furnace, and allowed the heat to seep through her sodden clothes. It increased her resolve to get some attire that was more suitable to flying. Men had it easy.

Khuwelsa had shut the hatch to prevent any more water entering that might get into the electrics. The battery spillage had been small; there was no risk of it happening again. Harry continued to huddle beside the fire. Her outer clothes were drying well, but she was wet to the skin.

Khuwelsa came through and unscrewed a panel in the floor. It was not that Harry was disinterested in how the *Pegasus* worked; she knew how her baby behaved in the air and what the Faraday could and could not do. But she was not interested in the details of the science. With the panel lifted off, Khuwelsa lowered the gas light into the hole.

Harry craned her neck to see in. There was a criss-cross mesh of fine copper wires connected to larger ones that carried the power. These in turn were wrapped around small white towers. They reminded her of something.

"What are those?" she asked.

Khuwelsa looked round. "What are what?"

Harry pointed. "The white things."

Confused, Khuwelsa looked back into the hold and pointed her screwdriver at the nearest small tower. "These?"

Harry nodded. "What do they do?"

"Insulators," said Khuwelsa. "The Faraday needs a lot of power; you need thick cables to carry it." She pointed at the copper wire almost a quarter of an inch thick that ran from tower to tower and wrapped round each. Grooves kept the wires from slipping. "These do the opposite of the lightning conductor, they won't carry electricity."

"Are they china?"

Khuwelsa tapped the metal of the screwdriver against the top. The sound was like a teaspoon against a cup.

"A bit fragile, isn't it?"

Khuwelsa hit it harder; Harry cringed, expecting it to crack or smash. "Not really. It's thicker than you'd get in a teapot."

"But it could shatter?"

"I suppose."

"What about hippo teeth?" said Harry. "Would they do the same job?"

Khuwelsa frowned in thought. "I don't think so," she said. "The tooth would burn if it got too hot, I think. Ceramics can get very hot without any damage."

But Harry would not be put off. "How hot does it get?"

"Not very, usually."

"Does it ever get hot?"

Khuwelsa shook her head reluctantly. "No."

"So you could use a hippo tooth as one of those insulating towers?"

"I suppose you could."

Harry looked up with a pleased expression on her face and realised three things in quick succession: She and Khuwelsa were alone in the *Pegasus*; the rain had stopped and light was pouring in through the windows; and someone outside was shouting Khuwelsa's name.

12

Harry got up awkwardly; her damp clothes were stiff and held her in a vicelike grip. Ahead of her, Khuwelsa reached the door. She called something in Bantu, waited for the reply, and then turned back.

"Bakari's found something he thinks will interest us."

Harry stretched her arms, trying to loosen her underthings.

"You know it wouldn't bother them if you took some of those off," said Khuwelsa with a grin. Harry knew she was just teasing her, getting her own back for having to pretend to be a native—or go back to being a native, whichever it was.

"Yes, well, I'm not going to."

Harry stepped out and looked around in confusion. Despite what she had thought when they landed, this was not the same place as where they had found the hippos before—yet it looked the same. More dead hippopotamuses: these too had gunshot wounds, but they had suffered more from the depredations of the carrion eaters. They had been dead longer by one or two days at least.

And there were more of them, perhaps a hundred.

Harry's heart sank. She knew she was right. The Germans were not seeking teeth to be carved into ornaments for sale. This had something to do with Faraday grids. She guessed, from what she had seen, the *Pegasus* must have fifty of those insulator towers under the deck, let alone the small ones in the feathers.

How many would the soldiers have collected now? Reluctantly she examined the broken jaw of the nearest carcass. She counted twelve teeth sliced off at the front; the ones further back were smaller and untouched. Just to be sure she checked another, and it was the same. Twelve each from a hundred and fifty animals: nearly two thousand. Enough for forty ships like the *Pegasus.*

If that's what they were doing. But what other reason could they have?

"Harry!"

She looked up. Khuwelsa was standing with their passengers a short distance away, waving Harry over.

Fighting with the wet clothes, Harry strode in their direction.

"What?" she said as she drew closer. Khuwelsa was pointing at one of the bodies. Harry scowled; she couldn't see what all the fuss was about. She rounded the body of one particularly large hippo and saw what Khuwelsa was pointing at.

A native arrow protruded from the chest of one of the hippos. It was buried deep but probably hadn't caused the animal's death. Killing a river horse took a lot; the line of bullet holes was more likely the reason.

"Bakari says it's an arrow belonging to their man," Khuwelsa said. "He must have joined up with the Germans."

"As a guide?" Harry was not convinced that was likely. They did not need a guide; all they had to do was fly around following rivers until they found a herd. It wouldn't be hard. Maybe they wanted a translator.

How many other groups of animals had they murdered and pillaged? Two thousand teeth might be a low estimate.

"Perhaps," said Khuwelsa. "But what about this?" She held out a necklace. Harry remembered that Bakari had been wearing it. It was composed of what might be snail shells strung on a cord, with an egg-sized polished green mineral as the pendant. The stone had a network of white veins running through it, like marble.

"Did your boyfriend give it to you?" said Harry.

Khuwelsa's face dropped. "What's wrong with you? He's not my boyfriend, though the way you're behaving he might be better company."

Harry wasn't sure what the problem was. She tried to shake herself free of the vague feeling of annoyance hanging around her. "Sorry. What about it?"

"It's malachite."

"If you say so."

"You get copper from malachite."

"As in copper wires?"

Khuwelsa nodded.

"And your friends come from the north."

"Our friends."

"If you say so," said Harry. "And the Zeppelin was heading north after picking up this fellow."

"Yes."

"Do we know if he had any of this malachite on him?"

Khuwelsa did not answer but pointed to the other warriors in turn. They all wore ornaments containing the green mineral.

"So they have thousands of insulators and a source of copper," said Harry. "They could be building a huge Faraday device."

"Yes," said Khuwelsa. "Or perhaps going into the ivory trade in a big way making necklaces."

"Either way we had probably better stop them," said Harry.

"Yes."

Harry hesitated and glanced at the men, who watched the girls talking without any comprehension or impatience. "Do your friends want a lift home?"

"Our friends."

"Do they?"

Khuwelsa turned and spoke to Bakari. There was a lot of gesturing, pointing at the *Pegasus* and then north to the distant mountains. Harry did not need an interpreter to see the initial reluctance, then the realisation of how much faster they would get home coupled with the fact they might catch up with their quarry.

Bakari bowed his head, first at Khuwelsa and then at Harry. He turned back to Khuwelsa and gave a long speech, occasionally looking over at Harry as he did so.

"Bakari says that he would be honoured to ride in the metal bird and he wants to apologise to both of us. He did not understand when I called you sister and thought I had used the wrong word. Now he understands that we are sisters and wishes to honour you equally with me."

"So he's a boyfriend to both of us now?"

Khuwelsa broke into a grin. "Probably. They practice plural marriage and he's a chief's son. I imagine he's allowed several wives."

"Lucky us," said Harry.

"He's particularly impressed with your red hair."

"You can tell him I'm taken."

"He might challenge Johannes to a fight to the death."

"Messy," said Harry. "Come on."

They headed back to the *Pegasus* with Harry and Khuwelsa walking together in the lead and the men following behind.

"Just as well they agreed to come with us," said Harry.

"Why?"

"Because we haven't the slightest clue where we're going."

13

"How's the coal situation?" Harry asked Khuwelsa.

The *Pegasus* was high over the southern Usambara Mountains once again. Harry had taken them up to five thousand feet but she still had to pay attention to avoid some of the peaks. Khuwelsa, standing beside her, had not had to stoke once. Bakari had a couple of his men do it. The machine fascinated them.

"Bakari says that their chief says they must learn the ways of the European to throw him out of Africa."

"Wise man," Harry said and glanced at Khuwelsa. She was grinning. "What?"

"I'm their ideal African," said Khuwelsa and giggled.

"Oh great," said Harry. "Well, don't let it go to your head. And you do realise"—she added with a malicious grin—"they'll be queueing up for your hand in marriage."

Khuwelsa made a rude noise. "If that's the case I'll be able to pick and choose, won't I?"

"I wouldn't count on it," said Harry. "You know what these things are like. It'll be a cattle market with you as the prize cow."

Khuwelsa slapped Harry across the top of her head.

"Anyway," said Harry. "How is the coal?"

"We'll need some if we're going up to Lake Victoria."

"And that's where we're going, is it?"

"Apparently."

The storm had veered off to the east, visible now as darkness covering the mountains on the horizon, occasionally lit from within by its powerful lightning.

Harry gave their course some thought. Once they were north of the mountains they would be in the British protectorate where—at least theoretically—no one would cause them any trouble. There was, of course, also the fact they had not got back home last night. If they chose to set down in a big enough town they could write a letter. There might even be a telegraph.

"We better send a message to Dad," said Khuwelsa as if reading Harry's thoughts.

"Better not say why we're away."

"Or that we went to see Johannes."

"Or where we're going."

Khuwelsa hesitated. "Perhaps we should stick to having a lovely time wish you were here."

"We could lie."

"We probably will."

Khuwelsa dug out a map of the Horn of Africa. Bakari became very interested as she unrolled it across the floor and held down his side. It was a square about a yard on each side, and covered Africa from the Red Sea down to Zanzibar. The printing in the corner indicated it had been created by the Ordnance Survey.

She ran her fingers over it, locating the town of Dodoma where Johannes was stationed, the location of their private valley, and the places where she thought they had encountered the dead hippos. As she described the places out loud to Bakari in Bantu there was a moment of realisation, and all the men gathered round to look.

"We can stop in at Ndungu," said Khuwelsa to Harry. "It's about a hundred miles north by northwest. There are good roads so we should be able to spot those even if we miss the town first time."

Harry checked the compass and brought the *Pegasus* round on a new heading. Khuwelsa spoke to Bakari again. The map did include the east coast of Lake Victoria. Harry heard him talking excitedly, and she could imagine him pointing at the map.

"Their village is not on the map," said Khuwelsa. "But it's near the coast, so if we stick to it he will be able to recognise the landmarks."

Less than twenty minutes later the mountains fell away beneath them and they were once more cruising across green valleys and hills below escarpments with steep cliffs. Harry angled the *Pegasus* into a gentle descent and reduced power to the propeller in order to save on coal.

It was one of Bakari's men who spotted the town from a starboard porthole. He called to Bakari, who relayed the message to Khuwelsa, and she informed Harry. Harry brought the ship round. The town was about twenty miles away but seemed be surrounded by some sort of haze.

"How are we for coal and pressure, Sellie?" Harry asked.

"Should be fine as long as we don't have to do any clever acrobatics."

"The sky's clear," said Harry. "Not a Zeppelin in sight." Or anything else, come to that, even the storm was now no more than a memory.

She studied the town and realised the sky was not clear after all. The haze was due to smoke rising from the town itself, smoke that went up several hundred feet before dissipating. She aimed the *Pegasus* at the town and accelerated slightly.

"What's wrong?" asked Khuwelsa.

"I don't know, how likely are all the buildings to be burning fires in their hearths in the middle of the day?" said Harry. "Just being careful."

"You?"

"Careful is my middle name."

Khuwelsa snorted in an unladylike fashion but went back and spoke to Bakari, returning moments later. "Bakari says it looks like a grass fire."

"Except there's not a lot of grass in a town."

It took them less than ten minutes to cover the distance. Every moment as they approached, the situation became clearer. It seemed as if the entire town was on fire.

As Harry brought the *Pegasus* in a wide loop around the buildings they could see great blast holes in the ground. At least three buildings had collapsed. As they came around the east side a tremendous cloud of smoke and flame shot into the sky as something exploded and another building collapsed in on itself.

The flames were out of control but townsfolk stretched in a chain from the river to the edge of the fire, passing buckets one to the next in a vain effort to put out the conflagration.

Bakari shouted again. Khuwelsa disappeared from Harry's side but was back in a moment. "There's a group of people trapped in a square of buildings, Harry."

Harry glanced at the steam pressure. They could land but they wouldn't be able to lift again. Without hesitation she turned in towards the middle of the buildings. Smoke obscured her vision but Bakari came up and pointed slightly to the right. She shifted her angle again and saw the target. They were only two storeys high but completely engulfed in flame.

She guided the *Pegasus* through the buffeting currents, smoke, and flames. Above the square she glimpsed the group of perhaps ten people. With strong strokes she arrested the 'thopter's motion and came down. The gusts of air from the wings pushed back the flames and people dodged out from under the beast as she landed.

Harry noted the steam pressure was almost depleted. They did not have enough to lift. What on earth would they do now?

14

Khuwelsa dashed to the hatch and flung it open. The heat from the burning buildings was like a pressure on her skin. The air was filled with the roaring of the flames and the constant crack of snapping timbers.

Heat didn't bother her; she faced the *Pegasus*'s furnace every day. She kicked the steps out and down, then descended into the square. A dozen people stood between the ship and the conflagration, unsure which was worse: being burned alive or risking the unknown ship.

"Everybody inside!" Khuwelsa shouted, but her voice was lost in the noise. She gestured wildly but the townspeople barely shuffled towards them. Khuwelsa tutted. It was because she was black.

She turned and saw Bakari standing in the hatch door. He was not helping; the people were probably terrified at the very sight of him. She thought quickly, beckoning to him and shouting in Bantu. "You and your men need to get out now!"

He hesitated.

"Come on! Quick! Or they will burn."

He disappeared for a moment. Khuwelsa looked round, squinting against the sun and the flames, looking for the townsperson that seemed to have the most authority.

The people shrank back even further towards the flames. She turned and saw that all five warriors had emerged. Bakari was at her shoulder. She had heard nothing above the crashing.

"They are afraid of you," said Khuwelsa.

"They should be."

"No, that's not what—" She thought of trying to explain but her knowledge of the language really didn't stretch that far. "You go to the other side; if there are people there, you must make them come around this side."

He nodded and stalked off around the front of the ship with his men in tow. Khuwelsa dreaded to think how they would persuade people, but if it meant they were rescued then 'how' didn't matter.

Her eyes lit on a woman sheltering two small children from the heat. Better than some officious man who would be bound to argue. Khuwelsa set off at a trot across the dirt, trying to avoid the sizzling embers that floated down.

The woman realised Khuwelsa was heading for her and looked round in panic. Nearby, a man moved to cut her off. Khuwelsa slowed to a walk and showed her hands as empty. Her frustration was about to boil over. Why did people act so stupidly when they were being rescued?

"We're here to help!" she shouted. "You need to get on board and we'll take you to safety." Surely the fact she spoke perfect English would allay their fears.

"Who are you?" shouted the man.

At that moment the building behind them collapsed in on itself with a thunderous crash. A cloud of sparks and burning wood thrust into the air and rained down on them. Khuwelsa pulled something hot from her hair. The cries from the children increased to screams.

"Just get in the bloody plane!" shouted Khuwelsa. "You're going to die if you don't!"

The mother finally made up her mind while the man and others who were gathering still prevaricated. She collected her children and, lifting them with an effort, pushed past the man. Khuwelsa held out her hands, and after a moment's hesitation the woman gave over the older one. A boy of about three, he silently stared around in awe. He latched on to Khuwelsa so tightly she barely even needed to hold him.

Together she and the woman ran back to the *Pegasus*. Once the dam of obstinacy and fear had been broken, everyone followed. Looking ahead, Khuwelsa saw a small group of five men running around from the other side. Khuwelsa hoped Bakari had not been too pushy.

She stopped at the hatch and handed the child into the plane while the people hurried up the steps.

Of course, thought Khuwelsa, there's no way she's lifting with this weight on board. Even if we had the steam, which we don't.

The last of the refugees climbed aboard and she was left with Bakari and his men. "Thank you," she said.

"They did not wish to move," said Bakari with a grin. "We persuaded them."

Khuwelsa smiled but inside she felt empty. How could they possibly lift off?

She looked around at the burning buildings.

Burning buildings.

Her heart leapt. "Bakari, we need wood to put in the fire."

"What wood?"

"That wood." She pointed at the burning buildings.

He nodded and with his men trotted towards the piles of burning timbers.

"Small pieces!" she shouted after him.

She climbed inside the ship and pushed past the crammed-in people to stand beside Harry's chair. "Can you tell the men to help get the wood, Harry?"

Harry seemed pensive but she turned in her chair and kneeled on the seat to give herself some height. "We need fuel to get out of here. You need to go and help the natives collect wood."

There was no rush for the door, for which Khuwelsa did not blame them. The *Pegasus* at least gave the impression of safety. Finally, though, the men left.

The heat from the burning buildings was intense but they soon had a system going, and blacks worked with whites to fill the furnace with wood. The pressure began to build.

Harry touched Khuwelsa's arm. When Sellie looked at her Harry glanced up and to the left. Khuwelsa followed her gaze. Above the ship was a building with a four-storey tower. It had not been burning very intensely when they landed but now flames licked around its base and up to the second floor. It had developed a pronounced lean—in their direction.

Khuwelsa squeezed through the crowd and checked the furnace. It would not hold any more wood; coal was far more compact. She shut and latched the furnace door. The pressure was high. It would not last, but they just needed to get out of here. Harry just needed to get them out of here, somehow.

She climbed out of the ship and gestured for the men to stop. They got the message and headed back at a run. More than one of them glanced up at the leaning tower. None of them mentioned it.

Bakari and his men were the last to squeeze in. There were one or two glances at them but there was no space, so physical contact was inevitable. Khuwelsa shut the hatch and clambered to Harry's side. She glanced at the tower as a flaming timber broke free and crashed onto the front of the *Pegasus*. There were gasps and a scream, very loud in such a tight place.

Harry put all the power into the propeller and its roar drowned out all other noise. Khuwelsa could almost feel the *Pegasus* trying to move even though the Faraday was not engaged, such was the propeller's power.

Harry engaged the Faraday without any warning. There were more gasps and screams. Another timber crashed down but this time with far less force. Harry beat the wings hard. The *Pegasus* jumped forward a short distance but there was no impression it was going to lift.

Using the technique she had developed back in the German-controlled town, Harry dug the wings into the ground, first left, then right. She walked the *Pegasus* laboriously forwards and then turned towards the base of the tower. The burning wall of buildings was directly ahead.

15

Khuwelsa trusted Harry, but she had no idea what her sister was doing. Unfortunately, neither did their passengers—and they did not trust Harry. A woman screamed as they moved inexorably towards the fire.

"She's going to kill us!" shouted a man. "Stop her!" Khuwelsa slammed into the display panels as someone behind heaved forwards. Then the pressure stopped, and she glanced behind. A man with a face full of anger was directly behind her, with the blade of a spear at his neck. He was no longer pushing.

At that moment they reached the tower with flames all around them. Harry killed the propeller and lashed out with the port wing. Khuwelsa cringed at the thought of the potential damage to the feathers. With a snatching motion, Harry brought the wings in around the fuselage.

For a moment there was nothing; then all sound was drowned out by the screeching, snapping, and crashing of the tower collapsing on top of them. It went dark.

Harry paused for only a moment. The Faraday remained engaged so the power was still available. Using the wings like legs again, Harry pushed the fuselage up and broke through, back into the sunlight. The collapsing tower had smothered the worst of the flames around them and the upper section, which had not been burning, now made a path through the buildings ahead.

Working the controls with a delicate efficiency Harry walked the *Pegasus* across the bridge she had created. There were flames on either side, and as they moved the wood of the tower beneath them began to burn. Despite the odds, they reached the highest point and could see a street ahead of them. The buildings were burning all along it but the road was wide and people could move to safety.

Harry brought them down to the other side and stopped. Khuwelsa opened the door and let down the steps. The people poured out.

Eventually only Harry and Khuwelsa remained on the ship.

Khuwelsa put her arms around her sister's shoulders. "You did it."

Harry put her hand on Khuwelsa's wrist. "That was close, Sellie," she said. "If it hadn't worked …"

"But it did."

Harry sighed. "The wing struts seemed stronger."

"After last time I thought I'd improve them a bit."

Harry gripped her arm tighter. "I think I'm going to cry."

Something rapped against the metal of the door. They both turned. It was the woman with the two children, her face streaked with soot. She shooed her older child up the steps and came in carrying the smaller one.

Her gaze darted around the interior of the ship and finally came to rest on Khuwelsa's face. "I, um …" she faltered. "I just wanted to say thank you. Both of you."

Khuwelsa glanced round at Harry who climbed out of her chair, wiping her cheek. Neither of them spoke; it was difficult to know what to say.

The woman looked embarrassed at their silence. "What are your names?"

"Edgbaston," said Khuwelsa. "This is Harriet Edgbaston."

The woman smiled and nodded to the red-haired girl.

"And this is my sister, Khuwelsa," said Harry.

A flicker of confusion crossed the woman's forehead.

"Khuwelsa Edgbaston."

She regained her composure. "Say thank you to Harriet and Khuselwa."

Khuwelsa said nothing about the mispronunciation of her name, it happened all the time. Even her nickname came from Harry's original misunderstanding when they were six years old. Instead Khuwelsa knelt down to the three-year-old. "Harry," she said pointing at Harry. "And Sellie."

"Thank you for saving us," said the child with great seriousness. "Harry and Sellie."

"Our pleasure," said Sellie.

The woman grabbed the child's hand and led him down the steps. She paused when she saw the five warriors standing outside but did not quite run to get past them.

Bakari climbed inside and stood straight in front of the sisters, his spear at his side.

"You and your sister are great warriors," he said in Bantu. There was no hint of insincerity in his voice.

"Thank you," Sellie said.

"My spear is your spear," he said. "All the spears at my command are your spears. If you need them, ask and you shall have them."

"What's he saying?" asked Harry. "He seems pretty serious."

"Um, well, apparently if we want an army, he'll supply it."

"That's nice."

"Yes, though I'm not sure 'nice' is entirely the right word," said Khuwelsa.

There was a commotion outside. Lots of talking. Through the door they saw a number of townspeople congregating.

"Oh, for heaven's sake," said Harry. "Now what?"

Bakari stood aside and the two of them climbed wearily out into the sun. The *Pegasus* was streaked with soot and showed some curious discolouration on lower areas of the fuselage.

It was a deputation of half a dozen men: none of them clean, most with soot marks and some wearing fire-damaged clothes. The cleanest of them was a rotund man with a large moustache. Khuwelsa had seen enough bureaucrats around her father to recognise the type. This was going to be a job for Harry; they wouldn't talk to a black girl, even if she had saved people's lives.

"Good afternoon," said Harry with a smile. "I am Harriet Edgbaston, pilot and owner of the *Pegasus*. I am daughter of Jonathan Edgbaston, of her Majesty's Foreign Office based in Mombasa."

She held out her hand to the man, who seemed taken aback.

"Frank Danby, mayor of Ndungu," he said as he shook her hand. He appeared uncertain, and Khuwelsa smiled inwardly. Harry was good at making people ill-at-ease. He looked past her at the Bantu warriors now ranged around the ship. "Who are they?"

"Passengers."

"And her?" he looked pointedly at Khuwelsa.

"That's my sister, Khuwelsa Edgbaston, the ship's engineer."

Khuwelsa was slightly shocked; Harry did not usually do that. Both of them usually went for the "possibly a servant but not precisely defined" approach when introducing her. She was surprised at how unsettling she found it to be thrust into the limelight.

"I believe I must thank you for your assistance," he said.

"We did what any decent person would have done," said Harry. "Would I be right in thinking you've been attacked by a Zeppelin crewed by German airmen?"

The entire group looked astonished. "How did you know?" said the mayor.

"We've been on their tail for a while."

Khuwelsa put her hand over her face to hide her smile at Harry's exaggerated account of the situation.

The mayor looked at Harry, then Khuwelsa, then the *Pegasus*. "You're chasing them?"

"That's right," said Harry. "Unfortunately for us, though luckily for your people, we ran out of coal. Have you got any?"

16

"It's going to take a couple of days to check everything," said Khuwelsa.

The sun was going down behind the high plateau to the west. The town, at least what was left of it, was situated in a wide and green river valley surrounded on three sides by mountains and high ground.

Where they'd been allowed to continue, fires had burnt themselves out. A few buildings had been deliberately brought down to prevent the spread, while the important structures that could be saved had been hosed down with steam-powered pumps.

The main warehouses, factory buildings, and shops had been saved where possible since they provided the town's wealth and ensured its survival.

Once the emergency had passed, the mayor gave them a tour. He almost had tears in his eyes when they reached a large wooden building with several bomb craters visible in the interior.

"Our copper smelting plant," he said waving his hand—at which action Harry exchanged significant looks with Khuwelsa. "They took all our stock."

"They didn't pay?"

"They violated my town," he said. "They arrived and offered friendship, but it was all lies. Once they had ascertained the locations of what they wanted, they simply took it."

"What form was the copper in?" asked Khuwelsa.

"Form?"

"Wire? Ingots? Rods?"

"Oh, we do not manufacture wire here," he said. "Just ingots." He paused and then added with interest. "Do you think we should?"

Harry noticed a sign from the original building now lying partially burnt on the ground: "F. Danby & Sons". The factory belonged to the mayor.

"There is great demand for copper in the world," he continued. "If we supplied it made into wire would we get a better price, do you think?"

Harry looked at the sky. Khuwelsa sighed. "It would not be as compact. You would not be able to transport it as efficiently."

"True, true." He looked thoughtful.

As they wandered on, the mayor pointed out the school next to the church, both of which had survived the bombardment though all the windows were shattered.

"Did they say anything?"

"Their lies."

"I mean anything about why they needed the copper?"

The mayor stopped stock-still in the street and made a great show of rubbing his head as if he were thinking hard.

"Well, of course," he said eventually. "It was considered odd that a German warship should float down into our town. There was nervousness at first; we sent up our own flyer to intercept them."

"You have a plane?" interrupted Khuwelsa.

He shook his head. "Not a plane, no. We have an armed launch. Alas, no more. They disabled it before their attack."

"Disabled how?"

"Why?"

"We may need some spare parts for our plane," said Harry.

The mayor spread out his arms as if he wanted to embrace them both. "Ask for whatever you need, if we can supply it then we will be happy to do so—at no charge!"

* * *

Harry was fairly sure that had the town not been in such a pitiable condition the mayor would have ordered a feast in their honour, which they would have been forced to endure.

"Is there anything you can do tonight?" asked Harry as the two of them returned through the rapidly cooling streets towards the *Pegasus.*

"Not really."

They walked past a collapsed building and felt the heat coming from it. Hopefully the night would cool it enough that it would not combust again.

"That airship must be very heavily laden by now," said Harry. "They might be using their thrusters to help keep them aloft. They'll be going more slowly."

"We don't know that."

"But it's likely."

Khuwelsa bowed to the inevitable. "Yes, it's likely." Once Harry got a thought stuck in her medulla oblongata it was impossible to shift, short of a blow to the head.

They approached the *Pegasus.* Flames still flickered in the smoking ruins nearby. "Perhaps we should have named her Phoenix," said Harry.

In the fast-deepening gloom they caught sight of their passengers sitting round a small fire of their own.

"You were amazing, Harry," said Khuwelsa. "We could all have died if you hadn't got us out of there."

Harry made a small groaning sound. "And if I hadn't landed at all, I wouldn't have put you at risk. What's Dad going to say when he finds out?"

"If you hadn't done it, knowing those people were trapped, how would you feel?"

"He's going to shout at me again."

"Probably," said Khuwelsa.

"Thanks."

"Then he'll tell you how proud he is you did the right thing."

The warriors did not stand as the girls reached the ship. Harry found it odd; men were supposed to stand when women approached. But they had different customs.

Instead Bakari spoke to Khuwelsa, apparently asking a question. She shook her head in response. He asked something else and she gave a long answer with the occasional hesitation. He spoke again in reply and Khuwelsa finished with a short response. She followed Harry towards the ship.

"He wanted to know if we wanted to sit at the fire."

"You said no."

"I did, although I think it's an honour to be asked," said Khuwelsa. "Then he wanted to know when we would be on our way."

They climbed aboard the *Pegasus* and pulled the hatch shut behind them with a firm clang. Harry threw the bolt. They sighed simultaneously as they cut off the world.

"What did you tell him?"

"I explained that *Pegasus* is hurt and needs to be mended."

"Hurt?"

"I don't know the right words, or whether they even if they have them at all," said Khuwelsa. "But he got the idea."

They made a bed alongside the furnace, forming pillows from their outer clothes; they shared the blanket.

"I hope things are better in the morning, Sellie."

But Khuwelsa was already asleep.

17

Breakfast had been supplied by their passengers, who must have risen at first light and gone hunting. They had returned with what had probably been a goat but had been skinned, gutted, and cooked by the time the sisters appeared.

Khuwelsa had drained some water from the boiler, still warm, for them to wash and they had spent some time brushing each other's hair. Their clothes were dirty but there was nothing they could do about that. Khuwelsa muttered something about keeping some spares on board in future if this gallivanting at the drop of a hat was going to continue.

Still, when they finally opened the hatch and the delicious smell of cooked goat wafted in, Harry felt ready to face the day with a renewed energy.

Bakari handed them crispy cuts of meat inside pouches of unleavened bread. Harry thought the addition of butter would make them almost perfect, perhaps some brown sauce too. Realising she was ravenous, she ate with gusto—she could not recall exactly when she had last eaten. Khuwelsa was the same and polished off three in the time Harry took for two.

"I'm going to check this armed launch the mayor mentioned," said Khuwelsa. "It might have something we can use depending on what they did to it."

"Anything I can do?" asked Harry.

Khuwelsa thought for a moment. "Not really. Oh, unless you can rustle up some heavy tooling like I have back in my workshop."

Then she headed off with Bakari and two of the others, leaving Harry with the remaining two with whom she could not exchange a single word. They did, however, consume several more sandwiches each. That seemed to have a strange bonding effect, especially when she kept asking for more.

Harry went back into the *Pegasus* and fetched her scarf. Only a few high-altitude clouds floated across the sky. Soon the sun would be beating down. She climbed down once more and shut the hatch.

She looked at the scorched town. In the light of morning it resembled a ruin, so few houses remained untouched, and those that still stood were smoke-damaged at best. A haze of heat and smoke made the farther buildings shimmer. Their governess had made them study the history of England, which included the Great Fire of London. It must have looked something like this, but without the sun; it always rained in England.

When she and Khuwelsa had walked around the previous evening most of the activity had been in the south of the town, so she headed in that direction. Hearing a noise behind her, she turned to discover the remaining two warriors were following her. They just grinned at her attempts to shoo them away.

Apparently sending them was Bakari's idea of respect, or perhaps he did not trust the people in the town. Either way, it was going to be difficult talking to anyone with those two in tow.

Rather than follow the route the mayor had taken them on, she took the first turning east that looked clear enough. She skirted a bomb crater. A thought occurred to her: would the captain of the Zeppelin have been so callous as to drop the bombs simply to lighten the load his ship had to carry?

It seemed unlikely, she thought. The next crater she encountered was off to the side and had destroyed a building. The debris of splintered wood and smashed bricks was strewn across the road. Fire had burnt out the buildings around it. Those a little further away were not in much better condition, as the fragments from the explosion had torn through their walls and windows.

They would have done this to Zanzibar, she thought. She had no idea how many people had been killed in this attack. Did the ones she had rescued balance the books compared to those who had died by her actions? She shook her head as if the question had been asked out loud. These books did not balance that way.

She came to a crossroads. The road directly across from her was lined with shops displaying signs for a grocer, barber, baker, and others. The shop row looked untouched; the only rising smoke was from chimneys. People moved with purpose along the street, some carrying baskets, others chatting with their companions. Except for the pervasive smell of burnt wood, it could have been a typical day.

She heard the sound of hooves before she saw the horse. Coming from the north, its firm steps thudded into the dry soil. The cart was moving at a fair speed, drawn by a blinkered Clydesdale which moved as if oblivious to the weight of the cart behind it. The driver wore the coarse clothing of a farmer.

She had been about to step out across the road and wander into the shops, but she waited for the cart. It did not slow at the junction and headed past. The driver was focused on his destination but must have caught sight of her and her small entourage. Whether because of her red hair or the tall black men behind her, his head whipped round to watch them as he passed.

Harry would have waved but caught sight of the cargo of the open cart. Bodies. Not only that, they were bodies dressed in German naval uniforms.

18

With sudden energy Harry hitched up her dress and took off after the cart at a run. She gathered disapproving looks from the people she passed, which were replaced by fear, horror, and possibly anger when those people saw the two warriors following. But if Harry ever cared what other people thought of her, this was not one of those times.

The powerful horse outdistanced her, but she did not slow down. The street was straight and wide, such that she saw the cart swerve round something she could not see and then turn right.

She was about a minute behind it when she reached the crater in the road the cart had swerved to avoid. From that, she knew the road to the right was the one she needed to take. She slowed to a walk and caught her breath. As her escort closed up behind her, she was annoyed to see that they were breathing as normally as if they had not been running for the last couple of minutes.

She looked around at this new part of the town. The damage here was minimal; the worst seemed to have been concentrated in the north, near to the copper works. Directly ahead, to the south, she could see the partially constructed tunnels of a terminus for an atmospheric train.

Either the people here were very hopeful or they were very prosperous. Considering the need for copper in the world to provide conduits for the fast-developing electrics, and for Faraday devices, she suspected it was the latter.

This attack, for all that it may have killed some people, was a mere blip in the fortunes of what would no doubt become a rich city in no time. As long as the copper continued to flow.

Following the route the cart had taken, she walked between warehouses and stores. They looked to have been built recently but stood empty. There were no business names on the exteriors. She peered in through a window. The inside was bare, just open space waiting for future businessmen to fill it with wares to be transported in and out on the atmospheric.

The road opened out into a square. A garden in its centre was laid out with greenery and fresh plantings of trees, still small. A wrought iron fence surrounded it, and the words "Danby Park" were engraved into the stone arch of the gate. She harrumphed at the mayor's arrogance.

She was not sure which way the cart had gone from here; there were routes in both directions around the garden.

"Harry."

She jerked around at the sound of her name, though it had been pronounced strangely. One of the warriors was looking at her and grinning. He pointed at the ground and then to the right around the square. She smiled; of course they would be able to track a horse and cart in a town.

"Thank you," she said and gestured for them to lead the way. Although, now she came to look, the track in the dirt really was very obvious—it just had not occurred to her to check.

Walking behind them, she realised she had never really looked at them. They wore a sort of skirt, which would have seemed strange on a European but not on them. Their skin was a deeper brown than Khuwelsa's, almost black, and their muscles were clearly defined beneath it. They wore necklaces and, apart from their spears, each had a vicious-looking club hanging from his belt.

She had had it drummed into her by Mrs Hemingway that looking at men in such detail would be frowned on polite society. This was not polite society.

They stopped. Ahead, the road they had been following opened out into another square. And in the middle of it, surrounded by men, was the cart. Harry came up beside them. She debated whether to try to make the two warriors remain where they were but decided they would be at risk if she left them alone.

She led the way forward.

As she approached the crowd, she realised from the cheerful sound of their voices the men were happy and in the process of looting the bodies.

"What are you doing?" No one took any notice of her query. A man came away from the cart holding a pair of boots. She recognised him as being one of the men she had rescued from the fire.

"Have you no shame?" she yelled. Her voice reverberated off the surrounding walls and silence fell.

The cart's driver pushed his way round to the front. He noticed the man with the boots. "That'll be ten shillings, mate." Then he turned his attention to Harry.

"Get lost, kid. This is nothing to do with you."

"What are you doing?" she demanded.

"I won't tell you again," he growled advancing on her. "Get lost."

At that moment she felt more than saw her escort move forward until they were flanking her. The cart driver hesitated.

"What kind of monster steals from the dead?" she said very loudly, just to make sure they all heard. "And when you stand up in church next Sunday, what will Christ, Our Lord, think of you?"

The man she had rescued dropped the boots as if they burned him. Other items fell to the ground and most of the men backed away.

"This is my business, girlie."

"My father is Jonathan Edgbaston, servant of Her Majesty's government in Mombasa," she said. "Perhaps you would like me to inform him of what's going on here?"

More items dropped. Several men left.

"These are the monsters, little girl," he said. "They're the ones who attacked this town." Murmurs of agreement rippled through the crowd. "They owe us."

"Perhaps that's true, but why should you be the one to make the money off of it?" she said. "If they truly owe the town, then you should be giving their goods away for free. To the townspeople who are owed."

The crowd seemed more on her side at that. She was not blind to the fact they would rather have the items for free than pay for them. She took a step forward and the warriors moved with her. The cart driver took a step back. The men of the town gathered round the cart began to decide there were better places to be at that moment, and their ranks thinned.

"Why shouldn't I make a penny or two when the opportunity arises?" he said.

"From the dead?" she said. "What sort of ghoul are you?"

"They're dead Germans," he said. "Who cares about the kaiser's hounds?"

"They are men," she said. "They deserve respect. Some of them will have left wives and children. Would you want to be treated like this if the tables were turned? Would you want to have your body defiled and left unburied?"

"I didn't say I wasn't going to bury them."

"You're willing to sell the shoes off their feet like a petty thief. You would just dump their bodies in the grass for the carrion eaters. Would you want that for yourself?"

He looked around for support, but only his horse remained. "Why do you even care?" he said in a tone of exasperated confusion. "Still, now that we're alone …"

He slipped his hand into his pocket and pulled out a small pistol.

"I think you should be on your way," he said. "Don't you?"

19

Harry stared down the barrel of the gun pointed at her head.

"Nothing to say now, have you?"

"Lambert, put that away."

The man called Lambert did no such thing. Harry looked up to see the mayor and one of the men she had rescued standing on the other side of the truck.

Mayor Danby moved more quickly than she would have thought him capable. He came alongside Lambert.

"Put that away now and we'll say no more about it," the mayor said quietly. "Do something foolish and I think those blacks will have you dead in a trice. And I won't stop them. Or string them up."

For a moment it was unclear whether the mayor's words had any effect. Then, without taking his eyes off Harry, the man called Lambert uncocked the gun and let his hand drop.

The mayor held out his hand. Lambert gave him the gun, and the mayor passed it to the other man.

"Go and get a drink, Lambert, and calm down."

"This is my cart," he said. "My horse."

"Nobody is going to steal it."

Lambert gave Harry another look of pure malice, turned away, and headed out to the main street.

The mayor smiled at Harry. "Don't let anyone tell you that being a mayor is an easy job, Miss Edgbaston."

She shook her head.

"Pretty speeches you were making. Ever thought of a career in politics?"

She frowned. "I'm no suffragist."

He laughed out loud. "Really? You may wear a dress, Miss Edgbaston, but we do get newspapers, even here. And your airplane and your recent escapades are not something you can hide. You are known. Then you arrive here and rescue my people from a raging fire. Quite the adventuress.

"Yet you are a mere woman and you say you're not a suffragist?" He could not suppress his laughter. "Well, you may not think of yourself as one but I can assure you, your exploits will be talked of by those particular women and will be held up as examples of what a woman can do. There will be many men who will not be happy with you at all."

Harry really could think of nothing to say on the matter. She just shrugged. "I just wanted to know how Mr Lambert had got himself a cartload of dead Germans."

This again seemed enormously amusing to the mayor; however, this time he seemed to bring himself under control more quickly.

"Yes indeed," he said. "That is an excellent question, and we will have to discuss the wherefores of that issue."

"Can I have a look at them?" asked Harry.

The mayor looked somewhat surprised. "You want to?"

"The reason I'm on their trail was that I found one before. He had fallen from their Zeppelin."

"Or was he pushed?" said the mayor with a wink. "I don't think people generally just fall from airships."

Harry came forward. From her first glance she knew she did not have to look any further. The clothes of the men—only five of them, though it had seemed more—were caked in dried blood crawling with flies. The blood came from bullet wounds.

"Shot," she said not really to anyone in particular.

"Indeed," said the mayor.

Harry looked more closely at the uniforms. She wasn't an expert but she did recognise the same badge as on the other man they had found. So they were from the same ship that had disappeared, or at least the same service. Four out of the five looked to be lower ranks, but one of them was at least a sergeant, perhaps even an officer.

She shook her head. It did not seem to make any sense. On a whim she looked at the hands that she could see. None were clasping anything.

Turning away, she glanced at her escort. She was glad for them now.

"Seen everything you wanted?" asked the mayor.

She nodded and pushed the question of the dead airmen to one side. "You are building an atmospheric terminus."

"Let us move away from these poor souls," the mayor said and offered his arm. She slipped her hand into the crook of his elbow and followed as he headed off towards the end of the road.

They came out onto a thoroughfare that paralleled the one down which she had chased the cart. This was the side of the town that had been the most damaged. The shattered buildings still smoked. People were clearing the road, making piles of the debris. Most of it would be used for reconstruction in one way or another.

"There is a great deal of hate in the world, Miss Edgbaston," he said. "Here we see the result of it."

"Did they drop their bombs before or after they took the copper?"

He glanced round at her with a sly look. "After."

"Why?"

"You do ask many questions."

"I'm sorry."

He patted her hand. "I daresay it is a fair question." But he did not continue; instead he guided her further into the south of the town. In the distance tents were being erected. Talking to the mayor was like boxing shadows, but she took another swing

"My sister would like access to some tools, the sort you probably have at the construction site."

"Your sister?"

"Khuwelsa is my sister, yes."

"And your escort are your brothers?"

"No, they are just passengers."

"They seem very protective for passengers," he said.

"Was there one like them on the German ship?" she asked.

The mayor stopped. "I did see a black man in their number. He seemed quite out of place. Was he related to these fellows?"

"They were in pursuit of him."

"So your paths merged and your purposes became united."

"Yes," she said, and realised he had deflected her again. "My sister would appreciate being given access to the tools you have at the terminus. Is that possible?"

"Will you recover our copper?"

"We can try."

"Then she may use the equipment."

"Thank you."

"Under supervision."

20

A considerable crowd gathered at the part-constructed terminus just after lunch the following day as they prepared to set off. Khuwelsa had outdone herself with the work she had put in, for which Harry was grateful as she could not stand the place any longer.

It was not the people themselves that bothered Harry. They either left her alone or wanted to thank her for saving their lives, or their loved ones' lives, or their friends' lives. Everybody knew everybody in a place so small.

The mayor and his hangers-on, however, were infuriating. The mayor seemed to want to be seen in her presence all the time and even implied on one occasion that the arrival of the *Pegasus* was somehow his doing.

She disliked the politicking intensely. It confirmed her in the opinion she had no interest whatsoever in being a suffragist or ever dealing with her father's friends and associates. Not that that would bother Jonathan Edgbaston; he always tried to find ways to keep her and Khuwelsa out of the way when he had people at the weekend.

Bakari and his men were aboard. Khuwelsa had installed additional seats with a barrier rail between the pilot's chair and the rest of the vessel, along with her other repairs and improvements. She had even found the feathers in the port wing that were not operating at full efficiency and fixed them. Harry was not sure whether the mayor was aware quite how much of the damaged launch Khuwelsa had scavenged. Harry had gone out to see it at one point and found it stripped bare, right down to the Faraday grid.

From the rear of the *Pegasus* Khuwelsa gave two short whistles: Steam's up. Harry glanced at the pressure gauge and confirmed it was at maximum. The mayor had provided a full load of coal for free as well. Once she had confirmed she would try to return their copper, he was full of cooperation.

The women of the town had provided them with cooked foods that would last a good amount of time, and Bakari's men had hunted and cooked several animals of their own. The *Pegasus* had never felt so full, almost bloated. Harry gave a long whistle, paused a moment, and engaged the Faraday.

She unlocked the wings, felt them unfold, and arched them as if she were a hawk readying herself to fly. The cries of amazement from the crowd that filtered through the hull made her smile. Harry knew her bird was beautiful and was pleased when she impressed.

Harry flapped the wings. They were perfect. She engaged the propeller at its lowest gearing and it spun up to speed. For some reason she wanted this to look good. She steadily increased the speed of the rotor until it was screaming. She gave the wings another couple of gentle flaps that would not shift them from the ground.

Finally she gave two long whistles, raised the wings and beat hard, tilting the wings forward as she did so. The front of the *Pegasus* lifted. The ship leapt upwards, the propeller caught the air and they shot into the sky.

She flattened out and they accelerated. Stroking the wings steadily to gain more height, she brought the *Pegasus* round until she was facing northeast and let her go. Their airspeed increased. She looked through the lower window of the cockpit at the newly installed mirror. The town was disappearing rapidly into the distance.

With the wings locked off in cruising position she reduced power on the propeller, and they cruised away from the town at a steady one hundred and twenty miles per hour as the day headed towards night.

"What do you think?" Khuwelsa leaned across the rail. She was grinning.

"Good as new," said Harry.

Khuwelsa's face fell. "Good as new? Is that the best you can offer?"

Harry laughed. "Better than new?"

Khuwelsa harrumphed. "Too late. I'm upset now. I slaved over our baby night and day for this."

"Well, if it's already too late I'll say no more."

There was silence between them for a while. The sky darkened and the stars stood out.

"Have you got a plan?" Khuwelsa could no longer stand the quiet.

"If I said yes, would you believe me?"

"Of course, I believe every word you say."

"Of course you do," said Harry. "Plan A: Find the German Zeppelin. Follow them to wherever they're going. Find out what's going on. Report back to Dad."

"Good plan."

"I thought so."

"It'll never work."

"We can try."

"So," said Khuwelsa. "Is there a plan B?"

"Improvise."

"I like plan B better."

Harry peered out into the deepening gloom. "Better put down before we lose all the light."

Khuwelsa disappeared into the plane while Harry reduced speed and lost height. There were some big mountains here on the upper plateau, including Kilima-Njaro. She certainly did not want to bump into that.

21

To the north the towering peak of Kilima-Njaro dominated the horizon, far taller than any surrounding peak, with its crown of glistening snow. Bakari and his men were glued to the portholes watching as the ship flew west into the setting sun.

"What's up with them?" she asked Khuwelsa, who spoke to Bakari briefly.

"Local god or something like that," said Khuwelsa.

Harry paused. "I've been thinking that if we get up as high as we can and our passengers can stand as lookouts we stand a better chance of spotting the Zeppelin. We can probably see for a good fifty miles in all directions."

Khuwelsa discussed it with Bakari. Harry, even lacking understanding of the language, saw he was happy with the idea. She increased power to the propeller and adjusted the attitude of the wings. The needle of the altitude gauge crept up.

Bakari posted two men at each of the port and starboard portholes then stationed himself and the remaining two at the front, leaning over the rail. Harry gestured for the two of them to climb under the rail and position themselves as far forward as possible. They moved forward and sat cross-legged on the deck looking out as the *Pegasus* continued to climb.

"What sort of speed do you think the Zeppelin will be making?" Harry asked Khuwelsa as they reached ten thousand feet.

"At best they could only manage sixty miles per hour, and with their additional weight it's difficult to say."

"But they have a big head start." Harry screwed up her face in concentration. "I have no idea how to work that out, even assuming they don't change course."

"It's easy," said Khuwelsa. "We'll assume they are in the air for the same amount of time as we are, and we're going the right way, otherwise there's no point. At worst we have twice their speed. First we have to cover the same distance they did in one day. It will take us half a day. They will have moved on a further half-day's travel but it will only take us quarter of a day."

"But they will have moved a further quarter-day's worth."

"Which we'll cover in an eighth."

"And they'll have gone a bit further."

Khuwelsa laughed. "Zeno's Paradox."

"What?"

"We can never actually catch them because they will always move forward a little bit in the time we cover the previous distance."

"That's ridiculous."

"Of course it is, it's Zeno's Paradox."

Harry sighed. "So when will we catch him?"

"No idea."

"Well, you're a bloody lot of use."

The sun was setting. Harry wanted to keep the *Pegasus* in the air as long as possible but landing in the dark was not ideal.

Just at that moment a beam of light pierced the twilight. It appeared to emanate from the ground, though from their altitude it was difficult to tell. Their passengers gasped in fear and amazement.

The light moved across the sky and came closer.

Harry knew exactly what it was: a searchlight from the Zeppelin. She cursed under her breath. Their quarry must have been going even slower than they thought and set down early. With the airship's engines off, the sound of the *Pegasus* would be very obvious. They had heard her coming and were now trying to find her.

There was no telling what sort of armament they might be carrying. If they had a searchlight then it was possible they could blow the *Pegasus* out of the air at ten thousand feet.

These thoughts flashed through Harry's mind in no time at all. She whistled five times in quick succession, then angled the wings so they went into a dive. Once they were heading down fast she pulled in the wings, killed the power to the propeller, and cut the Faraday.

Gravity took over.

With so far to fall, Harry had plenty of time for manoeuvring. She watched the airspeed increase until the needle was hard over against the pin. With practiced ease she opened the wings a fraction, just enough to gain some control.

They were diving straight towards the source of the light which had yet to find her, and now the enemy could no longer hear her. Quietly at first but increasing in volume, a whistling built up around the hull. She had no idea what speed they were making now. Probably over two hundred and fifty miles per hour.

With the spotlight as a reference point, she could see the ground was coming at them fast. She adjusted the wings. The *Pegasus* pulled slowly out of her dive, forcing Harry back into the seat. At the same time she gave them a slight tilt so they steered away from the Zeppelin.

The searchlight found them, lighting up the interior with a blinding glare. Then it went dark again as it lost them. Harry blinked to make her eyes adjust. Their high velocity had confused the crew manning the searchlight. But in that same moment a trail of white magnesium tracer bullets curved up and across the sky towards them.

As their trajectory flattened out the ship's airspeed fell. The needle moved back from the maximum of two hundred. Harry flipped the controls and they rolled to the right. The tracers flashed past on their port side. The Zeppelin passed beneath them and the searchlight lit them up again.

Harry applied power to the propeller and they shot away scarcely fifty feet above the terrain she could now barely see. Something exploded in light behind them, reflected in the mirror mounted below.

Artillery.

Harry rolled again as a trail of smoke went past the window. They were heading southeast, back the way they had come. There were no valleys she could hide in round here, but there were forests.

In the dying light she powered towards a thick stand of trees, with the wings fully deployed. She was sure the Zeppelin would not waste artillery when it had no chance of hitting its target. The *Pegasus* passed over a small lake. There was almost no shoreline between the water and the trees but Harry killed the propeller and brought the 'thopter round in a tight turn.

This landing would have been bumpy but instead they landed with a sticky squelch in the mud.

Khuwelsa went to work banking the furnace while Harry powered down everything. Their only hope was complete silence and no lights.

22

The night was filled with the choking grumbles of diesel engines and the penetrating glare of searchlights. It seemed this particular Zeppelin carried its own launch, perhaps more than one, and they searched through the night for Harry.

Bakari had asked to be let out shortly after the first launch went past, though it had missed them. Harry couldn't blame the warriors if they wanted to get out of the tin can which might come under attack at any moment.

But she was wrong. After less than fifteen minutes a large branch came down over the front of the *Pegasus* followed by repeated bangs and clangs as the warriors hid the vessel under a blanket of greenery. This process continued for half an hour, but the warriors did not knock on the door to be allowed back in.

"Will water get into the grid?" Harry asked after a significant bubbling noise emanated from beneath them and echoed in the cabin.

"It shouldn't be a problem," said Khuwelsa after a moment's thought. "It is proofed against rain. As long as we don't submerge it completely."

Harry sat in the pilot's chair watching lights of the searching vessels crossing the sky. With the furnace banked it would take time to get steam up. She knew she should sleep, but the fact they were sitting ducks if they were spotted preyed on her mind.

She jumped. Daylight filtered through the branches that covered the windows. In spite of herself she had slept and her neck was stiff. At a sound behind her, she turned her head and winced at the pain. Khuwelsa was unbolting the hatch. Bakari climbed in alone and had a long conversation with Khuwelsa which involved a great deal of repetition and hand signals.

"Well?" Harry had little patience, being tired and in pain.

Khuwelsa came over as Bakari exited through the hatch. "Don't be grumpy, Harriet."

"Don't you Harriet me, what's happened?"

"We're still here."

"I noticed," Harry said and dug her fingers into the muscles of her neck trying to get rid of the ache. "Can you thank Bakari for the disguise?"

"I did that."

Harry nodded and yawned.

"He says they waited until they were certain the flyers weren't going to find us, then went over to the Zeppelin for a look-see."

"And?"

"Not much to report, really," said Khuwelsa. "He thinks the ship has about thirty men. They tried firing an arrow into the balloon—"

"Well, that's not going to do anything."

"He didn't know that. He asked me if it would burn, I told him it wouldn't."

"Pity they stopped using hydrogen."

Khuwelsa tutted. "Are you going to let me tell you or just keep interrupting?

"Sorry."

"It's got two armed launches, five men and two machine guns on each."

Khuwelsa paused. A question burned in Harry's throat but she said nothing.

"What?" said Khuwelsa.

Harry shook her head. Khuwelsa laughed. "Spit it out."

"How do they know what machine guns are?"

"They described them, is that all right?"

"Yes."

"So anyway, Bakari has a plan."

"He has a plan?"

"He's allowed to have plans, Harry. I think it's quite a good one."

"What plan?"

"He wanted to know if the iron bird could destroy the enemy."

"You told him we couldn't."

"Harry, you're doing it again."

Harry put her hand over her mouth.

"Of course I said we couldn't, but we might be able to force it to stay on the ground." Khuwelsa paused, which drove Harry nuts; this wasn't a plan, it was a joke. "So, he said that he and his men can take care of the launches as they emerge from the ship. They'll just shoot the pilots. We damage the ship enough that it can't take off, and then we can follow its route to see where it was going. He and his men will pick off anyone who sticks his head out."

Harry hesitated before speaking. "Can I say something?"

"Yes."

"The ship will have lifted before we get there."

The distant sound of an explosion penetrated the cabin.

"No, they'll be too busy trying to fix the severed fuel and control lines."

If Khuwelsa was expecting Harry to be impressed she was out of luck. "In which case they'll know we're still around and send out the launches."

"Bakari's men are already on the case."

"Better get moving, then."

Khuwelsa executed a mock salute and headed back to the furnace. Harry went to the door just as a branch flew over her head and landed in the water. The surface was covered in a green scum which seemed to absorb the ripples. It smelt very bad.

She leaned out and looked up. Bakari was busy stripping the camouflage. Hampered by her dress, Harry did not attempt to follow. Instead, she went back to Khuwelsa who had put on her apron and gauntlets and begun fiddling around with the furnace.

"Maybe we should get a diesel engine," said Harry.

"It would help us to get going faster, but they don't have the power of steam." Khuwelsa's voice echoed inside the furnace which suddenly lit up. Khuwelsa pulled out and wiped the back of her gloved hand across her forehead.

"What if we had both?"

"That could work," said Khuwelsa. "Now, if you don't mind, I need to stoke."

"Stoke away," said Harry feeling like a cog without anything to mesh with.

She went back to her chair. And waited. Another explosion echoed through the forest. The airship had artillery guns as well, of course. But they shouldn't be a major worry.

The steam pressure gauge steadily rose. Harry went back to the hatch. "Hey, Bakari!"

She hoped that would be enough to bring him inside. She didn't want him near the propeller when they ran it up to speed. The propeller. She couldn't use it if they were sunk into the ground.

The lack of any visibility out of the rear was still a major issue. I need to sort out a list for Sellie, she thought as she hurried towards the hatch. The dark figure of Bakari swung in and bumped into her.

"Oh!" she said. "Sorry."

Infuriatingly he just grinned and got out of her way. She gathered herself, stalked to the hatch, leaned out for a look at the rear, and muttered a rude word. The propeller was half buried in mud and the roots of a tree. If she tried to spin it, it would either shatter, snap the drive shaft, or strip the gears.

She could only use it once they were free.

Returning to her chair, she studied the water in more detail: it was little more than a fetid pond and less than fifty feet across. She had never lifted on wings alone and certainly not over water. As Khuwelsa said, they could not afford to immerse the hull; otherwise the grid would get wet and short-circuit, and they would simply sink under their own weight. Just like the Zeppelins she had sunk off Zanzibar.

Her stream of thought was interrupted by two short blasts from Khuwelsa. She glanced at the gauge. Pressure was up. Harry replied with one long whistle, paused, and flipped the Faraday switch. The port side of the *Pegasus* seemed to rise a little.

Harry flexed the wings. The trees were close on the starboard side. She could not dip the wings in the water, but watching through the open hatch she pressed the tip of the wing against the biggest one and pushed.

There was a scraping sound along the bottom that sounded horribly like stone on metal. Harry cringed. But then the *Pegasus* glided gently out onto the water. Harry laughed out loud. With the Faraday engaged, she floated.

Still, they could not afford to remain on the water for long just in case there was a leak.

She flapped experimentally. The *Pegasus* lifted but then dropped back deeper. Harry panicked. She thrashed the wings frantically, trying to keep the bottom of the hull from going too deep.

"Sellie!" she shouted. "Engage the prop, Sellie! Now!"

There was a kerfuffle and Sellie appeared at Harry's side as she continued the frenzied flapping. Waves were rippling out from the ship as she rose and fell in the water. Sellie reached across and pushed the throttle hard forward.

The propeller whined. Harry lifted the nose fully and give the propeller something to work with. The pitch of the propeller dropped suddenly and the sound of it ripping the air vanished. Harry held her breath. The propeller was under the surface of the water.

But it still worked. If anything the pulse of thrust launched the *Pegasus* into the air with more violence than usual. Scattering water, the iron bird skimmed the tops of the trees opposite and made it into the air.

23

Sellie pulled the hatch closed once they achieved level flight.

Harry tried to relax. That was the worst take-off they had ever had. But we're aloft, she said to herself. Now all they had to do was fight a Zeppelin. How hard could that be? They'd done it before, and this one did not have a squadron of fighter planes to protect it.

Should be a walk in the park.

She found her own argument to be unconvincing.

There were plumes of smoke rising from behind the ridge ahead. The Zeppelin must be firing on Bakari's men to keep them away while they repaired their engines. Cutting lines was effective but relatively easy to fix.

The *Pegasus* was approaching the ridge at high velocity. Harry changed her mind. The moment they crossed the ridge the Germans would be able to hear her engine. She pulled the ship round in a hard turn to the right. It banked so much they lost a good percentage of the Faraday and side-slipped towards the grass cropped short by herbivores.

She headed southeast, hoping that no one would spot the smoke from their stack.

The ridge was lowering and they would soon become visible, so she cut the power to the propeller and glided just below the ridge line. She hopped the ridge and dived into the shallow dip in the landscape picking up speed again.

Adjusting the attitude of the wings slightly, she brought the *Pegasus* into the long slow turn heading northwest back up the valley.

A sound close by alerted her that Bakari was at her shoulder. His fingers gripped the rail tight as he said something she did not understand, but it sounded encouraging.

They were now gaining altitude and without the propeller the air speed was reducing. She skimmed the surface of the river, jumping its meanders and sliding round the larger boulders. Ahead of them another explosion erupted from the slope leading up to the ridge.

There was no way Bakari's men could keep the launches on the ground if they were that far away from the Zeppelin. She would have to keep an eye out for them; one of those Maxims could rip out enough feathers to stop them flying.

The airspeed of the *Pegasus* had dropped to the point where she needed the wings. With regular strokes she kept them aloft over the river bank. The top of the Zeppelin became visible above a small escarpment down which the river cascaded in a waterfall.

Harry pushed power back into the propeller and they rocketed over the ridge.

The airship was still on the ground; she could see a group of men gathered around the rear port engine. Several bodies lay on the grass, not moving. But what made her heart skip was a battery of half a dozen artillery pieces that had been mounted in the grass.

"We just need to disable it, Harry," said Sellie in her ear. "We don't need to take it down permanently. Bakari will do the rest."

"That's easy for you to say," said Harry. As if to echo her words, one of the launches emerged from the Zeppelin's hull. It had short wings for extra lift and twin diesel engines driving pusher-propellers, just like the *Pegasus.* This was no slow coach.

At over one hundred miles per hour the *Pegasus* flashed past the airship's envelope, making it billow in the plane's wake. Harry pulled round in a wide turn to the right, skirting the ridge on that side and losing speed.

"How's our Maxim?" asked Harry, referring to the gun Khuwelsa had purloined from the town and mounted under the fuselage.

"Wet and probably clogged with weed," said Khuwelsa.

"Yeah, that's what I thought," said Harry. "Great. The day we really need a gun we haven't got one that works. Should have boiled up some tar and screws."

"I did," said Khuwelsa. "And I have a delivery chute for them."

"Remind me to shake your hand when we get out of this." And at least no one will drown this time.

"I'll get it ready."

They were coming at the ship broadside but away from the deployed guns. That didn't stop the guns on the ship itself from firing at them. Harry knew it was very unlikely they would be hit so there was little point in trying to avoid the attacks. If they were hit, they would probably know very little about it.

Khuwelsa gave two quick whistles. Weapon ready.

Harry wondered if the Germans were ready for this trick. It didn't seem likely, because if Johannes was right this ship had disappeared before their unofficial battle of Zanzibar. Shooting one or two of the helium bags had little effect, but burning through a swathe of them with hot tar worked a treat.

The *Pegasus* was not at the right angle. They would be better attacking along the spine as they had before, but beggars couldn't be choosers. The sooner it was disabled, the sooner they could get out of artillery range.

She whistled, two short and one long. It really meant Attack dive but they would not be diving in this instance.

The *Pegasus* roared towards the Zeppelin. Three hundred yards out she killed the power to the propeller and flicked out the wings in a braking manoeuvre. Though the plane was slowing, Harry flinched.

The nose was coming up. If they lost too much headway they would crash tail-first into the ground. Their airspeed continued to fall; she flapped hard to gain a little height. Artillery shells and rippling gunfire filled the air around them. From the left the launch suddenly appeared from behind the balloon, the tracers from its twin Maxims tearing lines of destruction through the air.

They had to get out of its way but were, by now, almost motionless in mid-air. Harry cursed under her breath. She engaged the prop at full power to keep them up as long as possible. But the *Pegasus* was almost vertical, nose up. The only compensation was that the Faraday grid went up the rear wall to some extent, simply because the ornithopter had to tilt upwards to get into the air.

If the grid covered the entire ship it wouldn't matter what angle they were at. She pushed the thought away. The *Pegasus* could not do that.

The launch was still coming at them from the left. Harry pushed the port wing forwards and the right one back as hard as she could. The *Pegasus* spun in the air so the Zeppelin was to the side of her. Harry beat upwards with the wings flat. The fuselage turned as if the propeller was a fulcrum and was now horizontal, the Faraday fully effective again. Harry operated the wings madly to keep them aloft while the propeller gave them speed.

The launch was directly ahead, still spitting bullets. It was closing fast. Harry dived beneath it with an upstroke and then beat down hard. The iron bird came up under the launch. The deafening crash of metal against metal battered her ears, followed by horrendous scraping across the roof which stopped abruptly. The *Pegasus* lurched.

24

The mass of the *Pegasus* far exceeded that of the launch. She could feel the additional weight now attached to the top of the plane.

The sound of the wind grew loud as the hatch opened. Harry turned to see to see Bakari's foot disappearing upwards as he climbed onto the roof. There was another ear-battering screech. Harry worried that the launch might affect the propeller. If that happened they would all be dead. She adjusted the wings into a dive but reduced power to the prop.

The wind noise returned to normal. Harry risked another glance. Khuwelsa was dogging the hatch closed. They exchanged a momentary glance and Khuwelsa raised her eyebrows before heading back to her station.

Harry dived the *Pegasus* towards the ground, then brought the nose up and did a quick flip to the side. The sound of the launch scraping its way from the roof made Harry wince in pain. Her bird would need a good bit of repair. She paused, anticipating the sound of the propeller being ripped off. When it didn't happen she increased power to maximum.

A glance down into the rear-view mirror showed the blurry image of the launch hitting the ground. Someone with brown skin rolled off.

She hoped Bakari was not hurt.

An explosion erupted from the ground ahead of her. She gritted her teeth and brought the ship round in the tightest turn she dared. The artillery pieces were being dragged back inside. They must have repaired the engines. The top-mounted gun was firing at her; as she watched, the muzzle flared again. Harry growled.

Like a winged demon the *Pegasus* gained height with powerful beats. Harry whistled again: two short, one long. Khuwelsa responded with two short just to make sure Harry knew she was ready.

The *Pegasus* roared along the line of the Zeppelin, perfectly positioned. Its rear propellers were a blur of spinning wood to Harry's view. She wished she had the Maxim working as they rocketed towards the rear gunner. The muzzle flashed again. She imagined she felt the wind of the shell as it passed them. She whistled: one short, one long.

It took them barely three seconds to cover the length of the Zeppelin. She could see the faces of the men at the forward gun as the *Pegasus* whipped over it. Khuwelsa gave one short and one long whistle to indicate she had deployed the tar.

Harry kept up the speed and let her ship turn in a broad curve around the far side of the ridge. She powered down and reduced their speed, then brought them down to a gentle landing out of sight.

Staring at the motionless ground outside, Harry listened to the propeller wind down. She kept the Faraday engaged but folded in the wings. Khuwelsa went to the door, opened it, and kicked out the steps.

Harry took a deep breath and released the controls. She clenched and unclenched her fists, spreading her fingers wide. Her hands ached. She slipped out of the chair and onto her feet, feeling a little unsteady. Bakari's spear lay on the deck. She climbed under the bar and picked it up, then followed her sister outside.

She staggered slightly as she stepped down into full gravity. Khuwelsa had already reached the top of the ridge and was peering over. Harry caught up and looked. The middle section of the Zeppelin's balloon had collapsed, and its loose envelope flapped in the wind.

"We did it," said Khuwelsa.

Harry found she had nothing to say; her mind still felt numb.

The Germans were in the process of deploying the artillery again. Harry was not sure if they knew where she had landed, but she ducked down again, pulling Khuwelsa with her.

"We need to move," she said, and took a few steps down the stony ridge back towards the *Pegasus.*

"Wait," said Khuwelsa. "We should wait."

"What for?"

"Bakari."

Harry gave a slight smile. "You've have got a pash for him."

"I have not!" said Khuwelsa.

"I wouldn't mind, he is quite handsome," said Harry. "In a rugged, unrestrained sort of way."

"Sounds like you're the one with the pash," said Khuwelsa.

Harry laughed but without much energy. A movement along the ridge caught her eye and she wished she had brought the shotgun.

Two of Bakari's men appeared, grinning with their wide and toothy smiles. They were full of congratulations that Harry could not understand.

Exhausted, she sat down and then lay down. She would just close her eyes for a minute.

* * *

"Coffee, Harry?"

She smelled it before she opened her eyes. Seeing that the sun was in a different position, she sat up in a panic and then felt dizzy.

"How long was I asleep?" she demanded. "What are the Germans doing? Why didn't you wake me?"

Khuwelsa was crouching a couple of feet away holding a steaming mug.

"An hour. Consolidating their position. Because you were tired and needed to rest," she said. "Bakari's here and preening like a peacock. I think he's told the story of how he killed the men on the launch five times so far."

"He's all right?"

"Oh, he's fine. Some cuts of which he seems inordinately proud, and bruises, I expect, but he's not complaining."

"Men," said Harry.

Khuwelsa nodded and held out the coffee. Harry took it and sipped it, feeling its energy revitalising her mind.

"They've been quite complimentary about you too," said Khuwelsa.

"That's nice."

"Apparently it is. They're not big on female warriors, and apparently I don't qualify because all I did was tend the engine and drop the tar that actually did the damage."

"Sorry."

Khuwelsa shrugged. "I don't mind. Who wants to be in the limelight?"

"Not me," said Harry.

"Quite, but you have no choice," Khuwelsa said with a grin. "You get the fame and I'll get the fortune."

"Which fortune would that be?"

"No idea, but I think it's a fair division if it ever turns up."

Harry put down the tin mug and climbed to her feet. She glanced at the ridge, but resisted the temptation to see what the Germans were doing.

"We better be getting on," she said, almost to herself. "Come on, Sellie."

She glanced at the warriors who were all looking in her direction. She turned to Khuwelsa. "How do you say goodbye?"

"Sala hantle, I think."

Harry turned to the men. "Sala hantle."

They repeated the words although she was sure there was something of a laugh in their voices. Sellie and she probably had not got it quite right. Never mind; it was the thought that counted.

The sun was sinking in the west as they powered up the *Pegasus* again. Harry launched her down the ridge away from the Germans and hoped once more they would not notice the thin smoke trail. She swept low across the rocks and then the grass, scaring a small herd of goats. Turning northwest she kept the revolutions in the propeller low to reduce noise.

"What's Bakari going to do?" Harry asked Sellie after they had put a few miles between them and the Zeppelin.

"He's sent one of his men back to their home which is only a couple of days away now," said Khuwelsa. "He's mainly after his man, but he'll kill any Germans they can catch alone. If the man they're after makes a break for it, they'll go after him. Otherwise they'll wait for reinforcements."

"The Germans are a bit stuck, I suppose," said Harry. "They'll have to send out to get rescued."

"They might be able to lift if they abandon all their cargo."

"Or dump the cargo and leave an armed guard."

"Which would lighten the load even more."

They both thought for a minute.

"We better hurry," said Harry.

"Yes, we had," said Khuwelsa.

25

During the next hour the ground dropped away and they passed over some small lakes. This gave on to wide grasslands teeming with wildlife. The plains of the British and German protectorates were busy places when it came to nature, but this place was astonishing.

Herds of wildebeest, elephants, zebras, different types of gazelles, and giraffes roamed the plain. But at the speed the 'thopter was moving this soon gave way to swampier land. As that, too, came to an end, Harry blinked at what lay before her; it looked as if they had somehow reached the sea.

With the low sun reflecting from its calm surface they were faced with a wide expanse of water stretching to the horizon. Although, from their altitude, they could see mountains on the far side.

"Lake Victoria," said Harry almost in wonderment. It had been discovered over twenty years before by one of the early expeditions using balloon-lifted Faraday machines. The explorers had been searching for the source of the River Nile. This was it.

There was no time to think before they were across the coastline, dotted with herds of hippopotamuses, and then had nothing but water below them.

"Perhaps we should have stopped on the coast," said Khuwelsa, eyeing the setting sun.

"We'll be across in no time," said Harry. Dark shapes of islands grew from the shadows ahead. Then she saw lights on one of them. So bright, they could only be electric. Harry reached forward and pulled back on the throttle. The propeller's noise died away. Harry angled the wings and curved away from their northwesterly course that would have taken them directly across the island.

She headed west, reduced speed and kept them aloft with the occasional stroke of the wings. If they were spotted they might, just possibly, be mistaken for a predatory bird because there was no way to judge their actual distance.

They passed to the south of the brightly lit island at an altitude of a thousand feet, and a distance of ten miles. More than enough to be safe, Harry thought with her fingers firmly crossed.

They flew across the beach of the opposite coast at less than two hundred feet. Harry spotted a village and its natives staring up at the great metal bird flying over. She hoped they were not on friendly terms with the Germans, although they were a good fifteen miles away from the island and that was by boat.

She saw an open space in the middle of a forested area and without engaging the propeller made it to the ground with only a little bump. She switched off the Faraday and the *Pegasus* settled with a gentle groan from her metal bones.

Khuwelsa lit an oil lamp instead of the electric ones.

Harry got up and stretched.

"What's to eat?" she asked.

"Oh, so I'm your skivvy now as well?"

"Never mind," said Harry. She went to the wall rack that held the rolled-up camp beds. "Do you want yours?"

"I suppose so."

Harry pulled them both out and handed one to her sister.

"Roast gazelle sandwiches? Some pies. More sandwiches. Cooked meats. Fruit. Lots."

"Anything to drink?"

"Cold tea or water if you want it now, otherwise we can heat it all up."

While Khuwelsa sorted out the food Harry assembled their beds and pulled out the blanket rolls. Khuwelsa handed her a warm sandwich and a mug of cold tea which Harry consumed without really noticing the taste or the temperature.

"Do you think we could get a camera for next time?" Harry rested her chin on the rim of the mug. "Then we can take some pictures and just fly home to show Dad."

"You think the Germans will hold still for their portrait?"

"It's better than the alternative."

"The alternative being?"

"Capture a German? Blow up their base?"

"With one machine gun."

"Let's see what we have to deal with and then decide."

"By which time we'll probably have a squadron of fighters on our tail."

Harry sighed. "Old news, we've done it before, we can do it again."

"You seem to have forgotten how hard it's been. Every single time," said Khuwelsa.

Harry smiled. "I haven't forgotten." She swallowed the last of the sandwich and washed it down with the tea, then lay back on the bed. There was a squeak from the other bed as Khuwelsa did the same.

"This is really comfortable," Khuwelsa said.

Harry closed her eyes and a thought occurred to her. "Sellie?"

"Mmm?"

"I've had a few ideas."

There was no response.

"About the ship," said Harry.

Khuwelsa snored.

"Fair point," said Harry and rolled on her side. She gazed out the front window at the brilliant stars above the tops of the trees. "I'll tell you later."

* * *

Harry jumped at a metallic tapping noise. She opened her eyes. The sky was bright blue. The tops of the trees glowed green in the sunlight. There was a tap on the metal fuselage again.

"Sellie! Time to move."

"What?" said the muffled voice.

"Time for us to move," repeated Harry. "We have visitors."

"Germans?"

"Locals, I think."

The handle of the hatch turned, but it was locked so would not open.

"What about breakfast?"

"I'd rather get moving before they do any damage."

Khuwelsa headed into the back and Harry heard the door of the furnace clanging open.

A face appeared at the window peering in. They tapped on it with something metal. Harry muttered under her breath and looked around. It wasn't that she objected to any Africans, but she was very concerned about what they might do by accident. The feathers were vulnerable.

The figure outside peered in and caught sight of her. It gave a cry and slipped out of sight. They had probably heard of white people even if they hadn't seen any. Harry's eyes fell on the control cable down to the trigger for the heavy machine gun mounted under the deck, effectively below her chair. Khuwelsa had not been able to make it automatic in the short time she had had available, nor could they add more ammunition once it was exhausted. It was all they had against some sort of base that was bound to have defences.

She was tempted to try it just scare the curious locals away, but there were two problems with that: she might hurt someone, and it might jam because it had been submerged in water.

On the other hand she really didn't want to go outside in case the locals were not entirely friendly.

"You stoke," said Khuwelsa. "I'll talk to them."

Harry hesitated and then nodded. "But take one of the shotguns."

This time it was Khuwelsa that hesitated; then she nodded and extracted one from its box.

Harry went back to the furnace. The metal was already giving off a strong heat that pressed against her cheeks and forehead. Using the shovel she unlatched the furnace door and pulled it open. A wave of heat poured out. Harry picked up a shovelful of coal and tossed it inside.

Khuwelsa returned. The hatch was open. "They seem friendly enough," she said. "I'm going to check the Maxim."

So saying she collected some tools, the oil can, a cloth and left.

Harry went back to the shovelling.

26

"I told them to stay clear," said Khuwelsa as Harry powered up the propeller and engaged the Faraday. The clearing was empty of locals but their faces peered from between the trunks of the trees all around.

"I wish they weren't directly in front," said Harry.

"Can't have everything," said Khuwelsa. "Just try not to hit any of them."

"I'll do my best."

Khuwelsa put her hand on Harry's shoulder and gave it a squeeze. Then she gave two long whistles even though she was standing right next to her.

"Thanks," said Harry, wincing. She increased the power to the propeller, stroked the wings, and the *Pegasus* leapt into the air, easily clearing the trees. In the mirror she saw the villagers run out into the clearing to watch them leave.

"Any thought about how we're going to do this?" asked Khuwelsa.

"Plan B," said Harry.

"Right, plan B."

Harry poured on the power. As they left the woods behind, beach flashed beneath them, and the *Pegasus* shot across the flat calm of the great lake, skimming its surface like a seagull.

Harry looked at the low islands to the north of them. "Do you remember which one it was, Sellie?"

"Not from this angle," she said. "But I'm guessing it's the one with the smoke coming off it."

Harry peered ahead. Khuwelsa was right; northeast of their position, several lines of smoke streamed into the blue sky. Although the air around them was calm the smoke trails were rising to a few hundred feet and then veering almost horizontal as they hit a layer of air that must be moving fast.

Further to the north a mountain of cumulonimbus clouds rose high into the sky. Even as she watched, Harry saw its interior glow with light.

"Uh-oh," said Khuwelsa. "Look."

"Yes, thunderstorm."

"Not that," said Khuwelsa. "Those."

She pointed forward. Harry followed her fingers and saw a small group of fixed-wing fighters cutting across the sky heading south. The one at the front dipped its wings towards them and turned, the other two following suit. Now they were flying almost directly towards the *Pegasus.*

"You know," said Harry. "That's really not fair. How did they know we'd be here?"

Khuwelsa peered down into the mirror, then went to the porthole near the hatch and looked out. "We're creating a wake a mile wide in the lake."

Harry muttered a curse.

"Oh, if Mrs Hemingway could hear you now."

"Even she would be more concerned about how we're going to avoid getting shot down," said Harry. She gave the propeller the additional power she had kept in reserve, and the *Pegasus* surged ahead.

Harry edged the wings of the iron bird to line her up directly towards the island and brought her down even closer to the surface of the water, the wings arched over in the stable position. The island grew in size at a frightening speed. It was barely ten miles away, less than four minutes at their current speed.

"They've missed us," Khuwelsa shouted from the porthole. "Going too fast to turn."

Which is what Harry had been hoping for. The *Pegasus* was now faster than any German fighter they had encountered, but once they engaged the base the fighters would be on them.

She still had no idea what they were doing. She supposed that most generals would only authorise attacks when they had some idea of the terrain and their target. She knew neither, except for the fact the islands seemed to lie quite low in the water.

As far as she knew Lake Victoria was not tidal, and while it covered a huge area it did not have size enough to allow big waves to build up. It was, when all was said and done, just a lake.

Racing along barely two feet above the waves, through the controls Harry noticed that the *Pegasus* seemed to glide more fluidly. In fact their airspeed increased further, to nearly one hundred and eighty miles per hour.

She was pondering the effect so much she almost failed to notice that landfall was imminent. A gently sloping beach ran up to a stand of trees, just like on the mainland.

With a delicate touch she adjusted the angle of the wingtips only. She felt the power of her ship as it lifted, rocketed across the sand, and skimmed the tops of the trees. Their speed dropped back to normal now they were away from the ground.

"How far back are they?" she called to Khuwelsa.

"I can't see them, but they had started their turn before I lost sight of them."

"Can you come up here? I need your eyes."

The sun disappeared. Harry glanced up. High-level cloud from the thunderstorm crept across the sky. The flashing tower of cloud loomed in the distance, bigger than it had been before. This was the one thing that all Faraday fliers feared. A strike, just like the one they had received before, could fry all their electrics and turn the *Pegasus* into what it really was: a pile of iron. And piles of iron did not normally remain aloft.

Closer at hand, the rising columns of smoke became more distinct. Harry pulled back and they shot upwards, gaining altitude fast. The German base was laid out beneath them.

A space had been cut in the trees perhaps a quarter of a mile in diameter. Covering almost all of it was the skeleton of some massive construction of iron and wood. Even now Harry could see men at work, crawling and working in its interior. Arc lights made the inside glow.

She had trouble making out what it was. It was circular and at intervals around its perimeter were concentrations of metal. These looked like big tanks with massive pipes and tubes. From each of these protruded a long spike.

"Oh my," breathed Khuwelsa. "It's a *flyer*."

As she said it the parts clicked into place in Harry's head: a massive machine with engines placed at intervals around the edge that would drive horizontal rotors to give it lift. This was why they needed all the copper and ivory. The Faraday grid for this monster had to cover a vast area.

That was why the Germans had been so keen to take Zanzibar; they wanted the supplies and control of its trade. Harry and Khuwelsa's interference had stopped them, and it meant they had resorted to murdering hundreds of hippopotamuses and stealing copper.

It was the fault of the Edgbaston sisters.

27

The sun broke through the clouds and lit up something metallic hanging in the air. Without thinking Harry flipped the wings to avoid the wire. The *Pegasus* fell a hundred feet towards the skeletal monster before Harry regained control. She flapped the wings strongly as a curious pinging sound rattled off the fuselage.

Someone was shooting at them with a hand gun.

She almost laughed—but did not. Looking up, she saw the sky was criss-crossed with the metal wires they had barely avoided. She shook her head.

"Anti-aircraft wire?" said Khuwelsa.

"Effective," said Harry before something across the other side of the monster caught her eye. A familiar something. "That's how they knew where we were."

A battered Zeppelin, the middle section of its envelope sunken and deflated, sat on the far side.

"We were right," said Khuwelsa. "Of course, they knew they were nearly at their base."

A line of tracer curved above them.

Harry gave five quick whistles—grab something quick—and dived.

She took the ship round in a tight turn. She noted the positions of the six pylons supporting the high defensive wires and the three planes throttling back to combat speed above them. One had followed them into the space between the pylons while the other two circled above, their pilots probably thinking one would be enough.

It was getting dark as the clouds thickened. This is going to be interesting, thought Harry as a crazy idea took shape. A glance at the oncoming storm told her there wasn't a lot of time.

She poured power into the propeller and stroked the wings hard. The *Pegasus* gained altitude and speed. She slipped out between the pylons and turned on a wing so she was above the wires. The nearest plane was side on to her but lining up to intercept.

Reaching down her side, Harry took hold of the gun trigger and brought it back up to the wing controls. *Sellie needs to make this integral*, she added to her mental list. The *Pegasus* closed on the other plane. It was coming from the right; she was in a gentle curve that would intercept its path. She was not sure if the pilot had seen her, but she changed tack and pressed the trigger.

Silence. Just as she wondered if it would not work after all, a stuttering roar echoed through the ship and she could see her own tracers making a curved line through the sky. The other pilot may not have seen her but reacted instantly to the attack. He lifted his nose and passed unharmed above the line of bullets.

Harry frowned. This wasn't easy. Still, she could do things that he couldn't. The German had turned to the right and then came back to the left. He intended to get behind her, but Harry killed the propeller and back-winged, coming to a halt in the air. Using the propeller to maintain her height, she turned through ninety degrees just as the German came around—but instead of him being behind her, they were head on.

Harry pressed the trigger. The bullet stream intersected his path. He turned again but the tracers showed her attack ripping through his wing. His plane lurched. The Faraday grid shredded as the wing tore away.

He had power and the remainder of the grid still worked; he fought with his controls as the plane spiralled down. In the growing dark the magnesium glare of tracers cutting across her path blinded her. She blinked rapidly. The angle of the attack meant it came from behind her. She threw the throttle forward, brought down the nose, and leapt away.

She glanced down into the mirror. She could see the attacking plane's underside lit by the brilliantly white electric lights from below. Bullets pinged off the fuselage. She accelerated hard and then when she had gone beyond the edge of the open area she dived, confident there were no wires.

Her attacker followed. She allowed him to stay with her, not going at full velocity. They curved out across the lake as spots of rain began to fall. This was not going to help.

She curved back inland and accelerated a little just to make him chase harder. They were travelling in a straight line now, giving him a better chance with his guns. She wove back and forth tilting the wings first right, then left. Tracers passed them first on the left, then the right.

Resisting the temptation to go faster she throttled back again. The mirror showed nothing but blackness. But she knew he was closing, probably getting excited, holding back now until he could not possibly miss. As they crossed the beach the glow of the base was ahead of them. The fabric of the damaged Zeppelin rippled violently. The wind was getting up.

She had judged it well and returned into the light midway between two pylons. She gave the *Pegasus* full throttle and angled the wings into a climb. Just in time. Tracers poured through the space where she had been. Rain was coming down, each drop shining from the light below. She squinted and saw the crossed wires rushing towards them. Wires stretched between opposite pylons and met in the centre. If she got this wrong they would end up in several pieces.

She aimed for a point near the middle where two closed on one another.

At the last moment, as the ship rocketed upwards, she pulled in the wings. The 'thopter's momentum along with the powering propeller slipped them between the wires with barely any gap on either side. She slammed the wings out to stabilise the ship. She looked into the mirror, all but dazzled by the bright lights.

The German had followed her. She wondered at which point he realised his mistake as the wires on either side sheared off both his wings.

There was no time for dilly-dallying. She flipped the *Pegasus* around on her vertical axis and flattened out. The two nearest pylons wavered and slowly collapsed inwards from the impact, wreaking devastation on the skeletal ship as they came down. Many of the lights went out.

Flapping hard, Harry reversed direction again and headed to the opposite pylon. She dipped between the wires and descended fast. She opened up with the machine gun firing at the base of the pylon on this side.

The damaged Zeppelin stood a short distance away. They had dismounted all its artillery as well to save weight; it was a flying ruin.

She blasted away at the legs of the pylon. Although many shots missed, she was satisfied with the damage. It did not keel over, but she did not want that. Not yet.

28

The wind buffeted them, knocking the *Pegasus* to the side. Harry flapped automatically to recover their stability and then headed up again. Lightning lit up the landscape in white fire as a bolt sliced through the thundercloud. The storm was close now.

Harry brought them up to the top of the pylon where, despite being thrown to and fro by the uncertain wind, she settled the *Pegasus* onto its peak. The sound of creaking and cracking wood echoed around the interior.

"What are you doing, Harry?" Khuwelsa demanded in her ear.

"Do you trust me?"

Without giving her a chance to answer, Harry pushed the propeller to full power and flipped off the Faraday.

"Oh, no."

The tip of the pylon crunched under the weight and the ship dropped a foot, then held steady. The wire, along the ship's length, held the rear up while Harry balanced the iron bird against the wind with outstretched wings.

It was a testament to German engineering that the pylon lasted as long as it did. With the full weight of the ship on it and the propeller pushing hard, it was a good ten seconds before the first snap jerked the ship. The deck began to tilt forward. Harry raised the wings.

The pylon gave way, falling outwards from the centre of the work area. Harry held her fingers over the Faraday.

They fell. For a moment the pylon paused as the wire became tight, pulling against the remaining towers. Then it finally gave with a thrumming twang they could feel in the metal of the deck. As the pylon caved in, Harry flipped the switch and operated the wings, and the *Pegasus* pulled away. The tower crashed to the ground, pulling the remaining ones with it.

Harry brought the ship down to a bumpy landing and killed all the power.

"Grab the guns," she said. "Let's go."

"What? Where?"

"Hurry!" shouted Harry as she opened the hatch. The wind-driven rain lashed in. It was surprisingly cold. It was barely morning but the dense clouds made it black as night, except for the frequent brilliant white of the lightning.

With a confused Khuwelsa following, Harry rushed to the collapsed pylon.

"Can you grab the wire?" shouted Harry above the storm. She was wet through.

"It's as thick as your arm!" Khuwelsa shouted in return.

"We need to tie it to the Zeppelin!"

Khuwelsa peered through the pouring rain at the broken wood. They searched until they found the end, still connected to a metal bracket and bolted to a broken piece of wood. Together they lifted the wood and hauled the end of the wire towards the stricken airship.

Bullets and tracers ripped up the ground around them.

Harry looked up. She had forgotten the third plane. It shot over. At least it couldn't hover and would have to make runs in order to attack them. Ignore it.

They struggled on. There was a flash from a gun and the sound a moment later. Harry looked at Khuwelsa, who shrugged. Harry fired off a round from her shotgun in the general direction of the shot. It would be nonlethal at that range but she would almost certainly scare whoever had fired at them, and if she'd hit it would hurt. Perhaps he would be sufficiently discouraged.

A flash of lightning showed they had nearly reached their objective, but it was becoming harder and harder to shift the wire as they stretched it out. And it kept catching on broken pieces of wood and stone.

"See if you can get it attached," Harry said in her ear. "Doesn't have to be good, just so it won't pull free."

Khuwelsa nodded. She had given up shouting, as the wind and rain along with the rolling thunder made conversation all but impossible.

Harry went round the outside of the Zeppelin. It was tied down with ropes. She tried to undo the first one but it was too wet and slippery. So she lined up the shotgun and blasted through it. Her father would have been horrified. Harry glanced back at Khuwelsa who was staring in her direction, probably wondering about the shot. Harry gave her a thumbs-up and a lightning flash illuminated it.

There were three more ropes. Harry disposed of them in the same fashion, reloading twice. Once she had disposed of the penultimate one the airship began to move, blown by the wind. It swung towards her; she had to throw herself out of the way before it smashed into some rocks. The wooden part of the hull splintered.

The plane came back and shot at them but seemed to want to avoid hitting the Zeppelin. If he had realised the truth, the balloon would have been his target.

Harry got back to Khuwelsa, who had managed to loop the wire around the engine mount and passed the wooden piece through the loop, making an effective knot.

Harry unlimbered the shotgun again. Khuwelsa placed her hand on Harry's arm.

"May I?"

Harry withdrew and swept her hand in the direction of the final rope. Khuwelsa lined up the gun and blasted it. The airship hung for moment; then the wind pushed it towards Harry and Khuwelsa, who dropped to the ground as it went over them, rising slowly.

They jumped to their feet and ran back to the *Pegasus.*

Dripping wet, Harry climbed into her chair as Khuwelsa locked the door. There was a terrific metal clang and the ship jerked to the side. Metal scraped across the top of the ship. They followed the sound with their eyes as if they could see the airship moving across them.

Harry engaged the Faraday and launched them into the air.

The Zeppelin was about twenty feet up when the third German plane flew out of the black, shooting at it.

"Damn it!" shouted Harry. "He can't do that now."

She drove the *Pegasus* round in a circle and let fly with her machine gun as the German came around for another pass. He ignored her as the tracers showed her missing him by a mile. Harry cursed her inexperience.

The thunder cloud was directly overhead now. None of them should be in the air in these conditions. But the German did not fire his machine guns; something detached itself from the body of his plane and shot across the gap, leaving a trail of smoke. It passed the Zeppelin's balloon and exploded when it hit the ground on the far side.

"He's got rockets," said Harry. "If he hits the envelope with one of those he'll definitely bring it down."

She tried to follow his course but in the dark and the rain she lost him. She pulled the *Pegasus* up to give herself some height. He would probably come around and try the same thing again. The rockets did not look to be very accurate, so he would have to get close.

Making small circles she gained height keeping her eyes peeled. A flash of lightning finally revealed him coming in as slow as he could. Harry dived and then remembered to whistle five short blasts.

There was a crash. "Too late, Harry!"

Harry had just one thought: get him out of the sky. She hoped Sellie wasn't looking. The gun just wasn't good enough—or, more truthfully, she wasn't good enough with the gun. That first shot had been beginner's luck.

They were descending fast. She adjusted her angle and came down right on top of him, just as he fired the second rocket. She switched off the Faraday. Though parts of the *Pegasus* were now in his field, a lot of it wasn't and was now subject to gravity. With the extra weight, the planes plummeted.

The cabin was lit up by an explosion above them. In the light Harry saw the ground coming up at them, re-energised the Faraday, and took them up on powerful wings. The downward momentum of the German plane forced it into the ground, where it lay crumpled and broken.

Harry stared in despair at the flames on the Zeppelin, and then watched as part of its gondola detached itself and fell to the ground. Whether it was due to her attack or that the German pilot had simply missed, the rocket must have hit the body, not the envelope, and the now much lighter airship climbed into the sky trailing the metal wire.

Harry gunned the propeller and shot away through the rain. There was a tremendous flash from behind them. She glanced into the mirror to see the entire airship falling to earth. Explosions were erupting from different locations around the base, as well as from within the great skeletal ship itself.

Even as she watched, more bolts of lightning struck the Zeppelin as it fell. She had no idea what damage might have been done beyond the explosions, but with the collapsed pylons, crashed ships, and lightning damage the ship they had been building would be useless for a long time to come. Long enough for the British to arrive and deal with it.

Harry sighed. She was exhausted.

Minutes later they were out from under the thunderstorm and heading for the opposite coast of the lake in bright sunshine.

29

It was lunch time when they reached the valley where they had encountered the Zeppelin the first time. The smoke of several small fires curled into the sky around boxes of cargo and reflective piles of honey-coloured metal.

The sisters peered down trying to determine the situation. What had first appeared to be random boxes revealed itself to be a defensive circle. Twelve artillery pieces pointed outward in all directions and Sellie counted fifteen men within the circle. Some were on guard within the perimeter, while others sat nearer the center.

Although Bakari and his men had to be there somewhere, neither of the girls could see them. They were too well hidden.

"Can't say I really want to do this," said Harry.

"We can't leave them," said Khuwelsa. "Despite what we've done they'll probably be able to send reinforcements soon. Then they'll have all the copper and ivory."

Harry sighed. She knew her sister was right, but she was tired.

"It'll be like shooting fish in a barrel," Khuwelsa said.

"You're too blood-thirsty."

"Perhaps you're not blood-thirsty enough."

Harry folded in the wings and went into a curving dive. Khuwelsa was thrown to the side. "That blood-thirsty enough?" shouted Harry.

She picked up the gun trigger. "This needs to be part of the main control," she said as she lined up on the circle.

The Maxim spat bullets that threw up fountains of earth as she strafed the defences—careful not to aim directly at any of the sailors trapped in the middle.

They dived for cover on the far side of the circle.

Harry back-winged hard. The nose came up and with the prop roaring she landed. She kept the Faraday energised and walked the *Pegasus* closer to the wall of cargo, artillery, and copper ingots.

A couple of sailors fired their guns at her. She discouraged them with a barrage from the Maxim. It went straight over their heads and they dived for cover once more. They did not know that if she hit them it would be an accident.

Harry got a wing under one of the guns and flicked it upward. The gun lifted and toppled on its side. She punched a hole in the nearest crate and tossed it into the air. It ripped open and hippo teeth rained down on the sailors.

Like some stalking dragon she made the *Pegasus* turn along the wall and smash it down. She tossed the next gun into the air. It landed a dozen yards away.

She turned back towards the space in the middle. The sailors were cowering at the display of steam-powered destruction, their eyes fixed on the ship, waiting for her to unleash its power on them.

Harry looked up, beyond the men, and saw Bakari and a dozen warriors running fast in their direction. They must have found reinforcements sooner than expected. She just needed to hold the Germans' attention a few moments longer.

She powered up the propeller as she prepared to take flight again. She thrashed the wings and, like an avenging angel, the *Pegasus* reared up. It lifted into the air, the wind from the down strokes knocking the men to the ground and holding them there.

Harry executed a one-hundred-and-eighty-degree turn in the air and rose away from the circle with the air stream from the propeller pummelling them.

In the mirror she saw them falling away, and by the time they had recovered Bakari and his men were on them.

Harry brought the *Pegasus* down once more. Bakari had tied up his prisoners and was happy enough to hand them over to Harry. He had the one person he was chasing.

* * *

They went home via the town of Ndungu where they dropped off the Germans and provided the mayor with instructions as where to find his copper.

While some facts were not forthcoming from the prisoners, Harry and Khuwelsa were at least able to get answers to their most pressing questions. The sailor Harry had discovered was a thief who had fallen when he escaped from his original confinement. The other men had indicated they were not happy with the treatment of the town, for which they had been treated as mutineers and were immediately disposed of. "Immediately" still had given them time to partially disable one of the engines.

And with that the sisters headed home. By evening the Mombasa coast had come into view and Harry brought the *Pegasus* in for a gentle landing on the front lawn of their father's house.

The French windows of the lower part of the house opened and the menacing form of Jonathan Edgbaston emerged, flanked by Mrs Hemingway on one side and the butler, Raynes, on the other.

"What are we going to say?" asked Khuwelsa.

"I thought I might try 'We had a lovely time, wish you could have been there'."

"We're doomed."

BOOK 3

HARRY GETS HER WINGS

1

"I can't believe it," said Harry as she tossed another letter with its envelope into the fire. It blazed into cinders that balanced for a moment in the flames, then rocketed up the flue.

Seated in an armchair by the window, Khuwelsa glanced up from her book. Probably another scientific romance penned by *Monsieur* Verne. Harry had tried them, but they were far too dry.

It was still morning and the sun had not got around to this side of the house. The room was baking from the fire, but Harry needed to get through her correspondence and the fire was the most effective method.

"What can't you believe?" said Khuwelsa.

"Another proposal of marriage," Harry said. "Honestly, I have no idea what possesses these people."

"I imagine it happens to anyone in the public eye."

"It was another woman."

Khuwelsa shrugged. "Well, you do have a masculine *nom de guerre*."

"Not my idea."

"Be grateful we're stuck out here in the middle of nowhere. Imagine what it would be like in London or Manchester."

Harry kicked the postal sack that had arrived that morning. It keeled over and spilt its contents across the carpet. News of their latest exploits had leaked out and, with gross inaccuracies and pure invention from the members of the press, had been plastered across the broadsheets of England.

"Why did you tell them, Harry?"

"Me? I didn't tell them."

"Well, how did they find out?"

Harry shook her head. "I have no idea." She looked down at the pile at her feet. "It'll take me forever to get through this lot. I won't be finished before the next bag arrives."

"Want some help?"

Harry nodded.

Khuwelsa put down her book, gathered up her skirt and petticoats, and came over. She looked at the pile.

"You need a system," she said. She rummaged through her pockets and pulled out a notepad with a pencil attached by a string. "We'll make a list of the types of correspondence and the action to take with each. Then we'll take each one in turn, determine what it is, and put it in its appropriate pile. Finally we burn them all."

"If we're going to burn them all, why are we putting them in piles?" said Harry. "Why not just burn the lot now?"

"I'm curious as to percentages. Besides, you may decide to answer some of them. And there might be something important; perhaps Her Gracious Majesty would like to see you?"

Harry laughed.

"Or," said Khuwelsa. "Perhaps the prince would like to marry you?"

Harry pulled a face. "He's ancient and ugly."

"He's a prince."

"And he's married."

"He has mistresses, he might want to add you to his harem."

Harry made a disapproving noise and glanced at the clock on the mantel. It was just past ten thirty. "We have a lesson at eleven."

"All right," said Khuwelsa as she settled on the floor next to the letters. She wetted the tip of the pencil with her tongue and held the notepad at the ready. "What sorts of correspondence do you receive? Marriage proposals." She scribbled on the pad.

Harry picked up the next one, studied then sniffed it. "Smells of cigars, the hand pressed hard when writing the address, and it is angular. Angry."

Khuwelsa frowned. "Angry?"

Harry sighed. "Yes, some of them are not very complimentary."

Khuwelsa snatched it from her, tore it open and scanned the contents. "Evil man," she hissed. "You shouldn't read these."

"I get them from women too."

Her sister wadded up the letter and tossed it in the fire.

"I thought were categorising and making piles."

"Those go straight in the fire as soon as we know what they are," said Sellie. "What else?"

Harry picked a thicker and larger envelope from the selection. "This one will be a business requesting an endorsement of their product." She tore it open. "*Lady Lovely, support wear for the beautiful woman.*"

Khuwelsa laughed. "Are they offering money?"

Harry scanned the letter. "No, just free supplies."

"We'll make a category for business offers," said Khuwelsa, jotting down the name. She tapped on the table. "Put that here. If we get one that wants to give you money we will address it more seriously."

"I'm not sure how Dad will feel about that."

Sellie shrugged. "What he doesn't know can't hurt him."

Harry picked the next item. "Marriage proposal—oh, this one has a photograph." She giggled and handed it to her sister, who pulled a face.

"What do you want to do about these ones?" she said. "Do you want to reply?"

"If I do, it might encourage them."

"If you don't, they'll probably keep trying."

"We could do a form letter," said Harry. "*Miss Edgbaston thanks you for your kind consideration; however, she feels she is far too young to be contemplating marriage at this time.*"

Sellie giggled. "*Unless you have an annual income in excess of ten thousand pounds. In which case please come straight over.*"

Harry laughed. Khuwelsa noted down the new category and action to go with it.

"We should probably return their photographs."

"Yes," said Harry after a slight hesitation.

"What?"

"Occasionally they have no clothes on."

Sellie was aghast. "Really?"

Harry nodded. She could feel her face reddening.

"Any of them look nice?" asked Khuwelsa.

"Sellie!"

"Well, a girl can be interested, can't she?" she said. "And you didn't answer my question."

"Sometimes," Harry said in a very small voice.

"You should let me check those for suitability. And *then* we'll throw them in the fire." Sellie made notes. "Let's move on."

"Letters from admirers," said Harry. "These are in the majority."

"Form letter acknowledgement. Next."

"Business opportunities."

"Same as endorsements."

"No, these are people asking me to put money into business ventures."

Khuwelsa pulled a face again. "They can go in the fire after being checked."

"People wanting charity."

Sellie looked at her sister. "You can't."

Harry's heart felt heavy. "I know. I mean we don't even have any money to give. But it seems so heartless."

"Most of them will be chancers."

Harry nodded. "I feel like I should apologise."

"No," said Sellie. "No apology, not even an acknowledgement."

"Well, that covers everything."

Sellie wrote out signs and ripped the pages from her notepad. She laid them on the floor; then she and Harry went through the post. They managed to identify most of the angry people from the envelopes, and Sellie merely confirmed the contents before disposing of each letter.

They found they required one additional category: for genuine letters that required a reply.

Then the door slammed open, and Mrs Hemingway stood in the doorway, fuming.

"I believe you are overdue for my lesson."

2

Later Khuwelsa lay beneath the *Pegasus* and held out her right hand. "Small pliers."

She kept a tight grip on the ends of the wires in her left hand. There was a pause longer than she liked; she knew Harry would take a moment to figure out what she needed. It was not that Harry was not clever. In fact Khuwelsa agreed entirely with Mrs Hemingway on this point. Harry just didn't seem to try very hard. She was always a bit distracted.

Khuwelsa, on the other hand, drove herself despite Mrs Hemingway never disguising her disapproval of having to teach "the black girl". Sellie never expected to get any word of encouragement from their tutor, so she was never disappointed.

The heavy metal of the pliers fell into her hand. Khuwelsa focused on the wires in front of her. Their father, Jonathan Edgbaston, had cut off their pocket money again. It was the only pressure he could bring to bear since they were both too old to be spanked. So, she had spent the last few days tinkering with some left-overs in the workshop and turning them to a new use. Like the old Faraday grid she had picked up from one of the old plantation tractors.

Decisions about adding more equipment to the *Pegasus* were always difficult. Despite the gravity reduction, more weight was still an additional burden; if she added it in one place she really needed to take it away elsewhere. So the benefit of wrapping this old grid around the existing fuselage had to be balanced against the additional weight.

The problem was that Faraday grids did not add to one another. The best modern grid cancelled all but a quarter of the weight of anything above it. But if you put one grid on top of another and energised them both it was still one quarter, not a quarter of a quarter.

Nobody knew why. She had tried it herself, of course, but the experiment just proved what every engineer knew to be true. There were stories, of course; even Jules Verne had written *De la Terre à la Lune* ten years before the first ill-fated trip into the Void. In Verne's story, the inventor had succeeded in achieving complete nullification of gravity.

"We should be so lucky," said Khuwelsa to no one in particular.

"What?" said Harry.

"Nothing."

"What exactly are you doing?"

"Increasing the coverage of the Faraday effect so we can turn tighter without gaining weight."

"That'll be useful."

Khuwelsa tightened up the electrical connection with the pliers. She would have to come back and solder it later. Along with the dozens of other ones. It was going to be a long job. She replaced the cover and slid out from under the ship. Harry gave her a hand up and pulled her into a sitting position.

"You don't sound very enthusiastic about my improvements."

Harry looked pointedly across towards the front of the house. A line of steam-powered cars were puffing up the gravel drive. "Looks like we're going to be spending the weekend skulking in our rooms again."

"Dad didn't say he was having guests this weekend."

"Must be trouble."

"Well, we're grounded."

"It's all right for you; you'll just curl up with a book."

"You could."

Harry sighed. "I'd rather be flying."

Khuwelsa reached out and took her sister's pale hand in her own black one. She squeezed it. Harry just stared at the house. Sellie squeezed really hard.

"Ow!" said Harry. "What did you do that for?"

"Just trying to cheer you up."

"With pain?"

"Got to be better than melancholy." Sellie got up on her knees and poked Harry in the midriff.

"Ow."

Sellie poked again. Harry tried to bat her hand away but missed. Khuwelsa went all-out on a poking attack. Harry defended, but at least half of Sellie's pokes got through. Harry fell back into a flowerbed and rolled under the outstretched wing of the *Pegasus*. She tried to suppress her giggles, failed, and burst out laughing, but Sellie was remorseless in her attack.

Harry laughed and laughed. Khuwelsa grinned and kept up her relentless onslaught of poking fingers even though Harry's defence was in ruins and she could not see for the tears running down her face.

"Pax!" shrieked Harry. "Please! Pax!"

Sellie sat back on her heels, still grinning.

"I hate you," said Harry, though the grin on her face as she struggled out of the bushes belied her statement. "And I'll get you back."

Their moment did not last.

"Quite honestly, Miss Edgbaston, I despair." The highly strung wire that was Mrs Hemingway stood near the tail of the *Pegasus* with her arms crossed. Her hair piled high on her head gave her that extra height with which to dominate them (at least in theory).

Not that she needed it, thought Sellie, as she was quite a tall woman. Harry was only average height while Mrs Hemingway looked down on most men, both literally and figuratively. Perhaps that's why she remained single.

Harry stood and brushed some of the dirt from the front of her dress.

Mrs Hemingway shook her head. "You are not a child any more, Miss Edgbaston, you are a young woman and the sooner you behave appropriately the sooner you will find a husband."

"Yes, Mrs Hemingway," said Harry.

Khuwelsa rocked back on her heels and stood in one fluid motion. Mrs Hemingway was not addressing her, of course. There was no reason for Khuwelsa to behave in any fashion resembling that of a proper young woman because she would not be attracting a husband. Except perhaps one of the men working on the plantation.

From Mrs Hemingway's viewpoint, as soon as Harry was married off, Sellie could be dispensed with as a companion. Not that Harry thought that way, but every right-thinking British lady would come to the same conclusion.

"To what do we owe the pleasure of your visit, Mrs Hemingway?" said Harry. "If it's to tell us to keep clear of my father's guests we had already assumed as much."

Mrs Hemingway frowned. "Your assumption is completely incorrect. Your father requests your attendance at luncheon."

"What?"

Mrs Hemingway sighed. "Really, Harriet, you cannot say *what.* If you have truly misheard then the correct phrase is *I beg your pardon.*"

"I beg your pardon?"

"I said you must not say *what...*"

At which point she broke off with a look of powerless fury in her eyes. Khuwelsa turned away and hid her laughter in a cough.

"You will return to the house, clean yourself up, put on something respectable and present yourself at 1 p.m." She turned on her heel and flounced off.

Khuwelsa managed to suppress her giggles until Mrs Hemingway was, hopefully, out of earshot before they erupted from her. Harry turned with a look of fake innocence on her face. "What's funny?"

Then she dissolved into laughter as well.

3

Khuwelsa straightened her skirt for the umpteenth time and took a deep breath. Mrs Hemingway had insisted they take baths, which was not a problem, and then that they wore their best day dresses. Which *was* a problem because the only way they could get into them was to climb into the corsetry they preferred to avoid.

Not that Mrs Hemingway had given any instructions directly to Sellie herself, but since neither had she been forbidden it meant that she was also required to go to luncheon.

Sellie loved Jonathan Edgbaston, even though he wasn't her real father. He was never unkind, except when he was telling her off—and when that happened he would almost certainly be telling Harry off as well. He was genuinely unaffected by the colour of her skin.

Unlike everyone else, and that wasn't just the Europeans. Even her own people reacted badly to her much of the time. She was seen as unfairly privileged. If other natives couldn't have what she had, why should she be allowed it at all?

The fact that it was not her decision did not seem to have any bearing on the matter. Honestly Harry had nothing to worry about. At least she had a place in the world, while the only place Khuwelsa had was standing three paces behind her sister.

Khuwelsa looked down the long curving staircase and then back at Harry, who looked just as nervous as she. Mrs Hemingway had not been invited and that was another reason she had been in such a foul mood.

"Ready?" said Harry.

"Ready as I'll ever be."

Harry gave two short whistles and one long one: *Attack dive.* Sellie grinned, they linked arms, and as one they set off down into the hall.

The butler opened the door and they entered the morning room. The gazes of ten men turned on them. Five wore uniforms; Khuwelsa recognised both Navy and army. Of the others, three were in well-tailored suits and the final one was Mr Edgbaston. He was the only one who smiled.

"I thought they were chaps." The *sotto voce* whisper reverberated around the room. It was one of the military types, a fellow sporting a handlebar moustache on a face puffed and red from an over-indulgence in alcohol.

"My daughters, gentlemen," said their father. Khuwelsa's heart melted again. She loved it when he said that in front of people who would not only disapprove of her, but also of him for saying it.

Harry made a beeline for him and Sellie followed.

All eyes were on them.

Their father made introductions. They were not required to shake hands, which was probably just as well; only the younger men even looked at her. It was hard to imagine an event any more nightmarish than this.

The man who had been unable to keep a civil tongue in his head was Admiral Framington. There was a Lt Cmdr Laxton, a Lt Keating, two army majors, and four bureaucrats. After introductions there was a period of small talk where everyone spoke in low tones and no one spoke with the girls.

The food was brought in for a buffet lunch. The Edgbaston family did not maintain a large staff, and this sort of occasion was usually planned well in advance so they could draft in extras to deal with service. This meeting was impromptu.

No one moved towards the tables with the food, and it took Khuwelsa and Harry a few moments to realise that they were the reason. They had to go first.

"Come along, my dears," said their father and took each of them by the arm, guiding them to the table.

"What's this about, Dad?" hissed Harry.

"Newspaper reports."

Harry glanced at Sellie behind their father's back as he leaned over the table to get some food. She looked questioning. *Any ideas?* Sellie shrugged. *None.*

The torturous silence continued while they ate. Sellie had no appetite but pretended to eat. She noticed that Harry was scoffing hers down as if there was no tomorrow. Mrs Hemingway would not be impressed.

Subsequently they moved to the drawing room which had an attached conservatory. Khuwelsa went to the French window and looked out on to the manicured gardens and plantation beyond. The Edgbaston estate, while one of the larger ones in the area, was not huge. They cultivated grain with a staff of about thirty on the farm. That staff would all have been slaves at one time, but since the British had taken over slavery was abolished. The workers stayed because there was nowhere else to go.

"Miss Edgbaston."

Sellie turned towards the speaker only to realise that the Miss Edgbaston in question was Harry, and not her. Harry was sitting beside their father surrounded by the gentlemen. Khuwelsa was in two minds as to whether to stay safe where she was or be with Harry.

Her father solved the problem when he looked up and indicated she should come and sit. Her heart sank but she was an obedient daughter, most of the time, and did as he instructed.

She sat down decorously, as Mrs Hemingway had drilled them again and again. Perching on the edge and not sitting back. It was impossible to get out of a chair in an elegant way if seated all the way back. Though it defeated the point of there even being a back. Khuwelsa thought she would prefer to lounge like a bohemian than be so prim and proper.

The air was filled with the scent of cigars and alcohol.

"Miss Edgbaston," repeated the admiral, who appeared to be the one in charge. "Can you explain your involvement with the attack on Zanzibar?"

Harry cleared her throat. "There's a German lieutenant I like to dance with."

There were disapproving mutterings among the group.

"I met him at a dance organised by our army originally," she said. "We got on, so we would visit him from time to time."

"Without a chaperone?"

"I had my sister with me," said Harry. "And there was the whole garrison of soldiers."

"Oh, really?"

"Admiral," said their father. "I understand you wish to discuss the *military* situation with my daughters. I do not appreciate you impugning their honour."

"What? No," said the admiral. "Not intended."

"The point is," said Harry, "we arrived just as the Zanzibar invasion force was going through the town, and they imprisoned us. We escaped and got to Zanzibar to warn Daddy."

"And then you attacked and brought down four Zeppelins!"

"Outrageous," muttered someone.

Harry stood up. "Perhaps you would have preferred we let them attack and invade? Your two *boats* would not have stood a chance."

"But," said the admiral. "You're just a girl." It sounded like *gel*–with a hard "g"–the way he pronounced it.

"So what exactly is the problem, admiral?" demanded Harry. "That we saved Zanzibar or that a pair of girls brought down a German fleet with one unarmed ship?"

Sellie would have applauded but at that exact moment there was an explosion outside and all the windows blew in.

4

Khuwelsa could feel nothing save her blood pounding in her temples, see nothing through choking clouds of dust, and hear nothing but a shrill whistle in her ears. For some reason she felt it ought to be dark in the room, but there was plenty of light filtering through the dust.

She coughed again and reached out her hand to her sister. There was only an empty space. *Where was Harry?* She had been sitting right beside her but no longer. Sellie stood up, then sat down again abruptly; the explosion had done something to her ears and her balance was all wrong.

She did not hear but saw the main chandelier crash to the floor in front of her. One of the men in suits had been seated underneath it. Heedless of her lack of balance she got up again and staggered across to the chandelier, using the other furniture to stop herself from toppling over. Someone laid a hand on her left forearm, trying to hold her back. She shrugged them off.

The chandelier rope came tumbling down through the pulley. The cable for the electricity still ran up to the ceiling but must have become detached at the other end. The man under the chandelier had his eyes open and his arms were moving feebly as if he were trying to free himself, ineffectually.

Khuwelsa grabbed the upper arms of the chandelier and pulled. The heavy metal rolled towards her. It was caught on the other side. A hand tapped her on the shoulder. It was her father. He looked shocking, with his black hair a mess and his suit grey with dust. He held up a finger to her indicating she should wait.

He got the other side of the chandelier and lifted while she pulled. It rolled off completely. The electric cable went taut for a moment. Sellie glanced up to see it tear through the plaster ceiling, as the weight of the chandelier ripped the wire further out.

It hadn't become disconnected after all. Must have had a lot of play.

Her father was helping the man in the suit to his feet. He was not completely in his right mind; his head lolled and he staggered with his weight on her father's shoulder. However nothing seemed to be broken.

The ringing in her ears faded, replaced by weak cries for help and the occasional groan. Sellie looked towards the devastated windows and then the floor. There was remarkably little glass scattered about; it seemed the net curtains had retained most of the shattering windows, though they had themselves been ripped down by the weight.

The window frames were gone. The dust was clearing and there seemed to be no smoke. *Where was Harry?*

Khuwelsa tutted. Of the men, most appeared to have recovered the ability to move under their own power, although that meant limping, hobbling and leaning on one another. Two remained. Of those, one man looked as if he might be dead. Sellie plucked up her courage and went over to where he lay on the floor. A pool of blood was forming by his head. His eyes were open but lacked that vital spark of the living.

She closed his eyes. He was still warm, of course, which seemed strange: if he was dead should he not be cold? She shivered. Something structural snapped and its sound broke the unnatural quiet of the explosion's aftermath.

Sellie looked up. A gap several inches wide ran along the ceiling near the shattered wall. Even as she watched it lengthened. The ceiling bellied out as it lost it support.

The final man was Admiral Framington. He was awake, but his eyes were wandering. She hurried over and tried to get an arm under his shoulders.

"Come on, Admiral," she said.

His eyes focused on her. "Get away from me, darkie!"

Khuwelsa went cold. For a moment she was tempted to leave him to his fate. But only for a moment. She bent over him, her face close to his. "The ceiling is coming down, Admiral," she said. "Now, if you like, I'll walk away and leave you here. Or you can let me help you. Which would you prefer?"

She was surprised how long it took him to come to his decision but perhaps that was because his mind was still befuddled. He grabbed her left hand and let her pull him up. He seemed to have enough strength in his legs, which was just as well since she was not capable of carrying him. He did, however, need assistance with his balance.

A shower of plaster fluttered down on them as another crack rent the air. Something whipped Sellie's face, and she caught a glimpse of the end of the electrical wire from the chandelier.

It was a good thing they did not have gas in the house or the whole place might have gone up from an electrical spark.

A thunderous roar filled the air as the place went dark and they were again blinded by dust. The admiral tried to stop but Sellie kept him staggering forward by sheer strength. She could not see it, but the outer wall must have collapsed.

That meant the ceiling would not be far behind; it was already creaking ominously. Every few moments the crack of breaking timbers snapped through the air.

They must be almost at the door by now, surely?

Khuwelsa's arm banged into the wall. Good. The ceiling directly above should be supported by the wall. But the admiral seemed to be trying to move away from her, deeper into the room.

She held him but found herself being dragged. She realised it wasn't him, but the floor giving way. There were cellars beneath every room and the floor must be collapsing into them.

Sellie reached out her arm to find something to grab hold of, and found nothing but empty space where the wall should have been. They must have reached the door. She found the frame and hooked her fingers round it. Her other hand had a grip on the admiral's jacket, but he was very heavy. Still, she spent her life working with tools and shovelling coal. He was just a man.

"Help!" she called, though still able to see nothing.

"Sellie?"

"Dad! I'm at the door, I've got the admiral but the floor's going."

"I can't see you, sweetheart." She could tell he was trying to maintain a semblance of calm. "Keep talking."

"I'm here by the door. The whole outside wall collapsed and I don't know where Harry is. Dad, she's gone."

A hand found hers and grabbed her around the wrist. She felt her father move in front of her. He reached out, following her other arm with his hand until he touched the admiral. He took hold and, together with Sellie, they reeled the old man in and through the door to relative safety.

The air filled with the tearing and cracking of joists and boards as the floor behind them collapsed under its own weight plus that of the fallen ceiling.

5

The air cleared as the dust settled in the hall. Their beautiful house was a wreck. They had placed the admiral sitting up against a wall on the far side. He muttered something about anarchists but his eyes were wandering.

With one bureaucrat dead there remained the other seven visitors. The younger ones were on their feet but still confused. One of the army majors was checking his gun.

"See if you can find some of the staff, Sellie," said her father. "We could do with some assistance with this lot."

"What was it, Dad?"

He shook his head. "I don't know, sweetheart. I don't want to send you but you're the only one who knows their way around and"—he paused, considering how to say it—"I don't trust this lot not to shoot at someone who looked at them the wrong way."

"What about Harry?"

"She wasn't on the floor anywhere?"

"I didn't see her." Sellie went cold with the thought of Harry buried in the collapse. "I don't think she was in the room."

"No, she was gone by the time I managed to pull myself together." He thought for a moment, then shook his head. "We just have to assume she got out of there first."

Sellie glanced around and then decided she didn't care what the strangers thought. She flung her arms around her father and squeezed. It just felt so good to have him there and real before she headed off again.

She felt his arms enfold her and then he whispered in her ear. "I love you, daughter." She thought she might be overwhelmed from the feelings his words generated.

But emotions would have to wait. She stopped squeezing and he did the same; she stepped back. Normally he would have been smiling after a hug, but not on this occasion. Both of them were deadly serious.

Sellie had a sudden thought. "Mrs Hemingway?"

"I think she retreated to her rooms." Both of them glanced at the stairs.

"I'll go," said Khuwelsa.

"No, it's too dangerous," he said. "I'll send one of these chaps."

"I'm the lightest and, as you said, they don't know their way around."

He pursed his lips as he reached for an alternative, but he did not consider too long. He nodded.

She headed across the room at a fast walk. Running in the dress was almost impossible and now that the urgency was decreasing she began to feel the ache in her midriff where the corset pinched. She had been doing things in it that a proper young lady would not even contemplate. And for good reason, as corsets were simply not designed for those things.

The stairs creaked as she reached the halfway point. She glanced back. The men were all looking at her from the dusty wreckage of the hall. She noticed them looking above her head, she followed their gaze. The ceiling here was also cracked with a gap running the length of the wall.

"Gentlemen, we should move outside," said her father. "If two of you would care to assist the admiral?"

"Your girl?" said one of them, he clearly could not bring himself to say daughter.

"She's finding her tutor."

Sellie turned the bend in the stairs and they were lost to view. She reached the next floor. The passage ran the length of the house in both directions. There were suites on the same side of the building as the demolished outer wall. Those would be dangerous and the ones closest might not even have a floor.

On the other side were more bedrooms, and at the far end three rooms set aside for Mrs Hemingway. Harry and Sellie had two rooms which they still shared. Their father had offered them separate rooms but they did not want them—much to Mrs Hemingway's disapproval. Their tutor had to make do with the hope she could get Harry into a ladies' college at Cambridge. Sellie would have no chance of following her then.

But despite the woman's animosity, she needed rescuing.

Sellie hurried down the passage, her footfalls muffled by the carpet. She paused outside her own bedroom. Did she have time to get out of the corset? As if in answer the house groaned. Khuwelsa shot the wall an angry look as if it was deliberately forcing her to remain trussed up.

She looked back along the passage. It did not look entirely vertical. The way the whole corridor twisted convinced her she needed to move. She lifted her skirts and trotted the remainder of the distance.

At the last moment before ploughing directly into the room she decided to knock. She banged hard to make sure she received a response.

"Who is it?"

Sellie felt the floor shift.

"It's Khuwelsa, Mrs Hemingway," she kept her voice calm and normal. "I've come to escort you to safety."

"I am indisposed," came the reply. "I'll come down later."

Khuwelsa stared at the door.

"Mrs Hemingway, you really need to come now."

"Go away."

"The house is collapsing and you will be buried alive."

"Nonsense."

The house groaned and something cracked like a tree being felled.

Khuwelsa grabbed the door handle and pushed. For a moment she thought Mrs Hemingway must have locked it. But it opened slightly. The moving house had warped the frame and it was stuck. Sellie jammed her feet into the carpet and put her shoulder to the door. She shoved hard and it flew open only to come up short as it slid at an angle into the carpet inside. Nothing was straight any more.

Sellie squeezed through into Mrs Hemingway's sitting room.

6

Mrs Hemingway was one for frills and flower patterns. Lace covered every flat surface; an impressive aspidistra stood in the corner with its broad leaves folding out to catch the light while, by the window, there was another potted plant with patterned leaves.

Mrs Hemingway sat at a writing desk next to the door and her back to the window opposite. She was attempting to close it but the sliding cover seemed to have stuck. The reason was quite obvious from where Khuwelsa stood. The floor was warping and the otherwise sturdy desk was twisted slightly from the true.

"I told you I was busy," said Mrs Hemingway. Her voice was shrill, unlike its usual commanding tone.

"We have to get out, the house is collapsing."

Mrs Hemingway continued in her attempt to force the cover down across the desk. It was stuck tight. Sellie could see an unfinished letter, already covering several sheets, which her tutor had broken off from writing halfway down the page.

"Don't be ridiculous," she said again.

From the corridor beyond Khuwelsa came a low, thunderous roar. She glanced over her shoulder. Dust was billowing from under one of the opposite doors. Further along the corridor a door simply fell away and daylight poured through.

Khuwelsa shook her head. What idiot had built this house? Then she sighed. Who in their right mind would have expected it to be bombed? The fact was that the cellars undermined the entire building and the place was falling in like a house of cards.

"What have you done?" hissed Mrs Hemingway. Finally accepting that something was wrong, she gave up with the desk, grabbed sheets of the unfinished letter, and stood up.

Khuwelsa had had enough. "I'm so sorry, Mrs Hemingway. I had intended to assist you in your rescue but it is entirely clear that that is not what you want. So, if you don't mind I'll just leave you to it. You can find your own way out. As the house falls to pieces around you."

Sellie squeezed back through the door. The corridor was twisting and the floor dropped as she watched. Holding on to the door frame she turned towards the window at the end. As she watched the frame distorted and several of the frames fell out. They shattered as they hit the carpet.

Something grabbed her hand on the door frame.

"Don't leave me."

A tiny part of Sellie was grateful her tutor had relented. It would have been difficult explaining to her father how she had come to leave the ungrateful woman to her fate. Khuwelsa squeezed back through the gap into the tutor's suite.

The safest place was likely to be the corner of the house; it would be the last to go, if it fell at all. She took a step towards the bedroom with Mrs Hemingway still clinging to her hand. The floor lurched under them.

The tutor lost her balance and fell, dragging Khuwelsa down with her.

The floor was no longer flat and a gap yawned between it and the main wall. Mrs Hemingway squealed as another joist snapped and the floor shifted again. Gravity was pulling them across the carpet.

Sellie cursed silently; if Mrs Hemingway had not been there, she would have spoken out loud. Trying to crawl in these layers of petticoats and a corset was almost impossible. But if they didn't move, they would soon be dead.

They might not be able to crawl but there was another option.

"Mrs Hemingway, you must roll towards the bedroom door."

"Roll? I will not!"

"Die, then," said Khuwelsa. She was not in a good position to roll across to the bedroom—her tutor blocked her direct path—but she was considerably stronger, and rolling up the sloping floor should not be too much of a challenge. She could see the slope flattened out further towards the far wall.

Sellie twisted round on the floor and rolled uphill. It was considerably more difficult than rolling down a grassy slope. But by pushing with her arms she was able to make progress and it got easier.

Mrs Hemingway sobbed. The floor vibrated again. The wall that had once supported the floor was now bowing away from them. If she had been in the right place Sellie could have looked into the next room through the gap into which the writing desk was now leaning, as was the chair.

That must be quite heavy, thought Sellie as a potted fern toppled over and fell into the space between the wall and the floor. She stared at the writing desk. It teetered on the edge but its back still rested against the wall. Without help, it would not fall for some time.

She decided to give it the assistance it needed. She climbed to her feet and hitched up her skirts in a most unladylike way, tucking them into the decorative sash that served as a belt. Then she picked up a straight-backed chair—one of four around a small table suitable for card games—and descended the slope at increasing speed.

Mrs Hemingway was watching and screamed as Sellie took a suicidal route. As she reached the writing desk, Sellie jammed the chair ahead of her and the four legs struck the wall.

It was not Sellie's intention to move the wall but rather to use the chair as a support. It had been a risk, since the wall was clearly no longer the major structural feature it was intended to be but simply another card waiting to fall.

And yet, it held. And Sellie's downward motion was brought to an abrupt halt.

Having taken that risk, the next one was quite minor but far more alarming to her audience. She jumped up and down in an effort to dislodge the writing desk. Each jump vibrated the floor and the writing desk shifted slightly but it was taking too long.

There was a crumbling thunder further up the building and, about thirty feet away, Sellie could see the wall she was leaning against disintegrating. The ceiling above it was coming down as its support disappeared. The collapse was moving along the wall towards her.

Sellie threw herself to the floor. The chair, left to its own devices, tumbled through the gap into the dark below. Sellie put her feet against the carved ball-and-claw feet of the writing desk. The Mad Hatter's riddle from Alice in Wonderland came into her mind: *Why is a raven like a writing desk?* Sellie gave the legs an almighty shove. They slid across the carpet and the writing desk disappeared into the dark. With that weight gone, the floor sprang up several inches.

"Because they both have crow's feet!" shouted Sellie at the falling desk. She heard it crash.

She scrambled to her feet as the wall fell apart. She grabbed Mrs Hemingway by the arm and pulled her half-crawling half-stumbling towards the closed bedroom door.

The ceiling showered them with plaster. Sellie turned the handle and smashed her shoulder against the door. It did not budge but pain shot through her collar bone and upper arm.

The frame was too warped. Looking at it Sellie could see gaps where no gaps should be.

"The window!" shouted Sellie above the continuing roar of collapsing masonry.

Once more she grabbed her tutor by the wrist and dragged her across the room. She unlocked the sash window and flung the lower half up. Sellie had been aware of a background rumble among the rest of the noise, but with the window open that sound redoubled.

The growl of diesel-driven propellers. Above them a Zeppelin hung like a thundercloud threatening its worst.

"Friends of yours?" asked Sellie to Mrs Hemingway as they stared up at the airship.

"Of course not," said the tutor. "The only reason they will be here is for you and your sister."

"Thank you," said Sellie.

"What for?"

"For acknowledging we're sisters."

7

In the moments after the initial blast Harry sat with her mouth open. She had been in the middle of a word when the world exploded around her. She saw the admiral blown out of his chair.

The sound of thunder roared around her. The windows fragmented and shards of masonry splintered against the far wall. The room filled with dust and smoke. The sun shone down through it and Harry alone saw a shadow move across it. A shadow that meant something big had crossed in front of the sun.

It had not been fast, which meant it was not a plane. It could have been a British vehicle, but they would have heard the roar of its rotors. It had to be an airship—and only one sort of airship carried the artillery and bombs to destroy a house.

Harry did not know what state her sister and father were in but she guessed that, since she had been sitting between them, if she was not severely harmed then they would probably be the same.

Taking no time to make her decision she jumped to her feet and dodged across the room to the door to the conservatory. A remnant of the door was attached to the frame by a twisted hinge. The floor shifted slightly as she stepped out into the sunshine.

The conservatory was gone. Flattened. Not a single pane of glass remained; almost the entirety of its metal frame lay broken and twisted. The low wall that marked its perimeter was, for the most part, intact. A crater perhaps fifteen feet deep lay just outside the door. She stepped out onto its rim and the ground collapsed. It seemed to run away from her, descending deeper into the earth, like wave-washed sand on the beach.

She jumped away, stumbling as her foot caught on protruding bricks and landing face down in the damp soil. The artillery shell must have opened up a way into the cellar. She staggered away across the uneven surface. Craning her head she shielded her eyes against the sun. The Zeppelin, if that's what it was, had already disappeared over the roof of the house.

The house emitted a strange creaking sound. Its outer wall, where she had just exited, fell away, starting at the bottom. Harry gave her head a gentle shake just to be sure she was not imagining things. Then in a sudden rush a whole section gave way, showering her in dust and pieces of stone.

Fear for her sister and father gripped her but there was nothing she could do. A curtain of falling masonry barred her return. The wall looked none too safe and she was still within range if it decided to collapse. She must trust they would be safe.

She pulled up her inconvenient petticoats and staggered away around the crater, heading for what had once been the wide French windows leading to the lawns.

Once beyond the low wall she found herself walking through a carpet of shattered glass. She stepped gingerly. Her shoes were sturdy, but she did not need any shards getting into them and slicing her feet.

She had decided to go round to the front but was so busy picking her way through the devastation she was not paying full attention when she rounded the corner into the shadow of the house. Glancing up, she froze.

The Edgbaston home was essentially just a rectangle with additional kitchens and staff accommodation added at one end. She was at the other and standing on the corner. Only fifty yards away, down the gently sloping lawns from the main building, close to a copse with a white wooden summer house, stood a troop of German soldiers armed with rifles held in the ready position.

Behind her a piece of wall collapsed with a roar. More than one face turned in her direction at the sound. She stayed completely still. There was some discussion among the men but no cry went up. She was in the shadow of the house with the sun behind her

Not for one moment did Harry not think they had come for her and Khuwelsa. Sellie had received no post, so perhaps the newspapers did not mention her. But the Germans knew it was both of them.

Some of the letters had spoken in quite antagonistic terms about the Germans, which could only mean that those details had been included in the news reports. While she had never taken a great interest in politics she had become far more aware of it recently. And that was what the admiral and the rest of them had been here for, to discuss the newspaper reports.

And, she supposed with a wry smile as she watched the soldiers, the Germans wanted to discuss it as well. Though if they hadn't been so keen on starting a war, none of this would have happened.

She couldn't stay here; they were bound to see her eventually. The front of the house was out of the question now. The soldiers were probably waiting for either a signal to attack or for the people to come out.

Harry guessed they were not expecting to collect a bunch of British diplomats and top brass. Well, that meant she would have to rescue them. And that meant the *Pegasus.* The furnace should still be hot from this morning so if it was just one Zeppelin this should be easy, even without Sellie. Although she would much prefer it if her sister was with her.

The wall she was leaning against vibrated. Expecting another crash, Harry slipped back around the corner and out of sight. She was not disappointed. A whole section of the rear wall crumbled. She could see the exposed upper floor and watched as her father's bed fell from the edge into the accumulating masonry. She allowed herself to wonder why the house was falling to pieces just because of one bomb. It was probably something to do with the cellars. Sellie would know.

The house went quiet, but now she heard orders being given in German. Harry's command of German was good, as she had had lots of practice with Johannes so she understood perfectly: The soldiers were being told to check the rear of the house.

Pieces of shattered chimney pots landed beside her, one large piece embedding itself in the ground. It wasn't safe either. She dare not peek to see how close they were. She had to move.

Right now.

8

Harry cursed her skirts once more as she set off at the best run she could manage, diagonally away from the collapsing house. The fragments of glass twinkled in the sunlight. She could not worry about it, not this time.

Harry reached the low perimeter wall of the destroyed conservatory, paused for a moment and spotted a larger piece of glass. She picked it up and tossed it over the wall before throwing herself after it onto the bare earth.

She needed to crawl and that would be impossible in these clothes. She picked up the shard she had selected and rolled on to her back. She strongly doubted there would be anyone on this side of what remained of the house to see her pull up her skirt.

Her first action was to slice off a long section of a petticoat. She rapidly wrapped this around the glass to give herself something to grip more safely. She did not have time to cut all the layers short—which was a challenging idea—but she could slice up the side. She wished she had time to get rid of the corset.

She could hear nothing from the soldiers and it still took a couple of minutes to make a split in each layer up to her thigh. She hoped that would be sufficient. This method had the advantage that she would still look decent if she encountered anyone else.

Her instinct was to throw the glass into the corner but she decided to keep it with her, even though the petticoat wrapping was already stained red from where she had cut herself. It wasn't serious. She wanted to put it in a pocket but she had none until realising it could make its own if she pushed it through her dress and into the corset binding. Not entirely safe, but it freed up her hands.

Feeling very daring she exposed her legs and rolled over; her bare knees pressed into the ground. She was close to the wall and it was high enough to hide her even on her knees. She crawled as fast as she dared, every now and then touching the glass shard to make sure it remained firmly embedded. She did not relish the thought of running it through her knee if it fell out at the wrong moment.

There was another tremendous crash from behind her as another part of the house gave way. She knew the soldiers would be distracted by it, so she took a chance and poked her head up.

With the sinking feeling one gets when one discovers one has done something completely wrong unintentionally, she found herself staring directly at a soldier no more than ten feet away. Since all the lawns sloped down from the house, he was lower than she was and so his head was at a similar height to hers.

He must have caught her movement and turned. She ducked and in a single half-roll came up tight against the wall. She pulled the shard from her corset and covered her legs, then realised that might be a mistake. She shifted her left leg until she could feel the sun's heat beating down on her skin.

If she was lucky he would ignore the idea he had seen something. Or he would come closer and not see her. Or perhaps get called away.

Luck chose not to favour her. Instead the barrel of his rifle came over the top of wall slowly. Harry moved her left knee out a little more to make sure her leg was fully exposed to the thigh. Even she quavered at something so outrageous; she could not imagine what Mrs Hemingway would think.

It occurred to her that Mrs Hemingway was in her rooms, in the collapsing house. It seemed unlikely she would have the slightest clue what to do.

A hand holding the rifle appeared. It was the hand of a younger person, she thought. All the better. She contrived to look unconscious but kept her eyes open a tiny slit. Her glass dagger lay hidden in her hand under a fold of her dress.

His head came into view, and his eyes were directed at her leg. She felt a blush blooming in her cheeks. For some reason being a redhead meant she blushed far worse than most people.

The time had come to act. She reached up with her free hand and grabbed him by his collar. She pulled hard. He overbalanced and fell across the wall. She hoped he would not pull the trigger by accident. She lifted her other hand and pressed the glass against his neck, he flinched. She spoke in German.

"I don't want to hurt you but we have very little time. Do you understand?"

"Yes."

Another part of her home collapsed with the accompanying cacophony.

"Listen. You are going to drop your rifle and pistol. You will escort me to the far wall as if I am your prisoner. Then I will let you go. Just say yes and then do it; otherwise I will hurt you."

He did not bother with the *yes*. The rifle dropped beside her and then the handgun.

She stood carefully, keeping the glass blade at his neck. She grabbed his arm to keep him close and made sure he was aware she could cut into his neck in a trice.

They walked towards the far wall, away from the house and the other soldiers.

"Beckhardt!" shouted someone.

"Is that your name?"

"Yes."

"We'll just carry on walking, they won't shoot because they might hit you so we're both safe."

A bullet ricocheted from the wall as the sound of the shot reached them. Beckhardt jumped. Another error, perhaps they didn't like him.

"Please understand I have no ill will towards you," she said. "But your seniors will not be pleased with you if they think you simply gave in. Isn't that right?"

"It is."

They reached the wall as another shot, closer, slammed into it.

"I am sorry," said Harry. "But this is for your own good." She stepped away from him and slashed down his arm. The material of his shirt parted as did the skin beneath it. He cried out in pain and blood welled from the wound.

"Good luck," she said and once more jumped the wall.

9

Heedless of the glass, she charged down the slope. Gravity pulled her along so fast her legs could almost not keep up. The roof of the barn where they kept the *Pegasus* rose beyond the trees. Harry could see a thin line of smoke wafting upwards; her plane was still hot. Something whined past her ear as a gunshot echoed across the grass.

There were trees to the right and only a little out of her way, so she cut across into them. She did not look behind as it would only slow her down. Luckily, this was her domain. She knew exactly where she was going.

The trees thickened but she kept running. The level of freedom the split in the dress provided was impressive; it would be perfect if only she weren't so constricted by the corset. The little air-dock they had for the *Pegasus* had originally been a barn with a walled area for keeping animals safe from lions and other predators. She and Khuwelsa had inherited it even before her father had given her the *Pegasus* to silence her pleas for an air-plane.

She headed for the main gate first. She knew the Germans were not stupid. They would have mounted a guard on her baby. So she headed straight for it. It took less than a minute for her to negotiate the woods and come out on the track leading to the main gate.

"Halt!"

She almost smiled and dodged to the side back into the trees, heading away from the gate and the guard. He had now successfully scared her off and that was what he would tell his friends when they arrived.

But the main gate was not the only way in. She made her way through the undergrowth following paths that she and Sellie had made over the years, though mostly overgrown now. And then she found the tree that had grown up overhanging the wall.

With her newly freed legs she was up it in no time. It had been years since she had climbed it but her arms and legs remembered it. She balanced along the branch—though it was thinner than she recalled—and came to the drop-off. She knelt down on the branch, grabbed it with both hands, and swung down.

It was a further drop of three feet but that was nothing. She had done the same trick when she was half her current height. She brushed off her hands. The last part might be tricky.

An outbuilding stood between her and the yard in which her airplane stood. She took a deep breath and stepped round the corner of the brick wall. The *Pegasus* was exactly where they had left it. Smoke rose in a thin column from the stack above the furnace.

A roar of diesel engines grew filling the air, and with no clear source. Harry did not glance up; if anything the sound would mask any accidental noise she might make. She strode across the yard towards the open hatch of the plane. She glanced to her left. The guard was at his post, looking away from her.

"Look behind you!"

A small group of soldiers, the ones that had been chasing her, emerged through the trees. And she was in plain view to them. They were pointing at her past the guard.

She hitched up her skirt and sprinted as the guard turned. "Halt!"

She did not halt, nor did she look. He would no doubt be raising his gun in her direction. He was unlikely to try to kill her on the first shot. He would want to scare her.

The gunshot echoed round the yard and the bullet careened off the flagstone at her feet. Her blood ran cold. He was successful. She was scared. But the *Pegasus* was only a couple of steps away. Harry flung herself into the air, twisted and landed heavily inside the cabin on her side.

She whirled to grab the rope that held the steps. She yanked on it and pulled them up. A bullet ricocheted off the fuselage near her head. She reached out and grabbed the hatch. It resisted her before swinging closed. The guard was aiming directly at her. Would he really shoot a girl?

She did not know whether he hesitated or simply took too long but the door slammed shut before the next bullet struck the fuselage.

She was uncertain what to do next, she might have some steam but that would be exhausted quickly so stoking the furnace should come first. But there were soldiers directly outside and they could cause trouble.

A shadow passed across the sun. She glanced up through the glass. The Zeppelin was gliding past at about five hundred feet. They were unlikely to open fire with their soldiers so close, in which case it would be better if the men on the ground stayed nearby.

Furnace first.

Harry hurried into the back. She snatched up the shovel and used it to unhook the latch on the furnace door and pull it open. Heat streamed out like the beam of a searchlight.

As fast as she could, Harry shovelled. It was exhausting work,

A couple of bullets hit the fuselage but the *Pegasus* was tough. Then came the banging. Harry hoped they would not try to damage the Faraday.

There was no time to do everything. Harry slammed the furnace door shut and the latch engaged automatically. She flicked the switch that activated the forced airflow pump. Sellie had rigged an air-blowing device after she had read about them being used in the furnaces on the big ships to achieve higher temperatures. Hers was not as powerful and drained the battery but Harry needed all the steam she could get as fast as possible.

The banging had stopped, and that worried Harry. She hurried to the pilot's seat. She gave a long whistle without even thinking about it and flipped the Faraday switch.

There was a cry from up top as they went light. The whole squad of soldiers were in the yard, maybe ten of them including the one who had climbed up onto the plane.

They were looking at her through the glass; some were grinning. Harry took a gentle hold of the wing controls and glanced at the steam pressure gauge. Not enough for flight yet but it was moving in the right direction.

This was not a time for messing around, Harry decided. She rested her thumb on the button that Sellie had installed for the Maxim and pressed it. The *Pegasus* vibrated with the thudding of the machine gun.

That wiped the grins off their faces, she thought. Every one of them had hit the deck as the machine gun's bullets flashed over their heads. With the *Pegasus* on the ground the gun's angle meant there was no chance she would hit them.

It did not take them long to realise and within a few moments there were a dozen rifles pointing straight at her through the glass.

10

Harry glanced once more at the steam pressure. It was nearly enough. She felt the urge to just fight. Those times when the *Pegasus* became an extension of herself were when she felt powerful. But if she did that now, she might not have the steam to rescue Mrs Hemingway.

She needed to delay them until the pressure was up. Two minutes would be sufficient.

She raised her hands so that they did not shoot. She wasn't sure the glass could take multiple rifle shots. One in the wrong place would shatter a pane; then the jig would be up.

One of the soldiers stepped forward; he was a sergeant according to his stripes. He continued to point his gun at her and then gestured with it towards the hatch.

She acted dumb.

He stopped pointing the gun and used his hands. He pointed at her and then at the hatch. He gestured for her to leave the ship. Harry scrunched up her eyes as if she was crying, buried her face in her hands swayed as if she was sobbing.

Everything she knew about men told her this would provide an excellent delay. With her face hidden she could no longer see them so their gestures were useless. But they would assume a crying female just needed to be waited out, and that she would stop eventually.

She counted each breath. When she reached fifty-three, the banging on the hatch started again followed by something metal hitting the glass in front of her. She pretended she was crying even more heavily, though she wanted to shout angrily at the person damaging her baby.

Ninety-seven. She lifted her face from her hands but kept the saddest expression she could muster on her face. The sergeant was directly in front of the ship, holding his rifle as if he were about to strike the glass with the butt.

Ninety-eight. Harry let her hands fall to the controls; she shifted forward a little in the seat as if she were intending to get up. The sergeant took a deep breath and suppressed the anger that leaked out in the form of his frown and clenched teeth. He took a step back.

Ninety-nine. Harry placed her fingers around the control sticks. She looked the sergeant in the eye and grinned. His face changed to one of alarm, and he shouted something to his men.

One hundred.

Harry engaged the propeller, pushing it to its highest gearing. It screamed into life. Harry lifted her wings, and gave a powerful stroke. The *Pegasus* shifted a little, but Harry's intention had been to scare the soldiers.

Those to the sides were knocked to the floor by the strength of the air blast while the ones in front ran for cover. The sergeant did not move but reversed his gun and took aim.

Harry could tell by the pitch of the propeller that she was ready to fly. She beat down hard with the wings once. The *Pegasus* leapt up; the sergeant became inconsequential.

She was above the tree-tops in moments. A cloud of what she thought at first was smoke but then realised was dust rose from where her home had once stood. Only the two ends remained standing and even those were crumbling.

The Zeppelin was close to Mrs Hemingway's rooms although they were still moving round the house. As she watched, the sash window of Mrs Hemingway's lounge opened and she saw Sellie lean out and look up. Harry was so relieved she almost cried out with joy.

She reduced the power to the propeller and used the wings to hop the short distance in mere seconds. Sellie waved as she approached, pointed down and then disappeared back inside.

Harry knew what Sellie was thinking but this was going to be tight; the Germans would be on them as soon as she touched down. However, it was the only way.

* * *

Mary Odette Francesca Hemingway clung to the lighting sconce in terror. The house she had lived in for the past twelve years had crumbled away, leaving her and the damned black girl high and dry.

She could see the collapsed ruin of the house along its entire length. Only the corners at the other end and, she supposed, the extension still remained standing. Except for their corner.

Where the door and the passageway had been she could see across the lawns. Her employer, Mr Edgbaston, and his guests with various of the servants were surrounded by soldiers. Her room still had a roof but tiles rained down continually.

The whole world had gone mad.

"Come on, Mrs Hemingway. Our ride is here."

She turned to look; the black had gone insane and was grinning. Mrs Hemingway hated the way the girl's white teeth were in such sharp contrast to her black skin. It gave her an almost unreal appearance.

The girl walked across to her, casually grabbing the window frame and another light fitting so she did not overbalance.

"Don't be so ignorant. Someone must bring a ladder, and no one can bring a ladder with these soldiers."

The black girl's smile faded and she regarded her. "I know that if you had a means of escape you would leave me without a second thought," said the girl. "But I do not have that luxury."

"Of course not, I am your superior."

The black girl caught her by her wrist. "That being the case," she said, "allow me to assist you to the window."

"Is there a ladder?"

"Oh yes, there's a ladder."

Mrs Hemingway allowed herself to be led to the window. She leaned on the girl who was quite inordinately strong. No proper woman would be like that.

They reached the window. "After you," said the girl.

Mrs Hemingway looked out to see there was no ladder. The traitorous girl had lied! She turned to give her a good dressing down. Before she had a chance, the girl pressed her hand against Mrs Hemingway's stomach and shoved her out of the window.

11

Harry watched Mrs Hemingway fall backwards from the window and float slowly down—tumbling over and over like Alice down the rabbit hole—under the influence of the *Pegasus*'s Faraday field. Sellie did a hand-stand on the windowsill and pushed off with her legs from the window frame. She rocketed down, shooting past the gently rotating Mrs Hemingway.

Sellie twisted in midair, but misjudged her trajectory. Her dress billowed up and she landed on her behind with her skirts draped across the cockpit window, blocking out the sunlight.

"Elegant landing, Sellie," said Harry as she jumped to the hatch and unlocked it. She heard Mrs Hemingway's whimpering cry as she came in to a landing on the top of the fuselage. Harry grabbed Mrs Hemingway's legs when they appeared over the edge and managed to pull her inside as she fell off the roof. It wasn't elegant.

Harry saw soldiers approaching round the remains of the house and jumped back into the pilot's chair. She heard Khuwelsa land on the deck, followed quickly by the slamming and locking of the hatch.

"We need steam, Sellie."

"Aye, aye, skipper."

Harry felt the strain go out of her. She almost laughed out loud as she used her wings to walk the *Pegasus* backwards away from the wall. A couple of bullets hit the fuselage. She powered up the propeller and turned the *Pegasus*'s back to the oncoming soldiers. In the rear-facing mirror she watched the glass shards lift in the airflow, stream away in a cloud and pepper the soldiers. They retreated in disorder.

With two powerful wing beats they were airborne. The devastation of her home flashed past at increasing speed. She would mourn later. Right now she had a score to settle.

By the time the *Pegasus* had reached the far end of the building she had accelerated to the speed that no longer required the wings for lift. Harry glanced in the mirror.

The Zeppelin was putting down an anchor. It was not coming after her, nor were its guns firing. She growled and glanced at the steam pressure. It was climbing; Sellie was on her post.

Harry gave one long and two short whistles, and paused for a moment before snapping the wings into braking position and bringing the nose up. The *Pegasus* stalled and flipped over on one wing. There was a scream from behind her.

Mrs Hemingway. Drat the woman, she did not know their whistle codes. Well, it was too late to worry now.

The propeller was still at full power and, as they dived, they picked up speed, but now facing in the other direction and heading back towards the Zeppelin.

Mrs Hemingway whimpered as the ground came at them very fast. Harry pulled back gently and skimmed the grass.

She throttled back and pulled the nose up a second time. She back-winged hard, bringing them up to a position above the Zeppelin ready to rain molten tar on its envelope and send it crashing to the ground.

The *Pegasus* might not be able to hover but with the propeller cranked to full thrust, the wings beating, and the nose up, she could get the velocity down to a few miles per hour. She worked the wings hard, driving them with her anger.

"Stop!" shrieked Mrs Hemingway. "You can't."

Harry was not listening. *Two short whistles.* When Harry did it, it was a question: *Weapon ready?*

Four short from Sellie. *Prepare for landing.*

"What?" shouted Harry. "Get the tar ready, Sellie! We'll take it down."

"No, Harry."

Harry was getting out of position. "Sellie! Now!"

"No, Harry," said Sellie beside her. "They've got Dad."

Harry let the nose drop and curved away to the right. The *Pegasus* accelerated under the propeller's thrust but Harry reduced the power and they glided smoothly round in a tight arc. "We had them Sellie, we could have taken them. It's only one!"

"Stop it, Harry," said Sellie.

As the ship came around they could see the German soldiers with their guns raised, surrounding the military guests and Jonathan Edgbaston in the middle of them.

"You must land and give yourself up," said Mrs Hemingway. "Your behaviour has provoked an international incident. To do anything else could incite war and, Lord knows, we do not want that. Do we?"

Harry felt numb. Her anger was like the core of a banked furnace. Raging with heat but unable to flame. Without even thinking about it she brought the *Pegasus* down to a gentle landing on the lawn a hundred yards from the group.

"Good," said Mrs Hemingway. "I'm glad to see you have at least some sense. Even if it requires putting your father at risk to show it."

"Shut up."

"I beg your pardon, young lady?"

"As you have so often pointed out, Mrs Hemingway, I am very far from being a lady, and I am telling you to shut up."

"Really!" But if she intended to say anything further the words did not come.

Harry watched the unfolding scene. A young officer—she did not recognise his insignia—flanked by two guards and using a walking stick limped across the grass towards them. Her father was separated from the herd and brought forward as well but kept a little further back.

The officer stopped about ten yards from the *Pegasus* out of the line of fire of her machine gun. He made a slicing move across his neck. He wanted her to cut the power to the propeller.

Harry did not move.

"What are you doing, Harry?" asked her sister quietly.

The officer waited a short time before making the signal again, more vehemently.

Harry still did nothing.

"Miss Edgbaston, I strongly suggest you follow his instructions."

"And I strongly suggest you shut up, as previously mentioned. This is my ship, I am in charge." Harry did not turn around but kept her eyes fixed on the German officer.

The man took a few steps back and pointed at her father, who was dragged forward and pushed to his knees.

"Bastards," said Sellie in Harry's ear.

"Quite," said Harry. "I've had as much of this as I'm going to stand for."

She pushed the propeller to full power.

"We're leaving."

Either the shock of Harry's action was too much for both Khuwelsa and Mrs Hemingway, rendering them speechless, or their voices were drowned out by the sudden roar.

Harry stroked the wings and the *Pegasus* lifted. The soldiers ducked as she rocketed over them. They had barely enough space to gain sufficient altitude. Harry steered for the collapsed house and flew between the parts that remained standing then shot away across the grass.

"What have you done, Harry?" Sellie's voice cracked with tears.

"Well, you've certainly shown your true colours, Harriet Edgbaston, just like your mother."

Harry's anger rose up hotter than before. She gritted her teeth. She wished that she could force the *Pegasus* to fly faster but she had reached maximum speed. She did not bother gaining more height but assuaged her anger by flying low. Dangerously low, barely clearing the tops of the trees.

"Harry, we have to go back," said Sellie.

"No. Isn't it obvious?" said Harry. "You're the clever one. Can't you see?"

"See what?"

"They only had power over us when we could see him!" she said. "They didn't want Dad, they wanted us. They wanted the *Pegasus.* They want to humiliate us, take away our power. They want to make sure we know that the German military is better than we are. But they can only do that if we're there."

Sellie was quiet for a minute. "That's genius."

"It's bloody obvious."

"Miss Edgbaston, mind your language."

"Shut up, really, or I will gag you."

12

In the wardroom of the *Graf von Moltke*, its captain, Odhert Reichler, relaxed back into his chair. Across the table from him, *Hauptman* Liman Gerhardt fidgeted, repeatedly tapping the end of his cane on the deck. It was quite irritating.

Reichler placed his cigar between his lips and drew on it. He held the perfumed smoke in his mouth for a moment before blowing it out. There had been a time when naked flames were not permitted on airships. Those were the days before the Empire's trade agreement with the United States for their helium gas.

While the Americans were keen to keep a distance between themselves and the affairs of Europe he was not sure how they would react to a country declaring war. *Hauptman* Gerhardt did not seem to appreciate the seriousness of the situation but then he was a commoner. Though what he lacked in vision he more than made up for in drive.

"So, *Hauptman*, what are you going to do now?"

"We must chase them."

Reichler did not laugh. "That is impossible. Even if we had been ready we cannot keep pace with such a vessel and we have undertaken this mission without a fighter escort. Against my advice, I might add."

"What would you suggest?"

This time he did laugh. "Oh no, *Hauptman* Gerhardt," he said. "This is not my circus, even if we have been made into monkeys by a pair of young girls.

"No, I will not make your decisions for you. I will not provide you with an opportunity to lay any blame at my door."

He puffed the cigar and then pointed the bright embers in the Gerhardt's direction. "You are the ringmaster, it is you who will be thrown to the lions."

Gerhardt frowned. "What do you mean?"

Captain Reichler stood up, he was stiff. Perhaps he had been under the influence of the *reduzierter Schwerkraft*, what the English referred to as the Faraday effect, too long. "You and any of your men remaining on board will leave my ship immediately."

Gerhardt jumped to his feet. "What? You can't do that, you have orders!"

In a casual move Reichler pulled a pistol from his pocket: another device that would not have been permitted in the old days. He pointed it at Gerhardt.

"You, and your men, will get off my ship. I will not be part of any action that starts a war with Britain."

"It's too late for that," said Gerhardt, staring down the gun barrel. "We did not know the British were going to be here in such numbers."

"You have made the bed," said Reichler. "But I am not going to lie in it. It has your name carved into the headboard." He gestured with the gun. "Now, do I need to make myself any clearer on this matter?"

"But you cannot leave us here. We are in the heart of the British Protectorate."

"You should have thought of that before you followed such an ill-conceived plan," said Reichler. "And who was the officer in charge who signed those orders? I was unable to make out the signature. Was he drunk?"

Gerhardt did not take the bait. "You are condemning me, and my men, to death."

"Oh, I don't think the British will be upset enough to execute you," said Reichler with a smile. "This is, after all, a gentleman's game and it wouldn't be, what is it they say? *Cricket.* I have no doubt you will have your weapons confiscated, your knuckle's rapped, and an entirely justified fuss will be made of your stupidity. Then you will be returned to Germany in disgrace never to be heard from again."

"I don't mean the British," hissed Gerhardt. "I mean those girls."

"Ah yes, his daughters. They are a different kettle of fish," said Reichler. "After what you have done to their home and the way you treated their father, you must hope they don't catch up with you."

He lifted his gun once more. "By now my men will have rounded up the rest of your squad. It is time for you to leave."

On the ground, Reichler did not interfere with Gerhardt's men guarding the British, but he went to speak with Edgbaston.

He offered his hand but was not surprised when the man chose not to shake it.

Reichler looked up the lawn at the ruined house. A slight haze of dust hung in the air above it; there was a steady stream of smoke from a chimney of the servants' block that still stood on the far side.

"I am sorry about your house," he said to Edgbaston in English. "I assure you that we had no intention causing such damage."

"I'm sure if it had been of *German* construction it would have remained standing," said Edgbaston.

"I think you are making fun of me," said Reichler as he turned to face Edgbaston fully. "I find myself in an awkward position."

"You expect my sympathy?"

"I am explaining so that you better understand yours."

Edgbaston said nothing.

"I was not happy with the orders," Reichler continued. "However, your daughters have destroyed a considerable amount of German equipment and killed some of our men."

"You attempted to start a war."

"That was not my decision."

"You cannot escape responsibility by claiming you were following orders."

"Nor am I, Mr Edgbaston," he said. "That is why I am abandoning *Hauptman* Gerhardt and his men. My orders were to assist him in carrying out his disciplinary action on your daughters."

"The German military wishes to *discipline* my daughters."

"Mr Edgbaston, they are running amok."

The Englishman paused and looked down before he replied. "I have always encouraged my daughters to behave in the most decent and honest fashion, and to strive for the greater good. And, while you may disagree with their judgement, that is precisely what they have done."

"Be that as it may, Mr Edgbaston, I have assisted *Hauptman* Gerhardt to the best of my ability but now I find that there is nothing further I can do. Therefore I am returning to my base."

Edgbaston looked him in the eye. "But you're leaving that man here?"

"Yes."

"He will kill us."

"No, I do not think so," said Reichler. "He is already afraid of your girls. I do not think he is going to antagonise them further."

"Afraid of them?"

Reichler nodded. "Yes, I believe that is the case. Apparently he has encountered them before."

"What is he going to do?"

Reichler put his cap on and adjusted it. "That I cannot say, Mr Edgbaston. Nor do I wish to know. But you may rest assured I will be making a full report on my return and it will not be in *Hauptman* Gerhardt's favour."

"Well, I find that very reassuring, I'm sure," said Edgbaston.

"Good."

Reichler saluted, turned on his heel, and headed back to his ship.

13

The *Pegasus* tore through the air as if all the demons of hell were in pursuit. Harry had the wings pulled in as tight as she could while still maintaining sufficient lift to keep them airborne. Her anger still boiled inside.

The northern slopes, ridges, and peaks of the Usambara Mountains grew visibly as they ripped across the sky.

"*Graf von Moltke*," she muttered.

"What?" said her sister. Sellie stood beside but a little behind her, leaning on the bar that now separated the main cabin area from the pilot's chair.

"That Zeppelin," said Harry. "It was the *Graf von Moltke*."

"Oh." She glanced at the compass just to confirm what she thought: they were heading south by south-east. "Thinking of visiting Johannes?"

"Yes."

"I believe we've covered this point before," said Sellie. "And not that long ago. The Germans don't like us."

"I don't care."

"What was your plan? It better not include me stripping off again."

"There's no time to waste, we'll go straight in."

"Harry," said Sellie. "On a scale of one to ten, where ten is a good idea and one is a bad idea, that rates minus several thousand."

A bank of clouds hung over the peaks further into the mountains. Harry adjusted the wings and the *Pegasus* climbed.

"What would you suggest?"

Mrs Hemingway's voice cut across them. "If you give yourselves up to the Germans they will free your father."

"Why is she still on board?" Harry said.

"Who am I? The cat's mother? You will kindly mind your manners, Miss Edgbaston."

"And you will leave my sister alone," shouted Sellie with a level of anger that shocked even Harry.

"How do dare you? You little upstart. You cuckoo in the nest!"

"How dare I?" said Sellie. "This is your fault."

"My fault? How could this *possibly* be my fault?" Mrs Hemingway's tone was acidic but Harry recognised a slight waver in it.

Harry reduced power to the propeller and spread the wings into their full gliding arch. After locking them off, she turned in her chair. Sellie and Mrs Hemingway were facing off across the cabin. Sellie was much shorter, but in a physical contest there was no question which of them would come out on top.

"What's this about, Sellie?" Harry asked in a normal tone, in an attempt to defuse a situation that she did not understand.

"She's got a letter on her, why don't you ask her who it's addressed to?"

Harry frowned and looked at Mrs Hemingway. "Have you got a letter?"

"I don't think that's any of your business."

"That's a yes," said Harry. "If you had no letter you would just have said no."

Mrs Hemingway stared back with her lips pursed.

"I'll get it for you," said Sellie.

Harry put her hand on her sister's arm. "Who's the letter addressed to?" she said.

"It's private."

"I'm not asking what's in the letter. I just want to know who it's addressed to."

"It is my business and I choose not to tell you."

"It's to the *Manchester Guardian* newspaper. I saw it when she tried to hide it," said Sellie. "A man by the name of Ernest Tyndale."

Harry held out her hand for Mrs Hemingway to relinquish the letter. She showed no sign of intending to do so. Sellie adjusted her stance.

"You know, Mrs Hemingway," said Harry. "My sister would find great satisfaction in coming over there and relieving you of this letter. And I somehow doubt you would have the strength to resist her. Do you?"

Mrs Hemingway glowered at them both but reached inside her bodice and retrieved several sheets of writing paper. She moved forward with the uncertainness of someone unaccustomed to the Faraday effect. Angrily she slammed the sheets into Harry's hand.

Sellie was correct about the addressee. Harry skimmed the first paragraph, which was mainly platitudes but contained an exhortation not to reveal the source of the information. At the mention of the *agreed remuneration* Harry's blood began pumping hot again.

The following paragraphs contained a distorted and inventive account of their expedition to Lake Victoria. Except Sellie was nowhere in the narrative. Harry could not quite decide what made her most angry, the woman's betrayal of her father's trust, or the shameless omission of Khuwelsa from the story.

Turning away, Harry sat back the chair. She folded the sheets and tucked them into her dress. She took in the state of the ship's gauges at a glance; she could feel they were still climbing. They were at the same altitude as the cloud bank now. In the midday sunshine the mountains beneath the clouds were hidden in shadow.

"Why?" Harry said. She did not turn but her voice was clear and loud.

"I am not required to justify my actions to you," said Mrs Hemingway. "You are my charges, not my employer."

Harry spun around. If the barrier had not been there she was not sure she would not have reached across to the woman and slapped her across the face. "Why would you do this to my father?"

"Someone had to rein in your excesses," said Mrs Hemingway. "You and she are out of control, you have no discipline. I don't blame your father, of course; you have not had a proper woman's hand to show you how to behave."

Harry turned back to the view from the window. True, they had only had Mrs Hemingway as a female exemplar for the past few years. It had only convinced her that she had no desire to become a proper Englishwoman. Had she inherited her lack of discipline from her mother? Was it in her blood?

A dark dot against the hard blue of the sky caught Harry's eye. It left a dark trail in the sky. She glanced at the steam pressure. It was high.

"We've got company, Sellie."

Harry climbed back into her chair and watched the dot. They were not on a course that would directly intercept the *Pegasus* but that would change as soon as they saw her.

The question was whether this was a British or German plane; at this distance it was impossible to tell. The Usambara Mountains marked the uncertain border between the two protectorates with the British to the north and the Germans the south.

One of the reasons the kaiser had wanted to acquire Zanzibar, apart from the supplies and trade, was that it stood off from the shore of their part of Africa. It was inconvenient having a British stronghold controlling the routes across the Indian Ocean. That

Harry and Sellie had put a stop to his plans was one of the reasons they were so disliked.

Plus the fact that Mrs Hemingway had been plastering their adventures all over the British newspapers. How in the world had the woman come to the conclusion that making their actions public would stop them? Harry could ask her, but the answer would be ridiculous, something about being so embarrassed she would stop flying her plane. Or perhaps this visit from the admiral was the outcome she had desired.

Harry squinted at the dot, which was now more of a smudge against the blue. It appeared to have stopped moving, which could only mean it was heading towards or away from them. And it wasn't getting any smaller.

14

Harry whistled once long, once short. She heard Sellie telling Mrs Hemingway she would be better off sitting down.

"Why?"

"Because Harry's probably going to do something crazy and if you're not sitting in a chair you get hurt."

"What sort of thing?"

"Honestly," said Sellie. "I have no idea. She hardly ever does the same thing twice."

"Isn't that dangerous?"

There was a long pause. Harry could imagine her sister looking at Mrs Hemingway with a bemused expression wondering quite how to respond. But finally she said, in a balanced and even tone. "Oh yes. It's almost always dangerous."

Harry unlocked the wings and the ship rocked slightly as she took control. They were still a couple of miles from the cloud bank. If they had been over the plains she would have had no hesitation in plunging in. But here the clouds cloaked the tops of mountains, and rock was not known for its forgiving nature.

There was still the question of the plane's origin. The German military was not the only force that employed fixed-wing fighters and other craft of that nature; the Royal Navy had them too. The big British ships that lifted using adjustable rotors—they had never adopted the lift-bags of the Zeppelins—were impressive but they did not have the speed of the small ships.

The other vessel was getting close and their relative speeds meant they would pass one another in the next minute. The other pilot probably wanted to know who she was as well. Perhaps if she just kept flying straight he would look and then move on.

He flashed past and Harry saw the German cross emblazoned across the fuselage and wings. That settled that. She sighed. She had no desire to fight this fellow; she just wanted to talk to Johannes and find out what was really going on.

Then she was struck by a crazy idea. There were no whistles that could communicate it.

"Sellie!" she shouted.

Her sister was by her side in a moment, scanning the gauges to see what the problem was.

"We need to run out a white flag. And a sign saying 'Escort us to Dodoma'."

"This is going to involve my clothes, isn't it?"

"Did you bring any large pieces of white card?"

"I seem to have forgotten the white card this trip," Sellie said. "Why can't we use your petticoat?"

Harry raised her eyebrows as if surprised by the question. "I'm flying the plane."

"Oh yes, silly of me for forgetting."

Harry smiled. "You could ask Mrs Hemingway."

"Never mind."

"And be quick."

"Of course." Sellie ducked back into the main part of the cabin.

The other ship was nowhere in sight. Harry reduced power to the propeller to come down to a slow cruising speed and once more locked off the wings. She hoped she looked as if she was flying in a casual manner. Not threatening.

She took her hands off the controls and sat back. She forced herself to relax but jumped when the German plane flashed over them from stern to prow. She watched as he turned to port and flew round them in a great arc. If she was him she would be reducing power in order to come alongside.

She hoped he would do that instead of shooting her out of the sky. Right now they were a sitting duck.

* * *

Senior Pilot Hans Schmidt expected the British ship to react but it did not. It maintained its course directly into the territory of the German Protectorate. He recognised the vessel. It was notorious but he knew it from the very beginning.

Those girls had killed one of their top pilots—though he was a thoroughly unpleasant fellow and his loss had not been mourned—in a one-on-one battle, and they were not even armed. He corrected himself. The ship *had not been* armed then, but he could see the end of a large-calibre machine gun protruding from the front of the fuselage.

They had brought down the four Zeppelins of the Zanzibar task force using Greek fire. That was what the men were calling it, though it had been analysed and was just hot tar and metal fragments. Steps were being taken to protect the Zeppelins from any future attacks of that nature. From the information they had gleaned, the *Schwarze* was the clever one, but the redhead was an astonishing pilot. If they had a dozen like her they would be invincible.

Schmidt himself had been reprimanded for not attacking them when he had the opportunity. It had gone on his record and it probably meant he would never be promoted. He did not mind; he knew he had done the right thing.

The border patrols were something new. They did not have sufficient planes to patrol properly, which was why he was on his own. There were rumours the girls had been involved in something that had happened at Lake Victoria, but no one talked about that. At least not openly. Still, orders had come down from on high to patrol the border.

It was not known what had occurred but the rumours said there had been another Zeppelin downed. They described the ornithopter like a living creature tearing a camp to pieces, and even calling down lightning to destroy a ship the size of a town—though what ship that might have been, no one said. The girls were a legend—or a nightmare.

And here they were once more, in his power again. If he shot them down now, no doubt his promotion prospects would be restored. But he had daughters back home in Düsseldorf. He knew how he would feel if anything happened to Hannah or Greta. He wondered what these girls' names were. Perhaps he might get the opportunity to meet them.

No, he would not shoot them down in cold blood, and it was clear they did not intend to fight.

He throttled back and came alongside. He glanced along his long, wide wing at the cockpit windows; there was something obscuring his view inside. A white sheet with markings on it. He laughed out loud as he deciphered the badly written, but correctly spelt, German.

He opened up the power, pulled ahead then slid directly in front of them. He pushed his control stick left then right and the wings waggled. A glance at the compass showed their heading was correct so he accelerated again. A glance in his mirror showed the ornithopter keeping up. Knowing how fast the little plane could go would be a valuable piece of information, he thought, so he gradually increased his velocity.

The ornithopter did not fall behind although, if he was not mistaken, the shape of the wings had been changed: they were now more swept back. He shook his head. *Who in their right mind would build a plane that moved like a bird?* But then again, birds were the masters of the air, so why would you not?

He reached his plane's maximum speed and the ornithopter was still behind him.

He smiled. It was a thing to be admired.

15

Harry smiled. She knew the pilot of the German plane was testing her, and the *Pegasus* had come through with flying colours. However, they had reached maximum speed for level flight.

At this height, despite their speed, the Usambaras seemed to crawl away beneath them—but it was an illusion. They crossed into the German Protectorate proper within twenty minutes. There was now no question whose territory they were in.

They had no food on board since they had not prepared for this flight, but she had eaten well enough at the luncheon. It was another two hours to Dodoma.

"How do you see this working?" asked Sellie.

"What do you mean?"

"They'll want to arrest us and do whatever it was that Zeppelin wanted to do."

"Johannes will help."

"What if he's not there?"

"We'll cross that bridge when we come to it."

Sellie climbed under the bar and stood next to her. Harry could see the concern in her face. "It'll be all right, Sellie."

"I'm worried about Dad."

"Me too."

The speed they were flying at meant that Harry couldn't let go of the controls even though all she wanted to do was give her sister a hug.

"I want to know if this is official or just revenge by someone we've hurt," said Harry.

"Given the number of people you've killed it wouldn't surprise me if they were after your blood."

Harry had almost forgotten that Mrs Hemingway was still aboard.

"In case you have forgotten, madam," said Harry. "You too would have been a casualty of this incident if we had not rescued you."

"In fact," added Sellie. "If I hadn't ignored your instruction, you would have joined your writing desk under the rubble. Dead as a doornail and no one to mourn you."

There was no response. Harry wondered if that last comment was a bit too much but she was not about to criticise her sister in front of Mrs Hemingway. If nothing else, she deserved it.

Sellie sat on the ledge beside the pilot's chair and stared out at the terrain as it rolled away beneath them.

The German plane angled into a slow descent; Harry powered back slightly and followed. She spread the wings a little to provide braking against the pull of gravity.

The river came into view, a bright ribbon against the greens and golds of the savannah. Dodoma was a stop on the trade route from the interior lakes through to the coast. Before the Europeans arrived it had been a major town used by the Arabs with slaves, ivory and trade goods.

Now it was occupied by the kaiser's hounds.

Like the British to the north, the Germans had not taken over the country and did not rule it. But, like the rest of East Africa, there were no nations to take over; they were all simply tribal areas criss-crossed with caravan routes.

Instead of ruling, the empires simply "protected" the lands and their peoples. The end result was the same, though. The British owned a strip of Africa running from Egypt in the north to the southern tip. The Germans controlled a band across Africa from the west to the east.

The German Protectorate was where the two areas crossed. Her Majesty's government wanted to control this land, and the kaiser prevented it. If ever there was a place waiting for a war to happen, this was it.

Harry understood this now. Their father had given Harry and Sellie a long lecture as to why they could not interfere with the Germans when the risk of war was so close. He had not had a great deal to say when Sellie had pointed out that it was the German's who had tried to force the point at Zanzibar and the ship they had destroyed on the Lake Victoria island was clearly not a pleasure cruiser.

And that was why she had difficulty understanding what had happened today.

Receiving a deputation from the government in order that she and Sellie be "told off" made sense. They did not appreciate the war-mongering of the press along with the adulation of a mere girl making war on the Germans when the government did nothing. Fair enough.

But why the German force? Why would they risk an armed incursion into the home of a British diplomat? Granted they had not intended to demolish the house; it had only been one bomb and had been aimed at the conservatory. If they had struck only a few feet further away, the house would probably have remained standing.

That still did not explain why they were there. Politically it did not make sense. Neither nation wanted to be seen as the one who started the war. Besides, the kaiser was a blood relation of the queen.

This was why she was so certain that the attack had not been official, and why she felt justified in coming to Dodoma.

The town grew rapidly ahead of them and their escort turned to the south to land at the military air-dock. Harry did not have time to mess about; she needed to speak to Johannes as soon as possible. She did not follow the other plane but continued directly towards the town. She could see the utilitarian building that comprised the German administration. It had a forecourt she knew she could get in and out of.

"Harry, they've got artillery."

Sellie was right. At frequent and regular intervals around the town there were emplacements featuring large-calibre weapons. Just one shell would rip the *Pegasus* to pieces.

"Can't be helped," she said. "Can you see where our escort went?"

Sellie climbed back into the main cabin. "Can't see him in the direction of the air-dock—he's probably coming around to see what you're up to."

* * *

Hans Schmidt had not been entirely surprised when the ornithopter failed to follow him. Rather than land, he continued his turn until the girls were in view.

Sure enough they were heading into the town but they had not accelerated; in fact they were slowing still. He opened up his engine and his plane shot towards them. His diesel engine was considerably more responsive than their steam contraption, and he did not require a stoker. He tilted the plane into a sharp turn that lost him altitude. The pilot of the other plane did not know the artillery were under orders to shoot down any unidentified air-plane.

He was certain the girls did not intend to attack but there was no way the gunners could know that. So he poured on the power as the girls entered the artillery attack field.

A cloud of smoke plumed from a gun on the ground. He stared at the ornithopter and sighed in relief when it did not explode. Travelling fast it took him only moments to reach them. He powered back so as not to overshoot and positioned himself behind them but above and slightly to their starboard.

No other guns fired.

The ornithopter continued to slow over the town until it was below his stall speed and he overshot it. Pulling round he saw it disappearing into the forecourt of the administration building, wings stroking hard as it did so. He smiled. That was one thing he could not do, and it was a beautiful thing to witness.

16

Harry stood just inside the still-closed hatch and adjusted her dress to make herself as decent as possible. The way it draped hid the split she had made up the side but there were smudges of dirt in various locations that could not be disguised.

"I'll stay here," said Sellie, "and keep the steam up. I'll make sure that panel underneath is firmly fixed."

"Don't take any unnecessary risks," said Harry. "If it looks dangerous outside, stay inside."

"I'm not reckless like you," Sellie said with a smile.

Harry turned to Mrs Hemingway, who was so tall that she had to stoop slightly to prevent her hair brushing the ceiling. Her eyes looked red, as if she had been crying. "Would you accompany me, Mrs Hemingway?"

The woman looked up in surprise and then frowned. "Why would you want me with you?"

"A couple of reasons," said Harry. "The main one being that I don't think I can leave you and my sister alone together."

Mrs Hemingway sniffed. "And the other?"

"In this situation, I believe a mature woman would be an asset. You will be able to confirm the events."

"I will not lie to help you."

Harry put her head on one side. "No, I'm sure you won't. You only lie to help yourself."

Mrs Hemingway did not make any sharp retort but brought a kerchief to her eyes. "You people have no idea what it's like for those like me," she said. "We may enjoy your lifestyle for a while but when we are no longer needed we are cast out without a thought. I am only concerned with my future."

Harry thought perhaps she ought to feel sorry for her but she did not. "To be concerned with one's future may be admirable but to be so unconcerned with anyone else's is despicable."

Sellie handed Harry a metal rod with a square piece of her petticoat tied to it as a white flag. "You be careful," she said, and then in a quieter voice added, "Don't trust her."

Harry shook her head. "I don't."

She drew the bolts on the hatch and pushed it open, then gave the steps a kick so they folded out and down. Feeling a little foolish she held up the flag and stepped down on to the ground.

There were twenty or so infantry men in the forecourt. The *Pegasus* was surrounded on three sides by the four storeys of the utilitarian administrative building. The fourth side was the fence and main gate. Glancing around Harry could see the scrapes and grooves in the walls that had not been erased by the repairs: the marks of the *Pegasus*'s escape only a few months before.

Some of the men standing here might well have been ones she had injured as the *Pegasus* fought for her freedom. On an individual basis she felt the guilt since she had no grudge against any person here. But she and her sister had been imprisoned. They were simply taking the opportunity to escape.

She heard Mrs Hemingway descending the steps behind her.

There was a movement in the ranks and the familiar face of *Feldwebel-Leutnant* Johannes Schönfeldt emerged. Harry smiled. Johannes did not.

"Put down that ridiculous flag, Harriet," he said in English with his clipped German accent. He never called her Harry.

"I don't want to be arrested again," she said. "I need to talk to you and then I need to leave."

"Why do you always make things difficult?"

"You mean you'd rather I just handed myself in?"

"That would be easier."

Harry frowned. "This is not a joke, Lieutenant. I am here on a serious matter."

He studied her face for a moment and then stood up straighter.

"Very well, Miss Edgbaston, we will take the flag as read, shall we?" he said. "It is quite clearly somebody's undergarments and I would prefer they were not placed on show in this manner."

Harry tossed the rod and flag back through the hatch.

"My engineer would like to carry out some maintenance unmolested."

"You can tell Khuwelsa that no one will interfere with anything she wants to do as long as she stays close to the plane."

"Thank you!" shouted Sellie from inside.

"Now," said Johannes. "You have not introduced your guest."

"Mrs Hemingway is our tutor."

Johannes was unable to suppress the look of surprise which he directed at Harry. She had not been quiet about the unpleasant nature of the woman who taught them. Not a governess—she did not have that level of power—but a teacher who lived with them.

Harry gave the slightest of shrugs.

"If you will accompany me," said the lieutenant. He turned almost as if he were marching and headed through the ranks of men. Harry followed, showing rather more confidence than she was feeling. She wondered what on earth Mrs Hemingway would make of all this.

Johannes had got his old office back. He was no longer relegated to the cellar but returned to the second floor looking out over the nearby native buildings to the grasslands in the south.

He brought two chairs to the desk and assisted Mrs Hemingway into one while Harry sat in the other.

"Now," he said, sitting upright in his chair on the other side of the desk. "What is this about?"

"The *Graf von Moltke*," said Harry.

Johannes's face fell. "You haven't shot it down?"

Harry gave him an accusing look. "Why would you assume that?"

He raised his eyebrows.

"Yes, all right. But I *have* encountered Zeppelins that I haven't shot down, you know."

"Not recently."

"Look, Johannes, this is serious." She took a deep breath. "Did it come from here?"

"Captain Reichler flew out of here a couple of days ago."

"Is he a young man with a limp and walking stick?"

"No, that would be *Hauptman* Gerhardt."

"Well, your Captain Reichler and *Hauptman* Gerhardt came to our house, demolished it and have kidnapped my father."

"Impossible."

Harry sat back and crossed her legs. The slit in the dress opened up, revealing her leg to her thigh. She hurriedly covered herself but not before Johannes had seen. "Ask Mrs Hemingway."

Johannes looked at her. "Is this correct, *Frau* Hemingway?"

Mrs Hemingway glanced at Harry. "Miss Edgbaston's description of events, while abbreviated, is essentially accurate. It should also be pointed out that they have taken several senior British officers and bureaucrats prisoner as well."

Johannes sat back, nonplussed. "I was not aware of their precise orders."

"You knew they were coming after Sellie and me?" said Harry, the suppressed anger bursting out again.

"No," he said. "I knew Gerhardt had a mission over the border. I did not know it had anything to do with you and I find it hard to believe he would kidnap anyone."

Harry's eyes narrowed. "You're saying that with your mouth, but that's not what's in your heart."

"Gerhardt was in Zanzibar."

Realisation came to Harry. "The one who nearly managed to stop me in the sultan's palace."

Johannes nodded.

"I thought he seemed vaguely familiar," said Harry. "I couldn't place him. So this is personal."

"His orders were valid," said Johannes. Harry's glare made him continue. "However, it would seem this is a personal vendetta rather than a military or political operation."

"That's all I need to know," said Harry and got to her feet.

Johannes stood out of politeness. Mrs Hemingway looked as if she would rather not move.

Harry gave him a smile. "Would you do something for me, Johannes?"

"Something *else*?" he said. "I will not betray my country."

Harry effected an expression of sadness. "Feeding us would be a betrayal?"

"Feeding you?"

Harry shook her head for emphasis. "I'm starving, Sellie hasn't eaten since breakfast, and there's not a single jot of food on the plane."

17

"Try not to destroy another Zeppelin, Harriet," said Johannes. "They are very expensive."

Harry turned in the pilot's chair and looked at him seriously. "This isn't a joke, Johannes. Have you killed as many men as I have?"

He shook his head.

"I'm not a soldier," she said. "How well do you think I sleep, knowing what I've done?"

"I am sorry, Harriet," he said. "But I did not mean it as a joke either."

"No, well, it isn't."

"Even soldiers don't sleep well."

Harry turned back to the controls and checked the steam. It was in range for take-off. "You'd better go," she said. "You won't get in trouble, will you?"

"No more than usual," he said. He clicked his heels. The sound penetrated the noise of the steam generator and the bubbling of the pipes. He saluted, then turned and went down the steps.

Khuwelsa pulled in the steps and shut the hatch. The quality of sound in the cabin changed subtly. Harry felt her sister at her elbow.

"Perhaps you should kiss him," said Khuwelsa said quietly so that Mrs Hemingway would not hear.

"Why would I want to do that?"

"Perhaps because *you* want to do it."

"Sellie, nothing good could come of it," said Harry. "We're on opposite sides and they won't be able to hold off from making war forever."

"You should be happy."

Harry leaned back and turned her head. She put her pale-skinned hand on her sister's dark one. "I think we're doomed to become old maids together."

"Speak for yourself, white girl," said Khuwelsa with a wide grin. She gave Harry's hand a squeeze. "So what's the plan?"

"Get into as much trouble as possible."

"While trying not to break any German toys?"

"We'll see."

Harry gave two short whistles and then flipped the Faraday switch. The *Pegasus* creaked as the weight went from her structure. There was a short cry from Mrs Hemingway, though without justification since she was already seated.

After a couple of experimental wing beats, issued as a warning to anyone in the area, she ran up the power on the propeller. She did a visual check to ensure there was no one in their immediate vicinity but the guards had stepped back well out of range.

Three strokes of the wings later and they were accelerating northeast across the town. As they passed the final line of buildings she opened up full throttle but descended to a height of twenty feet. Through her reverse mirror she saw three German fighters in a diagonal in-line formation turn and follow.

She gave a grim smile, the other pilot had tested her speed, well, she would see if they could keep up with *her*. She stayed low and watched her velocity climb. As she passed a hundred miles per hour she felt the same additional lift she had over the water of Lake Victoria.

She frowned. She had never heard of anything like this. Their speed increased effortlessly this close to the ground. It was as if the *Pegasus* were sliding over ice.

The only problem here was the trees. Every now and then there would be one in their path and she would have to either hop over or steer around it. And as her velocity passed one hundred and sixty she had to focus every ounce of her concentration on the terrain streaming towards her. She had to negotiate every lump and hillock before it became a problem.

Step by step she pulled the wings in closer to her body, noticing every nuanced change in how she reacted to the air. They reached one hundred and seventy-five, and the air set up shrill whistles around the fuselage. With a flat stretch ahead she glanced into the mirror. Her escort was outdistanced and she could only see where they were by the three thin trails.

The mountains were growing fast in the north, and the storm clouds they had passed over earlier in the day were still there. Harry made a decision. With a slight touch to the controls she edged the *Pegasus* slightly more to the east.

"Where are we going?" asked Sellie. Harry almost jumped; she had been concentrating so hard she had not noticed her sister.

"The sea," said Harry. "It's flat so we can just run up the coast. If we can maintain this speed it will be quicker than going over the mountains."

"I noticed that," said Khuwelsa. "We really shouldn't be going this fast."

"I know."

"Are you all right?"

"It's tiring."

Sellie hesitated. "Slow down if you need to. I'd rather survive."

"I'm fine."

Harry calculated that at their current velocity it would probably be less than twenty minutes before they reached the sea.

But she was wrong.

They were following a road that led towards Tanga on the coast a short distance south of Mombasa when something much larger than a tree loomed out of the ground ahead.

The *Pegasus* rocketed beneath the Zeppelin so fast that Harry had no time to react. Mrs Hemingway screamed though her cry began after they had passed the other vessel. Harry dared not react suddenly. At this speed she could rip the wings off if she tried to use them for braking.

She gave them a slight up angle and Harry felt herself pushed down into her chair as they shot skywards, shedding velocity. She powered back on the throttle and turned the *Pegasus* on her wing. The Zeppelin was crawling along at barely fifty miles per hour. Not in any hurry.

Harry matched course and, conscious of what Johannes had said as well as the fact that their father might be on board, did not make any aggressive moves. Instead she brought the *Pegasus* down to fly alongside the Zeppelin. A glance at the lettering along the side told her it was the *Graf von Moltke.*

"Harry, we're sitting ducks," said Sellie. As they moved up beside the airship with its dozen artillery guns mounted along its side.

"Have you got a mirror?" said Harry.

18

Before they had a chance to use the mirror as a heliograph, the Zeppelin reversed its engines and lost altitude. Within minutes it came to rest a short distance from the road.

Harry brought the *Pegasus* down with her gun pointing directly at the airship's gondola.

"You were saying about not being aggressive?" said Sellie.

"Yes, well," said Harry. "There's non-aggressive and then there's lying on your back and inviting them to eat you for lunch. I'd like to have some negotiating power. You stay here and man the gun."

Mrs Hemingway stood up. "I should like to accompany you, Miss Edgbaston."

Harry looked at her. She had been much quieter since their visit to Johannes. In fact, she had said nothing at all apart from the occasional squeak of fear.

"Why?"

"Perhaps if I were to accept that this is all my fault?"

Harry took a moment to absorb what she had said. "That's very … noble of you, madam," said Harry. "But not this time."

Mrs Hemingway shifted her feet as if she were restraining herself. "Do you think I am lying?"

"No, it's not that. This is a different situation. I might have to run and you would be too slow, and besides, this really isn't your fault. If there's any fault here it's the British and German governments fighting over Zanzibar." Mrs Hemingway looked somewhat relieved until Harry continued. "You just made it a lot worse."

Well, thought Harry, *why should I excuse her despicable behaviour?*

"I'd tell you to be careful," said Sellie. "But I think we're far beyond that point."

Harry shrugged. "Still got that flag?"

Sellie produced it from behind a set of tools. It was streaked with coal dust. Harry tried to clean it but only succeeded in smudging the dirt. "It'll do."

She opened the hatch, pushed out the steps, and climbed down, poking the white flag out in front of her once more. No weapons were fired in her direction so she stepped away from the *Pegasus* and moved towards the Zeppelin.

From the ground, without her ship around her, it was huge. The great sheath that surrounded the individual internal balloons billowed in the breeze. The rotors were still turning, but with the majority of its Faraday grid turned off it sat firmly on the ground.

The three decks of the massive gondola stretched above her. From all the windows and portholes, men stared out at her. She crossed a third of the distance to the Zeppelin and stopped. There, she planted the flag in the ground beside her and waited.

Behind her she could hear the huffing of the steam generator inside the *Pegasus* while the engines of the Zeppelin were a constant beat in the background. It was like some sort of industrial music. The sun was pounding down but she had her scarf over her hair. She still wore the same dress, as dirty as the white flag, and the light breeze floated through the gap she had cut.

It must have been ten minutes before a door in the lowest level of the gondola opened. A crewman jumped down and took folding steps from someone inside. He then placed them against the hull and stepped back, standing to attention.

From the uniforms she knew it was the captain with two of his lieutenants who descended the steps and made their way across the long grass until they were standing a similar distance from their ship as she was from hers.

The captain alone continued until he was about halfway. Harry left the flag and walked up to him.

"Miss Harriet Edgbaston," he said in English, and bowed.

"Captain Reichler, I presume," she said.

His eyes narrowed. "You know who I am?"

"Yes, Captain," she said. "I understand you have been conveying *Hauptman* Gerhardt on his mission to teach my sister and I a lesson of some sort."

"You are remarkably well informed," he said.

"Where is my father?"

"Shall we move somewhere more comfortable, where we may talk?"

"This location is quite satisfactory, Captain," she said. "I just want to know where my father is. Is he aboard your ship?"

He shook his head. "No, Miss Edgbaston, he is not."

"You have withdrawn then?" she asked with some relief.

"Not exactly," he said. "I left *Hauptman* Gerhardt and his men back at your home."

Harry exploded. "You did what?" Captain Reichler took a step back in surprise at her vehemence. "That man has a personal vendetta against us. This has nothing to do with any enmity between your country and mine. It's personal! And you left him alone with my father!"

Harry turned on her heel and ran back to the *Pegasus*.

"Miss Edgbaston!" called the captain. She paused at the step. "I did not know."

She threw herself into the ship and froze with her hands on the bar. Her heart pounded in her breast, and she felt the tears streaming down her cheeks.

She sobbed.

"Harry?" Khuwelsa's arm went round her shoulder. "Harry? What is it?" There was an awful tremor of fear in Sellie's voice. "Is it Dad? Is he … all right?"

Harry rubbed her nose with the back of her hand and sniffed. "No, I mean, yes. I mean, I don't know." She sniffed again. "I just don't know, Sellie. The captain left Gerhardt and his men."

"With Dad?"

Harry nodded and tried to find a kerchief. She sniffed.

"Oh God."

They were distracted by a movement outside as the *Graf von Moltke* surged into the air. With its engines roaring it turned through 180 degrees before it had gained more than a few feet. Its massive body tore a tree out of the ground as it ran straight through it.

"I can't fly, Sellie," said Harry.

"Don't be silly, of course you can."

Harry held up her hands, they were shaking. She sniffed again.

A hand holding a kerchief appeared at her cheek. Harry took it from Mrs Hemingway and blew her nose.

"I'm so tired, Sellie," she said. "I can't do this anymore. What if he's already …?"

"What are you talking about, Miss Edgbaston?" said Mrs Hemingway. "Your father is one of the most resourceful gentlemen I have met. He deals with international situations using nothing but his wits and his tongue. Do you think some upstart German will be able to get the better of him?"

Harry blew her nose again and wiped her eyes.

"Better?" said Mrs Hemingway. Harry nodded.

She clambered beneath the rail and up into the pilot's seat. The Zeppelin was making its best speed back towards the coast.

Harry tried to whistle but nothing came. Her sister gave two short whistles, reached across and flipped the Faraday switch.

Harry gunned the propeller, beat the wings, and the *Pegasus* took flight.

19

"Five hours, Harry," said Sellie in her ear. "They can't have got far in that time."

They had torn past the *Graf Van Moltke,* hugging the ground as the speed indicator climbed steadily once more. Khuwelsa estimated they would reach home in less than an hour, though they would have to slow down when they reached Mombasa.

The small seaport of Tanga flashed past as they shot out across the sea. Harry angled north, bringing the *Pegasus* around in a slow turn.

Sellie turned as Mrs Hemingway approached the front of the cabin. The tutor put her hands around the bar and clung to it, though the ship was solid without the slightest tremor beyond the normal engine vibrations.

One hundred and seventy-five miles per hour.

The waves, as seen through the lower viewing glass, were a green-blue blur. Objects further off moved more slowly. The coastline was half a mile to their port; it was possible to focus on features before they slipped behind.

"This is remarkable," said Mrs Hemingway. "That is our velocity?" She pointed at the airspeed gauge. Sellie nodded.

"As fast as an atmospheric train."

"Faster," said Sellie. "They cruise at about one hundred and fifty. And they're being pushed by pneumatic pressure, not self-powered as we are."

"I had no idea it could go so fast."

"It shouldn't," Khuwelsa said. "There seems to be some effect that takes hold when we are close to the ground. We can go faster, yet we burn less coal in the process."

"I see."

They passed a village perched on a hill rising from the sea, below which was a promontory enclosing a bay filled with mangroves.

"I think that is Msambweni," said Khuwelsa. "It's less than twenty miles to Mombasa."

In response Harry angled the *Pegasus* away from the coast. She did not speak.

"Why are we going further out?" asked Mrs Hemingway.

"We can't do any sharp turns at this speed," Sellie said. "So Harry's moving out from the coast and will bring us round in an arc when we reach the city."

Sellie did not like Mombasa. Oh, she went when Harry wanted to go, but she did not enjoy it. There were too many bad memories and Mombasa brought them back.

She had been three weeks in the slave caravan walking the roads that they flitted past in the *Pegasus*. But although there had been precious little to eat, along with constant walking from dawn until dusk, those had not been bad days. Mombasa had been another story completely. She shuddered involuntarily and pushed the memories away. She focused on the distant coastline.

There was a haze above the city, it made it easy to locate even when it was just a smudge on the horizon.

Sellie glanced at the steam pressure gauge. They could do with a top-up, especially if Harry was planning any fancy manoeuvres. Sellie laughed at the idea of Harry *planning* anything. Planning? Not very likely.

She turned and saw that Mrs Hemingway was still standing against the rail.

"You should probably take a seat, madam. It might get a bit rough."

The woman jumped at her words. "It's mesmerising," she said quickly as if to hide her reaction, and then smiled. She turned away and went to the chair. Carefully, she adjusted her skirts and took her seat.

Sellie hurried into the back and pulled her leather apron over her torn and dirty dress. With Mrs Hemingway on board she was not going to strip to her undergarments as she usually did. It was practical and cooler, but their tutor would be outraged. Anyway, smut from the furnace was unlikely to make things much worse. The apron was there to stop sparks setting her aflame.

She pulled on the gauntlets, picked up the shovel, and unlatched the door of the furnace. Heat poured out. She loaded up the fire with half a dozen shovelfuls of coal, and once again wondered whether it wouldn't be a better idea to change to diesel. Trouble was, it just didn't have the raw power the wings needed.

She slammed the door shut just as she felt the deck tilt. Harry had started her approach to Mombasa.

Stripping off her gauntlets, Sellie went forward to the main cabin and opened the door to the cold store she had installed. Johannes had supplied them with some sealed jugs of water and, she noted, three bottles of wine. She retrieved one of the jugs and closed the door.

"Would you like some water, Mrs Hemingway?" she asked.

As a tremor rippled in the hull, she glanced out the front. The city was moving past the window. Harry had crossed the coast a little south of it but heading northwest towards their home. Mombasa had been built on an outcrop of rock surrounded by water on three sides. The fourth side, that led inland, was almost a swamp.

The *Pegasus* crossed the southern river estuary and headed inland. Harry was still very low and flitted across the tops of masts from the dozens of fishing vessels.

"No, thank you," said Mrs Hemingway. "I find the way liquid moves in a Faraday field to be most disturbing." She was referring to the way it rolled sluggishly instead of pouring.

Sellie smiled. "We use these," she said simply. She dipped her hand into a container set into the inner wall of the fuselage and pulled out three paper straws. "Much simpler and you don't have to wait for the water to get around to moving."

She ripped the waxed paper lid from the jug, dropped a straw into it, and handed it to Mrs Hemingway, who took it gingerly. She studied the idle ripples in the jug for a moment and then sucked on the straw. Under the force of the suction the water responded normally and she received a mouthful.

Sellie dug out another jug and went forward to Harry. She put in the remaining two straws and drank through one. She leaned on the rail.

And then said "Oh."

Ahead of them there was a cloud hanging in the air, a grey miasma that grew like a sickly tower above where their house ought to be. Knowing that their home was gone, even having seen it, did not prepare her for the approach. For so many years the building had stood atop the small hill and had been there to greet them when they came home.

Now it was not. Only a dusty ruin remained.

20

Harry did not slow down. Her heart was full of despair and pain. It was not that she had many precious belongings that had been lost in their home's collapse—the *Pegasus* was the only thing that would break her heart to lose.

But home was still home, and hers was no more.

Tears welled up in her eyes, blurring her vision. Angrily she brushed them away. She had no time for tears, and they would impair her ability to fly.

She did not try to hide their approach as they shot across the ruin. A group of men stood beneath the trees at one side. Some of the staff were moving between there and the part that remained standing.

No Germans in sight.

At the speed they were going, Harry could not see whether her father was in the group. She did not want to stop; if he was not there, she wanted to keep flying until she found him. But she knew that was foolish. How could she find him if she did not know where to look? And perhaps he *was* down there.

Though, in her heart, she knew he was not.

She brought the *Pegasus* around to a fast but light landing. She flipped off the Faraday and found Sellie pushing one of Johannes's jugs into her hand.

"No time for that."

"Drink it, Harry," said Sellie. "Take a deep breath and drink. You need it."

The men who had been under the tree were heading across the grass towards them. Harry did as she was told. The deep breath helped. Her hand and arm muscles ached from gripping the controls for so long. Now that she had stopped she could feel the sweat sliding uncomfortably down her back.

She used the straw even though the Faraday was off. The cool water slipped down her throat. She had not realised how thirsty she was, and hunger grew in her stomach. She checked the time. It was five-thirty. They had another hour and a half of light.

"Anything to eat?" she said.

* * *

Out on the lawn, standing in the shade provided by the *Pegasus*, with the ruin on the hill, the six remaining members of the original deputation explained what had happened after the girls' precipitous departure.

The Germans had been at a loss at first. The captain and the one in charge of the ground troops had gone into the airship for about twenty minutes, after which the *Hauptman* had been summarily ejected from the Zeppelin with his men and the ship had simply left.

There remained about twenty of them. After some discussion they had appropriated the cars and driven away with the admiral and Jonathan Edgbaston. The *Hauptman* had left a letter for Harry and Sellie.

The letter was hastily written and not entirely grammatical but the gist was clear: Do not pursue, and the prisoners will be freed once the Germans had reached a safe haven.

Harry crumpled the letter.

"I hadn't finished reading it," said Sellie over her shoulder.

Lt Cmdr Laxton had taken charge of the group now the admiral was gone. He took the letter from her and looked at it. "Can you translate it?" he asked Harry, but she wasn't listening.

"I can," said Sellie.

Harry turned away from the group and went to stand at the front of the *Pegasus*. She placed her hand on the glass and stared towards the horizon. She knew what her father would want. He would want her safe. But did she believe what the *Hauptman* had said in his letter? He was scared. Scared of her and Sellie.

That was strange.

She understood people disliking her, and she had had plenty of them being angry with her, including her father. But the idea that someone could be scared of her?

What did that mean? If he was scared enough to arrange a mission to … To what? Why did he come here at all?

"Penny for your thoughts," said Sellie. "Here, have something to eat." She put a heavy crusted pie into Harry's hand. She took it but just held it.

"Why did he come here, Sellie?" she said. "Why did he risk everything to come here? What was he trying to achieve?"

"Eat your pie," said her sister. "I'll talk."

Harry chose a place to start and bit into the pastry. It was thick but the inside was juicy with meat gravy.

"You're lucky, Harry. You're white. You belong to the people in charge."

"I didn't choose it," she said with her mouth full.

"I know and I'm not blaming you. I'm lucky in some ways; I got to be your sister and that doesn't happen much to people like me. Look, Harry, I'm going to tell you something and it's really important you don't fly off the handle."

Harry swallowed. "I won't."

"This is serious. You're going to get upset and I don't want you doing anything silly." Sellie glanced around. "In fact, let's go inside."

Harry had just taken another big bite and was unable to respond. She followed Sellie to the hatch of the *Pegasus*.

"Where are you going?" Mrs Hemingway's voice pierced the air.

"Nowhere," said Sellie. "We just need a private chat. I'll leave the hatch open just to prove it."

Their tutor said nothing more, so they climbed in.

Harry polished off the last remnants of the pie and pulled another jug of water from the cold box.

"Let's sit down," said Sellie.

They did so but Harry was getting impatient. "Come on, Sellie, spit it out."

"All right, Harry," said Sellie. "Don't rush me, I promised myself I'd never tell you."

Harry frowned. "Never tell me what?"

"Harry! Just shut up and let me say it."

Sellie waited but Harry remained silent. Sellie took a deep breath and tried to marshal her thoughts. "You remember Joseph the butler?"

Her sister simply nodded, making the point that she was not saying anything. Sellie looked at her hands, her skin the same colour as Joseph's.

"You know he was always short with me," she said. "Did you ever wonder why?"

Harry hesitated then shook her head as if it had never even occurred to her to think about it.

"Because he hated me, Harry." Sellie's eyes burned with tears. She rubbed them. "He used to kick me when no one was looking." Harry's eyes widened, Sellie touched her finger to her lips to make sure she stayed quiet.

"Did you really think I was so clumsy, Harry, that I was always spilling food and drink on me?" she said, upset from the thousand times no one had questioned it. Harry stopped chewing. "He would do it, or get one of the maids to do it. Drop stuff on me. Then Mrs Hemingway would notice."

Harry found her voice though it was no more than a whisper. "Did Mrs Hemingway know?"

Sellie shook her head. "I don't know. Doesn't matter whether she knew or not, you know what pleasure she took in criticising me."

"But why?"

"Because I was better than him—that's what he thought anyway. Women aren't supposed to be like us, Harry," said Sellie. "I think we make some men…scared."

"So he was just a bully?"

"'Just a bully', Harry? There was no 'just' about it." *It was years, Harry, he did it for years.* Sellie wiped the tears from her cheeks.

"I'm so sorry." Harry rubbed her eyes. "If I'd known…"

"What? Told Dad?"

"Yes."

"And he would have spoken to Joseph and *he* would have denied it."

Harry went silent. "I'm so sorry."

Sellie smiled through her tears and put her hand on her sister's knee. "Doesn't matter now, he's been gone a long time and we can deal with the cow." She nodded her head in the direction of Mrs Hemingway.

"So you're saying we scare *Hauptman* Gerhardt."

Sellie nodded. "We're heretics in his world. You know what they used to do with heretics."

Harry stood up and threw the remains of her pie out of the hatch. She held out her hand and helped Sellie to her feet. They put their arms around one another in a tight hug.

When Sellie finally pulled back she saw that Harry wearing a malicious grin.

"Well," she said. "Perhaps we better finish the job."

21

"You are not leaving," said Mrs Hemingway firmly. "In the absence of your father I am *in loco parentis*. You are not of age so you will do precisely as you are told."

Harry had to look up to Mrs Hemingway. But while their tutor might be imposing, Harry was not daunted.

"You can't stop me."

Harry glanced at the sun, there was not much daylight remaining.

"I do not need to, these gentlemen will do so." She indicated the remaining uniformed men, who were following the orders of Lieutenant Commander Laxton.

"Mrs Hemingway is correct, we cannot allow you to fly."

Harry felt the anger growing in her again. She pushed it down. "Why would you take an interest?"

"Miss Edgbaston, apart from the obvious fact that you have no idea where the Germans have taken your father"—unlike Mrs Hemingway's, his voice was not tinged with condescension—"we are also keen to recover the admiral. It will not look good on our records to have lost one." He smiled.

She softened towards him a little. He was not like *her* at all.

"There is not much daylight left and trying to find them in the dark is even more ridiculous than trying to find them in daylight."

"Quite so," said Mrs Hemingway.

"So we will see what intelligence can be gathered during the night and will set off at first light," he said. "I hope that will suit you."

Harry grinned. "Thank you."

"This is out of the question!" said Mrs Hemingway, though her tone suggested that she was now uncertain, having lost the ally she thought she had.

"On the contrary, madam," said Lt Cmdr Laxton. "It is the only sensible solution. We are stuck here and there is insufficient time for any official transport to reach us." He paused and glanced at the *Pegasus* reflecting the light of the setting sun. "Considering the distance this vehicle travelled in such a short time, I believe it is our best option as it combines high speed with the ability to land on any terrain."

"Sellie's the engineer," said Harry, glowing at the praise being heaped on her ship. "She's the miracle worker."

"Your companion?"

Harry's good humour vanished. "She is my sister."

"Adopted," said Mrs Hemingway.

"I do apologise, Miss Edgbaston and," he looked at Sellie, nodding his head, "Miss Edgbaston."

"Apology accepted," said Sellie, a little hoarsely.

"Lieutenant Keating here"—the other naval officer nodded at Sellie—"he came up on the engineering side, I'm sure he would be interested in your vessel."

"Um," said Sellie. She looked embarrassed when all eyes turned in her direction. "I was thinking, about the intelligence?"

"Yes, Miss Edgbaston?" said Laxton.

"Well, local people will have seen the horseless carriages leaving. We could send out some people to find out where they went."

Laxton smiled. "An excellent proposition."

He strode away to where the two army majors stood and spoke to them. They in their turn moved in the direction of the staff quarters. Laxton returned; he did not walk slowly but seemed always to be marching to some beat Harry could not hear.

"Mrs Hemingway," he said.

"I am not happy with this," she said.

"I understand and that is why I feel it is important for you to accompany us in the morning. It would not be proper for the young ladies to be without a chaperone. I'm sure you understand."

"Yes," she said weakly.

"Good, now I think if you ladies occupy the summer house for the night and we will make do," he said. "It will be rather more of a problem for the … ah … bureaucrats than for the military."

"Sellie and I will sleep in the *Pegasus,*" said Harry. "But I'm sure one of the more senior female staff will give up her room for Mrs Hemingway."

Their tutor looked horrified.

"Leaving us with the summer house. Excellent," said Laxton. "We will make it so, if you're sure you'll be comfortable in your vessel."

"Done it lots of times," said Harry.

Laxton nodded, and made it so.

* * *

A rapping on the hull jerked Harry awake. She groaned and opened her eyes.

"Rise and shine, ladies. It is oh-six hundred hours. We go light in forty-five minutes."

Harry groaned again.

"Welcome to the Royal Navy," muttered Sellie. "I don't think I'll pursue a career in the Senior Service."

"Any service," said Harry rolling onto her back and pushing herself up on her elbows. "I'm guessing they're both like this."

"What are we going to wear, Harry?" said Sellie. "Yesterday's are torn and filthy."

There was another knock. "Commander Laxton's compliments," said a younger voice. "He thought you might require suitable attire for the day."

Sellie looked at Harry. "I like this Laxton fellow, he's sensitive to a lady's needs."

"Just being practical, who'd want to be seen around a pair of scarecrows?"

"Just a minute!" called Sellie. Both of them were dressed in their underclothes. Sellie had unscrewed a panel from the wall and used it as a screen to hide the interior of the ship. She looked at her dress. Yesterday morning it had been a bright yellow but no longer. She grabbed it and held it in front of herself. "This will do."

She went to the hatch and then looked over at Harry, her arms and legs completely bare and her hair a disaster, standing directly across from the door. "I'm going to open this door," she said.

Harry seemed deep in thought and didn't respond.

Sellie tried again. "Is it your intention to display your nether limbs to the officer outside this door?"

Nothing.

"Harry!"

Her head jerked up. "What?"

"Get out of the way! I'm opening the hatch."

Harry hurried across the deck into a position where she would not be seen. Sellie unlocked the door and pushed it open a few inches. "Just squeeze them through."

"I have my eyes averted," said the officer. Sellie caught a glimpse of the khaki uniform of one of the majors as he pushed some coarse looking dark brown material through the gap.

"Thanks, Major Page" said Sellie.

"Thresher, Miss," he said without rancour. "The other one."

"Thanks."

She shut the door and the sisters pounced on the clothes.

"Oh," said Sellie.

Harry eyed the clothing with distaste. "Farm workers' overalls," she said. There were some shirts to go with them.

"Well," said Sellie. "They're practical."

Harry pulled a face.

Sellie dropped her arms, letting the fabric drag on the floor. "I thought you were the one who was always complaining about flying in a dress and how much more convenient it would be to wear trousers."

"I know, but …" she trailed off.

"Farm workers' overalls not good enough for you?"

Harry bit her lip.

"All right for the blacks to wear, but not next to your precious pale and freckly skin?"

Harry's freckles were not limited to her face, as Sellie knew but most of the rest of the world did not. Thankfully.

"Better make the best of it, Harry," said Sellie. "It's all we've got and we have just wasted ten minutes of our limited time. Commander Laxton might be thoughtful in one respect but there'll be hell to pay if we're not ready to lift at the appointed minute."

They got changed. Everything was too big but at least it was clean. Harry cut up the dresses and plaited strips of material into belts while Sellie got the furnace running up to heat.

They still had water in the cold store and plenty of food, which they ate as they worked. Harry opened the hatch and let the cold dawn air circulate through, clearing out the smells. They tidied up.

It was oh-six hundred hours and forty minutes when Lieutenant Commander Laxton and Lieutenant Keating with Majors Thresher and Page came down the lawn to the *Pegasus.* They looked clean and their uniforms fresh. Harry was envious. They were accompanied by Mrs Hemingway. Harry stood in the hatchway. Smoke drifted from the stack.

"Permission to come aboard, Miss Edgbaston?" said Laxton.

22

Feeling somewhat awkward in her manly clothing—the roughness of the material wrapped around her legs was distracting—Harry climbed into the pilot's chair. Commander Laxton and the other men took up positions along the rail. Mrs Hemingway sat in the chair, after giving Harry a curious look that could have been either satisfaction at seeing her in such embarrassing clothing, or possibly pity.

"Did you find out where we need to go?" asked Harry, turning in the chair so she could look at Laxton.

He smiled. "We found something," he said. "You know the station?"

"Of course."

"Head that way, if you would be so kind."

Harry glanced at the steam gauge from habit, though she already knew the *Pegasus* was hot. She gave two short whistles and then spoke. "Going light in five … four … three … two … one."

She flipped the switch. There was neither a murmur nor any other sort of reaction from the military men, and just a sharp intake of breath from Mrs Hemingway.

Harry tested the wings. Their powerful response to her movements gave her strength and confidence. She ran up the speed of the propeller.

Two long whistles. "Taking off," she shouted over the breathless pumping of the steam engines.

One stroke. Two. And they were airborne. She brought the *Pegasus* around and stared at the ruin of their home. It was a sharp reminder of why they were in the air and what they were planning to do.

She powered into the dawn as the sun rose across the Indian Ocean beyond Mombasa.

The station was barely a minute away. Almost immediately it was possible to see the pneumatic tube running across the landscape. The atmospheric ran from Mombasa to Nairobi, and then onwards to the north. Ultimately it was intended to link East Africa with Egypt and the Mediterranean.

Two of the military vehicles that had brought the group were parked outside the station.

"They took the atmospheric?" said Harry incredulously.

"What better way to outrun you?" said Laxton.

"To Mombasa?"

"North."

Harry gritted her teeth. "When?"

"Mid-afternoon."

"They have a fifteen-hour head start," she said in despair. "They could be in Khartoum by now."

"But not much further since that is where the atmospheric ends. The line from Cairo is not yet complete."

Harry said nothing further. She put her hand on the power and cranked the propeller to maximum. As their airspeed increased she descended until she was only a few feet above the tunnel of the atmospheric.

Across the plains of Africa the pumping stations were two to three miles apart. They could not keep up the kind of pressure in the tube to maintain the kinds of speeds they managed in Europe, but even an African atmospheric was no slouch.

That *Hauptman* Gerhardt had chosen to take the train meant that his trail was easy to follow. Unless he had got off, he could only be in the tube.

As they approached the top of the tube Harry felt the change in the air around them and under the wings. The *Pegasus*'s velocity slid higher on the dial, as if they were gliding on oil.

"That is impressive," said a voice in her ear. It was Lieutenant Keating. "How is it possible your vessel can make this kind of speed?"

"Ground effect," she heard Sellie answer. "Harry says it happens when we're close to the ground."

Harry focused on the tube. Every few miles she had to swing out to avoid the pumping stations, though they were easy to spot as they poured smoke from their furnaces. Here in the heat of Africa they ran water in pipes down the inside of the tubes to supply the steam for the pumps.

Their speed topped out at 175. That seemed to be the maximum they could reach. Still, it was nearly three miles, or one pumping station, per minute. Harry gave up riding above the tube but stayed to the side and simply followed its line.

Time passed and the sun rose. It was about half-past eight when they reached a place called Nairobi. It was nothing more than an outcropping at the edge of a swamp but it was well placed and there was fresh water nearby.

The town was composed of a selection of buildings. Maintenance for the atmospheric, sidings, and workshops. To support the workforce there were already shops, hotels, and other establishments. Harry climbed to kill their speed and brought the *Pegasus* to a gentle landing next to the station.

Laxton and the two majors went to make enquiries. Mrs Hemingway, who had been silent the entire trip, went to stretch her legs, as did Khuwelsa.

Harry climbed out of her chair and stretched. Her muscles were tense and ached, not just from this short flight but from her exertions on the previous day. The only other person in the cabin was Lt Keating who diplomatically looked out of the window while she performed her exercises.

"The commander thinks I should learn how to fly your vessel, Miss Edgbaston," he said, almost diffidently as if he had an inkling she might react badly to the suggestion.

She did not find the idea pleasant. "Why?"

"He does not wish to die."

Harry blinked. "What? Die?"

Keating now turned to face her. His face lacked any strong emotion. "Miss Edgbaston, how long has the Royal Navy had an air corps?"

"Twenty-eight years."

"Quite so, in fact exactly so," he said. "Since 1868, and there were air vehicles in use for three years before that." He took a breath. "In that time, do you suppose we learned anything about piloting Faraday craft?"

She frowned. "Well, of course, we have the most powerful vessels in the air and the Void."

"Then perhaps it may not come as a surprise that we soon learnt that a pilot flying for more than two or three hours, particularly under stress, becomes tired and likely to make mistakes."

Harry said nothing.

"And in a vessel such as this, that requires constant attention, travelling at a velocity far in excess of its design specifications would tire the pilot far more quickly."

"I …" she trailed off.

"Do you dispute my authority in this matter?"

After a moment's hesitation she shook her head.

"Then you see the value in my becoming your substitute pilot on this journey?"

"Yes." The single word was almost whisper.

Cmdr Laxton's voice penetrated the hull. "Prepare to go light! Immediately."

Harry dived under the rail and swung into the pilot's chair. Sellie entered and almost pulled Mrs Hemingway up the steps and inside.

"Going light!" shouted Harry counted one and flipped the switch. Pressure had dropped but they had enough. She could already hear Sellie shovelling coal.

Laxton and the majors tumbled inside. The last one in slammed the hatch and dogged it.

Harry ran up the propeller and, with two powerful beats, had them in the air.

"Which way?" Harry called.

"Keep following the tube."

Harry gunned the engine, thrust them forward with powerful strokes, and brought the *Pegasus* around. Within seconds Nairobi was no more than a memory.

23

Once they had settled into their course, Laxton related the information they had discovered. The atmospheric train had arrived on schedule the evening before. It had been due for a stop-over for the night so the passengers could, if they chose, find accommodation and food in the town.

However the flood of passengers escaping from the atmospheric once the tube doors had been opened was the first sign something was wrong. The local constabulary had investigated but were warned off by shots when they approached.

The Germans aboard kept the crew and their original prisoners as hostages, and had the train restocked and its water tanks filled—though an atmospheric was driven by air pressure, it still required its own power to drive the Faraday grid.

One passenger had been killed. He was ex-army and had tried to overpower their captors. He had expected the other passengers to assist but they were too scared, and his death confirmed their fears.

The atmospheric had spent a little over an hour at Nairobi before the train pushed on into the night.

Harry put the *Pegasus* to the ground and accelerated. They were soon roaring above the savannah at their maximum speed. To the north the horizon was broken by the green slopes and white top of a massive volcano.

"It's Kiri Nyaga, 'God's home'," said Khuwelsa. "Some of Bakari's people live around here."

"Well, it's more interesting than this place," said Harry. The terrain was flat as a pancake and the atmospheric tube ran straight as a die. The grasslands were filled with animals and birds that flashed past so fast the beasts had no time to react before the vessel was already gone.

Harry yawned.

An hour later, and they were running northwest up a valley with hills to the right and plains the other side. Every now and then they would pass a smaller volcano caldera. All of them were ages dead and filled with green.

"Perhaps this would be a good time for you to show me how to fly your plane," said Keating.

"We'll have to slow down," said Harry, realising that she sounded like a whiny child.

"Better than the alternative."

Harry adjusted the angle of the wings slightly and the *Pegasus* soared up.

Keating immediately enquired as to what she had done. She explained as best she could. It was only then that it occurred to her that she did not even think about flying. When she was at the controls it was as if she and the ship were one and the same.

She felt a panic. What if explaining it took away that oneness? Could analysing it make it stop?

But she went through the controls with Keating: the two sticks that controlled the wing position by pushing forward, back and to the sides, and how rotating them adjusted the feathering.

"No foot controls?" asked Keating.

Harry shook her head. "What would you use your feet for?"

"Fixed-wing craft use them for the rudder."

"The wings do everything," said Harry. "We don't need a rudder."

Reluctantly she had throttled back to sixty miles per hour, which almost certainly meant they were falling behind their quarry.

She locked off the wings, after explaining what she had done and how the arched position was very stable. Finally she relinquished her position. It was not leaving the chair while in flight that bothered her. She had done that before many times; the *Pegasus* just hung in the air like a gull or a hawk. No, it wasn't that.

It was that she had to stand by while someone else climbed into her chair. While that someone touched her controls, it was as if he was touching her, violating her privacy, her very person.

She pointed to the control lock. "Move that up, it's quite stiff, and make sure you put your hand on the control quickly."

They had climbed to three thousand feet, there would be plenty of time for her to get back in the chair even if he made a mess of it. Unless he flipped them over.

Harry tried, with only partial success, to suppress the anger that rose within her. She knew it was foolish but the fact that Keating did not mess up filled her with unjustifiable annoyance. He was cautious. He seemed to understand that the *Pegasus* was a delicate creature and that he had to work with her, and not try to enforce his will on her.

"May I increase velocity?" he asked.

Harry nodded but then realised he was not looking in her direction. "Yes. She will let you release the controls but only for a moment."

"You compensate before you let go," he said.

"I don't know what you mean?"

"You know how the ship will react when you let go, so you adjust for it before you do."

Harry thought about it. He was right. "Yes."

"I'll just try letting go," he said. And for the next two minutes he let go, felt the ship move, and then took hold again. He tried it with the other hand and then both hands. "I see," he said. He made a slight movement that brought the port side up, released the stick, and as the stick moved and the port dropped again he pushed the throttle forward.

Harry was grateful that he missed the stick and had to grab it.

She always knew where the sticks were. She sighed; yes, she knew, but that knowledge came with experience. He was doing very well for someone who had never flown a 'thopter before.

As he pushed the ship into a gentle dive, the airspeed increased. He moved the wings into the arched position. After glancing left and right through the portholes to check their position, he locked them off. He released the controls and sat back, rubbing his hands and arms.

"Aching," he said.

"You haven't done this before," she said.

"Well, I may be able to relieve you for short periods," he said. "But you'll still have to the most of the work."

"Good," said Harry. She had not meant to say it aloud, and embarrassment swept over her.

Keating laughed. "I know this is your baby," he said. "But we have to be practical." He climbed out of the chair. "The helm is yours, Miss Edgbaston."

24

For the rest of the day they traced the tube north across Africa. The terrain was largely unchanging, which was good because it meant they could maintain a high velocity. Every ninety minutes Keating would relieve Harry and give her a chance to rest. They flew slower at those times, as he was not going to risk the low altitude flight Harry could manage.

Three times they were forced to stop for personal convenience. It was extremely embarrassing for the ladies but the military men were practical about the matter. Though Harry and Sellie were used to using the wilderness for such necessities, they had always been alone. Poor Mrs Hemingway tried to deny nature for a long time until it became impossible for her. The situation was not discussed.

As to their temporary dress, Harry was satisfied despite the roughness. She found piloting the *Pegasus* to be much easier without having to fight her way through layers of restrictive clothing. She would have to have some flying gear made up when she got home.

Home. Her heart felt empty. They no longer had a home. Their father, stolen away and her mother, thousands of miles distant. Harry wondered why she had come to mind now. After all, she almost never thought about the woman. What was the point? Her mother had never been part of the home that she or Sellie remembered.

By mid-afternoon the mountains of Ethiopia had emerged from the landscape to the east. The lush grasslands of the equatorial country gave way to stony ground. It was still green here, but it was more like the lower slopes of the mountain, where the green had to fight to maintain its hold.

Harry had never seen the Nile before. Although there were plenty of bigger rivers around Mombasa, none of them was the mighty river of Egypt. The atmospheric followed it now, though it cut corners wherever appropriate. It even crossed the waters more than once. A fast atmospheric did not take corners quickly so the engineers took the straightest line they could.

The fabled Nile, the life's blood of Egypt and the river that fed the people of the Sudan. It would not be much further to Khartoum where the two major tributaries—the Blue Nile that they were following, and the White Nile that flowed from Ethiopia—joined to become the mightiest river in the world that flowed for another thousand miles into the Mediterranean.

To Italy. Perhaps that was why Harry thought of her mother; she now lived in Italy. Of course, Mrs Hemingway had mentioned her yesterday as well.

Harry felt strange thinking about her mother. She could barely remember what she looked like. There was the photograph she had in the bedroom but that had been taken a dozen years before.

"That's Juba," said Keating.

They were overflying a large Arab walled town with its low white houses tight together and the thinnest lines separating them showing where the streets lay. Packing them so close meant the narrow streets were in shade almost the whole day. A train of camels headed into the city through one of its gates.

Camels. They were approaching the southernmost reaches of the Sahara. And that meant sand. Harry was not sure how well the mechanisms of *Pegasus* would cope.

"How long to Khartoum?" she said.

"Three hours at a guess," he said. "We shall have to stop for the night before we reach it."

"No!"

Keating leaned on the rail and put his head close to her ear. So close she could feel his breath.

"Harry." It was the first time he had used her nickname. "This is a military operation, you cannot go against orders."

"It may be a military operation for you," she hissed, "but I am rescuing my father and every moment we delay we give them time."

"You cannot fly at night."

"Give me one good reason why not?"

"You won't be able to see where you're going," he said without raising his voice. "You'll crash at high speed."

"Am I allowed to present an alternative plan to your military operation?"

"Of course."

"You take over for an hour, so I can rest. Then I'll take us to Khartoum, if it gets dark before we reach there I'll reduce speed and take us up. We have a compass and we have both the Nile and the tube to guide us. We'll be able to see them even at night."

"If it remains clear."

"Yes," she said. "We will set down at Khartoum and find out if they've moved on. The tube stops there so they will be using the old style train, which is much slower. We can follow them in the dark perhaps even catch up or overtake them."

Keating thought for a few moments. "Very well, I will discuss this with the commander."

Harry calmed herself and brought the *Pegasus* down again. She stifled a yawn; she did not want anyone to know how tired she was.

"Getting on all right with the lieutenant?" It was Sellie's turn to talk in her ear, but she was grateful. She missed her sister; the only reason she knew Sellie was still there was that the steam pressure stayed up. "Those army boys are handy as stokers," Sellie said. "We should try to keep them on."

"I thought you were still doing the stoking," said Harry, almost offended that she had been wrong. That she, Harry, had been doing all the hard work while Sellie had been having it easy.

"Why would I shovel coal when I have a couple of strong lads to do it for me?" said Sellie. "Grateful to do it, I might add."

"Grateful?"

"I let them have some of the cold water."

"Can I have some?"

"Not while you're flying," Sellie said. "Tree."

The terrain had dipped and there was a tall tree directly ahead of them that had looked like a bush a moment before.

"Yes," said Harry as she lifted the *Pegasus* over it in a smooth motion. "I can see perfectly well."

"So, you and the lieutenant?" said Sellie again.

"You and the *two* majors?"

Sellie laughed. "Too old."

"Ditto."

"Excuse me, Miss Edgbaston," said Keating as he edged in on the other side of Harry. The ship really wasn't built for so many, although they had managed to carry Bakari and his men before, but it had not been for such an extended period.

"Cmdr Laxton is in agreement with your plan—"

"You have a plan?" said Sellie.

"I always have a plan."

Khuwelsa made a sceptical sound and muttered something about Plan B.

Harry brought the *Pegasus* up to five hundred feet and throttled back. Giving control to Keating was still uncomfortable but it no longer caused a wrench when he sat in her chair. She locked off the wings and climbed out.

It was odd the way things changed, she no longer worried about the fact people could see her as she stretched her tired muscles. She reached up, placed her hands against the ceiling, and pressed. When she relaxed her pressure, the strain ebbed away. She rolled her shoulders in both directions and stretched the muscles in her neck.

Beneath her feet she could feel the vibrations from the drive increasing and the way the ship tilted down towards the grass. She knew everything that Keating was doing without even looking at him. She may not be in the chair but she was still the *Pegasus*, and the ship was still Harry.

She glanced at Mrs Hemingway. She had her eyes closed.

Harry knelt beside her. The woman's eyelids opened.

"Why did you say I was as bad as my mother?" she said quietly.

25

"Shouldn't you be resting?"

"I am resting," said Harry. "Not being in the chair is resting."

"It's not my place to discuss your mother."

"You're the one who mentioned her in the first place," Harry said. "I believe I have a right to know why."

"No," said Mrs Hemingway. "You do not."

Harry moved a little closer, almost threatening. "I can't imagine you're keeping it from me to protect my feelings, Mrs Hemingway. So either it was simply a vicious turn of phrase intended to hurt, or it's a secret you should not have let slip.

"So which is it?"

Their tutor hesitated and then blurted out. "Your mother is a painter."

Harry blinked. "Is that all?"

"Of the Impressionist movement."

Harry was fairly sure they had not covered anything of the recent Impressionist movement when Mrs Hemingway had attempted to instill some art appreciation into them. As usual Sellie had lapped it up. Harry did not dislike the pictures but couldn't see why they had to be classified or, more particularly, why she had to know the difference.

Harry shook her head.

"The Impressionists are libertines and women of loose morals."

"So you're saying I have loose morals?"

"I did not say that."

"Yes, you did," said Harry. "You said I was as bad as my mother. Clearly the badness you see in her is that she is an

Impressionist painter and therefore a woman of loose morals. So you're saying I must be too."

For the first time Harry noticed a strain in the woman's face.

"I didn't mean it," she said.

"I think you did," said Harry. "I am not a lady by your rules. I won't sit and do needlework or play the piano and sing. I have a metal bird and I'm free to travel where I choose. I dance unchaperoned with soldiers. My sister is black. And I have a mother with loose morals."

Harry paused for breath. Every word seemed to make Mrs Hemingway shrink.

"I am everything you are not," she said. "And I will never fit the mould you have created for me."

Harry felt the tears running down her cheeks and her sight blurred.

Mrs Hemingway produced a kerchief and handed it to her. "You can be if you try," she said.

Harry sniffed. "I'm not crying for me," she said. "I'm crying for you."

The older woman looked as if she might break. Harry sighed, wiped her eyes once more and handed back the kerchief. She stood up and looked around the small cabin. The two majors were in the back by the furnace. Lt Cmdr Laxton was standing by the hatch, looking at her with concern.

Sellie was forward by the rail; her deep brown eyes also shone with tears. There was no way she could have heard the quiet conversation above the noises of the *Pegasus* but she and Harry were sisters, and Sellie knew something important had happened.

Harry gave a slight shake of her head to Sellie's questioning look.

The cabin seemed smaller as if Harry had grown, as if somehow she had become taller. Where before Lt Cmdr Laxton was a figure of high authority, she now saw him as someone who could get her what she wanted—when she had determined what, exactly, that was.

Harry took three steps and leaned on the rail beside Sellie. She looked out and down. They were still over green, but in the distance the horizon had taken on a yellow/brown hue. The desert was approaching.

"You should rest more," said Laxton.

"This is enough," said Harry.

Laxton did not press the point.

For a long time the desert colour remained on the horizon. But then it began to approach, with the appearance of a physical line between green and yellow. And they rushed across it.

The meandering Nile cut a groove in its wide flood plain filled with green, but beyond that winding strip there was nothing but sand and rocks. Through it all the man-made tube ran straight as if God himself had laid out a celestial ruler and drawn a line across the landscape.

"I'll take the helm," said Harry. Even she noticed the difference in her tone. It was not the parade ground demand of the military men, but it was a voice that brooked no disagreement. Harry had no idea where it had come from, but it was part of her now.

She glanced at Sellie, who raised an eyebrow and sported a slight smile.

Keating locked off the controls and climbed out of the chair. Harry slipped in and replaced him. In a smooth motion she unlocked the wings, opened the throttle and angled the ship towards the tube.

There were still the pumping stations but no more trees. The land here was intensely flat. The shadow of the tube, cast by the dying sun stretched out across the landscape. They passed over tiny groups of mud huts that could barely even be called villages. Small fishing boats with triangular sails skittered across the surface of the widening river.

From the edge of the desert to Khartoum was barely one hundred miles. The city came into view half an hour after she had taken her seat. But the sun had already gone down and, true to her promise, Harry had climbed to one thousand feet and reduced speed.

An air-dock came into sight to the south of the city. The dock itself was an intense grouping of lights, while the city beyond was partially electrified and had street lights that burned with a curious constancy.

Harry put the *Pegasus* into a wide turn around the dock, which carried them over the terminus of the atmospheric tube and the beginning of the old fashioned rails.

Tiny flashes of light caught her eye. "What's that?" she said pointing down.

She felt rather than saw Keating come to the rail. Something erupted in a ball of fire. Harry back-winged and brought the ship to a near stand-still in the air. She used her knee to push the throttle up to full power as she kept the ship in the air.

Sputtering lights created a flashing display as the sound of the explosion rolled over them.

Keating shouted over his shoulder. "Weapons fire at the terminus."

Harry had to adjust for the change in weight as everyone on the vessel moved to the rail at the front. The nose tilted down, and she had to veer off to gain some speed to stay aloft. When she brought the ship round again, a line of lights was moving off towards the north.

"They must have taken the train," shouted Harry. "Plan B!"

26

Harry increased power to the propeller and tilted the nose down.

"What is Plan B, Miss Edgbaston?" It was Laxton, he seemed remarkably calm.

"I have no idea."

"She just piles in and does her … thing," said Sellie. "That's Plan B."

"And how often does this work?" his voice held an irritating tone of amusement.

Sellie paused and then replied. "Every time, actually."

"If they haven't seen us, then we have the element of surprise," Harry said. "If they have we can't give them time to get organised."

"What of the hostages?"

"They won't hurt them," said Harry. She tried to think objectively but the idea of her father with that man's gun on him was upsetting. "They need them for bargaining."

Laxton said nothing for a few moments.

"Sir?"

"Keating?"

"Up ahead, sir."

Harry looked forward into the night. The sky was clear and the moon up, turning the desert silver. At least a certain distance, then the horizon became blurred. Without warning the *Pegasus* dropped away from under them, what little weight they had became nothing. Mrs Hemingway screamed.

"Air pocket!" shouted Harry, not entirely sure who she was trying to calm. The controls were unresponsive but then, as if they had fallen into water, they were pushed down into the deck and wings had something to beat against.

The ground was considerably nearer than it had been.

The railway lines gleamed in the moonlight. The fuzziness on the horizon had not gone away.

"Sandstorm," said Keating. "Not good."

"You're telling me," said Sellie. "We have to land, Harry, preferably inside something, a cave maybe? Or we go over it."

"They can last for days," said Keating.

"Right," said Harry. "We're going in."

She pushed the throttle all the way forward. A side wind buffeted them, and she compensated. Then she headed down to the metal railway lines.

She did not see the men behind her gripping the rail all the more tightly as the ground came up to meet them. She adjusted the wings and the *Pegasus* swooped into perfect alignment with the parallel lines of metal, less than a dozen feet above it. No one spoke.

The air seemed a little calmer close to the ground, but even here gusts knocked the vessel to one side or the other at random.

Harry focused on the rails, not looking ahead. "How far to the train and the storm?"

"Two minutes for both," said Keating. "What are you going to do, Harry?"

"You don't want to know," she said, failing to notice him switching to her nickname. "But you boys need to be ready."

"Shall I open the hatch?" asked Sellie.

"Not yet," said Harry. "Last moment, all right?"

"I'll be ready," Sellie said. "Majors? I'll need your help."

The blur on the horizon was growing fast, occupying more of the sky. Smoke from the train's engine scudded past them. They were going too fast but Harry did not want to slow down. Once they were in the storm they might lose the train, or the sand would bring them down.

"Come on, baby," Harry muttered.

Then it all happened at once. They were so close to the storm they could see the sand swirling in the moonlight. The train which had been in the distance seem to leap at them.

There was a risk, she knew, it might be that her father or the admiral were in the last carriage that was rushing towards them. But she thought they would try to keep everyone together in a group near the engine.

The hull hissed as grains of sand blasted against it. The final train carriage burst out of the dark at them. Harry killed the propeller's power, pulled up and back-winged hard. The *Pegasus* lifted over the carriage as the train's engine vanished into the swirling storm.

A blast of air ripped through the cabin as the hatch was forced open against the wind. The end of the train slipped beneath them as all light was blotted out by the sand storm.

Harry flipped off the Faraday. With its full weight, the *Pegasus* slammed down through the roof of the carriage. The passengers were thrown to the side as the ship lurched. Harry switched the Faraday back on and the air was filled with drifting sand that slowly made its way towards the ground.

A curious feeling of rhythmic movement transferred through the floor and into her body. Harry had never travelled on an old style train before. The regular pattern was not unpleasant. But there was nothing to see; they were in pitch darkness.

"Is everyone all right?" she called. Sounds of assent answered her, including an angry mutter from Mrs Hemingway. There was a flash of light outside and deafening thunder pounded their ears.

A dim glow filled the cabin as Khuwelsa lit one of the oil lamps.

"If we're lucky they might not have noticed," said Sellie.

"How could they possibly not?" said Keating.

"Their attention will have been on the storm. Listen to that." She waved her hand at the roaring and constant sighing of sand. "If they didn't see us, they would attribute any movement to the storm, and the noise likewise."

Keating nodded. "No one is shooting at us."

"Besides," said Sellie. "Who would land a plane on a train?"

Her comment elicited a smile from everyone except the commander and Mrs Hemingway.

Harry got out of the chair and rummaged in the chest behind it. She pulled out two electric torches. "They only have about half an hour of power," she said, handing one to Keating.

"We'll take it from here," said Laxton.

"You mean you don't want us to come?"

"More than that, I forbid it. Both you and your sister, Miss Edgbaston."

"We're coming," said Sellie. "That's our father."

"And I cannot possibly allow two young ladies to enter such a dangerous situation."

Harry looked at him, straight in the eye. "You're joking."

"If I gave the impression of humour then I must be more careful," said Laxton.

"You know what we've done before?"

"I don't believe I have read any reports," he said. "Apart from those sensationalised news items."

"We brought down four Zeppelins in one fight, and they had an escort of fighters," said Harry angrily. "In this!" She gestured at the *Pegasus*. "Not to mention destroying that giant flyer in Lake Victoria, in a thunderstorm."

"Yes, well," said Laxton. "This is entirely different. Here we have soldiers with guns."

The question as to whether they had been seen was answered moments later as the hull echoed to the sound of ricocheting bullets and one of the panes of the windscreen cracked.

27

The military men swung into action without a word. Keating grabbed Harry and Mrs Hemingway by the arm and pulled them to the engineering section, gathering up Sellie on the way.

Laxton and the majors went to the door. While one provided covering fire the other two squirmed their way out into the swirling wind and sand. They went up and over the fuselage. It was difficult to tell what was happening but whoever had been shooting at them ceased to do so. Whether he had been killed or had retreated was unclear.

Keating stood with his hands akimbo facing them. "Please do not leave the ship. I appreciate that you have accomplished astonishing feats for a pair of young girls, but it would be a terrible shame to lose you when you have so much to offer in the future."

"I am not afraid of dying, lieutenant," said Harry. Sellie gave her a *speak for yourself* look.

"There are worse things than dying, Miss Edgbaston," he said. "Living when someone you love is gone, for example. We are not alone in this world; we have people we would miss, and those who would mourn our passing. You cannot ignore them."

Harry frowned, but nodded.

Keating smiled, then stepped back and saluted them.

"Stay in the ship."

Then he was gone.

* * *

Hauptman Gerhardt sipped his glass of brandy. It was not a good brandy, just one from the kitchen. He was reasonably content. The whole situation was difficult, but he knew he had made the best of it.

Ever since that morning in Zanzibar when he had caught the girl trying to escape, only to have her ripped from his grasp by the damnable *Schwarze*. Ever since then he had vowed he would get his revenge on her.

Her deeds after that and the fact she had boasted to the world about them only intensified his resolve. The train was buffeted by the wind as they rattled along the track. It was slow but once they were on board he was more relaxed.

The father and the admiral sat further down the carriage. As it was much easier to jump from one of these trains than the one in the tube, he kept them tied up. He had lost another two men at Khartoum, which was unfortunate. However they had surprised the British by their arrival and were able to take control of this machine.

They had destroyed the telegraph office, so there would be no communicating with Aswan. Though perhaps it would be better to stop short of the town and leave the train. He would think more on that later.

With only six men remaining, he had stationed two with the train drivers and two in the rear carriages, and the others were with him here.

Thunder from the lightning inside the sand storm boomed through the carriage and disturbed his concentration. The oil lights juddered and swung above them as the train shifted and rocked.

There was a sharp crack behind him. He jerked his head round as the door burst open with a swirl of wind and sand, and one of his men staggered through. There was another crack and he collapsed. His blood spread across the floor.

Gerhardt tried to up-end his table, but it was screwed to the floor. There was movement in the dark beyond the door. There were gunshots from behind him as his men fired past him. Gerhardt drew his pistol and moved back along the train.

He grabbed Edgbaston and pulled him to his feet. A bullet splintered the wall near his head. Gerhardt pulled Edgbaston round as a barrier, holding him in place, then pointed the gun at the admiral. "Get up."

The admiral looked him in the eye and shook his head. Instead he slipped to the floor and lay along it. Gerhardt growled. He desperately wanted to shoot the man but his ammunition was limited. Instead, he kicked the admiral in the head as hard as he could, slamming it against the wooden wall.

The admiral's tense body slumped into relaxation.

Gerhardt pulled Edgbaston back further, until he moved past his men. The British took that moment to advance through the door and take cover behind the partition walls. But they were not firing.

"Preserve your ammunition," Gerhardt said quietly then retreated towards the rear of the carriage. He kept Edgbaston as a barrier but concentrated on the rear. There was no way of knowing how many they were, though he was fairly sure the two that had come in were from the group at the house—which implied there might only be those.

There was only one way they could have caught up. The girls and their plane. They must have dropped them onto the train before it entered the sandstorm. It would be a happy day if that act had resulted in their deaths.

The rear door opened. Gerhardt held his fire; he wanted a clear shot. With both doors open to the elements, the wind ripped through carrying a stream of sand with it. The door opened wide and a man threw himself through it. Gerhardt fired but the bullet lodged in the door frame as the fellow disappeared. The wind changed direction and the door slammed shut.

The storm was getting worse and the carriage rocked with frightening ferocity. It sounded as if the sand would tear away the ceiling and walls. Perhaps he should order them to stop the train. But that was no longer possible.

The new fellow at the rear popped out his head and Gerhardt took a shot at him. He missed again. Still, having Edgbaston prevented them from firing.

"To fight is foolish," he shouted in English. "You want your men and we simply wish to leave."

"It's not that simple any more, Gerhardt," said the Englishman. "You have kidnapped an official representatives of Her Majesty's government, never mind waging war on her subjects. We cannot allow you to leave."

"Then we are at an impasse," called Gerhardt.

The train carriage lurched and tilted. As he tried to stay hidden, Gerhardt lost his grip on Edgbaston, who fell against the opposite wall. There was a shriek of metal and a crash. The entire rear wall of the carriage ripped away leaving tattered edges. Wind-driven sand swirled through the gap. Gerhardt threw up his hands to cover his eyes as something huge and metallic lurched forward and crashed into the carriage.

From behind the glass windows of the *Pegasus* the red-haired girl glared out, her entire focus on him.

Gerhardt dropped his hand from his eyes and squinted against the driven sand. How was this possible?

The girl and her vessel. Here. On the train? She was going to kill him, he knew it. He jumped across to where Edgbaston had fallen and pulled him to his feet. A wing from the ship slammed down in front of him, piercing the wooden planks and twisting them. Then it ripped upwards, tearing away the roof.

He pulled the girl's father in front of him and pointed the gun at the man's head. Still holding the ace, he fixed the girl with a glare of his own. She met his gaze with one equally stony. The wing that had taken away the ceiling slowly folded back. Not into the body, but back into a position with its end feathers touching the shifting and rocking floor of the carriage.

Gerhardt could see the other girl, the *Schwarze,* standing beside the pilot. She was saying something. On the other side was a woman he did not recognise. The one they had rescued from the collapsing house? She too was talking at the girl, in her other ear. They would be telling her to control herself. That if she did anything then her father would die and it would be her fault.

Gerhardt slowly smiled. He would win this after all.

At that moment there was a movement from the man who had come through before. His gun appeared. Gerhardt took a quick shot in his direction.

The last thing he remembered was the iron wing flicking up at him impossibly fast. And the pain.

28

With the *Pegasus*'s Faraday switched on, the crane at Luxor station did not have any difficulty lifting the vessel from the broken train. The ship swung precariously as Sellie wrung her hands. She had insisted the foreman check the mounting points three times before she was satisfied.

A crew of naval engineers was waiting to go through every movable part of the ship and clear out any sand that had got into the works. She had to trust them because they worked in this environment all the time and knew what to look for. Still, she would check every seam and every joint after they had finished.

She also wanted to finish the job she had started with the extra Faraday grids.

Harry, their father, and Mrs Hemingway had all gone to the hotel. Dad needed to get some sleep, a good clean, and a change of clothes. Sellie had had a long discussion with Harry about it and they decided that Sellie should stay with the *Pegasus* while Harry went with him.

It had been a decision between them, and it was the right one, but Sellie could not help but feel she was being left out. The crane lurched and Sellie shouted at the foreman.

* * *

Harry got changed into proper clothes. She had never thought she would be so glad to put on layers of petticoats. Mrs Hemingway had helped her but this was a different woman to the one they had known half their lives. She did not boss Harry around, she asked and made suggestions—every one of which Harry agreed to.

She had slept on the train and had not been through the same ordeal as her father. She was tired, but not exhausted.

She glanced out the window. The train had emerged from the sandstorm after three hours and it had taken until the next morning for them to arrive in Luxor, though they had stopped briefly in Aswan and a message had been sent ahead.

A boy knocked at the door of their suite—provided by the British government—and handed them a card. Mrs Hemingway glanced at it and then passed it to Harry. She smiled on seeing it was from Lt Cmdr Laxton.

With Mrs Hemingway as chaperone, she made her way to the lobby where they were shown into a large room with wide and open windows. Both Laxton and Lt Keating were there, wearing clean and smart uniforms they must have acquired from somewhere, and there was another man, a bureaucrat by his suit and an important one by his bearing.

"Miss Edgbaston, Mrs Hemingway," began Laxton, "may I introduce His Excellency, Lord Walton. Her Majesty's Ambassador to Egypt."

Harry curtsied as well as she could remember. An ambassador was the monarch's direct representative and thereby deserved almost as much respect. She wondered how surprised Mrs Hemingway was by her manners—though there was the possibility she had got it all wrong and any surprise might be embarrassment.

None of the men reacted so she assumed she had got it right. The ambassador held out his hand and helped her to her feet.

"Miss Edgbaston, I have heard a great deal about you." His voice was deep and comfortable, like a feather bed, though Harry noticed there was nothing soft about his grip.

"Thank you, Your Excellency," she said.

"Not all of it was good," he added.

"I'm sorry."

"But, on balance, it was positive."

"Thank you."

The ambassador pulled out his pocket watch and glanced at it. "I'm afraid I do not have much time, Miss Edgbaston, as I have a meeting with the German ambassador directly."

"He's in Luxor, too?"

"You are in the middle of an international incident, Miss Edgbaston." His voice carried the tone of someone who was not at all pleased with the situation. "It's just as well you did not kill *Hauptman* Gerhardt."

"It was an accident."

"I somehow find that hard to believe."

"No, I mean 'not killing him' was an accident," she said. "I was aiming for his head."

The ambassador hesitated. "I see. Well, I believe I will not relay that part of the story. At least, not officially. But I wanted to meet with you to see what sort of a girl Miss Harriet Edgbaston is before I spoke with him."

"Am I what you expected, sir?"

"Truthfully? Not in the least."

The ambassador took his leave and Lt Keating left with him, shutting the door behind them.

"It's been a pleasure, Miss Edgbaston," said Laxton and held out his hand. Harry took it, though she was surprised.

"Really?"

"Except the part where you almost killed me ripping out the wall."

"Sorry."

"No harm done," he said. "The navy will ensure that your bird is ready to fly again as soon as possible, and you can go home."

Harry pulled a face. "I don't have a home anymore."

Laxton grunted. "Oh yes, and I have this for you." He reached into an inner pocket and pulled out two envelopes. He glanced at them and handed one to Harry. "And this one is for your sister." The second had Khuwelsa's name written out in full. Each envelope bulged slightly in one place.

"Thank you."

He smiled. "You can open it now."

Harry passed Sellie's envelope to Mrs Hemingway then ran her thumb up hers and tore it open. There was a letter with the Royal Navy seal at the top. It was an official acknowledgement for rescuing the admiral and her father. And a metal badge. Two wings mounted on the rectangle of the Royal Ensign, the official insignia of the Royal Navy Aerial Fleet.

"We do not hand out badges like sweets, Miss Edgbaston," he said. "These are to signify that you have the genuine gratitude of Her Majesty and the Senior Service. If you or your sister should ever wish to become a part of it we will endeavour to find you a place."

He and Lt Keating saluted and left.

Harry turned the badge over in her hands. There were no women in the Royal Navy.

Perhaps she and Sellie could be the first.

~ end ~

Don't miss Harry and Sellie in their next amazing adventure:

Harry Goes to Italy

In which Harry meets her mother after years of separation and the sisters get mixed up in the complexity of Italian unification.

To make sure you don't miss it,
join the mailing list at:

http://bit.ly/voidships

ABOUT THE AUTHOR

Steve Turnbull was born in the heart of London to book-loving working-class parents in 1958. He lived with his parents and two older sisters in two rooms with gas lighting and no hot water. In his fifth year, a change in his father's fortunes took them out to a detached house in the suburbs. That was the year *Dr Who* first aired on British TV, and Steve watched it avidly from behind the sofa. It was the beginning of his love of science fiction.

Academically Steve always went for the science side, but he also had his imagination—and that took him everywhere. He read through his local library's entire science fiction and fantasy selection, plus his father's 1950s *Astounding Science Fiction* magazines. As he got older he also ate his way through TV SF like *Star Trek*, *Dr Who* and *Blake's 7*.

However, it was when he was 15 he discovered something new. Bored with a maths lesson, he noticed a book from the school library: *Cider with Rosie* by Laurie Lee. From the first page he was captivated by the beauty of the language. As a result he wrote a story longhand and then spent evenings at home on his father's electric typewriter pounding out a second draft, expanding it. Then he wrote a second book. After that he switched to poetry and turned out dozens, mostly not involving teenage angst.

After receiving excellent science and maths results, he went on to study computer science. There he teamed up with another student and they wrote songs for their band, with Steve writing the lyrics. However, they admit their best song was the other way around, with Steve writing the music.

After graduation Steve moved into contract programming but was snapped up a couple of years later by a computer magazine looking for someone with technical knowledge. It was in the magazine industry that Steve learned how to write to length, to deadline, and to style. Within a couple of years he was editor and stayed there for many years.

During that time he married Pam (who also became a magazine editor), whom he'd met at a student party.

Though he continued to write poetry, all prose work stopped. He created his own magazine publishing company which at one point produced the subscription magazine for the *Robot Wars* TV show. The company evolved into a design agency, but after six years of working very hard and not seeing his family—now including a daughter and son—he gave it all up.

He spent a year working on miscellaneous projects including writing 300 pages for a website until he started back where he had begun, contract programming.

With security and success on the job front, the writing began again. This time it was scriptwriting: features scripts, TV scripts and radio scripts. During this time he met a director, Chris Payne, who wanted to create steampunk stories, and between them they created the Voidships universe, a place very similar to ours but with specific scientific changes.

With a whole universe to play with, Steve wrote a web series, a feature film, and then books all in the same Steampunk world and, behind the scenes, all connected.

Join the mailing list at http://bit.ly/voidships

Lightning Source UK Ltd.
Milton Keynes UK
UKHW020329070919
349238UK00004B/392/P

9 781910 34257